The Pri
Two prince

You are cordially invited to celebrate the
weddings of Xaviera's most eligible princes…

When Prince Dominic spends one night with
Ginny Jones it comes at a price… a marriage of
convenience in order to claim his heir!

Pregnant with a Royal Baby!
Available February 2016

Prince Alex has always believed royal rules
were made to be broken, but when his royal
duty comes calling it's time for Alex to
meet his Princess—and wife-to-be!

Coming Soon!

*For better or for worse, these gorgeous
princes are about to claim their brides!*

I2707027

PREGNANT WITH A ROYAL BABY

BY
SUSAN MEIER

First Published in Great Britain 2016
By Mills & Boon, an imprint of HarperCollins*Publishers*
1 London Bridge Street, London, SE1 9GF

© 2016 Linda Susan Meier

ISBN: 978-0-263-91962-2

23-0216

Our policy is to use papers that are natural, renewable and recyclable products and made from wood grown in sustainable forests.The logging and manufacturing processes conform to the legal environmental regulations of the country of origin.

Printed and bound in Spain
by CPI, Barcelona

Susan Meier is the author of over fifty books for Mills & Boon. *The Tycoon's Secret Daughter* was a RITA® Award finalist, and *Nanny for the Millionaire's Twins* won the Book Buyer's Best award and was a finalist in the National Reader's Choice awards. She is married and has three children. One of eleven children, she loves to write about the complexity of families and totally believes in the power of love.

To my own Prince Charming, and our marriage—
a journey of ups and downs that surprises me
every day. Usually in a good way. :)

CHAPTER ONE

WHEN THE DOORBELL to her condo rang, Virginia Jones, Ginny for short, had just gotten out of the shower after a long, long day at Jefferson High School in Terra Mas, Texas. Her school was the last on a list of places Prince Dominic Sancho of Xaviera, a small island country between Spain and Algeria, was visiting on a good-will tour. As guidance counselor, she'd shown him the school and introduced him to staff, then herded the kids into the gymnasium, where he'd given an hour-long talk on global economics: how the world was a much smaller place than it had been before the internet.

She'd loved the talk, but she'd liked looking at Prince Dominic even more. Tall and broad shouldered, he filled out the formal uniform of his royalty like a man meant to be a king. His dark eyes sparkled with amusement at the antics of "her" kids. His full lips had never stopped smiling.

If it were permitted for grown women to swoon, she would have made a fool of herself with him that afternoon. As it was, common sense had kept her pro-fessional. And now she was tired. Not up for a visitor.

Her doorbell rang again.

She gave her glass of wine a longing look before she rose from her sofa.

"I'm coming." She said it just as she reached the door. Going up on tiptoes, she peeked through the peephole. When she saw Prince Dominic, she gasped and jumped back.

Her doorbell rang again.

She peered down at her sweatpants and tank top, ran a hand along her still-wet long blond hair and knew this would go down in the annals of her life as one of her most embarrassing moments.

With no choice, she pasted a smile on her face and opened the door.

He laughed. "I caught you at a bad time."

"Unfortunately." Just looking at him made her heart speed up. He'd removed the royal uniform and replaced it with a lightweight white V-neck sweater and jeans. Not a hair of his shiny black curls was out of place. His dark eyes sparkled with amusement.

"You probably think all Americans are idiots."

"No, I think the United States is a very comfortable country." He paused long enough to lift his perfect lips into a warm smile. "Are you going to invite me in?"

She motioned for him to come in with a wave of her hand and kept hyperventilation at bay only by a miracle of self-discipline. She had a *prince* entering her house. A good-looking, good-natured, good *everything* prince.

As she closed the door, he said, "I'd actually come here tonight to see if you'd like to have dinner with me." He shrugged. "And show me your town."

She had to work to keep her eyes from bugging. He wanted to take her *out*? Then she realized his request made sense. She'd shown him the school. Of course, she was the prime candidate to show him the town. He was not asking her out.

"Then I thought maybe we'd fly to Los Angeles and go to a club."

She let her eyes bulge. Okay. He *was* asking her out. "You want to go clubbing?"

"Don't you like to dance?"

Her heart tripped over itself in her chest. "I love to dance."

He smiled. "Me, too. I'm afraid I don't get to dance often, though. Duty supersedes fun. Please say you'll come with me."

"I'd love to."

Though he was in jeans, he looked good enough to eat, so she slithered into her prettiest red party dress, put on her best makeup and slid into tall black sandals.

They had dinner at the local Italian restaurant, with his bodyguards unobtrusively eating at the tables beside theirs, then they actually got on his royal jet and flew to LA, where they'd danced until three. He should have dropped her off at her building lobby. Instead, he came up to her condo, and the few kisses they'd shared in his limo turned into passionate lovemaking. The best sex of her life. She'd kissed him goodbye at the door in her one and only fancy robe—which she'd retrieved from her closet when he made the call to his driver that he was ready. Then just when she was about to shower for school again, he called her.

"Thank you."

The sweetness of his words caused her throat to tighten. Her voice was soft and breathless when she said, "You're welcome."

"I'm sorry we'll never meet again."

"Me, too."

But in a way she wasn't. She'd had a wonderful fairy-tale night with a prince, something she could hold in her heart forever. There would be no need to worry if he would be a good king or a bad king; no need to know if he did stupid things like hog the bathroom; no need to worry if the stress of his job would make him an alcoholic, as her dad had been. No need to know the real Prince Dominic Sancho.

There had been one glorious, wonderful night. No regrets and no worries about the future. The way she liked all her relationships.

They hung up on mutual sighs. In the process of setting her phone on her bedside table, she realized that because he'd called her, she had his number. She clicked a few buttons and when the digits came up caller ID said private line. She smiled. She didn't just have his number she had his *private* number.

That pleased her enormously. If she ever got curious or lonely, she could call him…

Or not. Best to sit and stare at his number and imagine good things. Not bad. Never bad. She'd had enough bad in her life.

Knowing there was no time to sleep, she dressed for school, hugging her secret to herself. For two weeks she walked on a cloud of happiness, then one morning she woke and realized she hadn't gotten her period, and she knew there *really* was a good reason to have his private number.

"Thank God our country isn't like Britain used to be where the future king had to marry a virgin."

Prince Dominic Sancho held back the anger that threatened to rise up in him. He'd been the perfect royal for nearly thirty years and one slip, one reckless night in America, had wiped all that away. His father might be angry, but it was *his* life plan that had been changed.

In order to ensure the integrity of the line and the safety of his child, he had no choice but to marry Ginny Jones, a woman he didn't know.

"Yes. Thank God I'm permitted to marry the mother of my child."

"I was being facetious." Short and bald, with a round belly, his father, the king of Xaviera, was an imposing, strict man. He hated mistakes. Couldn't even tolerate slipups. Especially not from the son who was his successor.

"And I was being sarcastic." It wasn't often that he got smart with his father. In fact, he probably hadn't done it more than five times in his entire life, including his teen years. But discovering a simple one-night stand had resulted in a pregnancy had pushed him over the edge. His brother was the king of playboys but did he ever suffer a consequence for his actions? No. Yet the first time Dom stepped out of line, he was punished.

"I've arranged for you and Ms. Jones to meet with the protocol officials whenever you're ready. But no later than tomorrow morning." King Ronaldo caught his gaze. "Prepare your *bride*."

The insult in his father's voice cut through Dom like a knife. He just barely succeeded in not sniping back.

He rose from his seat across from the ornate desk that was the seat of power for the king. He should have said, "Thank you for your time, Your Majesty." A good prince would have done that. Instead he said, "I'll get back to you."

"See to it that this wedding is done right. I will not be so easy on you if you screw up again."

He bowed and headed out of the room. *I will not be so easy on you if you screw up again?*

Anger coursed through him. He stifled it. His father

was the king. Dominic was heir to the throne. He *knew* there were protocols and rules. He'd broken them. He deserved this.

Still…the penalty for one misstep was marriage? *Marriage.*

After the way his father had fallen apart when his mother died, Dominic understood why his dad was careful, rigid now. His grief had been so intense that he hadn't come out of his quarters for six weeks and in that time the country had begun to crumble. Parliament nearly took his crown, and, watching it all unfold, Dominic had promised himself he would never marry, never soften so much that a loss nearly destroyed him.

When an opportunity for a treaty had arisen, the price being his marriage to a princess of a country that had been an enemy for centuries, he'd thought why not? Not only was the feud between their kingdoms old enough that it was time to retire it, but also there'd be no real emotional ties in a marriage that was part of a treaty, and he'd get an heir who would be a prince in two countries. But now here he was. Forced to marry a woman he didn't know, ruining his design for a double royal heir, because of his own carelessness.

His life plan really had gone to hell.

He sucked in a breath and walked to the back stairway that led to his private quarters, buying time before he had to talk to Ginny. If he was angry, he couldn't imagine how she felt—

Unless she'd gotten pregnant deliberately?

The horribleness of the thought froze his blood, stopped his breathing, and he told himself to calm down. Too many things had to align for her to have orchestrated the pregnancy, including the fact that he was the one who had gone to her condo that night. And she'd been a cute mess. Wet hair. Sweatpants. She obviously hadn't been planning on seeing him that night.

Reaching the top floor of the east wing of Xaviera's palace, he strode in the direction of the white double doors with intricate scroll designs carved down the sides. The huge square "waiting" area between the top of the stairs and his apartment had scant furnishings, though the walls were adorned with art. Picasso. Rembrandt. Monet. Hidden treasures. Mostly for his viewing. Because that's what his life was. Special. Honored. In spite of the awkward meeting with his father, he knew that he was different. Some day he would be a king.

The click of his heels echoed as he walked along the marble floor. When he reached the doors, he took both handles and opened them onto his home, his haven.

Virginia Jones rose from the tufted bench seat in what served as a foyer for his apartment. Medium height, with long yellow hair and the kind of body that tempts a man to do exactly what he had done the night he met her, Ginny was every man's fantasy. When her striking blue eyes met his, he remembered how adorable she was at the Texas high school, a guidance counselor beloved by her students. He also remembered the hot little red dress she'd slipped into when he'd persuaded her to go clubbing with him. The dress had brought out the best of her figure, almost made him drool and turned him into a real live Prince Charming. Seducing her had been second nature. The sex had been amazing.

It seemed that was all he could think about when he looked at her. And now he was about to make her a princess.

"So?"

"So, my father and my kingdom wish for us to marry."

Those bright blue eyes met his. "Wish?"

He motioned for her to follow him into his formal living room. More marble floors greeted them, except these were covered by rich red Oriental rugs. White sofas flanked a white marble fireplace. Red pillows gave the room some color. He gestured for Virginia to take a seat while he strode to the bar and grabbed the decanter of Scotch.

"Can I get you a drink?"

She gaped at him. "I'm pregnant."

He winced. "Right." He took a breath. "How about some orange juice?"

"I'm fine." She held his gaze. "I'm more anxious to learn my fate than to pretend we're having a tea party."

He had no idea where the attitude had come from, but that was the truth of getting intimate with someone you didn't know. She could be the Wicked Witch of the West, or a woman who wanted to save the whales, or a woman who had no loyalties at all, a woman who was lazy, crass or stupid, and he was stuck with her.

"All right." He walked to the sofa across from the one on which she sat and set his Scotch on the glass table between them. "Maybe the better way to put it is that they are *requesting* that we marry."

"So I have a choice?"

"Not really. You are pregnant with the heir to Xaviera's throne. If you decide not to marry me, your child will be taken from you."

She gasped. "What?"

"He or she is the heir to our throne. There isn't a country in the world who'd dare supersede our laws with their own when it comes to royalty, especially royalty in line to rule the country."

She bounced from her seat. "That's not fair!"

He sat back, watching her long legs as she paced. Though she wore jeans and a snug sweater, he pictured those legs beneath the shiny red dress. "Try suing. Waste time. Ruin the chance for us to have a royal wedding. Ruin the chance for the gossip to die down and our child to be brought into the world with a celebration instead of whispers."

She stopped pacing and caught his gaze, obviously thinking through what he'd said.

He took advantage of her weak moment. "You won't win and you'll bring our child into a world of chaos for nothing because I have a plan."

"A plan?"

Ginny stared at the gorgeous man on the sofa. With eyes so dark they almost looked black and onyx hair, he was every inch a prince. A royal. A future ruler who lived a life of privilege. A man just a little bit above everybody else.

As they talked about a situation that would totally change her life, he very calmly sipped Scotch.

"My father wants the next king to be born in wedlock." He held her gaze. "Our subjects will, too. But that doesn't mean we have to stay married."

Relieved, she sat on the sofa across from him again. "It doesn't?"

"No. But it does mean we have to play a part for a while." He glanced at his Scotch then back up at her. "Over the next couple of days, as the protocol office begins planning our wedding, we'll be seen together in public."

Her heart thumped when he said *wedding*. She would be married to a guy who would someday be a king. Did that mean sleeping with him? They might be at odds now, but the night they'd gone out, they'd had a really good time. She had no idea how *that* factored into his plan, so she kept her face calm, simply kept her gaze locked with his, hoping to appear cooler than she was.

"Next week we'll announce our engagement, quick wedding and pregnancy all at once."

That didn't sound fun. "Oh, boy."

"Don't worry. I've thought this through. The people of Xaviera will be thrilled to see me getting married. But the only thing they love better than a royal wedding is a royal pregnancy. If we play this right, the next few months could be a wonderful time for the people of my kingdom."

"Okay." Her nerves popped and jumped, but she resisted the urge to bounce off the sofa and pace again. If he could be calm, she could be calm. And really what he said made sense. They were doing this for his people and their child, a future king, who deserved to be born amid celebration.

"So we'd get married next month and after that we'd spend the rest of your pregnancy making appearances as the happy couple expecting the next heir to the throne, then the baby will be born to a country excited and happy about his birth."

She could picture it. She'd seen enough of Britain's royal family's weddings, as well as their pregnancies, to have a pretty good idea of what she was in for. Except Xaviera was a small country, much smaller than Britain, so she could probably cut the exposure in the press and even in Xaviera itself in about half. Which wouldn't be *too* bad.

"After that we should stay married until the baby's about two. At age two, there's a ceremony that would induct him or her into the line of reigning Sanchos. We can be cool to each other at that ceremony, and then we can divorce without causing too much of a stir because after that nothing press worthy happens in his life until he turns twelve." He sat back. "If people want to say we married hastily, or even if they say we only married for the baby, we agree. But waiting until he or she is two shows we gave the marriage a good shot. Because we'll be fair and calm about it, everyone will support us."

"And what about the baby?"

"What about the baby?"

"Who keeps him? What kind of custody arrangements are we talking about here?"

"There are a few scenarios. I was hoping you'd let the years we're married go by without making any final decisions, but if you choose to take our child back to America, a contingent of bodyguards will be sent with you. Xaviera will purchase a home with suitable security."

"What about my job?"

"Your job will be mother to Xaviera's heir. At least until he or she is twelve."

"Twelve?"

"Up until twelve he can be homeschooled. After that there are mandatory boarding schools. He or she has to have a certain kind of education."

"No public school, huh?"

"Mock if you want, but that is the situation." He rose from the sofa. "Once he goes to boarding school, your life is your own again. Except you will be expected to attend all of his public functions."

She could see it. She could picture herself as the future king's mom, wiping grape jelly from her little boy's chin in private, and way, way out of the view of cameras when he was in public. Knowing that she'd easily slip out of the limelight settled some of her nerves. Still, there was more to it than grape jelly and hiding from cameras.

"I'll give you a week to think about it."

"A week?"

"The week you're at the palace. The time we're getting out. Being seen in public. Having a date or two."

Their eyes met. Their last date had been fantastic. But it was also what had gotten them into this mess.

"I think I still have some more questions."

"About the dates?"

She nodded.

"Like, will we kiss?"

A starburst of tingles exploded in her stomach. She nodded again.

"Yes. We have to pretend we adore each other. That we met and swept each other off our respective feet." He held her gaze. "Which we sort of did."

Memories of holding hands, intimate touches and those unbelievable kisses rippled through her, tightening her chest, sending her pulse into overdrive.

"But sex is off the table." He smiled. "Unless you're interested."

Her heart thumped. She tried to imagine herself resisting that smile, that charm—

Actually, he hadn't been all that charming in this chat, except when it suited him. That was the curse of getting involved with someone she didn't know. She'd met and made love with Prince Charming. She had no idea who the real Prince Dominic was. What if he was like her dad? Only pulling out the charm to get what he wanted?

Oh. No brainer. She could resist that like sour wine at a bad dance club.

"Ginny, this relationship can go any way you want."

And the stoic, respectable prince was back. "Behind the walls of this palace we can be as distant or as intimate as you wish. But make no mistake. If you marry me, it's temporary. Don't get stars in your eyes. Don't get any big ideas. This marriage will not become permanent. I had been promised to a princess as part of a treaty and that was what I wanted. A marriage that meant something, accomplished something. A real marriage doesn't work in my world. So this little arrangement will not turn permanent. You need to know that, too, before you decide."

CHAPTER TWO

"SO IT WILL be totally a marriage of convenience?"

Ginny lay on the bed in the suite across the great room in Dominic's palace apartment. Cool silk caressed her back. Fluffy pillows supported her. Rich aqua walls brought color and life to the cavernous space.

"That's it. Nothing but a marriage of convenience to bring the heir to Xaviera's throne into the world legitimately."

"Oh, sweetie, that's weird."

"I know, Mom. But you have to remember the child we created will be in the public eye his entire life. How selfish would it be for me to refuse to marry Dominic, and have the heir to Xavier's throne born in a way that causes whispers and gossip that follow him forever?"

"True."

"Besides, this might just be the best thing for me, too. I mean, seriously, I don't know Dominic. What he said today about not wanting to be married proves it. He was such a sweetheart when he came to the school that day that I thought he really was a Prince Charming."

"They're all Prince Charming on dates, Ginny. It's real life that brings out their bad side."

Ginny winced. Though Dominic and her alcoholic dad seemed to share the charm gene, her dad had been mean and emotionally abusive. Dominic just seemed formal. It wasn't fair to compare the two—even if she would be wise about the charm part.

"He's not a bad guy, Mom. He's just not the happy-go-lucky guy he was on our date. And, you know what? I'm probably not the starry-eyed, flirty girl I was that night, either. We were both just having fun. But this pregnancy is real. And that's why he's serious."

"Okay. You're right."

"I know I'm right, but I still don't know what to do."

"It sounds like you think you should marry him. What are you giving up? A year, a year and a half of your life?"

"About two and a half years, and my career. Apparently, my job for the next twelve years is to be the heir's mom."

Ginny's mom laughed. "Even if your child wasn't a prince or princess, your priorities would switch from your job to this baby." She sucked in a breath. "You know what? This isn't all that much different from having the baby of a commoner."

"Except for dealing with the press."

"Yeah, well, the press is different."

"And boarding school."

"There is that."

"And living in a palace."

"Right, palace." Her mother sighed. "But the situation is done, Ginny."

"I suppose."

"So what concerns you?"

"Well, I have to see if I can handle it. Dominic's given me a week to make up my mind. He said we'd go out in public a few times." She groaned. "Oh, damn."

"What?"

"I brought jeans and T-shirts. One sundress." She dropped her head to her hands. "I'm going to go out with a prince, in public, in my junky clothes?"

"Your wardrobe is fine. *You'll* be fine."

"Right." She hadn't even told her mom about kissing Dom, possibly sleeping with Dom. All she'd mentioned was not knowing Dominic and changing her life to suit a baby, and just that had scared her silly.

This was a mess.

Two quick knocks at her door brought her head off the pillow. "Yes?"

"It's me. Dominic. My father requests our presence at dinner tonight."

Ginny turned toward the wall and whispered, "Gotta go, Mom," into the phone before she rolled off the bed and said, "Sure. That's fine. What time?"

"Seven." He cleared his throat. "It's semiformal."

She gaped at the door, as discomfort swamped her. Not only did she not have a semiformal dress for dinner, but her suite had a private sitting room outside her bedroom. He had to be in that room to be knocking on her bedroom door. He might have knocked on the door to her suite before inviting himself in, but she wouldn't have heard him. The darned place was so big and had such high ceilings that sound either echoed or disappeared. He wasn't infringing on her privacy. She hoped.

"Semiformal?"

"I took the liberty of having the staff get some suitable clothes for you."

Pride almost caused her to say, "I'm fine." But when she looked down at her jeans and considered the contents of her suitcase, she knew this was the first step in many toward giving up her real life.

"You're right. I have nothing acceptable to meet a

king." She walked to the door, opened it and watched as four men brought in bags and boxes and armloads of dresses, including gowns.

"Oh, my God."

Dominic walked in behind the parade of men. "Even if you decide not to marry me, you're here for a week."

Her mouth fell open at the ease with which he spoke in front of staff, but the expression of not a single man even twitched. This was one well-trained staff.

She took a quick breath. "So I need to be semiformal."

He nodded. "Yes."

"Okay. Scram. I have some work to do to be presentable."

"I can have a hairdresser sent up. Manicurist. Masseuse."

"Why would I need a massage?"

"Maybe what I should get you is a rundown on my dad. Then you'd very clearly understand why you want to be Zen and you'd get the massage."

"Great."

She took advantage of the hairdresser and manicurist, and ten minutes before it was time to leave for dinner she wished she'd agreed to the masseuse.

Dressed in a lightweight blue dress that stopped midcalf, with her hair in an updo suitable for a woman of seventy and old-fashioned pumps dyed to match the dress, she stepped out of her bedroom.

Standing in the great room, Dominic smiled. Unlike her ugly blue dress, his tux appeared to have been made for him. Again he was every inch a prince. Handsome. Debonair. Regal.

While she looked like a frumpy old bat.

"You look lovely."

"I look like the Queen of England. Get me a hat and one of those sedate purses she carries all the time and people would probably get us confused."

He laughed. "You are meeting a king."

"Who wants to be reminded of his grandmother?"

"You do not look like a grandmother."

"Well, I sure as hell don't look like a twenty-five-year-old guidance counselor in the coolest school in Texas."

"Trust me. You will want the armor of a grandma dress when you meet my dad." He took her elbow and led her to the door, out of the apartment and through the echoing lobby to the waiting elevator.

As they stepped inside and the door closed behind them, she said, "You have some impressive art."

"We are royalty."

"I guess I'd better get used to that." That and ugly clothes.

"That's why we're giving you the week. To get accustomed to us."

She released her breath in a slow sigh. She knew that, of course. She also suspected the clothes weren't ugly as much as they were dignified.

"Who picked out these clothes anyway?"

He stared straight ahead at the closed elevator door. "I did."

She pulled the skirt of the too-big dress away from her hips. "Because you think your dad will like me better in baggy clothes?"

"I was a bit off on your size. But it's better to be too big than too small."

"Couldn't you at least have gotten something red?"

"Blue matches your eyes."

The sweetness of that caught her off guard. For a

second she'd forgotten he knew the color of her eyes. But thinking about it, she remembered that gazing into her eyes, making her feel special, had been his seduction superpower.

"Besides, red would have reminded me of that night."

Her lips lifted into a smile. "Oh?"

"You were devastatingly beautiful."

Her heart skipped a beat. He'd made her feel beautiful. "If you hadn't been staring straight ahead when you said that, it would have been romantic."

"We don't want to be romantic, remember?"

"So that means you're not going to look at me?"

"I'm not going to make eye contact. I'm pretty sure that's what got us into trouble on our date."

She laughed, but happiness bubbled inside her. He *liked* her. A *prince* liked her. At the very least, he liked her looks.

It was heady stuff.

The elevator bell rang. The doors opened. Dominic led her out. "The family dining room is this way."

They walked across a short hall to open doors that ushered them into a formal dining room. A table that could have seated forty dominated the space. Four places were set near the head. An older man dressed in a royal uniform and a younger man in a tux like Dominic's rose as they entered.

"Virginia Jones, this is King Ronaldo Sancho and my brother, Prince Alexandros. We call him Alex."

Ginny froze. What was she supposed to do? Curtsy? Bow? Damn it. Why hadn't she paid attention to etiquette—

What etiquette? Guidance counselors knew the basics but nothing else. And she certainly hadn't expected to someday meet a prince, let alone a king. She hadn't attended etiquette classes. Was there even such a thing anymore? She couldn't be mad at herself for not knowing something she'd never been exposed to.

"You hold out your hand," King Ronaldo said irritably. "And it's my choice to kiss it or shake it."

"Oh." She held out her hand. The king shook it.

Great. She'd already blown her first introduction.

Dom turned her in the direction of his brother. As tall as Dominic and every bit as good-looking—though his face had a roundness to it that made him appear kinder, with eyes that sparkled—Alex smiled warmly at her.

"It's a pleasure to meet the woman who snagged my brother."

King Ronaldo growled. "We do not speak that way in this house."

"Really, Father," Alex said, as he took his seat and opened his napkin. "This house is the only place we can speak like that." He smiled at Ginny as Dominic seated her. "It's a pleasure to have you in the family, Ginny, even if my brother does intend to dress you like a grandmother."

With a gasp, she faced Dom. "I told you!"

He almost smiled, but his father let out one of those low growls of disapproval again, and Dominic's face shifted, returning to his formal expression.

As a servant brought in salads, King Ronaldo said, "So, Miss Jones, tell us about yourself."

She swallowed. "Well, you know I'm a guidance counselor at a high school."

"Which is where you met Dominic."

She nodded. "My mother was a teacher. I loved the relationships she had with her students."

Alex said, "So why not teach?"

"I wanted a chance to meet all the kids, know all the kids, not just the ones I was teaching."

The king said, "Ump," but his tone of voice was positive.

She relaxed a bit. But when she glanced at the row of silverware, sweat beaded on her forehead. Seven forks. Just what in the name of all that was holy were they about to eat?

Remembering the rhyme she'd been taught in grade school, she started with the outside fork.

"What else should we know?"

"Actually, Your Majesty, since you've already decided the answer to our problem is to marry, and I'm the one who hasn't made up her mind, I think I should be the one asking questions."

Alex burst out laughing. "I like her."

The king growled again.

Dominic shot her a look of reprimand.

So she smiled and rephrased the question. "It's an honor to have been asked to join your family. But in America we have a saying about not buying a car unless you kick the tires."

Alex laughed again. "Now we're tires."

Not sure if she liked Dominic's brother or not, Ginny shrugged and said, "Or you're the used car. Be glad I didn't use the don't-buy-a-horse-without-checking-its-teeth analogy."

Alex laughed. Dominic groaned. But the king quietly said, "Fair enough. What would you like to know?"

"I don't really have to dress like this for the entire time Dominic and I stay married, do I?"

"You need to look respectable." King Ronaldo inspected her blue dress and grimaced. Even he thought it was ugly. "If we let you choose your own wardrobe, can you do that?"

"Of course, I can do that!"

"You also need to behave with the utmost of decorum in public."

"I can do that, too. Though I might need some help with protocols." She answered honestly, but she hadn't missed the way the king had turned the tables on her again, and she retook control of the conversation. "So what was Dominic like as a child?"

The king said, "Headstrong."

Alex said, "A bully."

Dominic said, "All older brothers bully their baby brothers. It's like a rule."

And for the first time, Ginny felt as if she was actually talking to people. A family.

Alex shook his head. "Do you know he agreed to marry the princess of Grennady when he was only twelve?"

She faced Dom. "Really?"

Their eyes met and memories of holding him close, whispering in his ear, being held and touched and loved by him rolled through her, and she understood why Dominic had been avoiding eye contact in the elevator. Looking into someone's eyes was intimate. In those few seconds, he wasn't just a name or a problem or a memory, he was a real person. The guy she'd made love with. Father of her child.

"My mother had just died. Our kingdom was in a state of mourning from which we couldn't seem to emerge. It was appropriate to do something that didn't just ensure peace—it also brought up morale."

She continued to hold his gaze as he spoke, and something warm and soft floated through her. At twelve, he had been mature enough to do his duty. Hell, he was mature enough to *know* his duty. It was remarkable, amazing.

Alex sighed. "Now I'm stuck marrying her."

She faced Dom's younger brother with a wince. "Really? You have to marry the princess Dom was supposed to marry?"

The king said, "You can't just back out of a twenty-year-old treaty. We promised a marriage. We will deliver a marriage."

Alex batted a hand. "Doesn't matter. The princess and I will have a marriage of convenience." He shrugged. "I'll run around on her. She'll run around on me. Nobody will really know who our babies belong to and we won't allow blood tests. It'll be fine."

The king scowled. "Once again, Alex, I won't have you talk like that at the table."

Silence fell over the foursome. Dominic didn't defend his younger brother, who seemed oddly cowed by the reprimand. Hoping to restart the conversation and shift everybody's attention, Ginny tried to think of a question to ask, but couldn't come up with one to save her soul. She wanted to. She wanted to lift the gloom of talking about a dead queen, mourning subjects and a younger brother resigned to a loveless marriage—his life made tolerable by affairs. But nothing came to mind, except an empty, hollow feeling that *this* was the family she was marrying into.

But even as she thought that, she realized there was a human side to this story. A man had lost his wife and raised two boys alone. One son had become a slave to duty. The other rebellious.

Was the pain of losing a wife and mom any less because they were royal?

In some ways she thought it might have been worse.

Dominic started a conversation about the country's budget and a quiet discussion ensued. When the dinner was over, the king took her hand, bent and kissed it. An apology, she supposed, for the long, difficult dinner. Or maybe an acknowledgment that the next few years of her life would be like this, if she chose to marry Dominic.

They walked back to Dominic's apartment in silence, her blue dress swishing against her calves, mocking her, reminding her just how out of her element she was and just how much she wished she were back at her condo, sitting by the pool, sipping something fruity.

When they entered Dom's apartment, he said, "We'll meet the minister of protocol tomorrow morning."

"Okay." She headed for the double doors of her bedroom suite. "Great."

"Don't let my family scare you."

She stopped, turned to face him. "I'm not afraid of you." She almost said, "I feel sorry for you." For as difficult as the beginning of her life had been, she'd redeemed it. She'd built a world of friends and meaning. Dominic, his brother and the grouchy king were stuck.

But the strange look in his eyes kept her from saying that. He didn't seem embarrassed by his family as much as he appeared interested in what she thought of them. He wanted her to like them. Or approve of them. Or maybe just accept them.

She walked over to him, her ugly dyed blue pumps clicking on the marble floor, echoing in the silence. "I'm very accustomed to dealing with ornery dads. I was fine. Your father and brother might be a little grouchy or stern or even too flip, but I'd have paid to have family like them."

He sniffed a laugh. "Right."

"I'm serious." She smiled slightly. "Your brother needs a week of time-out in his room to get his act together, or maybe a good friend to talk through his life. Your dad lost his wife and lived his grief in the public eye. And you just want to live up to what your dad wants. You're actually a very normal family." Something she'd longed for her entire life. Something that could suck her in if she wasn't careful. "Good night."

As she turned to walk back to her bedroom suite, Dominic whispered, "Good night," confused by what she'd said. From what his investigators had dug up, her father was dead. Her mother adored her and she had a billion friends.

So what was that sad note he heard in her voice?

And why the hell would she have wanted *his* family?

He told himself it couldn't matter and walked to his suite, removing his tie. But the next day when she arrived at the table for breakfast, he jumped to his feet, feeling something he couldn't quite identify. He didn't see her in the red dress, dancing provocatively, happily seducing him. He saw a fresh-faced American girl who had something in her past. Something his private investigator hadn't dug up, but something that made her more than accepting of his stiff and formal father, and sometimes-obnoxious playboy brother.

He pulled out the chair beside his. "What would you like to eat?"

"I'd like one of those oranges," she said, pointing at the fruit in the bowl on the buffet behind the table. "And some toast."

"That's it?"

She shrugged. "It's all I'm hungry for."

He rang for a serving girl and made her request for toast and a glass of water. She plucked an orange from the bowl and began to peel it.

"Did you sleep well?"

"Yes."

"You remember we meet with the minister of protocol this morning?"

"Mmm-hmm."

His nerves jangled and he cursed himself. They were entering into a pretend marriage for the sake of their child. It was her prerogative if she didn't want to get too chummy with him.

Still, it didn't seem right not to say anything while they ate breakfast.

"If you decide to stay and marry me, we'll have your mom flown over, not just for the wedding but for the preparations."

"My mom still teaches."

"Oh."

"I'm twenty-five. She had me when she was twenty-five. That makes her fifty." She peeked up from her orange and smiled at him. "Too young to retire."

"You said she likes teaching."

"She loves teaching."

And the conversation died. Frustration rolled through him. As her toast arrived, he tried to think of something to say; nothing came to him.

She pulled one of the many newspapers provided for him from the stack on the end of the table and began reading. Even as he was glad she was a smart woman who appeared to be up on current events and most likely wouldn't embarrass him, he scowled internally, realizing reading the paper was a good way to avoid talking to him.

After breakfast, they walked along tall-ceilinged corridors to the first floor of the palace and the office of the minister of protocol, their footsteps the only sound around them. If a servant caught a peek at Dominic, he or she froze in place and bowed as he passed by. He barely noticed until he caught a sideways glance at Ginny's face and saw it scrunch in confusion.

"I don't like the fuss."

She peeked over. "Excuse me?"

"I don't like the fuss. But respect is part of the deal. To be an effective leader, your subjects must respect you. Trust you to rule well. Bowing is a sign that they trust you."

"Interesting."

Annoyance skittered through him. "It's not 'interesting.' It's true."

"Okay. Maybe I said that wrong. What I should have said was it's interesting that it's true because it gives me a whole different perspective of you as a leader. It helps me to see you as a leader."

It shouldn't have relieved him so much that she agreed. But he told himself it only mattered because he needed for her to respect him, too, for the years they'd be married.

Finally at the back of the building, they took an elevator to the first floor to the working space of the palace.

"Holy cow. This is big."

"It's huge." He pointed to the right. "The king's offices are over there. My offices and my brother's are near his. To the left," he said, motioning toward a long hall, "are the general offices. This is where our ministers and staff work."

* * *

Not able to see the end of the hall, Ginny blinked. It went so far it was almost like looking at an optical illusion.

He smiled. "I know. Impressive."

She said, "Right." But when her gaze swung around to his, she was no longer talking about the size of the palace. Everything about being royalty was bigger, better, grander than anything she'd ever seen or experienced. The truth of being a commoner washed through her again. His family might have normal bickering siblings with a traditional disciplinarian dad, but she couldn't forget they were rulers. Rich, powerful. The kind of family she shouldn't even cross paths with, let alone marry into.

"This way."

He took her elbow to guide her and sparkly little pinpricks skittered up her arm. She didn't know which was worse—being incredibly attracted to him or her good reaction to his brother and dad. Either one of them could get her into trouble. She shouldn't have admitted the night before that she'd have loved to have had a family like his. She could see it had made him curious. She'd tried to downplay it by being distant that morning, but she knew they were going to talk about this and she knew he had every right to ask. The question was: How did one explain living with a cheating, lying, thieving alcoholic to someone raised with such structure, such finery?

The minister of protocol turned out to be a short older woman whose green eyes lit when Ginny and Dominic entered the room.

She rose from her seat. "Prince Dominic!" She

rounded the desk and hugged him. "I hear congratulations are in order. You're about to have a baby!"

It was the first time anybody had actually been happy about her pregnancy or spoken of her baby as a baby, instead of a ruler or a prince or the guy who would be king. Ginny's heart filled with warmth and she forgot all about her dad, her past, her rubbish upbringing and the fear that someday she'd have to explain it all to Dominic.

The minister turned to Ginny. "And you." Her smile was warm, but didn't reach her eyes. "Congratulations on your upcoming wedding. Welcome to our home."

Stifling the urge to curtsy and the vague feeling that the minister didn't quite think her good enough, she said, "Thank you. But I still haven't made a decision on the marriage."

Dominic took over the introductions. "Virginia, this is Sally Peterson, our minister of protocol."

"You may call me Sally." She motioned to the chairs in front of her desk.

"Because Virginia is on the fence, I thought perhaps you could better explain to her why our getting married is a good idea."

"Okay." Sally folded her hands and set them on the desk. "What's the best way to explain this?" She thought for another second, then said, "Because your child will someday be our ruler, there isn't a court in the world that would refuse us the opportunity to train him, to bring him up to be our king. Which means you have four choices. First, marry Dom." She smiled at Dominic. "Second, don't marry Dom but live in the palace with your child to help raise him or her. Third, don't marry Dom, move back to the United States with a contingent of bodyguards and household servants until the child is twelve and will attend boarding school, and fourth, give up all rights."

Her voice softened. "I'm certain you don't want to give up all rights. Not marrying Dom, but living in the palace and helping raise your child makes sense, but will expose Dom to all kinds of gossip. He could be perceived as being unfit as a ruler if he couldn't even persuade the woman he'd gotten pregnant to marry him."

The thought of the ramifications for Dom made her blood run cold. She might not really know him, but she knew him enough that she could not let that happen to him. "What would happen if we got married?"

"You would need to be seen in public together at least twice before you would announce the quick wedding. We will also announce the pregnancy at the same time so that the rumors of a pregnancy don't take the sheen off your wedding day. The theory is if we get it out immediately it won't be 'news' anymore."

Exactly what Dom had told her.

He caught her gaze and smiled at her.

Once again she saw a glimpse of the guy who had whisked her away the night of their fateful dalliance. Stiff and formal or not, almost-complete stranger or not, he was the father of her child and his needs had to be considered.

"Plus, if you marry Dom, your position gives you a bit of power so to speak. You can use your celebrity to support causes. As someone who'd worked in education, you may wish to host events to raise awareness or to build schools anywhere in the world."

"Oh." That was amazing. Something she hadn't considered and something that would give her a chance to impact the *world*. Just the thought of it stole her breath. "That would be great."

"Plus," Sally said with a chuckle, "a royal wedding is fantastic. Your gown would be made by the designer of your choice." She laughed. "And money is no object. The guests will be royalty and dignitaries from every country in the world. You would get to meet your president."

"The president of the United States would be invited?"

"And he'd attend." Sally smiled. "Our royal family is influential. We don't just control waterways. We have oil, which gives us a seat in OPEC."

It was hard enough to adjust to the knowledge that Dominic was a royal. Now she was being told his small, seemingly insignificant country was powerful?

Oh, boy.

Dominic's hand stealthily slid from the arm of his chair over to her hand. He caught her pinkie with his, linking them.

She swallowed. He'd done that in the limo on the way to the club in Los Angeles. A small, sweet, simple gesture that made her heart catch and her breathing tremble. He recognized that all this information was becoming overwhelming for her. And the pinkie knot? It told her he was there for her.

Damn, but he could be sweet.

"But, as I mentioned, you have choices. And as I understand the situation, you and Dominic plan to divorce two years after the baby is born."

Dominic quietly said, "Yes."

The small, sweet gesture suddenly felt empty. Pointless. There was no need for them to be close. They just had to be friendly.

She pulled her hand away.

"In that case, most of your options still apply. Except

Dom wouldn't suffer the negative press of being unable to persuade you to marry him."

"I could return to the United States."

Sally laughed. "If, after years of being influential in education, of being someone known to the entire world, someone impacting the world, you still want to go back, then, yes."

Ginny smiled. Something about the way Sally kept highlighting the good part about staying in the country told her there was a catch, and she knew it had to have something to do with her child. "But the baby would go with me?"

Sally rose from the desk and walked to the front where she leaned against it. Her voice was soft, gentle. "Yes. As I'd said, that is an option. But it will require heightened security and teachers for home schooling unless you can find a private school that passes our tests. Then every time there was a ceremony, a formal dinner, a holiday, he'd have to be flown home." She shifted against the desk. "Ideally, our future ruler should be raised here. In the palace. It just makes things easier."

"Right."

Dominic faced her. "Our child needs to be acclimated into the life of a royal. Not rigidly, but to realize all monarchs and leaders are people, too. Countries are made up of people. Troubles are borne by people. Ruling is about people."

Caught in the gaze of his dark, dark eyes, she remembered why she'd fallen so hard for him the night she met him. He always knew the right thing to say.

Even if it was a modification of the truth.

Yesterday, he'd been smart enough to let her believe

returning home would be possible, when in reality it sounded as if it would be very hard on their child.

He hadn't out and out lied. In fact, if the option really was available for her to return to the United States, then he hadn't lied at all. But he was counting on her love for their baby to help her to see that returning home might be an option but it was a poor one.

She couldn't decide if he was manipulating her or trusting her, but after eighteen years of a bullying, manipulative father, that misstep made her stomach roil.

She rose. "You know what? I'm a bit tired. I think I should go back to the room."

He bounced to his feet. "Of course."

She faced Sally. "I'll need some help with etiquette. I know the basics but the specifics are way beyond what a high school guidance counselor needs to know. Even if I decide not to marry Dominic, I have an entire week here and I don't want to embarrass him."

Sally grabbed her calendar. "I'll make appointments for you."

"Just let me know when to be where."

Dominic laughed. "The teachers will come to our apartment. You're not just a guest of a prince. You're pregnant. We want to take care of you."

She ignored his laugh. Ignored the smile on his face. Ignored that he was solicitous about her pregnancy. Her dad had been exceptional at being sweet, being charming, when it suited him. She didn't want to think Dominic was like her dad, but the facts were out there plain and simple. He'd told her a half-truth the day before.

Still, she could deal with this. She was unfortunately good at dealing with people who told her half-truths.

She straightened her shoulders. "That's fine. I'm happy to have the sessions in your apartment."

She held her head high as she walked out of Sally's office, but her stomach churned.

Why was she even *considering* marrying a man who was a manipulator like her father?

CHAPTER THREE

DOMINIC HAD TO run to catch up to her. "What was that all about?"

"What?"

"Your sudden need to leave as if Sally had done something wrong."

"It wasn't Sally." She turned on him. "*You* led me to believe I could go home."

"The option is yours."

"Oh, sure, if I want to make our child's life a miserable succession of plane rides between Texas and Xaviera."

Not waiting for a reply, she raced to the elevator, punched the button and was inside before Dom had wrapped his head around what she'd said. He jumped into the plush car two seconds before the door would have closed.

"I'm sorry if the truth offends you."

She turned on him again, poking her index finger into his chest. "The truth? You told me half the truth, so I would get false hope. When the situation looked totally impossible, you held out the offer of being able to return home. Now that I'm adjusting to you, to your family and to people bowing to you, I'm told the option exists, but, oh, by the way, it will make your child's life suck."

He caught her finger. "What did you want me to say? No. You can't ever go home again?"

"Yes! I'm twenty-five years old. I handled two thousand kids for three years. I can handle this!"

The elevator door swished open. She yanked her finger from his hand and headed across the big square marble floor to the regal double doors of his apartment.

He ran after her, but didn't reach her until she was already in the sitting room of their apartment. When he did, he caught her arm and forced her to face him. "I will not have you be mad at me for something I didn't do! We didn't talk a lot yesterday. I gave you your bare-bones options because that's all you seemed to want to hear. Sally expanded on those options today. If you'd wanted the entire explanation yesterday, you should have stayed for it! Instead you said something about wanting to go to your room. I was fully prepared to talk it all out. *You* left."

He could see from the shifting expressions in her blue eyes that she knew what he said was true.

She dropped her head to her hands. "Oh, God. I'm sorry."

"It's okay."

She shook her head. "No. It isn't." She sucked in a breath. "Look, my dad was a hopeless alcoholic who was always lying to me. I have trust issues."

Glad to have his real Ginny back, Dom breathed a sigh of relief. "We all have trust issues."

He motioned for her to sit, so they could talk some more, but she shook her head. "I'm fine. Really. Tired, but fine."

A trained diplomat, he read the discretion in her answer and knew she didn't want to talk about this. Who would want to talk about a father who drank so much he'd clearly made her miserable? But at least he understood why she'd absurdly said she would have taken his family when she was a child.

"I probably also should have told you that all of this will be set out in an agreement."

"An agreement?"

"Yes, the legal office will draw up an agreement that sets out everything. Your responsibilities. Our responsibilities. What's required of you as mother to our future heir."

"You're going to put all this into an agreement?"

He chuckled. "You wouldn't?"

She considered that. "A written agreement would make things easier."

"It's one of the few documents that will remain totally secret. Because it's considered private, no one but you and I, the king and both of our counsels will even know it exists. But your jobs and responsibilities will be spelled out and so will mine. Plus, we can provide you with counsel who can assure you the agreement is fair. If you don't like who we provide, you can choose your own counsel."

She nodded.

"We're not trying to cheat you."

"Right."

"Really. And we don't sign the agreement until the day of the ceremony. So right up until the day we get married, you can change your mind."

"I'll just be doing it publicly."

He shrugged. "Sorry. The press sort of comes with the territory."

She didn't answer, but she'd definitely calmed down.

A written agreement seemed to suit her, but she still looked tired, worn. "Why don't you go lie down?"

She nodded and walked into her suite, closing the door behind her.

He gave her the morning to rest. When she came out at lunchtime, he pulled out her chair and she smiled.

Relieved that she really was okay, he said, "A simple coffee date has been arranged for us this afternoon."

"Then you'd better get someone up here to help me with wardrobe because I went through the clothes you had sent up yesterday and there isn't anything in there that I'd actually wear out in public."

"What about the white pants with the sweater?"

"Seriously? That blue sweater with the big anchor on the front? My mother would wear that."

"Okay. Fine. Right after lunch I'll have a clothier come up."

"Great." She looked at the food, then sat back as if discouraged.

"You don't like ham sandwiches?"

"They're great. I'm just not hungry."

He sucked in a breath. They'd had a misunderstanding but worked it out, and she'd taken a rest. When she'd come out of her suite, it was to eat lunch. Now suddenly she wasn't hungry?

"You had an orange for breakfast. You have to eat."

"Maybe I can get a cookie at the coffee shop."

He laughed, thinking she was joking. Seeing she wasn't, he frowned. "Seriously? That's going to be your food for the day? A cookie?"

"I told you. I'm not very hungry."

He supposed their situation would be enough to make a normal woman lose her appetite, but being married to him wasn't exactly the third circle of hell. Everything and anything she wanted could be at her disposal. There was no reason for her to refuse to eat.

"Okay. From here on out, you choose our menus."

She nodded. He felt marginally better. But what man in the world could possibly like the idea that just the thought of marrying him had taken away a woman's appetite?

Was she subtly saying he made her sick?

After a visit from the clothier, an hour's wait for clothing to be delivered and an hour for her to dress, they left the palace in his Mercedes. He drove, surprising her.

"We don't need a bodyguard?"

"They're discreetly behind us. This is supposed to look like a casual date."

"Ah."

He tried not to let her one-word answer grate against his skin, but it did. She wouldn't eat around him and her conversation had been reduced to one-word answers. He'd thought they'd resolved their issue, but maybe they hadn't? Or maybe the reality of marrying a prince was finally sinking in?

"You know you're going to have to say more than one word to me when we get into the coffee shop."

"Yes."

He gritted his teeth. "We could also use this time to chitchat so that when we get out of the car, we'll already be engaged in conversation the way normal people would be."

"I know all about being a normal person." She flicked her gaze to him. "You, on the other hand, are wearing a white shirt out for coffee."

"I'm a prince."

"You're also a person, supposedly out with a woman he likes. A woman he's comfortable with. White shirt does not say *comfortable*."

"Oh, and scruffy jeans does?"

She laughed. "Are you kidding? Scruffy jeans is the very definition of *comfortable*."

"You look like you're going to the trash yard."

"I look like an American girl on a date with a prince she just met. I am playing the part. As our dates get more serious so will my wardrobe."

Unexpectedly seeing her reasoning, he sighed. "Okay. I get it. Just don't make fun of the white shirt."

"Fine."

He glanced in the rearview mirror and saw not just the Mercedes with his bodyguards, but also the usual assortment of paparazzi. Satisfied, he finished the drive to the ocean-side coffee shop.

Xaviera's warm sun beat down on him as he walked around to the passenger's side and opened the door for Ginny. He took her hand and helped her out, to the whir of cameras. She stepped out, one blue-jeans-clad leg at a time, wedge sandals, short blue T-shirt and big sunglasses, all looking very normal to him in the parking lot of a beach café.

She really had been right about her very casual clothes.

Standing in front of him, she caught his gaze and smiled, and his heart—which had been thundering in his chest from fear of the first step of their charade—slowed down. He hadn't forgotten how beautiful she was, but somehow or another the sunlight seemed to bring out the best in her rich yellow hair and tanned skin. She might not be royalty or someone accustomed to the public eye, like an actress or model, but she was every bit as beautiful—if not more beautiful because she was genuine.

The cameras whirred again.

She whispered, "What do we do? Do we wave?"

"We ignore them."

She peeked up at him. "Really?"

He laughed, took her hand and led her to the café door. "Yes. We know they are there. But we also know they are always there, even if, for us, they have no purpose. Unlike an actor or actress, we don't need them to enhance our visibility. We tolerate them. Thus, we ignore them."

"Got it."

He held the door open for her. The press rushed up behind them, but his bodyguards closed the door on them. Two things happened simultaneously. The press opened the door and crammed in behind the bodyguards, their cameras whirring. And Marco, café owner, greeted them.

"Prince Dominic!" He bowed. "It's an honor."

"Can I have my usual, Marco? And—" Oh, dear God. First complication. He could not order coffee for a pregnant woman. He faced Ginny. "What would you like, Ginny?"

As soon as he said her name, the reporters began shouting, "Ginny! Ginny! Look here, Ginny!"

She slid off her sunglasses. Doing as he'd told her, she ignored the press. "How about some water? It's hot."

The press laughed. "Did you not know our weather was hot?"

"Where are you from?"

"How old are you?"

"How did you meet?"

"How long have you been dating?"

Dominic also ignored them. "Just water? What about that cookie?"

Marco said, "I have a cookie that will make you happy to be alive."

Ginny laughed. "That'd be great."

"You sound American."

He saw Ginny waver. The questions directed at her were hard for her to ignore. And the press began closing in on them. Even with his two bodyguards standing six inches away, the reporters and photographers bent around them, shouted questions and took pictures as Marco made Dom's coffee, retrieved a bottle of water and wrapped a cookie in a napkin.

Dom took their items and turned to say, "Let's go out to the deck by the dock," but, as he turned, he saw her sway. Before he could blink, she began to crumble.

He dropped his coffee, the water and the cookie to the counter and just barely caught her before she hit the floor.

The cameras whirred. A gasp went up from the crowd. Dominic's bodyguards turned to help him as Marco came out from behind the counter, broom in hand.

"Get out of here!" He waved the broom at the paparazzi. "Get out, you brood of vipers!" He glanced behind the counter. "Antonella. I chase them out. You lock the door!"

Down on one knee, holding Ginny, Dominic cast Marco a grateful look as the coffeehouse owner and Dom's bodyguards shooed the press out of his shop and Antonella locked the door behind them.

Ginny's eyes slowly blinked open. "It's so hot."

He sort of smiled. She was so fragile and so beautiful, and holding her again took him back to their night of dancing in LA and making love in her condo. A million feelings trembled through him. Brilliant memories. A sense of peace that had intermixed with their fun. The wonderful, almost-overwhelming sensation of being able to be himself because she was so comfortable being herself.

"You're adding to the heat by wearing jeans."

"Trying to look normal."

Her skin was clammy. Her eyes listless and dull. His happy, beautiful one-night stand memories dropped like a rock, as his heart squeezed with fear. "We need to get you to the hospital."

"You're sending a pregnant woman to the hospital for fainting? You haven't been around pregnant women much have you?"

"That's all this is?"

She drew in a breath and suddenly looked stronger. "Heat. Pregnancy. Nerves. Take your pick."

He said, "Right." Then nodded at Marco. "Open her water."

The solicitous shop owner did as he was told. He handed the opened bottle to Dominic, who held it out to her. She took a few sips.

Dominic sighed, grateful she was coming back but so scared internally that he shook from it. His heart had about leaped out of his chest when he saw her falling. "You should probably have a bite or two of the cookie. I told you to eat lunch."

She smiled. "Wasn't hungry."

Antonella brought over the cookie. "You eat."

Ginny sat up a bit and took the cookie from Antonella's hands.

"Maybe we should get you to a chair?"

She laughed. "I feel safer down here. No cameras. No one can see me through the windows."

He felt it, too. Behind the tables and chairs between them and the doorway, he felt totally protected from the press.

She ate a few bites of her cookie, drank the entire bottle of water and held out her hand to him. "We can stand now."

"We're going to have to go back to the car though a crowd of reporters and photographers who just saw you faint. If you thought their questions were bad before this—" he caught her gaze "—now they are going to be horrific. A tidal wave of jumbled words and noisy cameras. Are you up for this?"

"I'm fine."

"Right. As soon as we get home, I'm having you checked out by the doctor."

"I would expect nothing less from a man accustomed to bossing people around."

His fear for her wouldn't recede and she didn't seem to be taking any of this seriously. "Stop joking. You fainted."

"On a hot day, after not eating." She smiled suddenly, pushed herself to her tiptoes and kissed his cheek. "I'm fine."

The unexpected kiss went through him like a warm spring breeze. He told himself not to make too much of it, but how could he not when color was returning to her cheeks and she was smiling, really smiling, for the first time since their argument that morning.

Wanting to get her home, Dominic said, "Let's go."

But before they could walk to the door, Marco hugged her and then Antonella hugged her. Dominic finally noticed the few stragglers sitting at the café tables, necks craned to see what was going on. One or two whispered, but in general, they'd given them privacy.

Leading her to the door, he addressed them, "Thank you all for your consideration."

People nodded and smiled and a few said, "You're welcome." Then they reached the door. The lock clicked as Antonella sprang it.

He said, "Ready?"

Ginny nodded.

He opened the door to the whir of cameras and shouts of questions. "How are you?"

"Why did you faint?"

"What's your last name?"

"Are you pregnant?"

Dominic's steps faltered.

But Ginny slid her sunglasses on her face and smiled at them. "I didn't eat lunch." She turned to Dominic and entwined her arm with his. "Dom told me to eat lunch but—" She held out a leg. "Look at these jeans. They are to die for and I wanted them to fit." She smiled again. "American girls, right? We love our jeans and we want them to look perfect."

Then she turned them in the direction of his Mercedes. His bodyguards created a path for them to walk.

He opened the door for her.

She slid inside. Before Dom could close the door, she gave a final wave to the press. "I'm fine," she called out to them. "And, I swear, I will eat before we come out again."

Walking around the hood of his car, he heard the rumble of laughter. He peeked up to see the smiles of approval on the faces of those in the crowd. And why not? She was beautiful, approachable, *likable*.

But he also saw a few reporters frowning in his direction. He saw the ones on their cell phones talking feverishly.

He slid into the car. "You know your pregnancy's out now, right?"

"Yup." She caught his gaze. "Looks like we won't need a second date."

"You're saying yes?"

She nodded.

He took her hand and lifted it to his lips. "Thank you."

"Oh, don't thank me. I have a feeling we're in for one hell of a ride."

CHAPTER FOUR

THEY SCHEDULED A press conference for nine o'clock the next morning in the press room of the palace. The king announced his son's marriage to Virginia Jones of Texas in the United States, a former guidance counselor. Then he gave the podium to Dominic.

As Ginny expected, the resounding cry that rose from the crowd was… "Is Ginny pregnant?"

Another man might have been cowed, embarrassed or even unprepared. Ginny knew Dom had rehearsed every possible scenario of this moment into the wee hours of the morning with someone from his staff.

So she wasn't surprised when he smiled and said, "Yes."

The swish and whir of cameras filled the room. Several people called, "Ginny, look here."

But she kept her eyes trained on Dominic because that's what *her* two hours of training the night before had been about. That and choosing something to wear. After a doctor had seen her and pronounced her well, a clothier had arrived with swatches and catalogs. Sally from the protocol office had wanted her in a raspberry-colored suit. The king had thought she'd look more dignified in a white suit. But she'd reminded them that she'd fainted because she was *pregnant* and had gotten too hot. Her choice for the press conference had been a simple green dress with thin straps and a pale green cardigan—which she could remove, she reminded the king—if she got too hot.

The king had scowled, but Dominic had suddenly said, "I think she's right."

All eyes had turned to him. He'd shrugged. "You're not the ones who had to watch her fall. I barely caught her. I don't think we want to risk having that happen again."

Nope. If there was one thing Ginny knew, it was that she did not want to faint again. Seeing ten pictures of herself crumpling to a coffee-shop floor in the newspapers that morning had been enough to cure her of ever wanting to faint in public again.

But Dominic standing up for her choice had caused her breath to quietly catch. Her simple pregnancy might impact an entire kingdom—and maybe someday even the world—but this was her *baby*. And Dom's.

When he stood up for her, he caught her gaze, and in that second a wave of feeling had almost made her dizzy. They'd created a child and were getting married—temporarily. He'd warned her not to spin fantasies of permanency with him, and she wasn't, but with a baby on the way and so many people telling them what to do, she didn't see how they could get through the next few months without forming a team.

Which made it a terrible, terrible thing that she'd compared him to her father. Because no matter how hard she tried, she couldn't stop doing it. Not because she genuinely believed Dom was like her dad, but because she was so afraid. Living with her dad had been a nightmare. Only a fool would deliberately enter that kind of situation again.

So he couldn't be like her dad. He *couldn't*. Yet something about this situation, and Dom, set off warning signals that would not let her relax.

Watching Dominic speak now, she waited for his signal for her to join him at the podium. He fielded a question or two about how they met, then, just as they'd practiced, he turned to her with a smile and said, "Why don't we have Ginny join us to help answer some questions?"

In her high-heeled white sandals that perfectly offset the pretty green dress, she carefully walked to the podium. He slid his arm around her waist, bringing her closer to the microphones. Questions filled the air.

"Have you found a dress?"

"Are you having morning sickness?"

She heard the questions, but looking up at Dominic, all she saw were those onyx eyes filled with expectation. Could she stand up for him? Would she stand up for him? Would she protect his reputation as the future king the way he'd stood up for her the night before? Was she willing to fully commit to the charade?

Just as she couldn't quite get herself to trust him, the question in his eyes told her he didn't entirely trust her, either.

Which made them even.

If there was one thing she'd learned about partnerships, it was that they ran best when the partners really were even. Oddly, this deal would work not because they trusted each other, but because they didn't.

"Are you a real live Cinderella?"

That question made her laugh and brought her out of her reverie. She faced the sea of press crowded into the small room.

"Yes. I do feel like Cinderella. No, I haven't even

chosen a designer to make my dress. So I'll need all four weeks before the wedding just to find something to wear." When the reporters laughed, she smiled. "And no morning sickness."

She paused long enough to give Dominic her best fake loving smile, deferring to him, the way she'd been taught to the night before. When their gazes met, she could see he was pleased with how she handled herself. She recognized that his happy expression was part of their act, but he'd looked at her exactly that way the night they'd gone clubbing. The night they'd created their baby.

Her heart kicked against her ribs. A flash of memories flooded her brain. Kissing in the limo. Laughing at stupid things. Not a care in the world. And for one foolish second, she wished they could be those two people again. Two people just having fun. Not making a commitment—

She quickly looked away. Things like that, staring into his fathomless eyes, longing for a chance just to enjoy each other, would get her into trouble.

She faced the reporters. "So I won't faint again." She winced. "That is if I listen to Dom and actually eat breakfast and lunch."

A quiet chuckle went up from the group as they scribbled in notebooks.

The questions started again.

"What about your job?"

"Will you miss working?"

"What was it like growing up with an alcoholic dad?"

"Did you spin daydreams as a little girl that you'd someday marry a prince?"

The room suddenly got hot. She hadn't expected her

dad's life to escape scrutiny. She simply hadn't expected it to come up so soon.

She pushed her hair off her face, buying time, hoping to cool her forehead a bit before sweat began to bead on it. "I love my job." She answered the first and second questions together since they were easy, as she dreadfully scrambled in her head to think of how to answer the third. "If it were possible to be a princess *and* be a guidance counselor, I'd do both. As it is, my duty lies with Xaviera and our baby." She laughed. "My mom reminded me that even if my baby wasn't a future king, he'd still take up all my time and shift my priorities."

Before she could deal with question three, two other reporters raised their hands and called out, "So you've spoken to your mom and have her blessing?" and "Where is your mom?"

"My mom is finishing out her semester," she said, then suddenly wished her mom didn't have to work. Being alone in a strange country, in a white-hot spotlight with a guy she'd liked a lot was making her crazy. She had to remember he wasn't fun-loving Dom. He was Prince Dominic. And this marriage wasn't real. Hell, this whole situation was barely real.

"She has a few more weeks of school, but she'll be here for the wedding."

"I'm still waiting for an answer about your childhood with an alcoholic father."

The sweat arrived, beading on her forehead. A hot, dizzying wave passed through her, weakening her knees, just as it had two seconds before she'd fainted the day before.

"My father was sick," she said quietly, praying her legs would continue to hold her. "He also died when I was eighteen. I barely remember that part of my life."

That wasn't really a lie, more of an exaggeration. She didn't want to remember, so she spent her days refusing to even think about those years.

"As for whether or not I spun fantasies about marrying a prince." She smiled. "I hadn't. I was a very pragmatic child, enamored with my mom's love of her classes and students. But I'm glad I met Dominic."

Again, not a lie. She *was* glad she had met him. She'd loved their night out. It was being in cahoots with him, putting so much of her life into another person's hands, that caused fear to course through her. Especially after the mention of her dad. After being reminded that trusting the wrong person could suck the life out of your soul, reduce you to someone who suspiciously weighed every word and soon didn't trust anyone. Someone who protected herself by staying in her room, alone and lonely.

She did not want that to be her life again.

This time when she turned to smile at Dominic, she knew her eyes were dull and listless.

She wasn't surprised when he said, "And that's all for this morning. Our press office has issued a release with all relevant information."

He led her off the podium and then out of the room, behind the king, who turned to her with a satisfied look. "You lasted much longer than I predicted."

She winced. "Thank you, I think."

"Well, it's a compliment to an extent. I'm still not sure I trust your fashion sense. And I'm not at all pleased that you didn't warn us about your dad."

Her stomach churned. She'd buried her dad seven years ago, but here she was hiding him again, protecting him again— "I…"

Dominic stepped up. "I knew about her dad. My

security detail investigated everything." He caught Ginny's gaze. "I admit we glossed over his alcoholism because he's been dead for seven years. But no one kept it a secret."

She swallowed. Every time she looked in his eyes, she had no question about why he'd so easily been able to seduce her. But every time he talked he reminded her that she didn't belong here in his life, and how difficult the next years would be. "I guess you did that while we were waiting for the paternity results."

"Actually, we investigated you when we were told you would be my liaison at the school." He faced the king. "And you have a full report on Ginny's life in your office. Her father is in there."

King Ronaldo said, "I don't know how I missed it."

"You missed it because he's barely a footnote. He was never arrested. Never in the papers. Never anything. And now he's gone. Ginny and I talked about this a bit yesterday and the end result was I decided there's no real reason to put her through the memories by insisting she give us details."

He smiled slightly at her.

She tried to smile back. But an odd feeling tumbled through her. Not quite a nudge that she should trust him, the feeling told her at the very least she should appreciate the way he'd saved her from having to relive a part of her life that was gone. Past. She shouldn't have to explain it.

Sally said, "Yes, well, Prince Dominic, you should have bought this to your father's attention instead of expecting him to find it in a report."

Dom faced Sally, who stood with her arms crossed, clearly unhappy with him. He said, "I'll remember next time," but when he turned to Ginny he winked.

The weird feeling tumbled through her again.

Sally lifted her clipboard. "Okay, Ms. Jones, you have a few people coming to the apartment for lessons today. Mostly protocols and etiquettes. At four, the clothier and I will be bringing catalogs of various designers' work so you can begin the process of screening designers for your dress." She flipped a page. "Dom, I believe you're due in parliament this afternoon."

Dominic caught Ginny's hand. "Then I guess we better get back to the apartment and arrange for lunch."

Sally said, "Fine—"

But Dominic didn't wait for the rest of her answer. He turned and walked away, leading Ginny down several halls. He walked so fast, she had to skip to keep up with him in her high, high heels, but the air that whooshed past them was cool, and she suddenly felt like laughing. Not only had they survived the press, but Dominic had taken her side—again.

When the elevator door closed behind them, Ginny said, "That was awesome."

"What? You liked being interviewed by reporters?"

She batted a hand. "I could take that or leave that. What I loved was you walking away from Sally."

Dom spared her a glance, then he grinned. "She's protocol office so she basically runs everything. It's fun every once in a while to remind her that she works for me."

"Oh, so you're a tough guy now?"

He laughed. "I told you being a king is all about being respected."

"Well, in that case, let me say you got some votes of confidence from me."

He turned. "Really?"

"Yes. Last night when you said we should use my

dress choice and this morning when you let me answer my own questions from the press—those were good. But not letting Sally push me around? Or your dad? Those were better. I… Well, I felt like a real person."

"You are a real person."

She laughed, but something inside nudged her to talk, to at least trust him enough to tell him the basics. "I know that. But my upbringing was awful. There are more chances that I'm going to embarrass you than make you proud."

"Are you kidding? Your first public act was to faint, then pretend it was no big deal when you walked back into the fray of reporters to get to the car. You waved and told them you were fine as if they were a bunch of friends hanging out on a street corner." He laughed. "I think they don't know what to do with you."

"So confusion is the way to go, if I can't beguile them with my good looks and charm?"

He sneaked another peek at her as the elevator door opened on the big square foyer before his apartment. "Oh, I wouldn't discount your charm just yet."

She looked up at him. He gazed down at her. With the huge hall just outside the door empty and quiet, the tiny elevator suddenly felt intimate.

Gazing into his eyes, she remembered how he'd pulled her to him outside her apartment door and kissed her like a man so crazy about a woman he couldn't resist her.

So maybe he did think she had charm.

The elevator door began to close and without looking away Dominic caught it, forcing it open again.

"We better go."

"Yeah."

Neither of them moved. Something hummed between

them. She'd say it was the same something that had brought him to her condo door all those weeks ago, the same something that drew them to her bed, except in the past two days she'd made him laugh and he wasn't going to make her talk about her dad.

He took a step closer to her and her breath shivered. Her lips tingled from wanting to kiss him. But he stayed where he was, close enough to touch, but not making a move to kiss her, though his eyes shimmered with need.

The air filled with something hot and tempting. She knew she could easily label this lust, but she knew something else was at work here. They really were forming a team. And the pull of that, the longing not to be alone in this deal, fighting for herself and her rights, but having somebody fight with her, was even stronger than the lust that had driven them that night.

That scared her silly.

But his gaze held hers.

And everything inside her trembled with yearning.

She longed for the day she'd met him, when she didn't fear their future because she didn't think they had a future, and she wondered what it would be like to let her guard down again—

But Dom had warned her not to spin fairy tales. And life had taught her that good things could turn bad in the blink of an eye. Not more than twenty minutes ago, she'd been worried about comparing him to her dad. Now she wanted to kiss him? To trust him?

Everything was happening too fast.

This was a ruse. Nothing more. And she was going to get hurt if she didn't stop trying to spin that fairy tale.

She turned and walked out of the elevator to the apartment and to her suite.

CHAPTER FIVE

DOMINIC ATE A very quiet, disappointing lunch. No matter how he tried to engage Ginny, she'd smile distantly and pop a bite of food into her mouth so she didn't have to talk to him. Glad to see her eating for the sake of the baby, he couldn't allow himself the luxury of being upset that she wasn't talking to him.

Still, it made him nuts.

They were perfectly fine in that elevator until the conversation about her charming the press. She *could* charm the press. And without effort. But something about that one simple comment had made her quiet. Distant.

He probably shouldn't have mentioned it. Her ability with them was so natural that if he hadn't pointed it out to her, she would have used it without thought. But he liked talking to her and he liked it when they were getting along. Their natural connection would be what would make the charade work.

Then they'd had that moment of looking into each other's eyes, and for twenty seconds he'd thought he wouldn't be able to resist kissing her. But he *had*. He'd remembered his dad, the weakness that plagued him after Dom's mother's death. He knew he couldn't afford a marriage with real emotion. And when he kissed her, he felt things he couldn't define or describe. So he stepped back, away from a kiss he wanted, to prove he didn't *need* it.

That should have made her happy. God knew it made him happy to see he could resist her. She should be happy, too. Instead, she was distant.

He left her after lunch and spent four grueling hours in parliament. Tired and somewhat disgusted, he returned to his palace apartment to find Sally and Joshua, the clothier, sitting on one sofa with Ginny alone on the sofa across from them. Though Sally was frustrated, Joshua looked to be the picture of patience as he ran down the benefits of a list of designers.

Ginny frowned. "I know what I like. I know what I look good in. It just seems so sterile to be picking a gown this way. I always imagined myself trying things on."

Joshua smiled patiently. "Most women would kill for the chance to choose a designer to make a unique gown."

Ginny only sighed and glanced at the photo array of designers and their creations.

Sally shook her head. "What difference does it make? For Pete's sake. This wedding is just for show. It's not real. The gown doesn't have to reflect *you*. It just has to be beautiful. Something fit for a princess."

Ginny finally noticed Dom standing in the foyer by the door, but she quickly looked away. Still, he'd seen the naked misery in her eyes.

She straightened her shoulders, as if seeing him reminded her of her duty to him, and she pointed at one of the photo arrays. "This one. I'd like this designer."

Sally sighed with relief and rose. "We'll contact him."

Joshua rose, too. He bowed. "I am at your service."

Sally said, "Good because she still has a wardrobe to choose. Two pair of jeans and a green dress with cardigan won't be enough clothes for two days let alone over two years."

Joshua on her heels, Sally headed for the white double doors. "You'll be required to meet with Joshua again tomorrow afternoon, Ginny."

"That's Ms. Jones," Dominic said, suddenly annoyed. "She may not be a princess yet. But she will be. And when she is she will be your boss."

Sally quietly gasped and stepped back, but she quickly recovered. Bowing to Dominic, she said, "Yes, Your Majesty."

Joshua all but quivered with fear. New to the palace, because the king and the two princes rarely required help in choosing suits or having them made, he glanced from Dom to Sally, wide-eyed.

Sally opened the door and left. Joshua scampered after her.

Ginny blew her breath out on a long sigh. "You shouldn't have yelled at her. It wasn't her fault that I'm having trouble choosing. And our time is running out. She's right to be annoyed with me."

He walked to the bar and poured himself a Scotch. "Oh, sweetie. You have so much to learn about being a princess."

"I'm not going to be vapid and spoiled."

"Of course, you're not. But you can't let staff belittle you."

"As I said, she was right to be annoyed with me."

"Again. No. You are the member of the royal family here. If you want to take until the day before the wedding to choose your dress, that's what you do. Then *they* scramble."

She laughed.

He sat beside her on the sofa. "So, are you really happy with the designer you chose?"

She shrugged. "He's as good as any."

He caught her chin and nudged her to face him. "As good as any isn't good enough. I want you to be happy the day you get married. It may not be forever, but it's your first wedding."

"That's what I keep thinking."

"So what would you do if you were getting married for keeps?"

"I'd have a lot of pink roses."

"What else?"

"My two friends would be bridesmaids."

"You can have that." He sipped his Scotch. "What else?"

"I don't know. I always imagined my mom and me picking things out." She peeked up at him. "She has great taste."

He laughed. "Really?"

"Well, actually, we have about the same taste. But picking a gown is just something a girl wants to do with her mom. You know. Second opinion and all that." She took a deep breath, blew it out, then looked Dom in the eye. "My picture is going to go around the world. I'd like for it to be a good one."

He nodded. "That's something I'm so accustomed to I forget that others aren't." He rose from the sofa. "I have a dinner meeting tonight that's going to segue into a bigger meeting with several members of parliament. Why don't you call your friends on Skype and invite them to be your bridesmaids?"

She looked up at him, her eyes round and blue and honest. She was one of the most naturally beautiful women he'd ever met. She was also being a much better sport about this marriage than a lot of women would be. She hadn't asked for anything. She just did as she was told. And if she didn't talk to him, maybe that was his fault? He'd told her not to expect a long, happy marriage. If she held herself back, maybe that's what she felt she needed to do.

"Really? I can have bridesmaids?"

"As many as you want." On impulse he bent down and kissed her cheek. "Would a wedding without bridesmaids really look authentic?"

She shook her head.

"So call them."

Ginny watched Dom leave the sitting room and head for his bedroom suite, fighting that feeling again. Except this time, she named it. She wasn't worried about liking him or even being attracted to him. What she was feeling—or maybe recognizing—was that he was a nice guy. A good person. She thanked God he'd reminded her that the wedding needed to "look" authentic to serve his purpose. Otherwise, she might have melted right there at his feet.

She could resist the solemn guy, the one who would be king someday, who wanted everything to be perfect. The other guy, the sweet one who tried to make her happy? That was the guy who had been staring at her in the elevator. The one she'd wanted to kiss. He was the one she had to watch out for.

She returned to her room, found her laptop and connected with her two best friends on Skype. They knew she was pregnant, of course. She'd gone to them for guidance. She'd also called them the day she'd fainted, when she'd agreed to marry Dom. They were not surprised to be receiving invitations to be bridesmaids.

That little piece of normalcy lifted her spirits. It wasn't going to be a real marriage but it was going to be a real wedding, and she was going to look pretty and have her friends with her. They would keep her occupied the week before the big day. And, in a good mood, she'd be better able to look happy for the ceremony.

The next morning at breakfast, she showed her appreciation to Dominic by asking him how his meetings had gone the night before.

He winced. "There are one or two people who fear we are making an alliance with the United States by bringing you into the royal family."

She laughed. When he didn't, she said, "Really? Seriously? They think marrying a commoner from the United States is a lead-in to a treaty?"

"My brother will be marrying a woman as part of a treaty. Why would you be surprised our government is questioning my marriage?"

She shook her head and went back to her oatmeal. "I forget that your country looks at marriage differently."

"It's not really my country that looks at marriage differently. It's the royal family and what's expected of us. I'll be spending weeks alleviating the fears of several members of parliament, assuring them that our marriage is not part of a big master plan."

Taking a bite of oatmeal, she nodded. "I get it. It's something you shouldn't think you have to do, but you will. Just like I'll be spending two hours with Sally's staff today, learning how to curtsy."

"I thought curtsying was out. Old school. Something nobody did anymore."

"According to Sally's morning memo, there are some

small eastern European countries that still believe in it. I just hope we don't run into any of those royal families when I'm big-as-a-house pregnant. I can't imagine curtsying and balancing twenty-five pounds of stomach."

He laughed. "You're going to make an interesting princess."

"Lucky for you, it's only for a little over two years."

He said, "Uh-huh," and went back to reading his newspaper.

Ginny didn't care. Their conversation proved that she could talk to the "nice" Dominic and not get carried away. They did not have to be best friends. But they did have to get along. They had to look good together in public. They needed to know enough about each other that their charade appeared to be real. And this morning it was clear they were succeeding.

If there was a little rumble in her heart about wasting her wedding, a beautiful wedding, on a fake marriage, she silenced it. She'd never imagined herself getting married. Living with her dad had scared her off that. She'd never allow herself to let her guard down with a man enough to get serious enough to get married. So this was her wedding. Her one shot at being a bride. She'd be a fool not to make it as perfect as she could.

At four o'clock that afternoon, Dom unexpectedly returned to the apartment. As they had the day before, Joshua and Sally sat on the sofa across from her. The photo arrays and designer lists were with them.

She faced the door with a smile. "I thought you had more glad-handing to do."

He walked in and said, "I do. But I was the one who told Sally and Joshua to bring the designer lists up to you again. I wanted to make sure we were all on the same page."

"They told me you said I wasn't sure about the designer." She bit her lip, not happy that something she'd told him had become an issue.

He caught her gaze. "I want you to be sure."

The feeling whooshed through her again. The one that told her he was looking out for her because he was a nice guy. He might not love her. He might not even know her well enough to like her. But he was a nice enough guy that he wanted her to be happy.

"Okay."

Even as she said that, the big double doors of Dominic's apartment opened. "Ginny?"

Ginny's head snapped up. "Mom?"

She blinked as she saw her tall, slim mother race into the sitting room from the echoing foyer. Wearing a tan pantsuit that the king probably would have loved for its dignity, she ran over to Ginny.

Ginny rose and was enfolded into her mom's hug. After a long squeeze, she said, "Let me look at you!"

"Why aren't you in school?"

"Dom called. He said you needed help with your gown."

Her throat closed and tears welled in her eyes. This act of Dominic's was a little more difficult to call the actions of a nice guy trying to keep her happy. Having her mother flown to Xaviera was so kind it made her chest tight.

"I don't exactly need help. I just love your opinions."

Her mom said, "Even better." Then she faced Joshua and Sally, both of whom had risen. "And you must be Sally and Joshua."

Sally bowed slightly. Joshua said, "She's actually very clear about what she wants. I think she just needs your reassurance."

"Joshua, Sally, this is my mother, Rose Jones."

Ginny's mom smiled broadly. Her pretty blond hair had a hint of pink in it, because—well, she was a Texas girl, who'd grown up dancing to the Beach Boys and riding horses, and that crazy part of her had no intention of dying. "Let me see the designers and the dresses."

Joshua immediately handed over the photo array panels, but Ginny stepped away and slid around to the back of the couch where Dom stood.

He raised his eyebrows in question. "What?"

"You told my mom I needed help?"

He shook his head. "No, I called her and said I wanted you to be happy planning this wedding."

The sweetness of the gesture filled her heart. "I would have been okay."

"And the wedding would have looked fake."

This time the reminder that he didn't want the wedding to look fake didn't go through her like a knife. It was their deal. He'd always been up-front about their deal.

The crazy feeling she got around nice Dom morphed into something soft and happy. "We're going to have a beautiful wedding."

He smiled. "Yes, we are."

The air between them changed. For a few seconds, she debated springing to her tiptoes and hugging him, but that wasn't really acceptable, either.

Holding his gaze, she took a step back, then another, suddenly realizing why she kept getting odd nudges. After decades of surface relationships that she'd ended before she even knew the guy she was involved with, she'd managed to never really know anyone, never get beyond platitudes. But planning a fake wedding? Living in the same apartment with Dom? Coconspirators to protect their child? She was getting to know him. And she liked him. A lot more than she'd ever liked any man.

And he'd warned her not to spin a fairy-tale fantasy because he didn't want a marriage with emotion.

CHAPTER SIX

TWO DAYS LATER, Dom strode down the marble-floored hall to the double doors of his apartment. Since Rose had arrived, his home had become like a beehive. Where Ginny might be shy about creating a wardrobe, Rose had taken to the task as if she was born to it. Designers had been called in. Dresses and pants arrived for fittings. Two styles of wedding dresses had been chosen and Alfredo Larenzo, an Italian designer, had been hired to create them.

With a wince, he partially opened one of the two double doors, sticking his head in far enough to see into the living room. Which was, mercifully, empty. For a second, he hoped that Ginny and her mom had gone out for lunch, but his chest pinched. Since Rose had arrived, he'd also barely seen Ginny.

Not that he missed her. He didn't really know her. They were in a fake situation. There was nothing to miss. The thing was, he liked seeing her. Usually, she was funny. After four-hour sessions in parliament, funny was welcome. So he didn't miss her. He missed her silliness.

Comfortable with that assessment, he walked past the double sofas, over to the bar. When he turned to pour his Scotch, he saw the door to Ginny's suite door was

open. And there she stood, in little pink panties and a
pink lace bra. A short man wearing spectacles and a
white shirt with the sleeves rolled to his elbows had
a tape measure around her hips. Her mom stood with
her back to the door, obviously supervising.

Dom stared. He'd forgotten how perfect she was.
With full breasts, a sweet dip for a waist and hips that
flared just enough for a man to run his hand along, she
had what most men would consider a perfect figure.

The short, dark-haired guy raised the tape measure
to her waist and Dom followed every movement of the
man's hands, remembering the smoothness of her shape,
the silkiness of her skin. The tailor whipped the tape
around and snapped the two ends together in the middle,
right above her belly button and Dominic's head tilted.

Right there…

Right below that perfect belly button…

Was his child.

His child.

His hand went limp and the glass he was holding fell
to the bar with a thump.

Ginny's head snapped up and she turned to see him
standing there, staring. Their eyes met. And it hit him
for the very first time, not that she was pregnant, but
that the baby she carried was *his*.

His baby.

He'd created a life.

Rose turned, saw him and walked to the door. "Sorry,
Dom. Didn't realize you were home."

And she closed the door.

Dominic stared at it. The whole thing about the baby
didn't floor him as much as the realization that the baby
was in Ginny's stomach. In a few weeks that flat tummy
of hers would be round. She'd gain weight. Be miser-

able. Probably grouchy. Her feet would swell. She'd be clumsy—in front of millions. And then she'd spend God knew how long in labor.

Because of his baby.

Ginny's suite door opened and she walked out, tying the belt of a pink satin robe around her.

"Was there something you wanted?"

He stared at her, his chest tight, his mind numb. Up until that very moment he hadn't really considered how much Ginny was doing for him. Oh, he understood the loss of her job, but he suddenly saw the other things— losing her friends, living away from her mom, stretching her tummy to unknown limits, changing everything.

For his baby.

"Dom?"

He shook his head to clear it. "Sorry. I'm taking a break and thought I'd come up and see if you're ready for the formal dinner tonight with the ambassador."

She angled her thumb behind her, pointing at her suite door. "That's what the little guy with the moustache is doing. Final fitting for a dress Sally tells me your dad is going to have a fit over."

A laugh bubbled up, but he squelched it. "You can't always push my dad's buttons."

She shrugged. "I'm bored."

His laughter died. "Really?"

"No! Absolutely not. I'm getting fitted for a billion dresses and three-point-five-million pair of jeans. I never realized how many clothes a princess was expected to have."

"So you're not bored?"

"No. I just have a style." She shrugged and the pretty, shiny pink robe shifted over her sun-kissed shoulders.

He remembered biting those shoulders, nibbling her

neck, rubbing his entire body over the length of her entire body.

"And, I swear, I'm not going overboard with sexy clothes. I'm just not going to dress like a grandma."

He cleared his throat. "I get it about not wanting to dress like a grandma. But be careful."

"You don't think it's time for someone to bring your dad into the twenty-first century?"

"If you can bring him in without the press having a field day, then give it your best shot."

She smiled, turned and walked back to her room. He watched every swish of the satin over her round bottom.

"Dinner's at eight, right?"

She called the question over her shoulder, her shiny yellow hair flowing to the middle of her back, accenting that curved waist that led to her perfect butt.

Dominic licked his suddenly dry lips. "Yes, eight. But we need to be in my dad's quarters at seven so that we all arrive in the dining room together, long before the ambassador so we can greet him."

"Piece of cake."

She opened the door to her suite and walked inside, leaving him alone in the living room again.

He tugged his tie away from his throat. A year of celibacy with her was not going to be easy.

He threw back the shot of Scotch and returned to his office for a few hours of admin work. When he entered the apartment again, Ginny's door was closed. He suspected she was getting ready for the dinner, so he went to his quarters, showered and put on the trousers and white shirt of his tux.

He managed the bow tie the way he could since he was eight, but the onyx-and-diamond cuff links, heirlooms with tricky catches, wouldn't lock.

He looked at his door and smiled. For the first time in his life he had a woman. In his quarters. About to marry him. Why shouldn't he take advantage?

Walking past the white sofas in the sitting room, he reminded himself that another man engaged to a gorgeous woman would find much better ways to take advantage of the situation, but he sought only help with cuff links. He was insane.

He knocked on her door.

"Yes."

"It's me, Dom." He sucked in a breath, suddenly feeling like a teenager trying to ask a girl to a dance. Idiocy. He cleared his throat and strengthened his voice. "The cuff links I'm wearing were gifts from the ambassador we're dining with tonight. They'd been in his family for a century. The clasps stick."

Before he could finish, her door opened. She stood before him in a pale blue satin dress. Sleeveless—strapless—it should have given him a delightful view, but she wore a little lace thing over it—sort of a jacket, but not quite long enough.

Her hair had been put up, but not in the grandma hairdo. It was more like a long, silky, braided ponytail with flowers woven through it.

She lifted her pretty face and smiled at him. "Heirlooms, huh?"

He said, "Yes," but his voice came out rusty again. Except this time he knew why he was dumbstruck. She wore almost no makeup, yet she was still the most beautiful woman he'd ever met.

"Let me see."

He held out his arm and she examined the cuff links that he'd slid through the buttonholes but hadn't locked. She took the first in her nimble fingers, her face pinching in concentration, and something warm and wonderful swished through him.

He told himself it was nothing but attraction, but when she finished closing and locking the cuff links, she glanced up and smiled at him, and he realized how nice she was. It was no wonder she was so good with the children of her high school. She was just plain sweet.

And he was a pampered ruler. Somebody so accustomed to getting his own way that he'd persuaded her to marry him. It was for the best, of course, but that was his pathology. Even if it hadn't been the best for Ginny, if it had been the best for his country, he would have tossed her feelings aside and worked things to his benefit anyway.

The warm, fuzzy feeling she inspired shifted into cold, hard steel. Because that's who he really was, and even as much of a bastard as he could be, he didn't want to hurt her.

Not after she was doing so much for him.

Dom and Ginny left their apartment at ten to seven. He was the picture of kingly gorgeousness in his black tux.

When she told him that, he cast a sideways glance at her. "Thank you. You look lovely, too."

Not twenty minutes before they had shared a happy moment over his cuff links. Now he was cool and distant? It didn't make any sense.

They walked to the elevator, which opened as soon as they arrived. Neither spoke as they stepped inside and Dom pushed the button for the second floor.

A guest of the palace, Ginny's mom was invited to join them for dinner, and she waited for them in the second-floor lobby beside the elevator.

When they stepped out, she hugged Ginny. "Very pretty."

Ginny displayed her newfound curtsy skills. "Thanks. Your outfit is gorgeous, too."

Rose smoothed her hand along the soft beige satin. The king had offered the services of their clothier, and her pragmatic mom hadn't had a qualm about using them. She had the tailor whip up a simple satin skirt and sequined top that sort of looked like a tank top. She'd swept her yellow and pink hair into a neat French twist. She looked simple, but elegant. More elegant than Ginny had ever seen her.

As Dom guided them in the direction of the king's quarters, Rose whispered, "I could get used to this."

Ginny's eyes widened in horror. She had no idea why Dom had suddenly become distant, but hearing her mom say she could get used to luxury wouldn't help things.

"Do not say that!"

"I was kidding! It's stuffy here." She glanced around at the paintings on the elegant walls. "Almost like a really fancy prison."

Though Dominic hadn't appeared to have been listening, he turned and said, "Protocols and security are necessary."

"For protection and respect," Ginny quickly told her mom, wanting Dom to see her mom hadn't meant any harm. She simply wasn't up to speed on the lives of royalty. "If somebody's going to rule a country in a part of the world that isn't always stable, they need to command respect."

Dominic gave her a look of approval that helped alleviate the sense that she'd somehow caused his bad mood.

But her mom waved a hand. "Give me the good old-fashioned life of a commoner any day of the week."

Ginny smiled nervously, as Dom shook his head. He'd been so cute when he'd come to her suite, asking for help with his cuff links. Now a world of distance seemed to be lodged between them. She wouldn't tell him, but it had been nice to have a chance to touch him. And there was nothing more intimate than fixing a guy's cuff links or his bow tie—as a wife would.

She told herself not to go overboard with those thoughts and knew she wouldn't. She didn't want to get hurt by spinning fantasies. Still, though she might be a fake fiancée about to be a fake wife/princess, she and Dom were in this together. She didn't like the fact that he was unhappy. Especially if it might be because of something she'd done.

Security guards opened the gold doors to the king's quarters and Dom invited Ginny and her mom to enter before him. The foyer ceilings had to be three stories high. Everything from lamps to picture frames was trimmed in gold.

Her mother immediately recognized a Monet. She gasped. "Oh, this is delightful! One of my favorites."

"I'd be happy to give it to you as my wedding gift to you."

All heads turned as the king entered the foyer.

He kissed Ginny's hand, then Rose's.

Rose frowned. "First, I do not have the kind of security I'd need to put that in my home. Second, I'm not the bride. I don't get gifts."

"It's our custom to give parents of people who marry into our family a gift…something like a welcome to the family."

Her mom's eyebrows rose as she glanced over at Ginny, who shrugged slightly.

She leaned toward the king and whispered, "We're really not going to be in your family long."

He bowed. "A custom is a custom."

Rose nodded. "Point taken. Do I have to get you a gift?"

King Ronaldo unexpectedly smiled. "Do you wish to welcome me to your family?"

Rose laughed noisily. "Well, honey, I guess I do. Except you have to come to my house to get the gift."

The king directed everyone to the door again. "Maybe I will. But right now we're going to the formal reception room to meet the ambassador."

The king took Rose's arm as Dominic tucked Ginny's hand in the crook of his elbow.

She'd never seen her mom flirt. Not even after her dad had died. Not with anyone. Ever. The sight of her mom and the grouchy king—well, flirting—made her want to say, "Aw," and shiver with revulsion simultaneously.

King Ronaldo peeked over his shoulder at Ginny. "By the way, Ginny, I approve of the dress."

"This old thing?"

He smiled patiently. "I know you're coming to understand our customs and our etiquette, so you can't tease me anymore by pretending you don't understand. Were I you, I would have said thank you."

Dominic gave her a look and, suddenly, desperately wanting to please him, she took a quick breath and said, "Thank you."

"I'm hoping your entire wardrobe and wedding apparel will follow a similar pattern."

"Yes, Your Majesty. I appreciate that you're allowing me so much say in the wedding plans."

"Thank your future husband," the king said as the reached the door of the reception room. "He pleaded your case. Something about pink roses and your friends as bridesmaids lending authenticity to the whole thing."

Two guards opened the doors. The king walked into the room and led her mother to a discreet bar.

Ginny turned to Dom. "So, you pleaded my case?"

He glanced back at his father. "Saving an argument."

She reached up and tightened his bow tie. "Well, I appreciate it."

He caught her hand. "That's fine. My tie is fine."

She nodded quickly, annoyed with herself for the intimate gesture and for upsetting him again. "I guess I'm just getting a little too comfortable with you."

He caught her gaze. "You shouldn't."

Ginny stared into his dark, dark eyes, suddenly realizing he wasn't angry with her. But if he wasn't angry with her, that left only himself. Was he angry with himself? For asking her for help with cuff links? Or because asking for help with his cuff links proved they were getting close? Becoming friends?

She saw that as a good thing. Within the cocoon of their conspiracy, for the first time in her life, she was taking the initial steps of trusting a man. She didn't have to worry about consequences. There were none. She knew they were getting divorced. There was no way he could hurt her. And the little bit of intimacy with the cuff links had been warm and wonderful.

But obviously, he didn't feel the same way.

The ambassador arrived and Ginny played her role exactly as Dom wanted her to play it. They had a toast with the ambassador and his wife, Amelia, who then toasted the newly engaged couple and wished them happiness.

The ambassador then handed them a small box. Dominic opened it, smiled and handed it to her.

She glanced inside and her gaze jerked to the ambassador. "Emerald earrings."

Amelia said, "Our country's gift to you on your engagement."

She said, "Thanks," but her stomach tightened. She hadn't considered that kings and ambassadors and entire countries would give her gifts. But really? What wedding didn't attract gifts?

At the end of the evening, when the ambassador and his wife retreated to their suite, she and Dom also took their leave. Rose had decided to stay and have one more drink with the king, and Ginny's head spun.

When they got into the elevator and the door closed, affording them their first privacy of the evening, she turned to Dominic. "I don't know if I should apologize for my mom flirting with your dad or groan over the fact that we're going to get expensive wedding gifts that we have no right to."

"We're getting married. We have every right to get gifts and well-wishers have every right to send us gifts." He frowned slightly. "Haven't you seen the stack of presents that have already arrived?"

Her mouth fell open. "We've already gotten gifts?"

"Many. The protocol is that they stay with Sally until she has an appropriate thank-you card printed up on the royal family's stationery."

"We don't write our own thank-you cards?"

He smiled briefly.

Ginny held back a groan. No wonder he didn't want

to be friendly with her. She was more than a commoner. She was a bumpkin.

She swallowed. "What are we going to do with the presents?"

"What do you mean, what are we going to do with the presents? The same thing other newlyweds do."

The elevator door opened and he walked outside. She stood frozen, feeling odd—feeling horrible, actually. While she was learning to trust him, he was walking away from her. She might be a bumpkin, but he was the one who had his protocols out of order if he wanted to keep gifts they didn't deserve. Technically, they were at the center of perpetuating a fraud. They would benefit from a lie.

She scrambled after him. "So we're going to keep these things?"

He stopped, spun to face her. "What would you suggest? That we tell our guests no gifts? That we all but let them know we plan on divorcing. Get your head in the game, Ginny!"

His tone was like a slap in the face. She took a step back, then another. "I'm sorry."

He cursed. "Why are you saying you're sorry! I'm the one who just yelled at you! Do you have to be so nice? So honest?"

"You'd rather I be dishonest?"

"I'd rather that your sanctimonious attitude not make me feel like I'm doing something wrong all the time."

He turned to the white double doors, marched over, opened them and walked directly to the bar.

She scampered after him. "Wait! What?"

"You're so nice. You spar with my dad, then say something so respectful, he knows you're coming around. You didn't want a new wardrobe until we insisted. You're nice with Sally. You're happy your mom is here and it's clear she loves you." He stopped, sucking in a breath.

"You're mad at me because the situation is working out?"

"I'm mad at you because every day it becomes clearer and clearer that I'm going to hurt you."

She tilted her head, not quite understanding what he was getting at.

"You say you don't want to get drawn into this life and I believe you. But you and I…" He downed the shot of Scotch and poured another. "We sort of fit. You feel it as much as I do. It's not something we plan or intend to do. It's that thing that happens at odd moments. The times we're on the same page or thinking the same thought and we know it with just a glance." He walked from behind the bar to stand directly in front of her. "And pretty soon we're going to start remembering how good we are together in other ways and then we're going to be sleeping together."

Her heart thumped. He *was* feeling the same things she was. That unexpected trust. That sense that everything was going to be okay. "You thought we were good together?"

"You *know* we were good together."

"And you think we fit?"

"I see those little things happen every day. You liked fastening my cuff links. I like fighting your simple battles over things like jeans versus white suits."

She searched his gaze. Ridiculous hope filled her chest to capacity. They really were getting to know each other and in knowing each other, they were beginning to genuinely like each other.

For once, having more than a surface relationship

didn't scare her. Maybe because she knew it had a time limit. She could get close, make love, get married, have a baby with Dom, knowing it was going to end. Secure in the fact that they would part amicably, she wouldn't suffer the pains of rejection. She would simply move on. And she would have had a chance she never thought she'd get: a chance to really be in love. To know what it felt like to share. To be part of something wonderful. All under the protection of the knowledge that it wouldn't last forever. She didn't have to be perfect forever. She didn't even have to be good forever. Or to suit Dom forever. She only had to make this work for a little over two years.

"And you don't think it's a good thing that we get along?"

"I have a job to do. I've told you that if you get in the way of that job, I will always pick the kingdom over you."

She swallowed and nodded, knowing exactly what he was saying, but her stomach fluttered. When they first decided to marry, he had been sure he'd always take the kingdom's side over hers. But this very argument proved that he was changing. And he clearly wasn't happy about that.

"Is this the part where I say I'm sorry?"

He sniffed and looked away. "Sorry again? Why this time?"

"Because I think I tempt you. I think that's why you're really mad. I think knowing me has made you feel that you'd like to be a real boy, Pinocchio."

"So I'm a puppet?"

"No. I think you'd like the freedom to make up your own mind, to make your own choices, but you're afraid of what will happen to your kingdom."

He caught her gaze. "You make it sound like an idiotic dilemma. But it isn't. We might be a small kingdom but we're an important one." He slid his hand across her shoulder and to her long ponytail. He ran the fat braid through his fingers as if it were spun gold. "One woman should not change that."

Even as he said the words, he stepped closer. He wrapped the braid around his knuckles and tugged her forward until they almost touched, but not quite. The air between them crackled, not with memories of how good they'd been together but with anticipation. If they kissed now, changed the terms of their deal now, the next two years would be very different.

And she wanted it. Not just for the sex. For the intimacy and the chance to be genuinely close to someone, even as she had the magical out of a two-year time limit.

He lowered his head slowly, giving her time, it seemed, to pull away if she wanted. But, mesmerized by the desperation in his black eyes, she stood perfectly still, barely breathing. He wanted this, too, and even though she knew he was going to kiss her, she also knew he fought a demon. He might want to be king, but he also wanted to be a man.

When his lips touched hers, she didn't think of that night two months ago, she thought of this moment, of how he needed her, even if he didn't see it.

She slid her arms around his neck as he released her braid, letting it swing across her back. With his hand now free, he brought her closer still. The press of her breasts to his chest knocked the air out of her lungs as his lips moved across hers roughly.

He was angry, she knew, because she was upsetting his well-laid plans. The irony of it was he'd been upsetting her plans, her life, from the second she'd met him. It only seemed fitting that finally she was doing the same to him.

Standing on tiptoe, she returned his kiss, as sure as he was. If he wanted to talk about unfair, she would show him unfair. The only way she could be intimate with someone was knowing she had an out. The inability to trust that her dad had instilled in her had crippled her for anything but a relationship that couldn't last. She wouldn't share the joy of raising children. She was lucky to get a child. She wouldn't grow old with someone. The best she would get would be memories of whatever love, intimacy, happiness they could cobble together in the next two years. And even as it gave her at least slight hope, it also angered her mightily.

They dueled for a few seconds, each fighting for supremacy, until suddenly his mouth softened over hers. His hands slid down her back to her bottom, while his mouth lured her away from her anger and to that place where the softness of their kisses spoke of their real feelings.

Like it or not, they were falling in love.

And it wasn't going to last.

But it was all Ginny Jones, high school guidance counselor from Texas with the alcoholic dad, was going to get in her lifetime.

So she wanted it. She wanted the intimacy, the friendship, the secrets and dreams.

The only problem was she had no idea how to go about getting any of it.

CHAPTER SEVEN

IT TOOK EVERY ounce of concentration Dom could muster to pull away from Ginny. He'd never before felt the things he felt with her, but that was the problem. He'd never experienced any of these things because he'd avoided them. Not because he'd never met anyone like Ginny, but because he'd always been strong.

So when he stepped away, it wasn't with regret. It was with self-recrimination. He did not want what she seemed to be offering. And if they didn't stop this idiotic game, just as he'd told her, he was going to hurt her.

"I'm going to bed. I'll see you in the morning." He turned and walked to his room, vowing to himself that something like that kiss would never happen again.

The next day, he left before breakfast and didn't come back to his quarters until long past time for supper. That worked so well he decided to keep up that schedule.

At first, she'd waited for him on the sofa in the sitting room. So he'd stride into the room, barely glancing at her, and walk right past the bar, saying, "It was a long day. I'm going to shower and go right to bed."

And pretty soon she stopped waiting up.

For two weeks, he managed to avoid her in their private times and keep his distance when they were in public, but he could see something going on in that crazy head of hers. Every time they got within two feet of each other, she'd smile so prettily she'd temporarily throw him off balance. But he'd always remind himself he was strong. And it worked, but he wasn't superhuman. If something didn't give, they'd end up talking again. Or kissing. Or just plain forming a team. And then she'd get all the wrong ideas.

A week before the wedding, her bridesmaids arrived and he breathed a sigh of relief. Jessica and Molly were two teachers from her school, both of whom had just finished their semester. Dom smiled politely when Ginny introduced them and he shook both of their hands, reminding them they had met when he visited their school.

Molly laughed. "Of course, we remember you. We didn't think you'd remember us."

He smiled briefly. "It's my job to care for a country full of people. Remembering names, really seeing people when I look at them, is part of that."

Jessica nodded sagely as if she totally understood and agreed, but his future bride tilted her head in a way that told him she was turning that over in her mind, putting that statement up against other things he'd said.

Good. He hoped she was. Because from here on out that was his main goal. If she wanted to be part of his life, and for the next two years or so she had to be, then she needed not just to hear that but to fully understand it. His country came first. She would be second. And then only for about two years. He did not intend to get personally involved with her. God knew he'd sleep with her in a New York minute if he could be sure nothing would come of it. But that ship had sailed. They were getting to know each other, getting to *like* each other. If they went any further, their breakup would be a disaster.

He turned and walked out of the apartment, on his way to his office, but Molly stopped him. "Aren't you going to kiss your bride goodbye?"

Dom slid a questioning glance to Ginny. Her eyebrows raised and her mouth formed the cute little wince she always gave when she had no defense. Obviously, she hadn't told her friends their marriage would be a fake. That was good news and bad news. The good news was if her friends believed this marriage would be real, there was no chance either of them would slip up and say the wrong thing. Unfortunately, that meant there was no rest from the charade for him and Ginny.

He walked over and put his hands on her shoulders. For two seconds, he debated kissing her cheek, but knew that would never work. So he pressed his lips to hers lightly and pulled back quickly, then he turned and walked out to the door.

"I'll be busy all day. You ladies enjoy yourselves."

Then he left. But the look on Ginny's face when he'd pulled away from their kiss followed him out the door. She hadn't minded the quick kiss. She was back to being on board with the charade. Back to fake kisses and no intimate conversations. They'd barely seen each other in two weeks. His doing. And she wasn't pouting. She didn't throw hissy fits the way he distantly remembered his mom doing to manipulate his dad.

He shook his head, wondering where that memory had come from. His mom hadn't been a manipulator. His dad had been brutally in love with her. So in love that the king had been putty in her hands. And so in love that when she got sick and died, the king's world had come to a crashing halt.

Not that he had to worry about that with Ginny. He was much stronger than his dad had been. He could always do what needed to be done. Always resist when he needed to.

With her guests in the palace and a charade to perpetuate, he phoned the kitchen staff and made arrangements for a formal dinner in their apartment, then had his assistant phone Ginny and tell her he was honoring her and her guests that evening with a formal dinner.

Hanging up the phone, Ginny pressed her hand to her stomach. After two weeks of him virtually ignoring her—except when they were in public—he was back to being nice again. She would have breathed a sigh of relief but Molly was two feet away and Jessica wasn't that much farther, standing with the fiftysomething female dressmaker who was measuring her for her bridesmaid's gown.

"So you chose a dress without even consulting us?" Molly groused good-naturedly.

"Yes." Ginny winced. "Sorry, but fabric had to be ordered."

Jessica said, "Oh! Special fabric!"

"It's just a nice silk."

"Listen to her," Molly teased, nudging her shoulder. "A week away from the wedding and she's already acting like a princess."

"I am not!"

Jessica stepped away from the woman who had measured her for her dress. "It's not a bad thing. I imagine that adjusting to being the most important woman in a country isn't easy."

"The most important woman in a country? Not hardly."

Molly fell to a club chair. "Well, Dom's mother is dead and he has no sisters. His dad doesn't date and his brother is some kind of jet-setter. You are the only girl permanently in the mix."

She hadn't thought of that, but when she did, her stomach fluttered oddly. It meant something that they'd brought her into the family. True, she was pregnant with the heir to the throne, but there were so many ways they could have handled this other than marriage. On some level, she'd passed enough tests that they'd brought her in.

"If that makes you queasy," Jessica said, "then you'd better toughen up."

"I'm not queasy."

Molly said, "Well, something's up. You let Dom believe we don't know about your situation. Almost as if you don't trust what he'd say if he knew you'd confided in your friends."

"That's true, Gin," Jessica agreed, slipping on her blue jeans and pretty peach T-shirt that showed off her Texas-girl tan. "If you don't grow a pair with this guy pretty soon, he's going to walk all over you."

"What if I think I have a better way to handle the next two years?"

Jessica cautiously said, "Better?"

"Yeah." She turned away, puttering around with picking up pins and tape measures, and putting them in the dressmaker's tote.

Taking the cue that Ginny wanted her to leave, the dressmaker grabbed her tote and said, "Thanks. I'll have dresses for you to try on tomorrow."

When she closed the suite door behind her, Molly gasped. "Tomorrow?"

She shrugged. "That's how it goes here in the palace." She walked to the table by the window and busied herself with straightening stationery and pens. "I say I want something, somebody comes up and measures, and the next day it's at my door."

Shrewd, Jessica narrowed her eyes. "You never told us your better plan for how to handle your situation."

Ginny looked up into the faces of her two trusted friends and decided it wasn't out of line to want a second opinion. "Okay. Here's the deal. You know how my dad sort of ruined my ability to trust?"

Molly nodded. Jessica crossed her arms on her chest.

"Well, I've been thinking that if Dom and I hadn't accidentally gotten pregnant, I probably never would have trusted anyone enough to have had a child."

Jessica said, "True. So I hope you're not about to tell us you want to make your marriage real with Prince Gorgeous. The very fact that you can't trust makes that just plain stupid."

"Not really. Because I don't want a permanent husband. But I do want this marriage."

Molly tilted her head. "What does that mean?"

"Well, we're stuck together for at least two years and he *is* gorgeous. Not only would I like the whole mother experience with my baby's father, but I just don't see why we can't sleep together and maybe be a real husband and wife for a while."

"How about because that's not what he wants."

"I'll still divorce him two years after the baby's born and gone through the initiation ceremony. That's the deal. But it's the very fact that I know we're getting divorced that makes me comfortable enough to, you know—"

"Want to have sex?"

"It's more than that. When he's comfortable with me,

we have fun. I think we could make very good parents. I think being a husband and wife for real for two years could pave the way for us to have a good relationship after we're divorced and I think all that is nothing but good for our child."

Molly mulled that over and suddenly said, "Actually, that makes sense."

Jessica turned on her. "How can you say that? She's going to get hurt."

Molly shrugged. "Or not. The situation is weird, Jessica. And not everybody's lucky enough to attract men like mosquitoes."

Jessica nodded at Ginny. "She could if she wanted to."

"That's the point. She doesn't want to. But she's going to marry this guy and have his baby. Why shouldn't she have two years of being a real princess before she has to let it all go?"

"That's like saying you should eat a whole cake before you start a diet."

Ginny laughed. "You mean, you don't?"

Jessica groaned.

"Look, I am never, ever, ever going to be married. The mistrust my dad instilled in me will never go away. But I am getting married. To Dominic. For a bit over two years. Not forever. So it'll be like playing house."

Jessica sighed. "Playing house?"

"Yes. Just another facet of the charade. Because I know it's fake, I'm not going to get hurt. But I also want to experience something I never would have if we hadn't gotten pregnant and decided to marry for the baby."

"I hope you know what you're doing."

Ginny sucked in a breath. "I think I do, but even if I don't, it's only two years. Once it's over, it's over. I will have no choice but to go back to normal. Especially with a baby to raise with him." Satisfied with her conclusion, she changed the subject. "Did you bring something to wear tonight, or do I need to call the clothier?"

"Clothier?"

"He's this guy, Joshua, who if you need something you call him, and he'll call a store or designer and have it in the room within hours."

Molly gaped at her. "So you can get us gowns for tonight?"

"If you need them. It's all about not embarrassing Dominic in front of his father."

Jessica shook her head. "I think you're enjoying this too much."

"Actually, this is the part I don't enjoy. The part I won't miss at all. There are lots of things about being a princess like the press and having a father-in-law who can have you deported that make this life hard. Not something I'd want to do forever."

Jessica drew a deep breath. "Okay. Now I think I get it. You know you don't want to be in this life forever, but you like Dom and you're going to make the best of it while you're here. So you'll have no regrets and be ready to move on."

Ginny sighed with relief. "Exactly."

"Okay. Then I'm on board, too. What do you want us to do?"

"Nothing. This is the part I need to handle myself. I just haven't figured out how yet." She couldn't exactly say, "Hey, let's sleep together." But she wasn't the queen of seductresses, either. She was going to have to wait for her moment and take it. Given that he'd managed to avoid her for the past two weeks, that wasn't going to be easy.

They called Joshua, who called his contact at a local boutique from Ginny's suite. Four gowns were delivered within two hours, and Molly and Jessica made their choices before they returned to their rooms to dress for the formal dinner.

Ginny took special care with her outfit that night, wearing a coral-colored gown. She fixed her hair in the long braid again, the way she'd had it the night he'd kissed her.

When she finally came out of her suite, everyone was already there, including her mom—and the king, who was his charming best, and anybody with eyes in their head could see the reason was Rose.

After cocktails, they passed the small dining room where Dom and Ginny ate breakfast and lunch, and entered a much bigger dining room, something almost as fancy as the king's. Dom let the king have the head of the table, taking the seat to his right and seating Ginny next to him.

The conversation ebbed and flowed around them as Ginny watched her mom, seated across from them at the king's right. They talked about everything from sports to politics, and the king took great delight in sparring with her.

"He's going to miss her when she's gone next week."

Ginny's gaze snapped around to meet Dom's. From the surprised expression that came to his face, she could tell he hadn't meant to say that out loud.

"It's okay. You can talk to me. We're a team, remember?" She motioned from herself to Dom. "In this together."

"Yes. But we don't want to go too far."

She turned on her seat, her taffeta gown ruffling and rustling, suddenly wondering if this was her moment.

Everybody at the table was deep in conversation. Her bridesmaids chatted up Dom's brother. The king and her mother were so engrossed, there might as well not have been anybody else at the table.

The best place for her most private conversation with him might just be in this crowded dining room.

She took a breath, caught his gaze. "Why not? We're in a mighty big charade. I think it's going to be impossible for us to set limits on how close it makes us."

"I told you that we don't want to get close because I don't want to hurt you."

"You think you're going to hurt me over a few shared comments? I'm not asking you to divulge state secrets. I'm just saying the charade works better when we're talking." She smiled slightly. "We haven't talked in weeks."

"And it's my fault?"

She shook her head. "Dom. Dom. Dom. You're so uptight. I'm not placing blame. That's the beauty of forming a team and maybe even the beauty of knowing this team doesn't have to last. We're only going to be together for two years or so. After that, we are the parents of your country's next heir who must get along."

Totally against the rules of etiquette, Dom picked up a fork and tapped it lightly against his plate. "So?"

She could think she made him nervous enough to do something out of line. Or she could see she made him comfortable enough to do something totally out of line.

She liked the second. She *believed* the second.

"So, I honestly, genuinely believe that if we would simply allow ourselves to be friendly—maybe even to get close—in these next few years, the rest of our lives would go a lot smoother."

He peeked over at her. "Really? *That's* what you think?"

"Look at it logically. How does it benefit us to never speak? It doesn't. It makes the charade more difficult and opens the doors for us to make mistakes."

"True."

"But if we talk at dinner and lunch, debrief about our days—"

This time when he peeked at her, he sort of smiled. "Debrief?"

"Sally and Joshua are rubbing off on me. I just mean we should talk about our days with each other."

"Ah."

"Then we won't make as many mistakes."

"It seems to me that just a few weeks ago, *you* were ignoring *me*."

"I was figuring everything out."

"And now you think you understand the whole situation?"

"I really do."

"And your answer is for us to debrief."

She met his gaze. "It's more than that."

His eyes darkened. "How much more?"

"I think we need to tell each other our reading interests, where we've been on vacation, a bit or two about our jobs. I think I need to fix your cuff links. You need to let me straighten your tie. I think we should be talking baby names and colors for the nursery."

He held her gaze. "That's going to take us into some dangerous territory."

She took a long breath and with all her strength, all her courage, she kept eye contact. "I'm a big girl. I'm also a smart girl. I sort of like knowing that this relationship will end."

His eyes searched hers. "So you've said."

"My dad was an alcoholic who made promises he never kept. He was his most charming when he wanted to manipulate me. If there's one thing I can't trust, it's people being nice to me. How am I ever going to create a relationship that leads to marriage if niceness scares me?"

He laughed unexpectedly. "You're saying you think a relationship with me will work because I'm not nice?"

"I'm saying this is my shot. Do you know I've never fantasized about getting married and having kids? I was always so afraid I'd end up like my mother that I wouldn't even let myself pretend I'd get married. So I've never had anything but surface relationships." She sucked in a breath. Held his gaze. "This baby we're having will probably be my only child. This marriage? It might be fake to you, but it's the only marriage I'll ever have. I'd love to have two years of happiness, knowing that I don't have to trust you completely, that you can't hurt me because we have a deadline."

"You really don't trust me?"

"I'll never trust anyone."

He glanced around the table at her bridesmaids, who were chatting up his brother, his dad and her mom, who clearly weren't paying any attention to them, and suddenly faced her again.

"No."

CHAPTER EIGHT

THE CATHEDRAL IN which Dom would marry Ginny was at least a thousand years old. It had been renovated six times and almost totally rebuilt once after a fire. The pews were cedar from Israel. The stained glass from a famous Italian artist. Two of the statues were said to have been created by Michelangelo, though no one could confirm it. And the art that hung in the vestibule? All of it was priceless.

But when Ginny stepped inside, her hand wrapped in her mom's, every piece of art, every piece of wood, every famous, distinguished and renowned person seated in the sea of guests, disappeared from Dom's vision.

She looked amazing.

She'd let her hair down. The yellow strands billowed around her beneath a puffy tulle veil. The top of her dress was a dignified lace with a high collar and snug lace sleeves that ran the whole way from her shoulders, down her arms, across the back of her hand to her knuckles. The skirt started at her waist, then flowed to the floor. Made of a soft, airy-looking material, it was scattered with the same shimmering flowers that were embroidered into the lace top, but these flowers stood alone, peeking out of the folds of the fabric and then hiding again as the skirt moved with every step Ginny took.

She'd managed to look both young and beautiful, while pleasing his father with a very dignified gown that took Dom's breath away.

His brother leaned forward and whispered, "I know you weren't happy about this marriage, so if you'd like to trade, you can have your princess back and I'll raise your love child."

Any other time, Dom would have said, "Shut up, you twit." Today, mesmerized by the woman who had already seduced him once, and if he'd read her correctly the night of the formal dinner with her bridesmaids, wanted to seduce him again, he very quietly said, "Not on your life."

Ginny and her mom reached the altar. Rose kissed his bride's cheek and then walked to her seat. Ginny held out her hand to Dom and he took it, staring at her as if he'd never seen her before. Because in a way he hadn't. He'd seen her silly and happy and playful the night of their date. He'd seen her dressed in jeans and T-shirts and even beautifully, ornately, for the night with the ambassador. But today, in this dress that was as beautiful as it was bridal, she was a woman offering herself to a man, as a bride.

Caught in the gaze of her pretty blue eyes, he was floored by the significance of it. Especially after their conversation about making their marriage real for their time together.

The minister cleared his throat. Their hands joined, Dom and Ginny turned to the altar and the service began. As the solemn words and decrees were spoken by his country's highest-ranking religious official, Dominic reminded himself that this wedding wasn't real. Even when they said their vows and exchanged jewel-encrusted rings, he told himself they were words he meant, truly meant, for a limited time.

But when the minister said, "You may kiss the bride," and she turned those big blue eyes up at him, his heart stuttered. She wasn't just a woman in a white dress, helping him to perpetuate a charade that would give legitimacy to Xaviera's next heir. She was an innocent woman, a bride...

She was his now.

She whispered, "You don't want to kiss me?"

His heart thundered in his chest and he realized he'd been standing there staring at her. In awe. In confusion. She wasn't just an innocent. She was someone who'd been hurt. Someone who couldn't trust. If he agreed to make this marriage real, no matter how much she protested that it wasn't true, he would hurt her. He *knew* he would hurt her. Because as much as he hated the comparison, it seemed being royal had made him very much like her dad. He was his most charming when he needed to get his own way, and selfish, self-centered, the rest of the time.

Still, he held her gaze as his head lowered and his lips met hers. He watched her lids flutter shut in complete surrender. Total honesty. His heart of stone chipped a bit. The soft part of his soul, the place he rarely let himself acknowledge, shamed him for being so strict with her.

They broke apart slowly. She smiled up at him.

He told himself she was playing a part. The smile, the expression meant nothing. If she was smart enough to realize she didn't trust anyone, she was also smart enough to play her role well. Smart enough to see he was doing what needed to be done not just for the next heir to the throne, but for *his child*.

The child in her stomach.

They turned to the congregation and began their recessional down the aisle to the vestibule, where they were spirited away to a private room while their guests left the church. They endured an hour of pictures before they walked out of the church, beneath the canopy of swords of his military's honor guard.

Dressed in black suits and white silk shirts and ties, his bodyguards whisked them into the back of his limo, to a professional photo studio for more pictures.

And the whole time Ginny smiled at him radiantly. Anyone who looked at her would assume—*believe*— this wedding was real. Because he was beginning to get the feeling himself. She wasn't such a good actress that she was fooling him. What she'd said haunted him. She wanted this to be real. At least for a little while. Because this, this sham, was as close as she'd ever get to a real marriage.

Her mother rode in the limo with his dad. Her bridesmaids rode with his brother and a distant cousin who served as his best man and groomsman.

Alone in their limo, he turned to her. Struggling to forget the bargain she'd tried to strike and come up with normal conversation, he said, "You look amazing."

She smiled, reached over and straightened his tie. "You do, too."

He shifted away, afraid of her. Not because he worried she was going to hurt him or cheat him. But because he knew she wasn't.

"Dominic, the straightening-the-tie thing is important. A piece of intimacy everyone expects to see. You need to be still and let me do it."

Because of her suggestion that they make this marriage real, and his desperate need not to hurt her, he was now the one who might ruin their ruse. "I suppose."

She shrugged, her pretty yellow hair shifted and swayed around her. "No matter what you decide, I intend to be a good wife for these two years."

His tongue stuck to the roof of his mouth. What did that mean? That he'd find her in his bed that night?

He remembered that yellow hair floating around them their one and only night together, remembered the softness of her skin, and wondered just how a man was supposed to resist that honesty or the sexual tug that lured him into a spell so sweet, another man would have happily allowed himself to be drawn in.

But he wasn't just any man. He was a prince, someday a king. Someone held to a higher standard. He did not deliberately hurt people.

They arrived at the palace. Bodyguards ushered them into the main foyer. They stopped in his father's quarters to have a toast with her mother and his dad and their wedding party. Then they took an elevator to the third floor of his dad's wing of the palace and stood on the balcony, waving to well-wishers.

A young woman edged her way through the crowd to the space just in front of security. She waved and called, "Toss your bouquet!"

Dom said, "That's odd."

Ginny laughed. "She's American. We have a tradition that whoever catches the bride's bouquet will be the next person to be married." She gave him a smile, then winked, before she turned and tossed the spray of fifty roses with strength.that would have done any weight lifter proud.

The flowers bowed into a graceful arc before beginning their descent. The crowd gasped at Ginny's whimsy. The people closest to the woman who'd called realized they could intercept the bouquet and they scrambled forward, but it landed in the young girl's arms. As the crowd pressed forward to grab flowers from the bouquet, security surrounded her.

Ginny faced him. "Have her brought up for an audience."

He laughed. "Seriously?"

"Yes." She bowed slightly. "My lord," she said, her eyes downcast, her tone serious.

Those crazy feelings of wanting her rippled through him again. He raised her chin. "You don't have to bow to me."

"The etiquette books say I do." She smiled. "And I'm asking for the wedding favor the book also says I get. I'd like to meet the woman who wants so desperately to be married that she'd risk arrest."

Dom faced his bodyguard. He made a few hand gestures. The crowd called, "Kiss the bride," and he did. But he did so now with curiosity that nudged his fear of hurting her aside. He liked being able to do something for her.

When they returned to the king's receiving room, the young woman awaited them.

Ginny walked over and hugged her. "I hope the whole bouquet thing works out for you."

Their guest laughed nervously. Her big brown eyes stayed on Ginny's face. "I never thought you'd do it."

"I waited years for my prince. I know what you're feeling." She squeezed her hand and said, "Good luck."

Dominic nodded, the security detail motioned her to the door and she left with a quick wave. But the way Ginny had said, "I know what you're feeling," struck him oddly. She didn't say, "I've known what you feel." She said, "I know what you're feeling." He heard the sorrow there, maybe even a loneliness that almost opened that soft place in his soul again. But he hung on. He could not let sentiment destroy his plan. He could not become his dad.

Ginny said, "You know crazy people are going to try to steal that bouquet from her. You're going to have to have someone escort her to her hotel and maybe even out of the country."

"Yes. Security will take care of it."

But he couldn't stop staring at her. He might have closed the soft place in his soul, but his brain was working overtime to figure her out. What she had done had been a tad reckless, but it was very Ginny. Very sweet. Very warm. She'd used the wish her groom was to grant her for someone else.

And *that's* why he knew he couldn't sleep with her. No matter what she said or did or how she phrased things, she was innocent. Too nice for him.

But she was also hurting. She really believed she'd always be alone.

He couldn't think about that. He had to be fair.

They received dignitaries for hours. Even Dom was tired by the time his father, brother, cousin and Ginny's entourage escorted them to the palace ballroom.

They entered amid a trumpet blast and after toasts and a short speech by his father welcoming Ginny into the family, they finally ate.

Still, in between dances, he managed to find time to speak to his detail and arrange for their luggage to be taken to the yacht that night, instead of the next morning.

There was no way in hell he was taking her back to

his apartment, where they'd not only had privacy, they'd had friendly chats and a wonderful kiss.

Even he had his limits.

The staff on the *Crown Jewel* was too big to be in on the marriage ruse, but precautions were easier there. He and Ginny would be sleeping in the side-by-side bedrooms of the master suite, but the yacht was also so big that he could keep his distance. They'd sail so far out onto the ocean that even long lenses couldn't get pictures. And the staff would rotate so the same people wouldn't see them twice and wonder why they weren't kissing or holding hands.

Not only would this work, but it would be easy.

Piece of cake, as Ginny would say.

When they had to take a helicopter to the yacht, Ginny knew why Dom had chosen it as their honeymoon spot. The pilot put the helicopter down on the landing pad, and Dom helped her out, gathering the skirt of her gown so she didn't trip over it as she navigated the steps.

Walking across the deck, under the starlit sky, she glanced around in awe. "It's the friggin' Love Boat."

He turned to her with absolute horror in his eyes. "What?"

"You never saw the television show from the eighties? *The Love Boat?*"

Clearly relieved that she was referencing a television show, not referring to something about their relationship, he said, "You weren't even born in the eighties, so how did you see it?"

"My mom watched reruns all the time. It's a show about a cruise ship."

His eyes narrowed. "So you're saying our yacht is big?"

"Your yacht is huge."

"If that's a compliment, I accept it."

It wasn't a compliment. She was telling him she knew his plan. He intended to use this big ship to avoid her for the two weeks they were to be away. But he didn't seem to catch on to what she was saying.

It didn't matter. She was happy to have figured out his plan. She'd thought the night of the formal dinner for her friends had been her moment, and when it turned out that it wasn't, she'd hoped her honeymoon might give her another shot. And here she stood on a boat big enough to rival an aircraft carrier. It meant her options for finding another moment were seriously limited. But at least she knew what she was up against.

A security guard opened the door for them and Dom motioned for her to enter first. She stepped inside, expecting to see stairs with metal railings painted white, expecting to hear the hollow sound of a stairwell. Instead, she entered a small lobby. Sleek hardwood floors led to an elevator. Gold-framed paintings hung on the walls.

She spun around to face Dom. "Seriously? Is that a Picasso?"

Dom said, "Probably," as the elevator door opened. She hadn't even seen him press a button for it.

They rode down, only a few floors, before the door opened again onto a room so stunningly beautiful it could have been in a magazine. Huge windows in the back displayed the black sky with the faint dusting of stars. A taupe sofa flanked by two printed club chairs sat in front of a fireplace. The accent rug that held them all in a group was the same print as the club chairs. A long wooden bar gleamed in a far corner. Plants in elaborate pots converted empty space into focal points.

She wanted to say, "Wow," but her chest hurt. Her knees wobbled. This was her wedding night. But unlike a normal bride who knew what to expect, every step of her journey was a mystery. She wanted one thing. Dom wanted another. And only one of them could win.

Security guards entered behind Dom, rolling the cart carrying their luggage. She'd packed her four bags with care. Even though Dom had told her she'd need only a bikini and some sunblock, she'd brought clothes for romantic dinners—and undies. Pretty panties, bras and sleepwear that she and Joshua had chosen from catalogs so exclusive that prices weren't listed beneath the descriptions.

Joshua had said, "If you have to ask the price, you can't afford it."

And at that point she decided she didn't want to know. Dominic could afford to buy and sell small countries. She wasn't going to quibble over the price of the nighties she'd probably need to seduce him.

The bodyguards disappeared down the hall with the luggage cart carrying their bags.

"Nightcap?"

She pressed her hand to her tummy. "I probably could use some orange juice."

He walked to the bar. "Tired?"

Was he kidding? Even if she was exhausted, nerves would keep her awake tonight. The last time they'd been in this position, she hadn't had to seduce him. They'd seduced each other. Which meant, she shouldn't be nervous. She should be herself.

Pushing the empty luggage cart, the bodyguards left with a nod to Dom.

And suddenly they were alone.

Straightening her shoulders, she faced him with a smile. "You know what? I think I'll just go change."

She glanced down at her beautiful wedding dress. It would now be cleaned and pressed to be put on display in the part of the palace open to tourists.

"It seems a shame to take this off."

"It is pretty." He smiled. "You were a stunning bride."

Her spirits lifted. No matter how strong he was, he liked her. He'd always liked her. She could do this.

She walked back down the hall to the room she'd seen the guards take their bags and found herself in another sitting room. She shook her head. "These people must spend a fortune on furniture."

The tulle underskirt of her gown swishing, she turned to the right—the side of the suite her room was on in the palace—and headed to that bedroom. She opened the door on another sitting room, this one smaller, and walked into the bedroom, only to find it empty. She glanced in the walk-in closet, thinking they might have carried her bags the whole way in there, but that was empty, too.

She walked out of the bedroom, through the small sitting room, then the big sitting room and to the hall. "Dom?"

He ambled to the front of the hall where he could see her. "What?"

"My stuff's not in my room."

"It has to be. I saw the bodyguards carting it back."

"Well, it's not here."

He huffed out a sigh. "Let me see." He walked back along the hall and through the sitting room into the second bedroom of the master suite. Doing exactly as she had done, he frowned when he didn't see her bags in the bedroom, then checked the closet.

"That's weird."

"Yeah."

He slowly faced her. "They might have put your things in my room."

"Oh?"

"Don't get weird notions. My instruction was for your things to be put in your room." He went into the master bedroom.

On impulse, she followed him. Nothing ever really went as planned with the two of them, so maybe the thing to do would be let things happen.

His room didn't have a sitting room. The big double doors opened onto an enormous bed. Beige walls with a simple beige-and-white spread on the bed gave the room a soothing, peaceful feel. But Dom didn't even pause.

"No luggage here," he said, finding the bedroom empty. He turned to the walk-in closet. He opened the grand double doors and sighed. "And there's everything."

"They think we're sleeping together."

"I told them we're not."

"You actually told them?"

"I told them this marriage is a show for the heir."

"Oh."

"Don't be embarrassed. I'm the one who should be embarrassed. This is my mess we're cleaning up."

"Oh, yeah. Every woman loves it broadcast that her new husband doesn't want her."

"It wasn't broadcast. A few key servants know the secret. It's why we're on the yacht, not at the villa. There are many servants here, and they rotate. None of them is going to see us enough to put it all together."

Suddenly weary, she decided this was not a seduction night. It was a total bust. How on earth could she seduce a guy who had told his servants his marriage was a sham? She turned to leave but stopped and faced him again.

"You know how we did that thing with the cuff links?"

He cautiously said, "Yes."

"Well, there are a hundred buttons on the back of this dress, most of which I can't reach. Can I get some help?"

His relieved "Sure" did nothing to help her flagging spirit. If anything, it made her feel even worse.

Just wanting to get this over with so she could race out of his room, go to her room and be appropriately miserable, she presented her back to him.

His fingers bumped against the first button. She felt it slide through the loop. When it took a second for him to reach for the next button, she realized her hair was in the way and she scooped it to the side, totally revealing the long row of buttons to him.

"That's a lot of buttons."

Holding her hair to the side, she said, "Exactly why I need help."

He quickly undid three or four buttons, then she felt his fingers stall again.

"Getting tired, Your Majesty?"

"No. I'm fine."

But his voice was pinched, strained.

Another two buttons popped through the loops.

"You're not wearing a bra."

"Didn't want the straps to show through the lace."

He said, "Ump."

Another two buttons popped. Then two more. But when his fingers stalled again, she felt them skim along her skin. Not a lot, just a quick brush as if he couldn't resist temptation.

When he got to the last buttons, the three just above her butt, his hands slowed. When the last button popped, she almost turned around, but something told her to be still. His fingers trailed up her spine until he reached the place where he could lay his hands on the sides of her waist. He grazed them along the indent to her hips, then back up again. When they reached her rib cage, they kept going, under her dress to her naked breasts.

Her breath caught. She wanted to tell him she was his. That she'd been his from the moment she laid eyes on him. But she knew this wasn't as easy a decision for him as it was for her.

"You are temptation."

She turned, letting the top of her dress fall as she did so. "I don't intend to be."

"Liar."

She shrugged. "Maybe a little." She raised her gaze to his. "But would it be so, so terrible to pretend you like me?"

He shook his head, as he lowered it to kiss her. Their mouths met tentatively, then she rose to her tiptoes and pressed her lips against his strongly, surely.

She might not get forever. But she wanted this two years enough that she was willing to reach out and take it.

He cupped his hand on the back of her head and dipped her down far enough that her dress slithered around her hips. When he brought her back up again, the dress fell to the floor.

"No panties, either?"

She stood before him totally naked. No lies. No pretense. When she whispered, "It was actually a very heavy dress." He laughed.

Another woman might have worried, but Ginny

smiled. Part of what he liked about her was her ability to make him laugh. She wasn't surprised when he slid his arms around her back and knees, and carried her to the bed.

CHAPTER NINE

GINNY AWAKENED THE next morning with Dom's arms wrapped around her waist. She squeezed her eyes shut, enjoying the sensation, then told herself she had to get her priorities in line before he woke up.

They hadn't talked the night before. They'd had an amazing time, but they hadn't spoken one word. She hadn't been expecting words of love, but she knew making this marriage real hadn't been what he wanted. Though she hadn't actually seduced him, which had been her plan, he could still be upset that he hadn't been able to resist the temptation of their chemistry.

She opened her eyes to find him staring down at her. "Hey."

"Hey." He searched her eyes. "I hope you know what you're doing."

And pragmatic Dom was back.

So she smiled at him and stretched up to give him a kiss. "I do."

"I'm serious about not wanting this to last and about us not getting emotionally involved with each other."

"I hate to tell you, but I'm pretty sure raising a child together will more than get us emotionally involved."

"I'm not talking about being friendly. I'm talking about being ridiculously dependent."

Even as he spoke, he rose from the bed. With the fluidity and ease of a man comfortable with who he was, he stretched and reached for a robe.

She sat up, almost sorry he was covering all those wonderful muscles when he secured the belt around his waist.

He picked up the phone and, without dialing, said, "Bacon, eggs, bagels, croissants, and the usual fruit and juices."

He hung up the phone and walked into the bathroom.

Ginny stared after him. The man really was accustomed to getting everything he wanted. But constantly seeing the evidence of it was a good reminder that he wasn't going to be persuaded to do anything, be anything, other than what he wanted.

He came out of the bathroom, took off the robe and to her surprise climbed back into bed. He leaned against the headboard and reached down to catch her shoulders and bring her up beside him.

Bending to kiss her, he said, "We have about ten minutes before breakfast gets here. Any thoughts on what we should do?" The sexy, suggestive tone of his voice told her exactly what he wanted to do.

She laughed. "I think I need to eat and get my strength back."

He sobered suddenly. "You know, we rarely talk about your pregnancy. Are you okay? Really?"

"Millions of women have babies every day. I'm not special or in danger because I'm pregnant."

"You're pregnant with an heir to a throne." He looked away, then glanced down at her again. "And even if he wasn't heir to the throne, he's *my* baby."

He said it with such a proprietary air that her heart stuttered and she realized something unexpected. "So, like me, if we hadn't accidentally gotten pregnant, you wouldn't have had a child, either."

"No. A baby was part of the deal with the princess of Grennady. But this is different."

"I know." She ran her hand along her tummy, which was no longer flat. Though only slightly swollen, after a little over three months, it was beginning to show signs of cradling a child. "Do you think we're going to be good parents?"

"I don't know about you but I'm going to be an excellent father."

She laughed. "Conceited much?"

"I am going to be a good father," he insisted indignantly. "I know every mistake my father made with me and my brother—especially my brother—and I won't do those things." He shifted against the headboard. "What about you?"

"My mother was aces as a mom." She laughed. "Still is. My dad left a lot to be desired."

"So you're not going to drink?"

She shrugged. "I sometimes think it's smarter to demonstrate responsible behavior than to avoid something tricky like alcohol."

"Whew. For a while there I thought you were going to tell me I was going to have to give up drinking until our kid was in college or something."

Thinking of all the times she'd seen him come to the apartment and head directly to the bar, she turned slightly so she could look him in the eye. "It wouldn't hurt you to cut down. Maybe not drink in the afternoon."

"My job is stressful."

"Scotch isn't going to take that away."

"But it makes me feel better."

She peeked up at him again. "Really?"

He shrugged. "Some days. Others not so much. Those days it's better to keep a clear head."

"You deal with some real idiots?"

"Most of the people in our parliament come from old oil money. They care about two things. Keeping their families wealthy and keeping our waterways safe so that they can keep their families wealthy."

She laughed. "You're making fun, but it makes sense."

"Right after my mother died there was a problem with pirates."

"Pirates!" For that, she sat up and gave him her full attention. "I love pirates!"

He gave her a patient look. "These pirates aren't fun like Jack Sparrow. They're ruthless. Cutthroat. There was a particularly nasty band all but making it impossible for tankers to get through without paying a 'fee' for safe passage. The papers exploded with criticism of my dad for not taking a firm hand. Parliament called for his resignation. And he sat in his quarters, staring at pictures of my mom, having all his meals brought up, not changing out of sweats."

"Holy cow." Entranced now, she shimmied around to sit cross-legged on the bed so she could look directly at him as he spoke. "What happened?"

"On the last second of what seemed to be the last day before he would have been required to face down parliament, my dad sent the military to destroy the pirate ships. It was a war that lasted about forty-five minutes. He bombed the boats until there was nothing left but smoke and an oil slick."

"Wow."

"Then he sent the military to the country that was

aiding and abetting, and just about blew them off the map."

Two raps sounded on the door. Dominic pulled away. "That would be breakfast. You wait here."

"You're bringing me breakfast in bed?"

He tilted his head. "It looks like I am."

She saw it then. Not just his total confusion over his feelings for her, but the reason for it. He'd said before that his dad had made a mistake that he did not intend to repeat. This was it. Except she couldn't tell if the mistake was grieving his dead wife or being in love with his wife so much that he'd grieved her.

Dominic returned, rolling a cart covered with a white linen tablecloth into the room. He pulled a bed tray from beneath the cart and said, "I'm about to put bacon and eggs on this tray, so get yourself where you want to be sitting."

Still cross-legged in the middle of the bed, she patted a spot in front of her. "I like to be able to look at you when we talk."

"So you're going to want me to take off the robe while we eat?"

She pointed to herself. "I'm not dressed."

"You're certainly not dressed to receive company. But I like you that way."

The warmth of his feelings for her sent a shudder of happiness through her. He put the tray on the bed in front of her, lifted a lid from a plate of food and set that on the tray.

He motioned to the cart. "There's a variety of juices, pastries, toasts, fruit. What else would you like?"

"Just a bottle of water."

One of his eyebrows rose. "No fruit?"

"Oh, so suddenly you're not so unhappy with me eating fruit."

"I wasn't unhappy that you were eating fruit the day you fainted. I was unhappy that you seemed to be eating only fruit. You and the baby need a balanced diet."

Her spirits lifted again. She liked talking about the baby as a baby, not the next heir to Xaviera's throne. She patted her tummy. "I know exactly what to eat."

Though Dom took three calls after they ate and while Ginny showered, he couldn't shake the glorious feeling that he really didn't have to do anything for two whole weeks.

When she came out of the bathroom, dressed in a pretty sundress, he caught her shoulders and kissed her deeply before he pulled away and said, "I love the dress, but why don't you slip into a bikini and we'll sit on the deck and get some sun?"

She smiled cautiously. "Okay."

Unexpected fear skittered through him. "What's wrong?"

"Honestly, I have no idea what we're supposed to be doing."

"We can do anything we want, which is why I suggested sitting on the deck, getting some sun. I haven't had a vacation in a long time and just sitting in the sun for a few hours sounds really nice."

She bounced to her tiptoes and brushed a quick kiss across his mouth. "Bring a book."

He laughed. "I'm not *that* unaccustomed to taking a break."

"Good." She turned to go back into the bathroom/ dressing room, closet area.

Needing to get dressed himself, he followed her.

She stopped in front of a rack of clothes—her clothes—that now hung there. She frowned. "Did you unpack for me while I showered?"

"No. Servants must have done it. There's an entrance in the other side of the closet. Obviously, they came in, did what needed to be done and left."

She turned slightly and smiled at him. "So your privacy isn't really privacy at all."

"I have minions scurrying everywhere."

He meant it as a joke, but his comment caused her head to tilt. That assessing look came to her face again, but he took it as her trying to adjust to everything.

He was glad for that. Two years was a long time, and she'd need to be acclimated to everything around them—around him—in order to be casual in public.

Honesty compelled him to say, "You really won't get much in the way of privacy."

She smiled. "Do you think a guidance counselor in a school with two thousand kids ever gets privacy?"

He laughed. "At home." He winced. "At least I hope no one bothered you at home."

"It was never a bother to have someone contact me at home. If one of my kids thought enough to call me or come by, it was usually because they were so happy about something they wanted to share." She raised her gaze to meet his. "Or they were in trouble. And if they were, I wanted to help."

"That sounds a heck of a lot like my job. But multiply your two thousand by a thousand."

She nodded. "That's a lot of people."

He said, "All of them depending on me," then watched as she absorbed that.

"That's good for me to know."

"And understand. These people depend on me. I will not let them down."

As easy as breathing, she slid out of the sunny yellow dress and, naked, lifted a bikini out of one of the drawers.

He'd seen her naked, of course; they'd spent the night making love and the morning talking on his bed. What was odd was the strange sense of normalcy that rippled around him. He'd never pictured himself and the princess of Grennady sharing a dressing room. Even if they made love, she'd be dressing in the suite across from his, if only because she was as pampered as he was. Her wardrobe for a two-week cruise wouldn't have been four suitcases. It would have been closer to ten.

But Ginny was simple. Happy. And so was he. Not with sex. Not with the fact that living as a man and wife for real would make the ruse that much easier. He was happy with the little things. Breakfast in bed. The ability to be honest. Dressing together for a morning that would be spent reading fiction.

It was the very fact that these things were so foreign to him that grounded him to the reality that he shouldn't get used to them. In two years all this would be gone.

For the first time, he understood why Ginny had campaigned to make this marriage real. They'd never, ever have this again. He'd be a divorced prince, eventually king, who'd take mistresses while he ran a country and raised a son. And she'd be the king's ex-wife, mother of the heir to the throne.

"You know it's really going to be hard for you to get dates after we divorce."

She turned with a laugh. "Excuse me?"

"Nothing." He walked back to the section of the

dressing room that held his clothes and pulled out a pair of swimming trunks. He couldn't believe he'd thought of that. What she chose to do when they separated was her business. But he knew it might be a good thing for *her* to start thinking about that. Not just to remind her that this wasn't going to last but to get her realizing the next stage of her life wouldn't be easy.

They spent a fun, private two weeks on the yacht, with Dom called away only three or four times for phone calls from members of parliament. Otherwise, he'd been casual, restful and sexy.

When the royal helicopter touched down on the palace grounds, Dom and Ginny were greeted by the whir of cameras and a barrage of questions from reporters who stood behind the black iron fence surrounding the property.

Stepping out of the helicopter, helped by Dom, who took her hand to guide her to the steps, she smiled at the press.

"You look great! Very suntanned!"

She waved at them. "Don't worry. I used sunblock."

The reporters laughed.

Dom said, "We had a great time."

Ginny watched the reporters go slack jawed as if totally gob smacked by his answer. Then she realized they weren't accustomed to him talking to them outside of the press room or parliament.

As they walked to the palace behind bodyguards dressed casually in jeans and black T-shirts—with leather holsters and guns exposed—she turned to him. "That was kind of you to talk to them, Your Majesty."

He sniffed. "I'm rested enough that I threw them a bone."

She laughed. "You should rest more often."

They reached the palace. A bodyguard opened the door and they stepped into the cool air-conditioned space.

She took a long breath of the stale air. "I miss the ocean."

He dropped a quick kiss on her lips. "The yacht is at your disposal anytime you want."

"Are you trying to get rid of me?"

"No." He stopped walking and caught her hand. He kissed the knuckles. "No."

When their gazes met, she knew he thought the same thing he did. Two years would be over soon enough. But she couldn't be happy, be herself, make this relationship work, if it was permanent. And neither could he.

They'd been granted a very short window of time to be happy, but two years of perfection was a lot more than some people got.

So she raised herself to her tiptoes, kissed his cheek and said, "Go visit your dad. Get the rundown on what happened while we were away and I'll be waiting for you for supper tonight."

CHAPTER TEN

THEY SETTLED INTO a comfortable routine that was so easy, Dominic forgot this was supposed to be difficult. Dressing for the royal family's annual end-of-summer gala, he held out his arms to Ginny as naturally as breathing and she locked his cuff links.

"I heard your mother made it in this afternoon."

Ginny glanced up at him, then shook her head. "She didn't want to miss too much class time, so she only took two days off. Your father sent the jet and she got here about an hour ago. She almost got here too late to dress because she keeps forgetting that we're seven hours ahead of her."

He grunted. "She'll get used to it."

Her tummy peeped out a bit when her dress flattened against it as she turned to walk away. He caught her hand and spun her to face him again, his hand falling to the slight swelling. "What's this?"

She laughed. "I thought the flowing dress would hide the fact that I'm starting to show."

Emotion swelled in his chest, but he held it back, more afraid of it than he cared to admit. "You shouldn't hide it. Everybody's waiting to see it."

She groaned. "Everybody's waiting to see me get

fat? Thanks for the reminder that I'll be getting fat in front of the world."

He grabbed his jacket and motioned her out of their bedroom. "That's one way of looking at it. The other is to realize that since everybody's so eager to see you gain weight, you now have full permission to eat."

She stopped and pivoted to face him. "Oh, my gosh! I never thought of it that way. For the next five months I can eat on camera."

"Subjects will love seeing you eat on camera."

She rubbed her hands together with glee. "Bring on the steaks."

He opened the apartment door and led her into the echoing foyer. "Should I tell them to give you two from now on?"

She inclined her head. "Might not want to start big. I should work my way up to the second steak."

They entered the elevator. As it descended she slid her arm through his. The door opened and they made their way to his father's quarters, where her mother was holding court. He thought it odd for the real royal, his dad, to be letting Ginny's mom monopolize the conversation. Still, he walked into a room to the sound of his brother laughing and his dad trying to hide a laugh.

"Mother, please tell me you're not telling off-color jokes."

Rose gasped at the sound of her daughter's voice. When she turned and saw the same thing Dom had seen that evening—the slight evidence of a baby bump— her eyes misted. She raced over and put her hands on Ginny's tummy.

"Oh, my gosh."

As she had with him, Ginny groaned. "Great. Just great. Everybody's going to notice."

"Subjects are eagerly waiting for this," Dom's father said, sounding happier than Dom had ever heard him.

"That's what I told her." He nodded to the bartender to get him a Scotch but stopped midnod and shook his head. He didn't need a drink. Didn't want a drink. Not out of respect for her sensitivity because of her dad's alcoholism. But out of a sense of unity. This child was both of theirs, but technically she was doing all the work, all the sacrificing. He walked to the bar, got two orange juices in beautiful crystal and handed one to Ginny.

Alex laughed. "You're drinking orange juice?"

He glanced at his brother's double Scotch. "Maybe I'd like to have a clear head in case we go to war?"

"Bah. War!" The king batted a hand. "That miserable old sheikh who's been threatening had better watch his mouth."

Ginny spun to face him. "A sheikh's been threatening?"

"Rattling his saber." Dom took a sip of his orange juice.

She stepped back, tugging on his sleeve for him to join her out of the conversation circle. "Is that what the orange juice is about?"

He looked at the glass, then at her and decided to come clean. "No, as my dad said, the sheikh is just being an idiot. I realize you're doing all the heavy lifting with this pregnancy. I thought I'd show a little unity, if only in spirit."

"Oh." She kissed his cheek. "Now, there's something you should tell the press."

"Are you kidding?"

"No. If they like baby bumps, they'll love hearing that you're sacrificing your Scotch."

"This sacrifice isn't permanent. It's only for tonight."

"Still, it's charming."

"Oh, please. It took me decades to lose the Prince Charming title. I'd rather not go there again." He pointed at his brother. "Alex lives with it now."

"Still…" She sucked in a breath and caught his gaze. "Thank you."

He displayed the glass. "It's a little thing. Not much really." Yet he could see it meant a lot to her, and knowing that gave him a funny feeling inside. Add that to his ability to see her baby bump every time she shifted or moved and he couldn't seem to take his eyes off her.

His father led them to the ballroom, where they entered to a trumpet blast. After an hour in a receiving line, he noticed Ginny looked a little tired and was glad when they walked to the dais. His father made a toast. As minister of finance, he gave a longer toast.

The press was escorted out as dinner was served and, relieved, Dom sat back. Watching Ginny dig into her pork chops with raspberry sauce served with mashed potatoes and julienned steamed carrots, he laughed.

"You're going to be finished before I get three bites into mine."

"Everyone said pregnancy would make me hungry all the time. They should have said ravenous."

He chuckled.

She eyed his dish. "You got a bigger serving than I did."

"Wanna switch plates?"

She sighed. "No."

"Seriously. I'll save some. If you're still hungry you can have it."

"I'm gonna get big as a house."

"In front of the whole world," he agreed good-naturedly. But when she was done eating, he slid a piece of his pork to her plate. "I don't want you to faint from hunger while we're dancing."

But as he said the words, he got a funny sensation. A prickling that tiptoed up his spine to the roots of his hair. He glanced to the left and right, not sure what he was looking for. He saw only dinner servers in white jackets and gloves. People milling about the formal dining room.

Calling himself crazy, he went back to the entertainment that was watching his wife eat and didn't think of the prickling until he and Ginny were on the dance floor an hour later. With everyone's attention on his father and Ginny's mother, who were doing their own version of a samba, he felt comfortable enough to enjoy holding Ginny, dancing with her. He'd spun her around twice, then dipped her enough to make her laugh, and there it was again. A tingling that raced up his back and settled in his neck.

Still, he didn't mention it to Ginny. They danced and mingled with the dignitaries invited to their annual gala, including the sheikh currently giving them trouble.

She curtsied graciously when introduced. "I was hoping you could settle your differences tonight."

The sheikh's gaze bounced to Dominic's. Dominic only shrugged. She hadn't really said anything *too* bad.

The sheikh caught Ginny's hand and kissed it. "We don't talk business at the gala."

She bowed apologetically. "I'm so sorry. But since I was hoping that settling this agreement might get me two weeks on the yacht with my husband I guess I didn't see it as business."

The sheikh laughed. "I like a woman who doesn't mind asking for what she wants."

Ginny smiled. Dominic took the cue and said, "Perhaps we could meet first thing Monday morning."

"If your father's schedule is free."

"I'm sure it will be for you."

An hour later, seeing that Ginny was tired, Dominic excused himself to his father who—along with Ginny's mother—thought it was a good idea for her to leave.

He took her hand and led her down a few halls to their elevator. When they were securely behind the door of their apartment, he tugged on her hand and brought her to him for a long happy kiss.

"You do realize you just accomplished what diplomacy hasn't been able to get done in three weeks."

"Does this mean I get my three weeks on the yacht?"

"I thought it was two."

"I want three."

"You're getting greedy."

She curtsied. "I just like my time with you, Your Majesty. And your undivided attention."

He scooped her off her feet and carried her to their bedroom. "I'm about to give you all the undivided attention you can handle."

The next morning Ginny awakened as she had every day since their marriage, wrapped in his arms. At six, Dom rolled out of bed and used the bathroom. He slid into a robe and, from seeing his daily routine, Ginny knew he'd gone to their everyday dining room. Sliding into a pretty pink robe, Ginny followed him.

"Not sleepy this morning?"

Rather than take her chair, she slid to his lap. "I feel extraordinarily good."

"So maybe we should do what we did last night every night."

"Maybe we should."

The sound of the servant's door being opened brought Ginny to her feet. As she walked to her side of the table, a young girl wheeled in a cart containing his breakfast of bacon and eggs, plus bowls of fruit, carafes of fruit juices, and plates of pastries and breads.

She smiled at Ginny expectantly. Knowing she was waiting for her breakfast order, Ginny said, "I'll just eat what we have here."

Dom glanced over. "No bacon? No eggs?"

"Wait until you see now many bagels I eat."

He laughed as the serving girl left.

As always, their meal was accompanied by fourteen newspapers. She grabbed *USA TODAY* as he took London's the *Times*. Their table grew quiet until Dom flipped a page and suddenly said, "What?"

Busy putting cream cheese on a bagel, Ginny didn't even look over. "What's the *what* for?"

He slammed the paper to the table and reached for the house phone behind him. "Sally, get up here."

Ginny set down her bagel. "What's going on?"

He shoved the paper across the table. She glanced down and saw a picture of her and Dom with their heads together as their dinners were served, a picture of her and Dom dancing, a picture of Dom leading her out the back door of the ballroom. All beneath the headline: The Affectionate Prince.

"At least they didn't call you Prince Charming."

He glared at her.

"Dom, I'm sorry. Your picture gets in the paper almost every day here in Xaviera. I'm missing the significance of this."

"First, no press is allowed in that ballroom once dinner starts. So one of our employees got these pictures."

As the ramifications of that sank in, she said, "Oh."

"Second, look at that headline."

"'The Affectionate Prince'?" She caught his gaze. "When you want to be, you are affectionate."

"No ruler wants to be thought of as weak."

"Weak? It's not weak to love someone." Instantly realizing her mistake in saying the *L* word, Ginny shot her gaze to his. For a few seconds they just stared at each other, then he bounced from his seat, almost sending it across the room.

"This was exactly what I didn't want to happen!"

Ginny said, "What?" not quite sure if the unexpected anger coursing through her made her bold or if she was just plain tired of skirting the truth. "Are you mad that your happiness shows? Or are you really that surprised or that angry that we fell in love?"

"I can't love you."

"Oh, really? Because I think you already do."

There. She'd said it.

Their gazes met again, but this time his softened. He took his seat again. "Ginny. I can't love you."

Since she'd already made her position clear, she said nothing, only held his gaze.

"My dad loved my mother."

"Oh, damn him for his cruelty."

"Don't make fun. When my mother got sick, my dad slipped away, let our country flounder because he was searching the globe for someone, *something* that could save his wife."

"And you think that was weakness?"

"Call it what you want. Weakness. Distraction. Whatever."

"How about normal human behavior?"

"Or a lack of planning."

"You think your dad should have had a contingency plan in case his wife got sick?"

"I think he let pirates get a foothold because he put my mother first."

"Oh, Dominic, of course he put his sick wife first."

He shook his head as if he couldn't believe what she'd just said. "A king cannot put anyone ahead of his country. At the first sign of those pirates he should have involved the military."

"Even though his wife, the woman he obviously adored, was dying? How could he have avoided scrambling to save her?"

His gaze rose until it met hers. "By not falling in love in the first place."

Something fluttered oddly in her stomach. The conversation was making her sick and sad and scared. But the feeling went away as quickly as it came. "I see."

"The stakes of this game, my life, are very high, Ginny. We don't govern or rule our people as much as we protect them. I can't afford a slip, a lapse." He combed his fingers through his hair. "When I'm king I won't get two private weeks on a yacht. I'll get vacations that include video conferencing and daily briefings. I'll get two hours, at most, in the sun. A twenty-minute swim." He sucked in a breath. "And this is why I warned you. Even if I wanted to love you. Even if I fell head over heels for you...coming in second to a country isn't like being second to a hobby. You would get very little of my time. It wouldn't be worth loving me."

Stunned, Ginny watched him toss his napkin to the table. "Where is Sally?"

Then he stormed out of the dining room because he didn't have anything to give her.

And that was the truth he'd been trying to tell her all along.

CHAPTER ELEVEN

GINNY SAT STARING at her bagel when there was a knock on the apartment door. She expected it to be Sally, so when her mom walked into the dining room and said, "I thought we were going to swim this morning," Ginny dropped her bagel to a plate.

"I'm not much in the mood."

Her mom took a seat, grabbed a Danish pastry and popped a bite into her mouth. "First fight?"

"You know this isn't a real relationship."

"Oh, sweetie, of course it is. Get any man and woman involved in a plot or plan of any type and what results is a relationship."

"Yeah, well. It's short-term."

"Why is this bothering you suddenly?" Her eyes narrowed. "You want to change the rules."

Ginny rose from her seat. "I'm in my robe. I need to get some clothes on. Sally's supposed to be coming up."

"Dom was on his way out when he let me in."

"He must have called Sally and told her he would come down to her." She headed toward the bedroom. "I need to get dressed anyway."

She wasn't surprised when her mom followed her out of the dining room and into Dom's bedroom.

Seeing the entire bed was happily rumpled, she faced Ginny. "Well, this is a change of plans."

"You don't really think we were going to be married and not sleep together, Mom." She put her hand on her stomach and the strange flutter happened again.

"Honey, I knew you'd be sleeping together. I just didn't think you realized it would happen." She walked over. "What's up with your tummy? You're not sick, are you?"

"I don't know. I don't think so. But every couple of minutes this morning I've been getting this strange flutter in my stomach."

"Oh, my gosh! The baby's moving!"

"He is?"

"Or she is!" She plopped her palm on Ginny's stomach. "Let me feel." Her eyes filled with tears. "Oh, my gosh. Oh, Ginny. I'm going to be a grandma."

Ginny fell to the bed. "That fluttering is my baby?"

Rose sat beside her on the unmade bed. "Yep." She nudged Ginny's shoulder. "Mama."

She pressed her lips together. "Mama. I'm going to be somebody's mom."

Rose slid her hand across her shoulders. "Yes, you are. And whatever nonsense is going on between you and Dom, you have to straighten it out."

"There is nothing to straighten out. The deal is made. I leave two years after the baby's born."

Rose studied her face. "But you don't want to go now. You love him."

"And I think he loves me, too, but he doesn't want to."

"Oh, what man willingly falls in love?"

Ginny laughed.

Rose said, "Give him time."

"Time won't heal the fact that he thinks love makes a ruler weak."

"Really?"

"You know his mom died, right?"

Rose winced. "Kind of hard not to see that Ronaldo's wife isn't around."

"She was apparently sick for years with cancer." Ginny sighed. "He tried everything to save her and in that time the country fell apart."

"So?"

"So, parliament called for his resignation. Had he not snapped out of it he would have lost his crown."

"Oh."

Ginny rose from the bed and paced to the dresser. "I never realized how difficult their job was."

Her mom leaned back, balancing herself with her hands behind her. "How so?"

"Their location forces them into a position of needing to protect the waterways. While Dom's dad was scrambling to save his wife, pirates began attacking ships, demanding money to pass."

"That's not good."

"The press crucified the king. Parliament called for removal of his crown."

"So you said." She sat up. "But I still don't get how this means he can't have a wife."

"He doesn't want to be weak."

"You know the marriages I've seen that work the best are the ones where a husband and wife form a team."

"If you're suggesting that I should help him rule, you are out of your mind. Not only would he *never* let that happen, but I can't rule. I could make a suggestion or two, but I couldn't rule."

Rose batted a hand. "You're good with people,

sweetie, but not that good." She stood up and walked over to Ginny. "You love this guy."

Ginny didn't even try to deny it.

"So how in the hell could you possibly be willing to let him live this demanding, difficult life alone?"

Ginny blinked.

"You're looking at this from your side of the street, but what about his? Ronaldo told me that his wife was the treasure he came home to at night. That when the world was rocky, her silliness was his salvation. She was beautiful, elegant and could charm the birds out of the trees. But he didn't care about any of that. He liked that she played gin rummy with him until the sun came up on nights he couldn't sleep. He liked that he could talk about anything with her, knowing she'd never abuse the power of his confidences and that no one would ever know she'd heard things that were supposed to be secret."

Rose took a breath and patted Ginny's shoulder. "Do you really think Dom will live much past sixty if he doesn't have a friend, a buddy, a confidante, a lover who's willing to be whatever he wants without making demands?"

"No."

"And can you see the lonely life he'll have unless you try to work this out?"

She sucked in a breath. "Yes."

"Ginny, you always believed that being a guidance counselor was a calling. But what if this is your calling? Not just being Dom's true partner, but also raising your child so that he or she isn't buried under the stress of ruling?"

"Maybe I have been looking at this selfishly."

"Not selfishly, but ill informed. Now that you know

how difficult all this is, you've got to do whatever you can to make Dom's life easier."

Dom and Sally easily found the serving boy who had taken the pictures, but that didn't change the fact that the damage was done. Dom looked at photos of himself on the dais, on the dance floor and leading Ginny to the rear entrance to return to their apartment, and even he saw it—the weakness. The ease with which he stepped out of his role as leader and into the role of what? A smitten lover?

He could not have that. He would not be his dad. If anything, now was the time to prove that he was stronger than his father.

He didn't have lunch with Ginny, didn't return to the apartment until after eight that night. When he opened the door and entered the sitting room, he found her on the sofa, reading a magazine. Dressed in a soft red robe with a floral nightgown beneath it, she rose when she saw him.

"Did you catch the creep who took those pictures?"

He headed for the bar. "Yes."

"Want to talk about it?"

"No."

She returned to her seat. "Okay."

Silence descended on the room. He looked at the Scotch with disgust, remembering the orange juice he'd been drinking for "unity." What was wrong with him that he'd been such a schmuck? All he'd been doing since their honeymoon was giving her the wrong idea.

He set the glass on the bar and didn't even tell her he was going to get his shower. He let the water sluice over him, reminding himself that he was a ruler, royalty, someone set aside to do the noble task of keeping his people safe. He stood in the shower until he began to feel like his old self.

He put on a pair of pajamas and crawled into bed with the latest popular thriller. He might not be a television guy or a movie buff, but he liked a good story, a good book. He read until ten when his eyelids grew heavy. He set the book on the bedside table at the same time that Ginny entered the room.

He wanted to suggest that she go back to her old room, but couldn't quite bring himself to be that mean. Eventually she'd grow weary of him ignoring her and she'd come to the decision on her own.

Soundlessly, she slipped out of her red robe, exposing the pretty flowered nightie. His gaze fell to her stomach, which peeped out every time she moved in such a way that the gown flattened against it. She said nothing. Just crawled into bed.

But she rolled over to him. She put her head on his shoulder and her hand on his stomach.

He resisted the urge to lower his arm and cuddle her to him. This was, after all, part of how he'd get her to see the truth of their situation and go back to her own room. But when her breathing grew even and soft and he knew she was asleep, he let his arm fall enough that he could support her.

Then he laid his hand on her stomach.

He closed his eyes, savoring the sensations of holding her, and fell asleep telling himself that it wouldn't hurt to hold her every once in a while.

Dom's life became a series of long days and empty meals. With Ginny's mom deciding to retire to help Ginny care for the baby, he didn't have to worry if she had company or if she was being cared for or entertained. In fact, the way she slept in in the morning and had lunches and most dinners with her mom made him feel they were establishing a great system for being together without being together.

The thing of it was, though, she was in his bed every night. She never said a word. Didn't try to seduce him. She just rolled against him, put her head on his shoulder and her hand on his chest and fell asleep.

He didn't resist it. Not because he took comfort from the small gesture, but because she was pregnant with his child, and he was hurting her. It almost seemed that this little ritual was her way of easing away from him. And if this was what she needed to do to get through the next months, he would let her have it.

But one night, she rolled against him and something bounced against his side. He peered down. The stomach beneath her thin yellow nightgown looked much bigger when she was on her side.

The bounce hit him again. He stiffened but she laughed.

"That's your baby."

He sprang up. "What?"

"Your baby." She took his hand and set it on her stomach. "He's moving."

The rounded stomach beneath his hand rippled. His jaw dropped. He smoothed his fingers along the silken nightie.

She sat up. "Here." She wiggled out of the nightie and tossed it. Sitting naked in the dark with him, she took both his hands and positioned them on either side of her belly.

The baby moved. A soft shift that almost felt like a wave.

He laughed, but his throat closed. "Oh, my God."

She whispered, "I know."

The desire to take her into his arms overwhelmed him and he pulled her close, squeezing his eyes shut. "Thank you."

She leaned back so she could catch his gaze. "For showing you the best way to feel the baby or for actually having the baby?"

Her eyes warmed with humor. The tension that had seized his back and shoulders for the past six weeks eased and he laughed. "It's a big deal to have a baby."

"Millions of women do it every day."

He sobered. "But not under such ridiculous conditions."

She took his hand, pressed it to her stomach again. "The conditions aren't that bad."

"You're not going to have a life."

She shrugged. "I know. I already figured out it'll take some hellaciously special guy to ask out a woman who's divorced from a king and mother to a child who's about to become king." She met his gaze. "Very few guys will want to get on the bad side of a man who can answer the question 'you and what army?'"

With the baby wiggling under his fingers, he said, "I'm so sorry."

She waited until he looked at her again, then she whispered, "I'm not."

"Then you haven't fully absorbed the ramifications of this mess yet."

"First, I don't think it's a mess. I told you. I didn't think I'd ever become a mom. This baby is a great gift to me." She shrugged. "So I have to give up dating permanently?" She put her hands on top of his. "This is worth it."

"It is."

He didn't mean to say the words out loud. He now hated doing *anything* that gave her false hope. But she smiled and lay down.

"I'm sorry. Are you tired? Do you want to go to sleep?"

"Sleep?" She laughed and pointed at her stomach, which still rippled with movement. "You think I'm going to sleep with the Blue Man Group rolling around?"

He laughed, too, and settled on his pillow again. "Have you thought of names?"

"I pretty much figured your country would name her."

He sat up again and looked down into her eyes. "The country?"

She shrugged. "Parliament." She shrugged again. "Maybe your dad. Maybe tradition."

"Tradition plays a role but essentially we get to name the baby."

Her eyes lit. "Really? So if I want to call her Regina Rose, I can?"

He winced. "Sure."

"You don't like Regina?"

"I'd rather she just be Rose. It's a good solid name."

"It is." She paused a second before she said, "And if it's a boy?"

"I've always been fond of James Tiberius Kirk."

"*Star Trek!* You'd name our baby after someone in *Star Trek*?"

"Not just any old someone. The captain. Plus Tiberius is an honorable name." He met her gaze. "So is James."

"I might not mind it if we dropped the Kirk."

"I think that goes without saying."

He lay down again. She snuggled into his side.

"You know the sheikh still asks about you."

She laughed.

"He wanted to know if you got your three weeks on the yacht."

"Did you tell him I didn't?"

"No."

"Did you explain that we had a fight?"

He sat up again. "This isn't a fight. It's the way things have to be."

She said, "Yes, Your Majesty." Not smartly. No hint of sarcasm and he knew she understood.

It should have made him feel better. It didn't.

He lay back down again. "Have you thought about what you're going to do in two years?" He couldn't bring himself to say *after we divorce*. He knew that would hurt her too much.

"I'm still debating something Sally said about using my notoriety to bring attention to my causes."

"Education?"

He felt her nod.

"You know, you can still live in the palace."

"I know."

That would be hard for her, but having just felt his baby move for the first time, strange emotions coursed through him. He couldn't imagine Ginny gone. Couldn't quite figure out how two people raised a child when they lived in separate houses. He'd been so cool about this in the beginning. So detached. But now that he'd felt his child, was getting to know Ginny, he saw all those decisions that were made so glibly had sad, lonely consequences.

"I just think it would be easier if I lived on the other side of the island. I'd be close, but not too close."

He swallowed, grateful she wasn't taking his baby

halfway around the world. Still, an empty, hollow feeling sat in his stomach. "Makes sense."

She said, "Yeah," but he heard the wobble in her voice. She fell asleep a few minutes later, but Dom stayed awake most of the night. Sometimes angry with himself for hurting her. Other times angry with life. An ordinary man would take her and run with the life they could have together.

But he was a king—or would be someday. He didn't get those choices.

CHAPTER TWELVE

THE FIRST DAY of every month, Dom and Ginny made a public appearance that always included questions from the press. With her eight-months-pregnant stomach protruding, Ginny struggled to find something that wouldn't make her look like a house while Dom attended to some matters in his office.

She finally settled on straight-leg trousers and a loose-fitting blue sweater—knowing it would make her eye color pop and hopefully get everybody's attention on the baby. After stepping into flat sandals, she walked into the living room just as there was a knock at the door. Her mom entered without her having to answer the door.

"You're not glowing today."

"Nope. Why didn't anybody tell me that pregnant women didn't get any sleep when they got close to their due date?"

"Nobody wants to scare women off," her mother said with a laugh as she entered the sitting room. She bent and kissed Ginny's forehead, then sat beside her on the sofa.

"Dom not coming around?"

"Nope. And I'm out of tricks. We talked baby names. I've shown him how to feel the baby move. We eat breakfast and dinner together every day, and nothing. I'm out of ideas, short of seduction." She pointed at her stomach. "And we both know seduction would be a little awkward now."

"I'm so sorry, sweetie."

"It's fine. But I've gotta run. I get to play loving princess now, while he ignores me."

They left through the front of the palace so long-range lenses could pick up photos of Dom opening the door for Ginny.

Every inch of Dom now hated the charade he'd created. It was working, but it was also a strain on Ginny. When she was just a normal woman, a one-night stand, he didn't see the strain as being as much of a big deal, though he knew it was a sacrifice.

But now that he could see the effects of her sacrifice, her swollen stomach, the sadness that came to her eyes every time she realized how empty, how hollow their relationship was, it burned through him like a guilty verdict pronounced by the gods. She had been the sweetest woman in the world, and in spite of the way he was using her, she was still sweet, still genuine, still helping him.

If he didn't go to hell for this, it would be a miracle. Because he certainly believed he deserved the highest punishment.

She slid into the limo and blew her breath out in a long, labored sigh.

His gaze darted to hers. "Are you okay?"

She placed her hands on her basketball stomach. "I'm not accustomed to carrying twenty-five extra pounds." She laughed good-naturedly. "Sometimes I get winded."

The funny part of it was she didn't look bad. Wearing slim slacks that tapered to the top of her ankle and a loose blue sweater that didn't hide her baby bump but didn't hug it, either, she just looked pregnant. Her arms hadn't gained. Her legs hadn't gained. She simply had a belly.

A belly that held his child.

"If the trip is too much, we can go back to the palace."

"Only to have to reschedule it for tomorrow?" She shook her head. "Let's just get this over with."

The guilt pressed down again. He glanced at her feet, pretty in her pink-toned sandals. Her whimsy in the choice of color made him smile.

"You have an interesting fashion sense."

She gaped at him. "I have a wonderful fashion sense, Mr. White-Shirt-and-Tie-Everywhere-You-Go. You need to read *Vogue* every once in a while."

The very thought made him laugh.

Her head tilted as she smiled at him. "It's been a long time since I heard you laugh."

"Yeah, well, our saber-rattling sheikh is back and he isn't the country's only problem. It's hard for me to laugh when I have business to attend to."

Her pretty blue eyes sought his in the back of the limo. "Is it really that difficult?"

He turned his head to the right and then the left to loosen the tension. "Yes and no." Oddly, he felt better. He could twist his neck a million times, sitting in the halls of parliament, and nothing. But two feet away from her and the tension began to ebb.

"Ruling is mostly about paying attention. Not just to who wants what but also to negotiating styles and nonverbal cues. There are parliamentarians who get quiet right before they walk out of a session and spill their guts to the press. There are others who explode in session." He caught her gaze again. "I'd rather deal with them."

She smiled and nodded, and the conversation died. But when he helped her out of the limo at Marco's seaside coffee shop, she was all smiles.

A reporter shouted, "Coming back to the scene of the crime?"

She laughed. "If fainting was a crime, tons of pregnant women would be in jail." She smiled prettily as she slid on the sunglasses that made her look like a rock star. "Just hungry for a cookie."

With his bodyguards clearing a path, they made their way into the coffee shop. Standing behind the counter, Marco beamed with pleasure.

He bowed. "It is an honor that you love my cookies."

She laughed. "The pleasure is all mine. Not only do I want a cookie and a glass of milk for now, but I'm taking a half-dozen cookies back to the palace."

Marco scurried to get her order. Dominic frowned. "Don't you want to hear what I want?"

"Hazelnut coffee," Marco said, clearly disinterested in Dominic as he carefully placed cookies in a box for Ginny. Antonella brought Dominic's coffee to the counter.

He pulled a card out to pay, but Marco stopped him with a gasp. "It is my honor to serve our princess today."

Dominic said, "Right."

Because Ginny didn't faint this time, Dom could actually lead her out to the long deck that became a dock. He set her milk on the table in front of her, along with her single cookie. He handed the box of six cookies to a bodyguard.

Ginny said, "There better be six cookies in that box when we get back to the palace."

Dominic's typically staid and stoic bodyguard laughed.

After a sip of coffee, he said, "They love you, you know?"

She unwrapped her big sugar cookie as if it were a treasure. "Everybody loves me. But there's a reason for that. It's not magic. I'm a child of an alcoholic. I *know* everybody has something difficult in their life so I treat everyone well."

"I treat everyone well."

She lifted her cookie. "Yeah. Sort of."

"Sort of? I never yell at anyone. And if I reprimand, it's with kindness."

"You're still a prince."

"Dominic?"

Dom glanced up to see his boarding school friend, Pietro Fonichelli. The son of an Italian billionaire and a billionaire several times over in his own right, thanks to his computer software skills, Pietro was probably better known around the globe than Dominic was. He was also on Dominic's list of friends, the people his bodyguards were told to allow access to him.

Dominic rose. "What are you doing here?"

As he said the words, Dom noticed Pietro wore shorts and a big T-shirt.

"Vacationing." He faced Ginny. "And this is your lovely bride."

It was the first time Dominic was uncomfortable with the ruse. Engaging in a charade to help his subjects enjoy the birth of the country's next heir? That was a good thing. Fooling someone he considered a friend? It didn't sit well. Pietro had been at the wedding, but there had been so many people that at the time it hadn't registered that he was tricking a friend.

He politely said, "Yes, this is Ginny Jones."

Pietro laughed. "Ginny Jones? Is she so American that she didn't take your last name?"

Ginny rose, extending her hand to Pietro. "No. Dom sometimes forgets we're married."

Laughing, Pietro took the hand she extended. Instead of shaking it, he kissed the knuckles.

Something hot and fuzzy whipped through Dom. The custom in Xaviera was that a man had a choice. A handshake or a kiss. He should not be upset that his friend chose a kiss. It was nothing more than a sign of affection for the wife of a friend.

Holding Dom's wife's gaze, Pietro said, "I'm not entirely sure how a man forgets he's married to such a beautiful woman."

Ginny smiled as if she thought Pietro's words were baloney, but Dom had never seen his friend so smitten before. Just as Dom had been tongue-tied and eager the day he'd met Ginny, Pietro all but drooled.

Ginny said, "Dom's a great husband."

"Yeah, well, if he ever isn't—" he let go of Ginny's hand and pulled out a business card "—this card has my direct line on it."

Ginny laughed, but Dom said, "What? Are you flirting with my wife?"

"Teasing," Pietro said. He pulled Dom into a bear hug, released him and said, "It was great to run into you." He glanced at Ginny, then back at Dom. "We should do dinner sometime."

The air came back to Dom's lungs and he felt incredibly stupid. He knew Pietro was a jokester. He knew his friend loved getting a rise out of Dom. It was part of what made them click. They could joke. Tease. "Yes. We should."

With his coffee gone and Ginny's cookie demolished, they walked back to the limo, one bodyguard conspicuously holding a box of a half-dozen brightly painted sugar cookies.

He helped Ginny into the limo, then sat beside her, realizing Pietro was the kind of man who wouldn't care if her ex was a king. He would pursue Ginny. With the money to buy and sell loyalty, her connection to a king would mean nothing to him. Once Ginny was free of Dom, it wouldn't even cross Pietro's mind to care that she'd been his wife. He'd pursue her.

His nerves endings stood on edge like the fur of a hissing cat. *Not out of jealousy*, he told himself. Out of fear for her. Pietro might be a great friend, but he wouldn't be a good husband. Like Dom, he took what he wanted. Discarded it when he was done.

His nerves popped, and he suddenly knew another consequence of this fake relationship. In two years, he was going to have to watch his wife with another man.

That night in bed, the tension that vibrated from Dom rolled through Ginny. She considered shifting away, going to her own side of the bed, but she couldn't. Her baby would be born in thirty-two days, give or take a week for the unpredictability of first babies, and in two short years she would be gone. She wouldn't give up one second of her time with him. Even if it meant she wouldn't sleep tonight because the muscles of Dom's arm beneath her head had stiffened to concrete.

Finally, unable to take the tension anymore, she said, "What's wrong?"

"Nothing."

"Right." Knowing they weren't going to get any sleep anyway, she ran her fingers along the thick dark hair on his chest and said, "So I'll bet it was nice seeing your friend today."

He laughed. "Yeah. Nice."

"You know he was only teasing."

"Yes. He's a jokester and if he'd do something stupid at a bar, the press would love it and it could take the heat off of us."

"I don't mind the heat."

He didn't say anything for a second, then his arm tightened around her shoulders. "I know you don't."

"So we don't need for your friend to get punched out at a bar."

"Especially since I would like to have dinner with him. Actually, he's somebody I'd like to have in the baby's life. He started off wealthy, could have bummed around the world forever on his dad's money, but he knew the importance of being strong, being smart. I might just make him the baby's godfather so he's here for more than the big events."

She nodded but tears came to her eyes as an awful scenario ran through her brain. In two years, she and Dom would be divorced, but Dom and the baby's lives would go on—without her. She would come and go for those big events in the baby's life. She'd even be a part of things, but not really. After her two years were up, she'd be an outsider looking in.

"Are you crying?"

Dom's soft voice trickled down to her.

She swallowed. "It's just a pregnancy thing."

He sat up slightly and shifted her to her pillow so he could look down at her. "Is there anything I can do?"

You could love me, she thought and wished with

all her heart she could say the words. But she'd seduced this guy twice. She'd agreed to his plan to have
their child born amid celebration. She was good to his
family, good to his employees, good to the press and
his subjects. She didn't spend a lot of money, but she
did spend enough that she looked like the princess he
wanted her to be.

And what did she get for her troubles? The knowledge that in two years she'd be nothing to him.

She sniffed.

Dominic's eyes widened with horror. "Please. Silent tears are one thing. Actually crying will make us
both nuts."

"Really? I'm fat. I'm hungry. I'm *always* hungry. I'm
always *on*. I've been good to you, good to your family,
good to your subjects and you can't love me."

He squeezed his eyes shut. "It isn't that I can't love
you."

"Oh, it's just that you *don't want to love me*. That
makes it so much better."

He popped his eyes open. "It isn't that, either."

"Then explain this to me because I'm tired but can't
sleep. And I'm hungry even though I eat all the time.
And I just feel so freaking alone."

"We could call your friends."

"I want my husband."

"The Affectionate Prince."

"I don't give a flying fig what the press calls you.
This is our baby. Half yours. You should be here when
I need you."

"I am here when you need me."

"Yeah. Right. You're here physically, but emotionally you're a million miles away."

"I rule a country."

She shook her head. "Your dad rules the country. You work for him. Technically you're just the minister of finance."

"I need to be prepared for when I take over."

"Really? Your dad is around fifty-five. He's nowhere near retirement age. You and I could have three kids and a great life before your dad retires."

He laughed. "Seriously?" But she could tell from his tone of voice that the thought wasn't an unpleasant one.

She sat up. Holding his gaze, she said, "Would it be so wrong to ease off for the next ten years?"

He shook his head with a laugh. "First you wanted two years...now you want ten?"

"Yes." A sense of destiny filled her. The this-is-your-moment tug on her heart. There was something different in his voice. He wasn't hard, inflexible, as he usually was. In some ways, his eyes looked as tired as hers.

Could he be tired of fighting?

"I'm asking for ten years, Your Majesty, if your dad retires at sixty-five."

Dom frowned.

She plowed on, so determined that her heart beat like a hummingbird's wings. "What if he works until he's seventy? What if he's like Queen Elizabeth, keeping the throne until he's ninety? We could have a long, happy life."

Dom shook his head. "My dad won't rule until he's ninety." He caught her gaze. "But he could—will—rule another ten years."

"Doesn't ten years even tempt you?"

"You tempt me."

"So keep me. See if we can't figure this whole thing out together? See if we can't learn to have a family—be a family—in ten years."

* * *

It sounded like such a good plan when his heart beat slow and heavy in his chest from the ache of knowing he was about to lose her. He lowered his head and kissed her. Her arms came up to wrap around his shoulders and everything suddenly made sense in Dominic's world.

The buzz of the phone on his bedside table interrupted his thoughts. He didn't want to stop kissing Ginny. Didn't want this moment filled with possibilities to end. So he let the phone go, knowing it would switch to voice mail after five rings, only to have it immediately start ringing again.

The call of duty was stronger than his simple human needs. He pulled away from Ginny with a sigh, but didn't release her. Stretching, he retrieved the receiver for the phone and said, "Yes?"

"One of our ports has been taken by the sheikh. We are at war."

CHAPTER THIRTEEN

DOMINIC DIDN'T JUMP out of bed; he flew. "I don't know how much of this is going to hit the press or how soon, but the sheikh has taken one of our ports. He's telling people we're too weak to protect our waterways, so he's taking over. Which means that port is the first step to all-out war."

Ginny sucked in a breath. On top of all the other odd things she was feeling tonight, having her husband go to war made her chest hurt. She grabbed his arm as he turned to find clothes and get dressed.

"Where will you be? You don't actually have to lead troops into battle, do you?"

"No. There's a war room. My father and I will direct the military from there." He pursed his lips for a second as if debating, then sat on the edge of the bed. "I'll be fine. It's our military who will suffer casualties. Because we don't want to attack our own facility, we have to try diplomacy first. Worst-case scenario happens if he tries to move farther inland or take another port. Then there will be battles, casualties." He caught her gaze. "And then you might not see me until it's over."

She nodded, but the tears were back. No matter how strange or odd she felt, she didn't want to stop him from doing his duty. In fact, there was a part of her that was proud of him.

She leaned forward and kissed him. "Go stop that guy."

He nodded, dressed and raced out of the room.

Ginny lay in bed, breathing hard. Her stomach felt like a rock. Everything around her seemed out of control. So she did some of the breathing she'd been taught in the childbirth classes Sally had arranged for her. Even though Dom was supposed to be in the delivery room, he hadn't attended the classes. But since most of it was about breathing and remaining calm, he really hadn't needed to. Nobody could remain calm and detached the way Dom could.

She breathed again, in and out, and her stomach relaxed. Knowing she wouldn't sleep, she got out of bed and grabbed her book. Sitting on the sofa—with all her lights on because she was just a little afraid, and stupid as it sounded, the light made her feel better—she read until three o'clock in the morning. Her stomach tensed often enough that a horrible realization sliced through her. Still, with weeks until her due date, she didn't want to think she was in labor. So she let herself believe these contractions would pass.

But at seven, she couldn't lie to herself anymore. She picked up the house phone and dialed her mom's extension. "I think I'm in labor."

"Oh, no! Ginny, sweetie…this is too early."

Her stomach contracted again and she doubled over with pain. "All right. I no longer *think* I'm in labor. I know I am."

"Did they tell you what to do?"

"I have to call the doctor, but—" She doubled over again. "Oh, my God, this hurts."

"That'd be labor. Okay. I'm coming over. I'll call Sally who will tell Dom."

"He's in the war room. We're at war."

Her mom was quiet for a few seconds, then she said, "Didn't know if you'd been told, but, yes. I saw the news this morning. We're at war."

"I don't even know if Dom can come out for this."

"Oh, dear Lord, of course, he can. You just go get some clothes on so security can get you to the hospital. I will take care of calling Sally who will get Dom to the hospital."

Ginny did as she was told. The week before she'd been advised by her birthing coach to pack a bag for the hospital "just in case." So after sliding into maternity jeans and a sweater, she lugged the bag from Dom's room to the sitting area.

Then pain roared through her stomach and she fell to the sofa. She tried to breathe, but the fear that gripped her kept her from being able to focus. Her new country was at war and she was in labor. Four weeks too early. She didn't even want to contemplate that her baby might not be ready, but how could she not?

When she was almost at the point of hyperventilation, her door swung open and her mom raced in. "I talked to Sally, who said she will talk to the king. She said not to worry. She'll take care of everything."

She rose from the sofa, the pain so intense, tears speared her eyes again. "Good."

The doors opened again and Dom's top security team ran in.

"Ma'am? Can you walk?"

She caught her mother's hand. "Oh, jeez. Now I'm ma'am."

Her mother led her to the door. "That's right, sweetie. Keep your sense of humor."

Her labor lasted twelve long hours. Every twenty minutes she asked where Dom was. Every twenty-one minutes her mother would say, "He's been told you're in labor. He'll be here any minute."

She gave birth to a healthy, albeit tiny, baby boy. The happy, smiling doctor, a man who'd clearly gotten sufficient sleep the night before, joyfully said, "Can you tell me his name?"

She blinked tiredly. "For the birth certificate?"

He laughed. "No, just because I'm curious."

She swallowed. "We didn't really pick a name yet." But she remembered James Tiberius Kirk. There were some times Dom could be so much fun, so loving, that she *knew* this war had to be god-awful to keep him away from his son's birth.

The doctor placed her little boy, her little king, in her arms, and the tears that fell this time were happy tears. "Look at him, Mom." But she wished she was saying that to Dom. She should be saying, "Look at your son."

But they were at war. And he was needed.

Still, the sting of giving birth to their child alone caused tears to prick her eyelids.

"He's beautiful." Her mom kissed her cheek. "But you're tired."

"Have you heard from Sally?"

"Not a peep."

"Okay."

The doctor walked to the head of her bed. "The nurses need to take your son to be cleaned up and examined. You can have him back in an hour or so."

"You're taking him?" She hadn't been told this protocol, but it just didn't seem right to hand over the future king to people who were essentially strangers.

The doctor laughed and pointed outside the delivery room doors where her security detail stood guard. "Don't worry. He's already been assigned security. He might be leaving your sight but he won't be leaving the royal family's sight."

Her mom took the future king from her arms. "Why don't you go to sleep, honey?"

She said, "Okay," and felt herself drifting off as her mom handed her little boy to the doctor.

When she woke forty minutes later, she took off the ugly hospital gown they'd insisted she give birth in, and with her mom's help put on a pretty nightgown. She prayed Xaviera's war didn't last long, and also knew that when he could Dom would slip out and see his son. She wanted him to see she'd done okay. That she was fine. She was being the stiff-upper-lip princess she needed to be in this difficult time.

Nurses brought her baby back almost exactly an hour after he'd been taken away. The royal pediatrician came in and told her that her son was in good health, but he was small, so a few precautions would be taken.

The pediatrician returned the next morning and gave her the same report. She squeezed her hands together nervously. With her mom there, security outside her door and very attentive nurses, she shouldn't feel alone, but she did. They wouldn't let her see a newspaper so she knew whatever was going on had to be terrible.

She wondered how safe the war room was—how safe the palace was? The sheikh had barrels of money, and money bought weapons and soldiers. She knew very little about Xaviera's army and worried that Dom would have to bomb his own ports.

The next day she noticed security outside her room had been doubled. That's when it dawned on her that she hadn't seen any press. When she got out of bed and looked out her window, the world looked calm. Peaceful. Knowing that everybody in the kingdom was waiting for this baby, it seemed odd that the press wasn't climbing the walls, trying to get pictures.

She asked her mom about it when she arrived for a visit and her mom said the baby's birth hadn't been announced.

She gave Ginny a weak smile. "If anyone knew he'd already been born, he would be a target. The king told Sally he believes it's for the best that this news not yet hit the press."

She swallowed, but her fears mounted. "So things are bad?"

"Actually, things aren't bad at all. The way I understand it, the whole mess involves one port and some hostages. Which is why Sally thinks the king believes it's so important that we protect the baby. He would be the kind of leverage the sheikh needs to get himself out of this mess."

"So it's a standoff?"

"According to Sally, it's hours of drinking coffee and waiting."

Incredulous, Ginny gaped at her mom. "They're waiting, but Dom hasn't been able to get away to see me…to see *his son*?"

"Honey, I wasn't supposed to tell you any of this, but I could tell you were worried and it's not right for you to worry."

She fell back on her bed. "No. It's better for me to feel like a complete idiot."

Her mom fluffed her pillow. "You're not an idiot. Anybody would have worried."

"That's not the part that makes me feel like an idiot. I've been sitting here for three days, waiting for my husband, who apparently doesn't care to show up."

"He's dedicated."

"So is the king, but he's talked to Sally, who's gotten messages to you."

"Have you checked your cell phone? Maybe he's tried to call?"

She gasped. "I never thought to take it. I was in so much pain I just left the apartment."

Her mom pulled out her phone. "I'll call security and have someone bring it over."

That brightened her spirits for about an hour. But when the cell phone arrived and there were no calls, they sank like a rock.

"How could he not care?"

Rose busily, nervously, tucked the covers around her. "I'm sure he cares."

"No, Mom. He doesn't." And it took something this extreme to finally, finally get that through Ginny's head. Her husband did not love her. He probably didn't really love their child. He most certainly wasn't curious about their child, who had been born early and who could have had complications.

But a war came first—

Didn't it?

Not when the war wasn't really a war. When there were stretches of time and waiting. When her husband wasn't even king yet. When there was a king who should be doing the decision making but he had time to call one of his staff—not even a family member.

She got out of bed. "Help me pack my bag."

"Ginny, you can't go home yet! You just had a baby."

"My friend, Ellen, had a difficult birth and was home in forty-eight hours."

"But the baby—"

"Is fine. You heard the pediatrician this morning. He's gained the two ounces he needed to put him over five pounds." She grabbed her suitcase and tossed it to the bed. "If he'd been full-term he probably would have weighed eight pounds."

Her mom put her hand over Ginny's to stop her from opening her suitcase. "You cannot leave."

"The hell I can't. And let them try to stop me from taking my own child." She motioned around the room. "As long as I take the thirty bodyguards, I'm fine."

Rose grabbed her cell phone and hit a speed-dial number.

Ginny snatched her phone out of her mother's hands and disconnected it. "What are you doing? Tattling on me to Sally?"

"Ginny, you can't just leave."

"Mom, this isn't about Xaviera or my baby someday being a king. This is about me knowing that if I don't get out of this country with my baby, I'm going to be stuck here forever with a guy who doesn't love me and a king who thinks he's God." She tossed her mom's cell phone to the bed and took her hands. "I have a baby to protect. I'll be damned if my child will grow up to be a man so stuck to his duties that he can't even see his own babies born or love his wife."

She took a long breath and stared at her suitcase. "To hell with this junk! I didn't want these clothes in the first place."

She poked her head out the door and motioned for the two bodyguards to come inside. "I want a helicopter on the roof of this hospital in five minutes. Then I want flown to the nearest safe airport and one of the royal jets waiting for me there." She sucked in a breath. "I'm going home."

The buzz of the king's cell phone had all heads in the war room turning in his direction. Cell phones had been banned. Too many opportunities for picture taking, voice recordings and just plain dissemination of their plans. In fact, no one but the king had left these quarters.

They slept on cots in a barracks-like room, ate food that was made in the attached kitchen and hadn't had contact with the outside world except through the video feed they stared at.

He missed Ginny. More to the point, he *worried* about Ginny. Something had been wrong the night they came here and he just wanted to fix it. But he knew he couldn't, so maybe it was better that he spend three days cut off from her so he didn't make promises he couldn't keep.

His father walked over to where Dom sat in front of a computer, staring at the feed of the port, feed that hadn't changed in twenty-four hours.

His father sat. "What do you think they're doing?"

"Undoubtedly, trying to figure out how to distance themselves from the sheikh since he seems to have deserted them."

"Should we give them a chance to surrender?"

He caught his father's gaze. There was a look in his eye that told Dom this was a test. A real-life hostage crisis for sure, but a chance for his father to test him.

"I'd say we offer them generously reduced prison

terms for surrender and testimony against the sheikh, and go after the sheikh with both barrels."

"You want to kill him?"

"I'd rather arrest him and try him for this. I think making him look like a common criminal rather than a leader who'd started a war he couldn't finish sends a stronger message to the world."

His dad laughed unexpectedly. "I agree." He bowed, shocking Dominic. "Now what are you going to use to negotiate terms?"

He pointed at his father's cell phone. "This might be appropriate. Except I think we should get hostage negotiators from our police to do that. Once again making it look more like a criminal act that a military one."

"Agree again."

Dom called Xaviera's police commissioner and within the hour the rebels had surrendered, all hostages safe. The sheikh was in hiding, but he was too accustomed to luxury to stay underground for long. Dominic had every confidence they would find him, and when they did, he would stand trial.

The fifty military and security personnel in the war room cheered for joy when they received the call that all rebels were safely in jail.

But Dominic didn't want to stay around for the party. He might not be able to love Ginny, but she was pregnant with his child and not feeling well. He needed to get back to her.

He tapped his dad's shoulder. "I'm going to get going."

"Tired?"

"And I need a shower but I need to see Ginny."

As Dom turned to walk away, his dad stopped him. "Dom, there are a few things you need to know."

Expecting more details or facts about their problem, he faced his dad again.

"Ginny has gone home."

"What? Of course, she's home. She's in the apartment."

"No. She's gone back to Texas." He shrugged. "Some women can't handle war. She got a helicopter to take her to a safe airport this morning and took a jet back to her old hometown."

He gaped at his dad. "She's never mentioned wanting to leave before. She was committed—"

"Like I said, some women can't handle war. We've never been at war when she was with us."

"This is absurd. This was hardly a war. It was an ill-conceived attempt to take over our country by a guy who we clearly gave too much credit to."

"She didn't know that."

"How could she not know that! It's been all over the papers!"

"We weren't letting her see the papers."

"What! Why?"

"Because she had the baby the first day we were in here."

This time, Dom fell to a chair in disbelief. Absolutely positive he had not heard right, he looked up at his dad. *"She had the baby?"*

"Yes."

His kept his voice deceptively calm as he said, "And you didn't think to tell me."

"Duty comes before family."

Anger coursed through him. "But I notice you had your phone."

"I did."

"You talked to staff."

"Quite often. I had to keep track of the baby. Because he was born too soon, he was small. They monitored him. I made decisions."

The anger in Dom's blood went from blue to white hot. *"You made decisions."*

"You were at war. And duty comes before family."

Dominic bounced from his chair and punched his father in the mouth so hard the king flew into the wall behind him.

Fifty military men and ten bodyguards drew their weapons.

His dad burst out laughing. He waved his hands at the military and bodyguards. "Stand down."

But nobody dropped his weapon.

Not giving a damn about the sixty-plus guns trained on him Domini roared, "You think this is funny!"

"No. I think it's about time."

He grabbed his father's collar and yanked him off the floor.

"Dominic, you're the one who's always said duty comes before family."

"So you kept my baby from me!"

"I was showing you that what you were doing with your life was wrong. What you thought you wanted didn't work." He calmly held Dom's gaze even as Dom tightened his hold on his collar. "I'd tried hundreds of things over the years to get you to see that you couldn't live the life you had all planned out. I thought Ginny would break you. When she couldn't and the sheikh took our port and then Ginny went into labor, I saw a golden opportunity."

Dominic cursed and squeezed his eyes shut.

"I loved my wife, your mother. And I was neglectful of my duties but I never dropped them the way you were so sure I had. All those months, we were in private negotiations, trying to avoid a confrontation with the pirates, trying to keep from going to war. Because of your mother's death, they did get a few extra weeks. But in the end, I didn't attack until I knew it was the right thing to do. Loving somebody didn't make me weak. Your mother's love made me strong. And you're a fool if you think you can do this alone."

"So you took my baby from me, made Ginny go through labor and childbirth alone."

"For years I'd been talking to you and for years you've ignored me, treating me like somebody who only deserved respect because I had a title. I had to do something drastic or know you would ruin your life."

He released his dad as if he were poison he didn't want to touch.

"Maybe the lesson I learned, Father—*Your Majesty*—is that I no longer want to be connected to you."

His dad very calmly said, "Go after, Ginny. Bring the baby home."

"And then what? Let you torture him the way you tortured me and Alex?"

"When you see the lesson in this, you're going to apologize. Not just for hitting me but for not trusting me."

Dom sincerely doubted it.

CHAPTER FOURTEEN

GINNY'S CONDO HAD long ago been sold. And because her mom had decided to move to Xavicra for the two years Ginny would live there, her mom's house had also been sold. But the new owners hadn't taken possession yet, so that was the sanctuary Ginny targeted. Unfortunately, when her bodyguard unlocked the front door, they found two women and a man, packing her living room lamps.

"Excuse me, this house has sold."

Ginny patted her baby's back. "I know. It was my mom's. It doesn't close for a few weeks. Until then I can use it."

"Your mom hired us to sell the furniture."

"Well, I'm sure by next week I'll have my own house and you can do that. Until then, the house is mine."

The tall woman looked ready to argue, but when she looked at Ginny with her twelve bodyguards and very tiny baby, she sighed.

"Fine." Disgruntled, the two women and one angry man headed for the back door, clipboards in hand.

Ginny turned to Artemus, the leader of her detail. "I don't even know if there's food in the house."

"I have credit cards. I'm authorized to get you anything you want."

"Really? I ran away with the next heir to the throne and they're feeding me?"

"Yes, ma'am."

She glanced around at the small house that wouldn't sleep herself and twelve bodyguards. Plus, she didn't have a crib. And she was beginning to feel bad about taking the baby from Xaviera before Dom even saw him.

Worse, she missed Dom.

She wondered if her rash decision hadn't been caused by postpartum depression, but reminded herself that her husband hadn't wanted to see his child. He'd never loved her, didn't want to. And he planned on bringing their child up to be just like him. She couldn't let that happen.

Still, that didn't mean this was going to be easy.

"This is a mess."

Artemus agreed. "Yes, ma'am."

Just as her mother said, she hadn't really thought this through. But she had to forget about everything except setting up a household. She'd worry about Dom, what she would say to him, how she'd keep her baby safe from his ridiculous rule, when she had the house set up with beds and food.

"I guess I should feed the baby and get on the phone to find a crib."

Artemus nodded. "And I'll send two guys out for groceries."

She took the baby into her mother's small bedroom, breast-fed him and then made a bed for him out of a drawer from her mother's dresser. With the baby secure, she went online and ordered a crib to be express delivered the next day, along with linens, baby clothes, diapers and some sweatpants and T-shirts for herself. Then she started exploring the real estate sites, looking for a house. The baby woke up twice and she fed him once, changed him the other time. Artemus came in and offered her food, but she refused it. She couldn't eat until she got at least something in her life settled.

Dom showered on his father's private jet. Taking the plane had been another way he'd vented his anger, but though he was bone tired he couldn't sleep in the luxurious bed.

Even after a few hours for his dad's duplicity to sink in, Dom still wanted to punch him. He couldn't believe his father had treated Ginny so cruelly, but unexpectedly realized *he'd* been treating Ginny cruelly all along.

And what would he have done while she was in labor? Coached her? Helped her? Or held himself back because he didn't want to give her false hope? He'd have ruined that moment for Ginny every bit as much as his father had ruined it. Maybe more because she'd see him there, but feel the distance between them, the tangible reminder that he didn't want her in his life.

Which was a lie.

He did want her in his life. The feeling of fury that thundered through him when he realized what his father had done hadn't just shocked him. It had been so pure, so total that Dominic hadn't had a chance to mitigate it. In that moment of blazing-hot anger that resulted from white-hot pain, he knew what it was like to miss out on something so important he couldn't even describe it.

His father was right. Dom never would have felt this if his dad hadn't orchestrated it. He'd have covered, hidden, pretended, postured—whatever it took to fool himself into believing he was fine.

But faced with the raw truth of having those moments snatched away from him—he felt it all. The pain. The loss.

And he knew that pain, that loss, that horrible empty feeling truly was the result of the life he'd built.

He also knew that if he wanted Ginny back, all he had to say was that his bastard father had kept him from seeing the baby's birth, from being with her, and he'd be free in her eyes. She loved him. She'd believe him. She'd take him back with open arms.

He fell to the corner of the big, big bed in the outrageous jet that he could use because he would someday be a king.

The only problem was his dad was right. Even if he'd known his baby was being born, he wouldn't have rushed to Ginny's side. He might have seen the final few minutes of the baby's birth. But even then he would have raced back to the war room.

But what his father had done hadn't just opened his eyes. It had changed him. And he didn't want Ginny to take him back on something that wasn't quite a lie, but was a way to get out of being honest.

He had to be honest with her. He wouldn't even hint that she should come home—that he intended to love her—if he didn't know for sure he wouldn't hurt her again.

And that he couldn't promise.

After hours of combing through real estate sites, Ginny heard Artemus enter her room again. Staring at the computer screen, she said, "How big of a house should I get? I mean, should there be rooms for all of you or does the crown pay for separate quarters for you?"

"We pay for separate quarters."

Hearing Dom's voice, she spun around on her seat.

His chin and cheeks bore dark shadows, evidence that he hadn't shaved in days. His eyes looked pale and hollow from lack of sleep—even though he'd just had a ten-hour flight, which was perfect for catching up on sleep. But the killer was that he wore jeans and a T-shirt.

The desire to tease him almost outweighed the desire to jump into his arms and weep. Except this was the man who didn't love her. Who hadn't thought enough of her to come out of a bunker when apparently he could have. Who hadn't been with her for the birth of their child.

This was also the man she'd have to fight for their child. If he thought he'd just fought a war, he was in for a rude awakening because she was about to show him what real war was.

"Get out."

He peered beyond her to the bed, where their son lay in the bottom drawer of her mom's dresser. "Is that my son?"

His voice was soft, reverent.

She tensed her face to stop the muscles from weakening or tears from forming in her eyes. She would not be weak in this fight. Her child would not grow up afraid to love.

Still, they might ultimately get into a battle over this child, but Dom also had a right to see his son.

"Yes. That's our baby."

He caught her gaze. "You didn't name him."

"I didn't think James Tiberius Kirk was your final answer."

He laughed. She didn't.

He took a few steps closer to the bed. "Oh, my God. He's so little."

She had to fight the tremor of emotion that ripped through her at the awe in his voice.

"You would know that if you'd been there for his birth."

He took another step toward the bed. "My father didn't tell me you were in labor."

That sucked the air out of her lungs. "What?"

He paused and faced her, preparing to answer her, but her heart ached for him. His ridiculously pompous dad had kept his baby from him? She saw the anguish on his face. Knew there might be bigger reasons he hadn't shaved, hadn't slept and suddenly wore blue jeans and a T-shirt.

She rose from her chair, took the baby out of the drawer and watched his little face scrunch as he woke. "Hey, little guy, here's your daddy."

She presented the child to Dom and he stared at him. "Wow."

"Yeah, wow." She smiled. "Hold him."

"He's just barely bigger than my hand." He caught her gaze. "Won't I break him?"

She laughed. "I'm going to trust you to be careful." She nudged the blanket-wrapped baby to him. "Put your one hand under his bum and the other under his head."

Dom did as he was told and took the baby. He bent and pressed a kiss to his forehead. Ginny stepped back, unable to handle the sweetness of the meeting anymore. Or Dom's confusion. He was so new to the baby business that it would have been fun to watch him learn and grow with the baby—their baby. But even though his dad had kept the news that she was in labor from him, he'd always said the kingdom would come first. And they'd just lived the reality of what that meant.

She deserved better than that. Her baby deserved better than that.

He caught her gaze. "My dad said something about complications."

"He was just small, so they monitored him."

"You know his birth hasn't even been announced."

"No. Not at first. Eventually my mom told me."

"It seems my dad was teaching me a lesson."

The pompous old windbag.

"I'd always said the kingdom came first. I'd said I'd never love anybody." He glanced over at her. "I said I wouldn't do what he did when my mom died. Apparently that insulted him. So when the war and you going into labor just sort of happened, he saw it as a chance to show me what my attitude really meant."

"Oh." So maybe the king wasn't so much pompous as interfering. Not good, but at least not god awful. She wanted to ask Dom if he'd learned anything. But he looked so sad and so broken. And she didn't want to soften to him.

"I missed the birth of my son."

"If you'd known I was in labor, would you have come out of that bunker? In those first hours before you knew the threat wasn't as bad as you and your dad had believed…could you have come out?"

"I'd have pushed it." He unexpectedly hugged the baby to him. "I'd have given instructions for the hospital to let me know when you were close—"

"So you might have missed it anyway?"

"Maybe."

His honestly hit her like the swell of an ocean wave. The king might have kept the news from him, but he probably would have stayed away anyway. "Well, that certainly shines a light on that."

"That's why my dad's lesson was such a good one. I had to see what it felt like to have all my choices taken away from me. When I thought…knew…he was behind my not seeing the baby's birth, I felt the unfairness of it and ridiculous anger. But flying over on the plane, I realized what I just told you. That I might have pushed it back and put it off until I missed it by my own doing. I would have been disappointed but I would have made those crazy royalty excuses about duty, and I'd have forgiven myself. I had to experience it this way to feel the real loss."

He met her gaze again. "It gave me a totally new perspective."

Her heart jumped a bit. "So you're going to be a good dad?"

He laughed. "Yes."

And suddenly her war with him lost some of its oomph, too. Even as his changing attitude made her glad for their baby's sake, it also made her very sad. Very tired. Technically, she and Dom were back to where they were when they made this silly deal.

She said, "That's good," but her heart absolutely shattered. She'd have loved to have raised her baby with this Dom.

"Can you forgive me?"

"For missing the baby's birth? Since it means you're going to be a better dad? Yes." She tried to smile but just couldn't quite do it.

"What about for the other stuff?"

"Like…" The man had been sweet and kind. Attentive in a way that might not have been romantic, but he'd been good to her the whole time they were together. He'd always told her he didn't want to fall in love. She was the one who'd pushed. "…what?"

"You wanted me to love you."

Oh, great. Just what she wanted to talk about again. How he didn't love her.

"It's okay."

"Not for me. If you decided you don't want me to love you anymore, I'm in real trouble, because I realized flying over that ocean that I've probably always loved you."

Tears stung her eyes. "Really? Because I've told you that."

He chuckled. "I know you did. But just like the lesson my dad gave me, I sort of needed to lose you—lose everything—before I could realize what I had."

He laid the baby in the makeshift bed. "We're putting a future king in a dresser drawer."

She tried to laugh but a sob came out. He walked over and enfolded her in his arms. "I am so sorry."

She wanted to say, "That's okay," but she couldn't stop sobbing. She'd been alone for days, making decisions she didn't want to make, trying to get food in a house that was way too small. And she'd missed him. And felt betrayed. Alone.

He let her cry until her sobs became hiccups. Then he whispered, "Shouldn't you be in bed, too?"

"I'm fine."

"Right. Just like you were fine right before you fainted in front of poor Marco." He shifted the baby drawer to one side of the bed and pulled down the covers. "Come here."

She did. He helped her lie down, took off her shoes, pulled the covers to her chin and she fell into her first sound sleep in days.

When she woke, it was to the sounds of her son crying.

Dom lay beside her on the bed, watching her. "I think our son wants to be fed."

"Sounds like."

"We are going to have to name him sometime."

"I'm starting to think of him as Jimmy."

"He'll be King James…like in the Bible."

"Better than captain of the starship *Enterprise*."

She slid out of the bed, got James from his drawer, opened her shirt and began to nurse.

Some of the strain appeared to be gone from Dom's face. "You napped?"

He stretched and said, "A bit."

"Do we have to go home right away?"

His eyes leaped to hers. "You're coming with me?"

"We are raising a king together."

"Yes, we are."

"And your dad is nuts with his rules and his tests."

"I think he's going to let us alone with the tests."

"Yeah, wait until you see the dress I'm going to have made for his next formal dinner. He's not the only one who can push people's buttons. Except this time I owe him."

He laughed and for the first time in days, Ginny felt normal. She nudged her head, indicating he should join her and the baby. "Come watch."

"Really?"

"Sure. He's cute. It's fun to watch him eat like a little horse."

Dom scooted down the bed and looked at their baby suckling. He waited a few seconds, then his gaze rose to meet hers. "There is one thing we haven't sorted out."

She smiled. "What?"

"I love you."

She closed her eyes, savoring the words, then she laughed. "You already said that."

"Yes, but I wanted to say it by itself. You know…so you get the real meaning."

She laughed again. And the quiet, two-o'clock-in-the-morning world of Terra Mas, Texas, righted itself.

EPILOGUE

THE DAY GINNY and Dominic returned from Texas, the baby's birth was announced in the papers. It was reported that he'd been born in the time of crisis for the country, and to keep him safe, his birth had been concealed. Most of their subjects had agreed that keeping his birth a secret had made sense. Others yammered on and on about it on talk radio.

Ginny didn't care. Her life was perfect. She just wanted one more promise from her husband.

Rolling Jimmy into a tiny onesie, she said, "This is our last lie."

Dom pulled his sweater over his head before he said, "It isn't a lie. Technically, Jimmy *was* born in an insecure time for the country. Technically, my dad *had* been working to keep him safe. Technically, I *had been* too involved to leave to witness his birth."

"Now you're stretching things." She picked up the baby and he cooed with delight. "I think he likes these pj's."

Dominic put a quick kiss on her lips. "Or he likes his mom."

"He'd better. It'll take me decades to get my figure back."

"I like you a little rounded."

She sniffed. "Right."

Carrying the baby, she walked to the sitting room, Dom on her heels.

"Sally says it will look better if I hold the baby while we're standing on the balcony, waving."

"Drat. I was hoping to do a Princess Kate and strategically place the blanket so no one can see I still have a baby bump."

Diaper bag over his shoulder, Dom held the apartment door open for her. "You're paranoid."

"Isabelle doesn't think so," she said, referring to the nanny who had just been hired by Sally. "She perfectly understands wanting to look my best in public."

They entered the elevator. Dom pressed the button for the second floor. When the doors opened, the king and Ginny's mom stood waiting for them.

Rose said, "I get to hold him first."

The king nudged her aside. "You held him first yesterday."

Bodyguards silently, expressionlessly stood by doors, glanced out windows.

Rose sighed. "Fine."

Ronaldo said, "Maybe I should be the one to hold him on the balcony."

Dom and Ginny simultaneously said, "No!"

"I need him and a long blanket to cover my baby weight."

"And Sally says my holding Jimmy will go a long way toward repairing my image for not being around for the baby's birth."

The king laughed as he led the three adults to his quarters. "You're a war hero."

Dom blew out his breath disgustedly. "Some war hero."

"Hey, you made the choice to call in the local police rather than send in the military. Technically, that was the big decision of the conflict."

Jimmy squirmed and began to whimper. Rose immediately took him from Ronaldo's arms. "Come to your Grammy Pajammy, sweet boy," she crooned, patting his back.

Dom said, "Grammy Pajammy?"

His father sighed. "It's a long story."

Ginny rolled her eyes. "I called her Mama Pajama until I was about ten."

Dom laughed. "Really?" Then he frowned and glanced at his dad. "And how do you know this?"

The king slid his arm around Rose's shoulders. "I suppose this is as good of a time as any to come clean about our relationship."

Ginny laughed but Dom's mouth fell open. "What?"

Rose grinned. "Second chance at love, honey." She leaned over the baby to put a kiss on the king's cheek. "There's nothing like it."

Dom stood shell-shocked, and Ginny held her breath. She'd suspected a little something was going on with her mom and the king, but buried in their own problems, neither she nor Dom had actually seen it.

Finally, Dom's lips lifted into a smile. His simple heartfelt "Welcome to the family" warmed Ginny all over. So did the realization that her mom would be staying. Forever.

She had a family.

They walked through two sitting rooms and a den to get to the balcony. Ginny put a blanket over her arm in such a way it draped in front of her stomach, and Rose placed the baby in her arms.

But right before they would have stepped out onto the balcony, she stopped and smiled at Dom. "Here."

"You're letting me hold him?"

"He's yours as well as mine." She sighed. "Besides, the bigger I look today the easier it will be for people to notice I'm losing weight."

He laughed and stepped out onto the balcony, but he stopped, too.

He caught his dad's gaze. "You and Rose come with us."

His dad waved a hand. "No. No. You and Ginny and Jimmy are the stars here. Have your moment in the sun."

"I'd rather we looked like a family."

Rose said, "Mmm-hmm."

Ginny pressed a finger to her lips to keep her still-humming hormones from making her cry. They hadn't had a big discussion about the king keeping Ginny's labor from Dom. When they'd returned the day before, Dom had simply said, "You were right," and King Ronaldo had nodded. Dom wanting them to be a family spoke volumes.

The king said, "I think that would be nice."

They stepped out onto the balcony to present their son to the kingdom and in the last second, Alex came racing through the door. "I heard this is a family moment."

Dom said, "It is."

Alex straightened to his full height, grinning like an idiot.

Ginny leaned over to Dom and whispered, "What's up with him?"

"Our father and Princess Eva's father are having a phone call tomorrow to talk about the wedding. He's trying to get on Dad's good side, hoping he'll give him another year of freedom."

Ginny winced. "Do you think your dad will do it?"

Dom glanced at his father, who beamed at little Jimmy and laughed. "Nope. I think my dad likes being a grandfather." He cuddled Jimmy to him, then waved to the crowd below.

Ginny nestled against him. "We'll give him another one soon."

Dom glanced down at her. "Really?"

Ginny laughed and snuggled more tightly against him. "Sure, we'll have two kids, and then I'll get my figure back, and then it's Alex and Eva's turn."

Cameras whirred and flashed, but Ginny didn't care. For twenty-five years she'd longed for a family and she'd finally gotten one.

* * * * *

She was leaving?

"Let's not part this way," Marshall protested. "We should talk."

"About what?"

"You're supposed to be the expert."

"On pregnancy?" she asked.

"On relationships."

"Well, here's my opinion," Franca said. "We're not compatible, Marshall. I wish we were, and sometimes… No. I refuse to delude myself. Let's just leave it at that."

Her footsteps rapped across the tile floor toward the hall. Then he heard the door latch behind her with a loud click.

He sat at the counter, bewildered. How could she deny the intimacy they'd shared last night? Yet judging from her words, she regretted the whole night with a man she could never love. What had seemed a transformative experience to him had been entirely one-sided.

He and Franca had always been opposites. Why expect things to be different now?

Because, in a few weeks, they'd learn whether they were going to be parents…

THE WOULD-BE DADDY

BY
JACQUELINE DIAMOND

First Published in Great Britain 2016
By Mills & Boon, an imprint of HarperCollins*Publishers*
1 London Bridge Street, London, SE1 9GF

© 2016 Jackie Hyman

ISBN: 978-0-263-91962-2

23-0216

Our policy is to use papers that are natural, renewable and recyclable products and made from wood grown in sustainable forests.The logging and manufacturing processes conform to the legal environmental regulations of the country of origin.

Printed and bound in Spain
by CPI, Barcelona

Medical themes play a prominent role in many of **Jacqueline Diamond**'s one hundred published novels, including her Safe Harbor Medical series for Mills & Boon Cherish. Her father was a small-town doctor before becoming a psychiatrist, and Jackie developed an interest in fertility issues after successfully undergoing treatment to have her two sons. A former Associated Press reporter and TV columnist, Jackie lives with her husband of thirty-seven years in Orange County, California, where she's active in Romance Writers of America. You can sign up for her free newsletter at www.jacquelinediamond.com and say hello to Jackie on her Facebook page, JacquelineDiamondAuthor. On Twitter, she's @jacquediamond.

To Hunter and Brooke

Chapter One

It was unfair, dangerous and cruel. That poor little girl. If Franca Brightman didn't figure out a way to rescue four-year-old Jazz, she'd burst into a fireball that would bring down the Safe Harbor Medical Center parking structure on top of her.

She'd tried to work off her fury by staying late on a Friday night at her office. She'd spent hours reviewing the patient files that had come with her new job as staff psychologist. Plunging into the records and assessing patients' need for additional treatments should have blunted her pain and outrage.

Instead, the click of her medium-high heels on the concrete floor rang in a fierce staccato as she tore through the nearly empty lower level of the garage toward her aging white station wagon. At least at this hour she didn't have to feel embarrassed by her car, which was dented and old compared with the others, particularly the sleek silver sedan parked a short distance up the ramp.

Franca's last glimpse of Jazz had been riding off in a junkmobile far worse than this. The decrepit state of the car had intensified her fear about where and how the child would be living now that she'd gone back to her biological mother.

Where was Jazz right now? Had her mom bothered to fix dinner, or were they eating out of a can? Crammed into a rent-by-the-week motel unit, the four-year-old must miss her beautiful princess bedroom. Did she believe Franca had relinquished her by choice?

White-hot rage swirled inside Franca as she unlocked her station wagon and dropped into the driver's seat. It was a wonder that, despite the chilly March air, she hadn't already set the building ablaze.

Franca wished she could figure out a safe way to vent her anger, which had been simmering all day. With a PhD in psychology and years of counseling experience here in Southern California, she ought to be an expert on releasing emotions.

Instead, her mind returned to an image of the black-haired little girl, her blue eyes brimming with tears. Handing Jazz over to her unstable mother at the lawyer's office this morning had nearly torn Franca apart. How could she expect her foster daughter to understand why the planned adoption had fallen apart?

I shouldn't have come to work today. But being new at her job, Franca didn't want to ask for personal leave. After a lifetime of careful control, she'd assumed she could handle this.

She'd been wrong.

On the steering wheel, her hands trembled. She hated to drive in this condition, but she couldn't sit here indefinitely. Sucking in a breath, she switched on the ignition.

A rock song from the radio filled the car. The singer's voice rose in a ragged lament: "I can't take it anymore!"

There must have been half a dozen songs with similar lyrics, but right there, right then, this one seemed meant for her. Smacking the dashboard, Franca cranked up the volume and sang along in shared disgust, her voice ringing through the garage.

"I can't take it anymore! I can't take it anymore!" That felt good. Childish and self-indulgent, but good.

A drum solo followed, which Franca accompanied by thumping the steering wheel. When the chorus returned, she howled even louder: "I can't take it anymore!" The acoustics in this garage were odd, she noted as she paused for a breath. It sounded as if the music was echoing from up the ramp, underscored by…could that be a man's voice rasping out the same lyrics?

It might be her imagination, but to make sure, she muted the radio. The music continued in the distance, with a ragged masculine voice trumpeting, "I can't take it anymore!" over the recording. The words and melody were emanating from the silver sedan.

Although Franca had done her best to meet her fellow professionals at the hospital during the past few months, she couldn't identify them all. Maybe it was best if she *didn't* recognize her fellow sufferer. She hadn't meant to intrude on anyone's privacy.

Embarrassed by her outburst, Franca adjusted the radio so it played at a lower volume. The man, little more than a silhouette against a safety light, turned in her direction, as if he'd registered the change.

Had he heard her singing earlier? She hoped not.

Franca was about to pull out of her spot when the silver sedan shot in reverse. In a moment, the car would drive past her parked vehicle as it headed for the exit. The driver would be able to identify Franca by the reddish-blond hair floating around her shoulders.

How awkward for the staff counselor, who was supposed to be strong and supportive, to be caught screeching like a teenager. Should she try to beat him out of the garage and pray he hadn't already figured out who she was?

Too late. His car was closing in, and she might back into it by accident.

Hunkering down, Franca trained her gaze on the concrete pillar visible through her windshield. *Just zip on past, whoever you are.* He was probably as eager as she was to pretend this scene never happened.

But she couldn't resist sneaking a glance in the rear-view mirror...at precisely the wrong instant.

Brown eyes, surprisingly clear in the dim light, locked onto hers. That angular face had thinned since they'd first met fifteen years ago in college, but she experienced the same jolt of electricity, the same powerful sense of connection.

Why did this persist, this ridiculously misguided notion that they meant something to each other? She wished Dr. Marshall Davis hadn't come home to California. He'd spent more than a decade out east, completing his medical training and earning respect as a skilled men's fertility surgeon. Even though he had grown up around here, he should have stayed put.

Instead, Marshall had joined Safe Harbor's urology program last fall, she'd discovered when she was hired about a month later. Encountering him had been inevitable. At the cafeteria and staff meetings, they'd chatted pleasantly but impersonally.

Given her professional acquaintance with Marshall, there was no reason for her to react so strongly when their eyes met, yet electricity snapped through her. Did he feel it, too?

Apparently not. As cold as ever, Marshall whipped his gaze away and drove out of the parking structure. Gone in a flash of silver, he left her shivering.

So much for setting the building on fire.

Exiting the garage into the hospital's circular drive, Franca spotted his car skimming onto the street. Nothing else stirred. Only scattered lights glowed in the windows of the six-story main structure and the adjacent medical building.

She struggled to put the weird encounter out of her mind. She and Marshall had always had an inexplicable habit of stumbling into the same place at the same time, as with their hiring at Safe Harbor. It meant nothing except that they'd both been drawn to an exciting place to work.

The former community hospital had been remodeled to specialize in fertility treatments and maternity care, featuring the latest high-tech facilities and outstanding physicians hired from around the country. Across the drive, the recently acquired five-story dental building stood dark save for safety illumination. It was undergoing renovation to serve as a center for the expanding men's fertility program, in which Marshall played a key role.

There he was again, popping into her brain with his sharp, intelligent gaze and rare, brilliant smile.

Their first meeting at a student party near the UC Berkeley campus was as clear in Franca's mind as if it had been weeks instead of well over a decade ago. Tall and broodingly handsome, Marshall had stood out in the crowded room. She'd been a freshman and he, she later learned, a junior.

Franca's breath had caught when he'd started toward her. She'd been rooted to the spot, overwhelmed by the sense that something life-altering was about to shake her world. Until then, she'd never considered herself the romantic type. To her, boyfriends had been just that—boys who were friends.

As Marshall wove through the tangle of beer-drinking undergrads, the intensity of his gaze had made her acutely aware of her Little Orphan Annie red hair—now dyed a less strident shade—and her curvy figure beneath a tank top and jeans. She'd read his response in his parted lips and the warmth infusing his face.

As she started to greet him, however, a nerdy guy from her psych class darted up and tugged her hair. Startled, Franca spilled her plastic cup of soda and ice.

By the time she finished cleaning it up, Marshall was deep in conversation with her roommate, who'd been at her elbow. Tall and slim with ash-blond hair and tailored clothes, Belle radiated cool sophistication in contrast to Franca's scruffiness.

When Belle introduced them, Marshall had responded with a brief "hello" and a nod, nothing more. *Okay, so I'm not his type after all,* she'd thought. And had been reminded of that for the next two years as he and Belle dated.

Yet they kept running into each other at events that would have bored her roommate: a lecture on recent archaeological finds, an experimental theater performance, a poetry reading. Afterward, she and Marshall had shared fervent discussions over coffee, discussions that only revealed their different opinions on everything from politics to the value of therapy to attitudes toward family.

His views on child rearing were almost Victorian, while Franca had an affinity for hard-luck kids and a desire to become a foster parent. As with Jazz.

Steeling her nerve, Franca turned left onto Safe Harbor Boulevard. No sign of Marshall's car ahead, but then, she'd lingered for quite a while.

She remembered Belle's tear-streaked face when he'd broken it off with her after his graduation. Apparently Belle hadn't met his high standards because she was struggling academically. Never mind that her troubles had stemmed from her attempt to cram in extra classes and finish early so she could move to Boston to be near him.

Although the way he'd treated his devoted girlfriend had been cruel, it would be unfair to call him heartless, Franca reflected as she headed for the freeway and the half-hour drive to her apartment. Especially in view of his rumpled hair and distraught expression tonight.

What could have reduced him to screaming in a parking garage? Well, one thing was certain: he wouldn't be calling Franca Brightman, PhD, for a consultation.

IF LIFE WERE as precise, clean and well-structured as an operating room, Marshall would be a much happier man, he reflected the next morning as he performed microsurgery. Although he wasn't fond of working on Saturdays, the scheduling was necessary due to the shortage of ORs. That would change once the new building opened, thank goodness.

The patient, Art Lomax, a thirty-three-year-old ex-marine, suffered from a low sperm count and reduced sex drive. He longed to be a father and to satisfy his wife in bed. A man who'd fought for his country deserved a break, and Marshall was glad to be able to provide it.

Seated at the console of the microsurgical system, he trained his eyes on the 3-D high-definition image of the patient's body. Marshall enjoyed the way the controls translated his slightest hand movement to the instruments inserted into Lomax's body. The delicate procedure, a varicocelectomy, would repair blood vessels attached to the patient's testes, which produced both sperm and testosterone. Restoring them to normal functioning would enhance Lomax's ability to father children and improve his sex drive, along with muscle strength and energy level.

Around him, the surgical team functioned with smooth efficiency, from Dr. Reid Winfrey, the urologist assisting him, to the nurses who ensured that the right tools were ready to be attached to the machine's robotic arms. The OR was a technophile's dream. The overhead lighting generated no heat, while suspended cameras recorded the surgery for later review. An adjacent pathology lab allowed tissue to be tested during surgery so the surgeon could review the results without leaving the sterile field.

Early in Marshall's medical training, he'd felt uncomfortable in clinical settings because he lacked the gift of relating easily to people. The discovery of his talent for surgery had revolutionized his dreams.

Focusing on the screen, he took little notice of the chatter among the surgical team. Then a name caught his attention.

"Isn't it awful about Franca Brightman's little girl?" a nurse, Erica, commented to the anesthesiologist.

"What about her?" The slender fellow, who sported a trim gray beard, perked up at the prospect of fresh gossip.

"She was adopting this adorable four-year-old girl whose mom's a convicted drug dealer," the nurse said. "Apparently the mother had agreed to the adoption, but then she got sprung from prison due to an evidence snafu at the lab. Just like that, *wham*, she took the little girl away."

"That's rotten." Reid, an African-American urologist who shared Marshall's office suite, frowned at her. The man did volunteer work with underprivileged kids, and had more than once described the harsh impact of parental drug use on children. "Surely a court wouldn't hand a child over to a mother like that."

The petite blonde shrugged. "She isn't a convict anymore, and the adoption was voluntary."

"How long was the girl with Franca?" asked Marshall. Belatedly, he realized he should have used the title Dr. Brightman. But it was too late, anyway, to keep their acquaintance a secret. When he'd referred several staffers and patients to Franca for consults, he'd mentioned they had a prior acquaintance.

More than an acquaintance. Her anguish last night had shaken him. But he had no clue how to comfort anyone, especially a parent deprived of a child.

He'd never fathomed why Franca planned to become a foster and adoptive mom to troubled kids when she could presumably bear children of her own. Sure, Marshall sympathized with the youngsters Reid counseled; he'd donated scholarship money to an organization his colleague recommended. But no matter how much he sympathized with their plight, wasn't it natural to yearn for a little boy or girl who was yours from birth?

"She's been with Franca for a couple of years, half the kid's life." Erica peered up at the high-definition screen that showed the same image of the patient's body Marshall was viewing on his terminal. Observing it helped the staff anticipate Marshall's needs, plus many nurses took an interest in anatomy and physiology. "Jazz was pretty wild when Franca became her foster mom,

I gather, but she was learning to trust that the world is a safe place. Until now."

"You seem to know a lot about it." Marshall registered that the anesthesiologist gave him a speculative look due to his uncharacteristic show of interest, but he was too curious to care.

"Jazz's been attending the hospital day care center these past few months," the nurse explained. "My son Jordan is friends with her."

Erica and her husband had a toddler, Marshall recalled. Recently, he'd become more aware of who had children.

Part of the reason stemmed from learning he had a young nephew, and part of it from turning thirty-five. Many doctors delayed marriage and parenthood during their long training, but he'd moved past that stage. As his medical practice showed, men as well as women experienced a powerful urge to procreate. That was an intellectual way of rationalizing his gut-level desire to be a dad.

But Marshall couldn't consider fatherhood until he sorted out the shock he'd received less than a week ago. He'd never imagined that everything he thought he knew about himself could disintegrate with a single stunning revelation.

That didn't excuse him for howling like a banshee in his car last night. Luckily, the only person who'd overheard had been Franca, and he respected her discretion.

With the last of the blood vessels repaired, Marshall yielded his position at the controls to Reid, who would close the tiny incisions. The surgery was only minimally invasive, so the patient should be able to go home later that day.

As for Marshall, he was heading home now, having completed three operations this morning. Much as he loved the two-story house he'd bought here in Safe Harbor, though, he was in no hurry to get there.

In the hallway, his footsteps dragged. Marshall needed someone to talk to, someone who could set him straight and provide perspective. Someone like Franca.

That would be a big mistake. In college, he'd recognized almost immediately that his attraction to her was wrong for them both. Instead, he'd tried in vain to fall in love with her roommate, who met all his requirements, or so he'd believed.

He'd survived for more than a decade without Franca to bounce ideas off. And he would continue to manage just fine.

At the elevators, Marshall punched the down button. A second later, the doors opened to reveal the *other* person he didn't care to face right now. A man almost the same height, build and coloring as Marshall himself.

Dark circles underscored Dr. Nick Davis's eyes from an overnight shift in Labor and Delivery that had obviously run long. He gave a start at the sight of Marshall, and for a moment, the air bristled between them.

Stiffly, Marshall stepped inside. "Hey."

"Hey back at you," said the cousin he'd disliked and resented all his life. And whom he'd just learned was his biological brother.

As the elevator descended, Marshall searched for a polite way to break the silence. "Rough night, Nicholas?"

"Buckets of babies." Nick cleared his throat. "Say, I have a question."

Marshall braced for whatever barb might come next. "Shoot."

"Will you be the best man at my wedding?"

Chapter Two

After meeting with a family at her private office in Garden Grove, fifteen miles north of Safe Harbor, Franca drove to her nearby home Saturday morning with her mind in turmoil. She'd insisted on retaining her old practice when she'd joined the hospital staff, partly in case the new job didn't work out and partly because she refused to drop loyal clients.

She wasn't sure how much good she'd done today, though; it had been an effort to concentrate on the conflict between an adolescent girl and her parents. However, they'd shown progress in their ability to set reasonable boundaries while respecting the teenager's right to privacy.

At her apartment complex, Franca followed the walkway between calla lilies and red, purple and yellow pansies. In the spring, Jazz had been unable to keep herself from plucking the flowers until Franca explained that the blooms were for all the residents to enjoy. After that, the child had taken care to avoid picking or trampling them.

What a change from when she'd entered foster care. Jazz had lacked self-control, even for a two-year-old. Having a regular bedtime, eating three meals a day at a table and following rules about storing toys after use—

everything was a fight. But beneath the stubbornness, Franca had sensed the child's anger over having her world torn apart and her hurt at feeling abandoned. Distraught about facing trial, her mother, Bridget Oberly, had been a frequent no-show at arranged visits.

As a foster parent, it was Franca's job to prepare the child to return to her mother's care. The more self-sufficient Jazz became in terms of potty training and dressing, and the more she was able to obey rules, the better she'd handle her mother's unpredictable lifestyle. Since her father had died in a gang shooting, her mom was parenting solo.

Gradually, she'd bonded with Franca, running to her for hugs and curling in her lap for story time. When Bridget agreed to an adoption, Franca had been deeply grateful.

She'd never imagined that her world could shatter so utterly.

Now she stepped inside her second-floor unit with a sense of entering paradise lost. She'd tried to enliven her simple apartment with personal touches: a multi-colored comforter crocheted by her mother was draped over the couch, while on the walls, she'd hung framed photographs shot by her brother, Glenn, of the wildflowers and summer meadows near his Montana home.

At the doorway to Jazz's bedroom, tears blurred Franca's vision. The fairy-tale bedspread and curtains that she'd sewn herself, the shelf of books and the sparkly dolls remained unchanged, yet their princess was gone. Bridget had told Jazz she could take only a single suitcase because of their cramped unit. Franca wished she could drop by to check on the preschooler's well-being and reassure her.

The ringing of the phone drew Franca back to the

present. The caller was Ada Humphreys, owner of the Bear and Doll Boutique, where Franca had often taken Jazz to pick out toys and books.

"I just got a new catalog of doll-clothes patterns," Ada said after they exchanged greetings. "That little girl of yours will adore them."

Franca kept running into people who hadn't heard the bad news. Despite a catch in her throat, she forced out the words, "Jazz is…gone."

"Gone?" Ada repeated.

Franca summarized what had happened. "She trusted me to take care of her and I let her down."

"I don't mean to be nosy, but with her mother's history of drug use, couldn't you sue for custody?" Ada asked.

"My lawyer advised against it. He said there was no guarantee I'd win, and it might be counterproductive."

"In what way?"

"Jazz's mom may face retrial on the same drug charges," Franca explained. "If that happens, it's better for me to stay on good terms."

"So if she's convicted, she might relinquish Jazz to you again," Ada said.

"Exactly." Franca couldn't keep the quaver from her voice. "Otherwise, my little girl could end up in the foster care system and I'd have no claim on her."

"How awful," Ada said. "But it's fortunate Jazz had you during such an important part of her childhood. You've prepared her to succeed in school and life." The mother of a second-grade teacher, Ada understood a lot about learning and child development.

"That's a positive attitude." Franca wandered into her own bedroom. On a side table, her sewing machine sat idle, threaded with pink from the Valentine's Day dress she'd stitched for Jazz.

"I can understand you might not be making doll clothes for a while," Ada said. "It's too bad. Sewing is such a relaxing hobby."

"I do enjoy it." A puffy blue concoction on a hanger caught Franca's eye—the bridesmaid's dress from Belle's wedding. Considering Belle's usual good taste, why had she chosen such ugly gowns for her attendants?

Last month, Belle had pulled out all the stops in her wedding to a likable CPA. Franca had been glad to serve as a bridesmaid, despite the strain on her budget to pay for this awful creation, its bows and lacy trim more suitable for a Pollyanna costume than for a woman in her thirties. She wondered what the rest of the half dozen attendants would do with their froufrou getups. Donate them to charity? Use them in community theater productions? Clean the garage with them?

"Well, don't be a stranger," Ada said. "You never can tell when you might need a gift, or be in the mood to sew for fun."

On a shelf, a couple of dolls that doubled as bookends caught Franca's eye. How shabby they'd become, as had the dolls in her office. They underwent plenty of wear and tear in play therapy, where she used them along with stuffed animals, coloring materials and building blocks.

Franca hadn't planned to drive to Safe Harbor today, but she refused to sit here and stew in her unhappiness. A visit to the Bear and Doll Boutique was exactly what she needed.

"You're an inspiration," she said to Ada. "My dolls deserve a new wardrobe, and I have a perfectly hideous bridesmaid dress to cut up."

"Some of these new patterns are darling." A bell

tinkled in the background, signaling the arrival of a customer. "I'll see you soon."

After clicking off, Franca changed from her skirt and jacket into jeans and an old sweater. Since her hair was frizzing out of its bun, she shook it loose and ran a brush through it, which did little to tame the bushiness. But Ada wouldn't care about Franca's appearance, and she doubted she'd run into anyone else she knew.

Out Franca went, her mood lifting.

"Best man at your wedding?" Marshall repeated. He wasn't ready to answer, nor to ask the question uppermost in his mind until he had a better grasp of the situation. "Have you set a date?"

"Yep, three weeks from now." When the elevator arrived at the ground floor, Nick let him exit first. "There's nothing like an April wedding, Zady says. Lucky for us, the Seaside Wedding Chapel had a cancellation."

"Not so lucky for the couple who canceled, I presume," Marshall said.

"Maybe they decided to elope instead." How typical of Nick to look on the bright side.

As they passed a couple of nurses' aides in the hall, Marshall heard the murmur that often greeted their rare appearance side-by-side: "Are they twins?"

He'd been irked in school by the striking resemblance between him and his cousin, who was a year younger. Wasn't it obvious that Nick's brown hair was a shade lighter, and that at six feet tall he lacked an inch of Marshall's height?

Nevertheless, people considered them look-alikes. And since they were also close in age and shared a surname, teachers at their magnet science high school had often compared them academically. How unfair that Marshall had studied until his head hurt to earn top grades, while Nick, with his quick grasp of essentials and his unusually good memory, sailed from A to A.

After attending different colleges and medical schools, they'd accidentally landed at Safe Harbor Medical at almost the same time, which had created confusion among their colleagues. Good thing they specialized in different fields, Nick in obstetrics and Marshall in urology, or their patients might wind up in the wrong examining rooms. Or worse, the wrong ORs.

Nick must have heard the muttering, too. Rather than stiffening, he draped an arm over Marshall's shoulders. "If they want to yammer about us, bro, let's show 'em what pals we are. Okay if I mess up your hair?"

"No." Marshall eased away from his brother.

Nick removed his arm. "Loosen up, man."

"I'd rather not." However, Marshall had no desire to renew the friction that had flared between them over the years. His perfectionist, high-achieving parents had encouraged him to scorn his freewheeling cousin and Nick's irresponsible parents. They'd hidden a dark secret, though: unable to have children, Upton and Mildred Davis had adopted Marshall, their nephew, as a toddler. In exchange for their silence, Mildred and Upton promised to help pay the younger Davises' household expenses.

That silence had lasted for nearly thirty-five years, until last Monday. Out of the blue, Uncle Quentin had confronted Nick and Marshall with the truth, explaining that he wanted to repair past wrongs. Instead, he'd simply dumped his burden on his sons, then taken off for his home a hundred and fifty miles away in Bakersfield.

Everything Marshall believed he knew about himself and his parents had been thrown into turmoil. Why had they been ashamed of his origins? Had they been so strict because they feared he'd turn out a mess like his birth parents?

As they exited the hospital via a side door, Nick asked, "Is that a no? I assure you, I have the bride's approval."

"Considering that Zady's my office nurse, I should hope so." Marshall didn't wish to offend either his brother or the future Mrs. Davis, whom he liked and respected. Besides, being invited to serve as best man was an honor. "Of course I'll stand up with you."

On the path toward the parking structure, their strides synchronized. "Maybe we should rent different color tuxes," Nick said cheerfully. "I'd hate for the bride to get confused and marry the wrong guy."

Leave it to Nick to find humor in their embarrassing resemblance. "What exactly does a best man do?" Marshall asked. "Aside from making sure the groom shows up and doesn't lose the ring."

Halting in his tracks, Nick whipped out his phone. "Let's see."

"I didn't mean for you to research it now."

"We've only got a few weeks." He tapped the screen.

Marshall gazed across the curved drive to the newly acquired building, where construction equipment buzzed. The Portia and Vincent Adams Memorial Medical Building—popularly referred to as the Porvamm—would provide much-needed operating suites, laboratories and other facilities for the men's fertility program.

A little over a week earlier, two groups of doctors had nearly come to blows over how to allot the two floors of office space. Marshall and Nick had taken opposite sides, with Marshall in favor of keeping the entire Porvamm for the men's program, while Nick and his comrades protested that they deserved a break from their cramped quarters.

Before open warfare could break out with scalpels flashing in the corridors, they'd reached a compromise. Encouraged by Zady, Marshall had proposed a concession, and last Monday the administration had agreed to assign a quarter of the offices to obstetricians and pediatricians.

"Duties of a best man," Nick read aloud from the phone. "Serve as the groom's adviser on clothing and etiquette. I think we can skip that part."

"I know nothing about weddings, so I concur," Marshall said.

"Organize the bachelor party," his brother continued.

"Okay to video games and pizza," Marshall said. "I draw the line at strippers."

Nick laughed. "I'd love to see you plan a party with strippers, just to watch your face get redder than a blood specimen, but you're off the hook. Because of the tight time frame, Zady's skipping the bachelorette party, too."

What other land mines lay in wait? Co-opting the phone, Marshall scanned the list. "I can make a toast at the reception, and I'll be glad to dance with the bride and the maid of honor. Should I be squiring around the other bridesmaids, too?"

"There aren't any." Reclaiming the device, Nick resumed their walk toward the garage. "Just Zora as matron of honor." The bride's twin sister was an ultrasound technician. "You might have to ride herd on my future mother-in-law, though. She's reputed to be a dragon."

"You haven't met her?" Marshall had presumed that introductions to the bride's parents would be a priority.

"Zady doesn't plan to invite her until a few days before the ceremony. That's enough notice for her to fly down from Oregon but short enough to minimize the damage." Nick shrugged. "I've heard many stories about the woman's drinking and trouble-making. Zady's plan seems sensible."

Marshall hadn't given any thought to what kind of wedding he'd have. If he'd ever spared a moment's reflection on the subject, however, it wouldn't include misbehaving in-laws. That brought up a delicate subject. "Will my mother be invited?"

"I put Aunt Mildred on the guest list." Inside the parking structure, Nick halted beside his battered blue sedan. "Unless that's a problem for you."

"I doubt she'll accept," Marshall blurted. In response to his brother's quizzical expression, he explained, "I tried to talk to her after Uncle Quentin dropped his bomb, and got nowhere."

He still couldn't refer to Nick's father as "Dad." That title belonged to Quentin's older brother, who, to be fair, had been as hard on himself as he'd been on his adoptive son. A brilliant inventor of medical devices and a savvy businessman, Upton Davis had amassed a fortune. After his death five years ago of an aneurysm, he'd left half his estate to Marshall, along with a request to take care of his mother.

Marshall had done his best. How sad that his mother no longer wanted his help.

"You told her that you now know you're adopted?" Nick leaned against his car.

"Uncle Quentin beat me to it."

"How did she react?"

"Badly." When Marshall had called Thursday night to confirm their usual dinner date on Sunday, she'd dismissed him coldly. "She said now that I've learned I'm not really her son, not to bother. Then she hung up."

"That's harsh, even for Aunt Mildred," Nick said.

"I've called but all I get is her voice mail." How could his mother reject him for something that wasn't his fault? She was the one who should be apologizing, yet Marshall hadn't asked for that.

To him, Mildred would always be Mom. His birth mother, Adina Davis, had died of lung cancer two years ago. Thanks to the family's secrets, Marshall had never had a chance to know the woman who'd given birth to him except as a charming but volatile aunt.

"Give her a chance to recover," Nick said. "She's never been the warm, cuddly type."

"There's an understatement." Might as well raise the other issue on Marshall's mind. "I suppose your father is on the guest list."

"Yes. Zady requested it. She's more generous than I am after he let us down." In addition to hiding the truth about Marshall, Uncle Quentin had abandoned his wife and son when Nick was ten. "I may tolerate his presence, but that doesn't mean I forgive him."

For once, the two of them agreed on something, Marshall thought. And for all that he'd lost by his parents' deception, at least they'd been there for him.

Mercifully, neither he nor his brother showed signs of their parents' mental instability. Although about 50 percent of the children of bipolar patients suffered from a psychiatric disorder, sometimes the odds worked in your favor.

"The important thing is that you and Zady enjoy your wedding." Curiosity propelled Marshall to ask, "How's Caleb reacting?"

Although his nephew's conception four years ago had

been an accident, he'd proved a blessing to Nick. Named after their grandfather, the boy had come to live with his dad after his mother's death in a boating accident.

"He's excited about being the ring bearer." Nick grinned. "That's another duty of the best man—supervising my son. Hope that's okay."

"It's fine. More than fine." Marshall had felt an immediate attachment to his nephew when they'd met a few months ago. If he had a kid, he'd relish every minute of the boy's—or girl's—childhood.

"I'll email you with whatever we decide about tuxedos. I'd prefer a dark suit, but I doubt Zady will go for that," Nick said.

"I'm sure she'll keep me informed." Noting the exhaustion on his brother's face, Marshall remembered that the man had been on duty all night. "Go home."

"Gladly." Lifting a hand in farewell, Nick ducked into his car.

Marshall surveyed the scattering of vehicles for a familiar white station wagon. Its absence brought a pang of disappointment. What had he expected, a repeat of last night's impromptu karaoke duet?

Recalling what the surgical nurse had said about Franca's foster child brought a wave of sympathy. She must be grieving.

While Marshall respected her decision to take in a troubled child, he had to be honest. If he and his future wife were unable to have kids, he'd be happy to adopt, but only if they nurtured the child from infancy. He'd never invite trouble by taking in a foster kid. The discovery that his own parents had been so ashamed of adopting him that they'd kept him at arm's length reinforced his reservations.

His footsteps slowed as he neared the silver sedan,

his earlier reluctance to go home closing over him. He could call Franca to offer his support, he mused. He had her cell number, which she'd provided to the staff.

Then he got another, better idea. Since his best-man duties involved Caleb, why not buy the boy a gift? A teddy bear dressed in a tux, perhaps.

Marshall recalled passing a shop on Safe Harbor Boulevard…the Bear and Doll Boutique, that was the name.

And since Franca was no doubt clearing away reminders of her foster daughter rather than acquiring more toys, he didn't have to worry about an awkward encounter, or the possibility of a heart-to-heart conversation. As he'd learned from his father, it was his responsibility to deal with his own problems, and he intended to do just that.

Chapter Three

The rainbow colors of the toy store brightened Franca's mood. What a joyful array of bears, dolls, accessories and children's books, plus there was a large craft table that Ada used for classes. Although the store appeared small from the front, its depth encompassed several rooms, which was part of its charm: you never knew what delightful surprise lay around the corner.

Near the front counter, stuffed animals in fairy-tale outfits filled a shelf. A pink-gowned Cinderella pig beamed at her porcine prince. A polar bear Snow White shepherded an assembly of penguins, while a Little Red Riding Hood sheep held out her basket to a wolf in fleecy clothing.

"They're darling!" Franca told the owner.

At the compliment, Ada tipped her head of champagne-colored hair. "I ran across them last week in the storage room. I try to rotate my stock."

"They're too precious to hide." Wary of soiling the merchandise, Franca avoided picking up the wolf, despite her curiosity about how its fleecy costume had been constructed.

"I'll fetch that new catalog," Ada said. "Hang on." She ducked behind the counter.

From within the store appeared a familiar dark-haired woman. As the hospital's public relations director, Jennifer Serra Martin had interviewed Franca for the employee newsletter a few months ago. Discovering that they had a lot in common, they'd started meeting for lunch and scheduling play dates for their little girls.

"I heard about your daughter," Jennifer said. "Franca, I'm so sorry. I can't imagine what I'd have done if Rosalie's birth mother had changed her mind."

The five-year-old, a cutie with blond ringlets, trotted after her mother, clutching a panda. "Where's Jazz?"

"I told you, Rosalie, she's gone to live with her birth mommy," Jennifer reminded her. "Honey, can you read a story to your new bear for a minute? I'm busy with Dr. Brightman."

"You're just talking!"

"Remember what I said about that?"

Rosalie screwed up her face as she searched for the answer. "Talking is how grown-ups play."

"That's right. And you hate when I interrupt *your* play," Jennifer said.

"Okay, Mommy." Rosalie perched on a chair and, panda in lap, picked up a picture book.

With her daughter settled, the PR director turned to Franca. "Have you thought any more about what we discussed?"

Franca's memory yielded no clues as to what the woman was talking about. Suppressing an instinct to screw up her face like Rosalie, she asked, "What was that?"

"Ideas for new counseling groups," Jennifer reminded her.

"Oh, yes. I've been reviewing possibilities." The previous psychologist had established programs for infertile couples, for surrogate moms and for several other categories of patients. However, the hospital was expanding into many areas, and Jennifer had volunteered to brainstorm new groups with her.

"I had an idea I meant to share. Now, what was it?" Jennifer sighed. "Too bad I forgot to write it down."

"It'll come back to you," Franca assured her.

"Probably at a totally inappropriate moment." The dark-haired woman smiled. "When it does, I'll text you immediately."

Ada joined them with a pattern catalog. "I can order these at my discount—I'll split the difference with you."

"I'll pay full price," Franca told her. "I want you to stay in business."

"Every little bit helps," the older woman admitted.

Jennifer peered at the catalog. "What adorable little dresses!"

"Here's the fabric I plan to use." On her phone, Franca clicked to a photo of Belle resplendent in white, flanked by a half dozen attendants bedecked in frothy blue. "I'll never wear my bridesmaid dress again."

"Oh, dear," Jennifer said. "Those are fascinatingly hideous."

Ada took an amused peek. "Some insecure brides try to enhance their image by making their attendants as ugly as possible."

Franca shook her head. "I doubt Belle did it intentionally."

She halted as the shop's glass door opened to admit a tall and much-too-handsome man with a shadowed expression. Even though Marshall instantly assumed a polite smile, her heart twisted. What was troubling him?

Still, his rumpled appearance from last night had yielded to smooth hair, pressed slacks and a navy polo shirt—a marked contrast to Franca's scruffy state. She wished she hadn't worn her oldest jeans and stained sweater. As for the condition of her hair, the less she thought about that, the better.

Distractedly, she said hello, and after Marshall exchanged greetings with Jennifer, Franca introduced him to Ada. She'd forgotten the phone in her hand until the picture caught his gaze.

"Belle got married?" His voice rang hollow.

"Last month." Was this the cause of his distress? But that didn't make sense after all these years.

Franca supposed she ought to mind her own business about whatever was troubling Marshall. But it wasn't in her nature to ignore friends' distress...even if they hadn't consciously sought her input.

How ironic, Marshall mused as his pulse quickened. He'd been naive to believe himself safe from running into Franca here. Not that he was sorry.

In college, they'd frequently bumped into each other, as if drawn to the same locations. In truth, it hadn't always been a coincidence. If he learned Franca was attending an event that interested him, he'd make a point of going, too. But there'd also been a synchronicity at work, he believed.

Now here they were. And Belle was still between them. Speaking of Belle, she appeared happy in the picture. No doubt she'd long ago forgotten her disappointment in him.

"She's beautiful." That was true of all brides, but especially of Belle, with her blond radiance. Yet her image failed to eclipse one particular bridesmaid. "As are you."

Peripherally, he observed the PR director taking her little girl to the counter to pay for their purchases. He was glad not to have to include them in the conversation.

"No one could look beautiful in that dress." Franca chuckled. "I plan to cut it into doll clothes. I'm here to pick out patterns."

Marshall decided to explain why he'd stopped in, as well. "I figured my nephew, Caleb, might like a bear in a tux."

"You have a nephew?" A pucker formed between her eyebrows. "But you're an only child."

They'd had a conversation once about the advantages and disadvantages of their situations, him as a singleton and her as the middle of three kids. How odd that the normally hyperactive hospital grapevine hadn't yet broadcast the news to her.

"Nick and I were raised as cousins. We just learned that was a lie." To his embarrassment, he had to clear his throat. *Pull yourself together.* "The short version is, we're brothers and I was adopted by my aunt and uncle. Anyway, Nick asked me to be best man at his wedding next month, and Caleb's the ring bearer. He's engaged to my nurse, Zady. Nick is, not Caleb. But you got that." He rarely stumbled over words. How embarrassing.

"Zady told me she was engaged," Franca said. "I was honored that she asked me to save the date."

"I see." Up close, her cloud of reddish-blond hair made her amber eyes appear extra large, but Marshall noted there was something different. "Why did you change your hair color?"

Franca shrugged. "I was tired of feeling like Raggedy Ann."

"I liked it."

"You liked that I resembled a rag doll with red yarn for hair?"

"It was...you."

"Exactly," she said. "A mess. And I'm not fishing for compliments."

"May I offer a word of advice?" Marshall plunged ahead before she could respond. "I realize you're the expert on psychology, but you shouldn't put yourself down."

"Where's this coming from?" Franca asked.

"From…" He broke off. In college, he'd been aware that Franca felt eclipsed by her stunning roommate. But he'd been in no position to explain that whenever he was around her, Belle faded. Nor did he wish to bring it up now.

Fundamentally, nothing had changed. Marshall had recognized from the start that his attraction to Franca was destructive. They were opposites who disagreed on many important topics, and whenever they were together for long, their arguments brought out the worst in each other.

"Never mind," he said. "I shouldn't have spoken."

"Actually, you're right," she responded. "I was indulging in either self-pity or false modesty."

"Nothing about you is false." That skated too close to flattery for Marshall's taste. He decided on a quick exit. "Good luck with your patterns."

"Happy bear hunting."

"Thanks."

Before he could escape, Jennifer Martin turned from the counter and cried, "I remember!"

"Remember what?" Franca asked.

"I'll leave you two to chat." Marshall started to retreat.

"Wait, Dr. Davis!" Jennifer protested. "This concerns you."

"Excuse me?"

"I have an idea for a new therapy group," Jennifer burst out. "For men undergoing fertility treatments. How perfect if the pair of you ran it as a team!"

Teaming up with Franca to plumb patients' emotions? The concept struck him as anything but perfect. "I'm not a counselor," Marshall said. "Dr. Brightman is well qualified to lead such a group."

"Men might hesitate to talk freely with a woman," Jennifer said. "Also, while she's a counselor, you have medical expertise. You'd be a great team."

"She has a point," Franca conceded.

"Any male urologist would do." That was the best argument that came to mind. "Preferably one who has better people skills than mine."

"Such as who?" Jennifer demanded.

Marshall's mind skimmed over the urology staff. The head of the department, Dr. Cole Rattigan, had no spare time, since he and his wife were juggling fifteen-month-old triplets. Marshall's suitemates were even newer to the hospital than he was and still honing their surgical skills under his supervision. It seemed wrong to pressure them into the job.

So how did he get out of this?

Franca sympathized with Marshall's deer-in-the-headlights reaction. However, she couldn't dispute Jennifer's reasoning.

"It's worth considering," she said. "Dr. Davis and I will discuss it."

"Great!" Jennifer said. "Okay if I mention it to Mark?" Dr. Mark Rayburn was the hospital administrator. "Oh, and Cole, too?"

"What's the rush?" Marshall asked irritably.

"Things are slow after the holidays. There's not a lot

happening in March. I'd love to publicize a new therapy group in the newsletter," Jennifer explained.

"Give us a chance to consider how we might organize it and whether it fits into Dr. Davis's schedule," Franca said firmly. "Nice to see you and Rosalie."

"Nice to see you, too." To the obvious relief of her daughter, who was hopping up and down, the PR director departed.

"She doesn't take no for an answer, does she?" Marshall growled.

"She's not usually pushy," Franca assured him. "But if we don't want this foisted on us willy-nilly, we'd better present a united front."

His jaw twitched as if he were about to dismiss the notion entirely. But Ada was observing them from the counter, and other voices were approaching from outside. "Let's finish shopping and meet elsewhere to resolve this."

"Good idea." Not at her apartment, and Franca wasn't about to suggest his place. "How about the Sea Star Café down by the harbor? I haven't had lunch."

"Is that still there?" Like Franca, Marshall had grown up in inland Orange County, but must have visited the harbor town over the years. "Yes, I'm hungry, too."

Into the shop surged a couple of women shepherding children.

"See you there," she said.

"Done." He drew himself up to his full, rather impressive height. "Let's get this squared away before it blows up in our faces."

Would it be so terrible for them to coordinate a weekly group? she wondered, watching him move deeper into the store. Surely they could maintain a professional distance, despite her awareness of him as a man. And despite his disappointment in her new hair color. The picky comment reminded Franca of how exacting Marshall could be.

Franca flipped through the catalog and selected half a dozen patterns with adjustable fastenings, easy to remove for washing. After writing the pattern numbers on a notepad, she handed it to Ada.

The shopkeeper promised to order them that day. "I'll text you when they come in."

"Great."

In an angled wall mirror, Franca spotted Marshall in the next room, lifting a formally dressed bear for inspection. Yearning transformed his face as he fingered the soft fur.

With a start, she recognized that look. She'd seen it on the face of her older sister, Gail, when one of their cousins had brought her baby to a family gathering. Gail had been devastated by repeated miscarriages.

Was Marshall eager to be a father? Perhaps Belle's wedding photo had reminded him of how much he'd thrown away. But whatever promptings he experienced toward parenthood, Franca doubted he'd understand her torment over losing Jazz.

Marshall had made it clear long ago that he saw no reason to "invite trouble," as he put it, from a foster child. For him, fatherhood meant a traditional home with two or three genetic children.

To Franca, motherhood meant loving children regardless of their origins. Despite growing up in a happy household with a psychologist father and a devoted mother, she'd had an immediate bond with the neglected and abused youngsters she'd met as a teen volunteer, along with a sense of destiny. In her twenties, she'd gone through the process to qualify as a foster mom. After caring for several youngsters, she'd given her heart to Jazz.

She had no desire to return to her lonely apartment. In contrast, eating lunch with Marshall didn't seem so bad.

Reminded of their plans, Franca said goodbye to Ada and went out.

Chapter Four

Marshall inhaled the crisp sea air as he swiped his credit card in the parking meter. On a Saturday afternoon, he'd been lucky to find a space.

Seagulls mewed overhead as he descended the steps to the quay. Surf and souvenir shops lined the inland side of the wooden wharf, while small piers thrust outward into the harbor, tethered boats bobbing beside them in the water. In the breezy March sunshine, white sails filled the harbor.

To his right, past a tumble of rocks, stretched a beach dotted with a few brave sunbathers. During his teens, the beach had been popular with Marshall's classmates, but he'd been too busy with Advanced Placement and International Baccalaureate classes to hang out at such places. However, he'd enjoyed the sounds and smells of the ocean on rare jaunts with family friends who'd owned a powerboat.

Ahead, at the Sea Star Café, outdoor diners basked in the comfort of warming devices shaped like metal umbrellas. No sign of Franca.

Inside the café, the scents of coffee and spices greeted him. Families and couples had claimed all the tables, and he was wondering if they should have chosen a less popular locale when he spotted a tumble of red-gold hair at a booth.

Hands cupped around a mug, Franca gazed out the window to her left toward the open ocean. In profile, she had a straight nose, a determined chin and long lashes. When she swung toward him, her mouth curved in welcome. She waved at almost the same moment that the loudspeaker squawked her name.

"I went ahead and ordered," she explained when he reached her. "Hope you like pita sandwiches. You can have either the falafel and hummus or the Swiss and turkey."

"Take whichever you prefer." Marshall usually picked items that could be trimmed, such as sandwiches on bread. Still, he refused to become one of those fussy eaters who drove everyone around them crazy. He had even recently discovered the pleasures of pizza. "I'll pick up the order."

"I'll hold down the table," she said. "Either sandwich is fine with me."

Marshall claimed their tray and on his return, handed her the falafel and hummus pita—definitely messier. He slid several bills across the table to cover his check. "No arguing."

"Wasn't going to," she said.

He removed the plates, utensils and glasses of water from the tray, then carried it to a disposal station. "You're always so neat," Franca remarked.

"As opposed to?" He raised an eyebrow.

"Me." She indicated a glop of hummus she'd spilled on the table.

"A little mess doesn't bother me as long as it's not mine." Marshall had the sense he was being perpetually judged, thanks to his parents' habitual criticism. He tried, not always successfully, to cut others more slack.

After a few bites of pita, he brought up the proposed counseling group. "Any suggestion for how to get out of this?"

"Are you sure we should?" Responding to his frown, Franca said, "This would benefit many patients. It also could reinforce Dr. Rattigan's view of you as a key player in the department's expansion."

Marshall mulled the idea as he ate. Adding such a group did seem logical. "What exactly happens in a counseling group? If that isn't a bonehead question."

"It's more a reflection on what medical schools teach doctors, or fail to teach them," she said.

"I took courses in psychopathology and clinical psychiatry," Marshall countered. "As well as serving a rotation in psychiatry." Psychopathology was the study of the genetic, biological and other causes of mental disorders, along with their symptoms and treatments.

"Dealing with psychotics and how to medicate them?" Franca summarized.

"Basically, yes."

"I figured." Her nose wrinkled. "We won't be dealing with psychotics. We'll be helping ordinary people whose infertility creates problems for them." Having finished her pita, she wiped her hands on her paper napkin.

Marshall reached across with his own napkin to dab the corner of her mouth. "Missed a spot."

Startled, Franca lifted her chin, and her cheek brushed his hand. An electric tingle ran along his arm. "I could use an aide to follow me around and clean me up," she said.

"Why bother, when I'm here?" he teased.

She smiled. "Promise you won't do that in front of patients."

"Promise you won't eat a pita in front of patients."

"It's a deal."

He returned to their topic. "I don't mean to be dismissive, but why not refer troubled patients to Resolve?" The national organization assisted people coping with infertility.

"It's a terrific group, but it's a complement to therapy," Franca said. "It doesn't replace it. But I never answered your question."

"About what happens in counseling?"

She nodded. "Infertility is a stressful experience. People often feel out of control and that they've failed. There's loss and grief as well as financial concerns." Fertility treatments could cost tens of thousands of dollars and were rarely covered by insurance. "Sharing your pain with others who are in the same boat can be a relief."

"But why have a separate group for men?"

Franca took a sip from her mug. "Most infertility counseling focuses on the woman or on the couple's relationship. But when the man is the source of the infertility, that can affect his feelings of masculinity and self-worth. And men in general have a harder time expressing their emotions."

"That's true of me," Marshall conceded. Although he wasn't entirely convinced, he'd run out of arguments. Moreover, an earlier comment of hers was rattling inside his head.

He'd assumed that by adopting, his parents had put to rest the issues associated with their infertility. Perhaps he'd been wrong. "Could those concerns persist after the couple adopts?"

"Certainly." Sunlight through the window brought out the sprinkling of freckles across Franca's cheeks. "A lot depends on the patients' self-esteem and how they view adoption."

"And therapy can help?" Too bad his parents hadn't availed themselves of it. But that wouldn't have suited their superior, stiff-upper-lip attitude.

"It isn't a cure-all, but yes," Franca said. "For example, adoptive parents worry whether there'll be a temperamental mismatch and whether the child will bond with them as strongly as with a birth parent."

"Or whether they'll bond with the child?" Marshall asked.

"That, too."

"You raise interesting points," he said. "To me, therapy has always seemed unscientific, perhaps even…" He paused as a couple moved past them to claim an empty table.

"A weakness?"

"Yes." He regarded her steadily. "I realize patients find it helpful. I've just never understood why."

"I wish doctors underwent therapy the way psychologists do," Franca said. "It's part of our training."

"Was it helpful to you?"

"Very."

"In what way?"

"I learned to stop assuming I'm responsible for my mother's happiness." She tilted her head as she reflected. "Ten years ago, after my father died, my brother went his own way. My sister was already married and living out of state. So Mom focused her energies on me, insisting we talk for an hour every night. Sometimes she'd phone at lunch, too. It was intrusive, but I couldn't bear to disappoint her. She'd always been more invested emotionally in her children than in my dad, despite their good relationship."

"Why was that?" It had never occurred to him that children could be more important to a parent than the husband-wife bond.

"My mother had been married once before and had several miscarriages." Franca hesitated, as if reluctant to confide too much. Odd, considering how readily she invited *his* confidences. Then she continued, "Her first husband couldn't handle the disappointment and left. Mom never entirely recovered from that betrayal. So as you can see, I know about the fallout from fertility problems in my own family."

"Surely things changed after she married your father, right?" He'd liked the elder Dr. Brightman when they'd met once at a campus event, although the man hadn't spoken much. He'd puffed on an aromatic pipe and listened attentively to the conversation involving his wife, Franca and Belle.

"Yes," Franca said. "Fortunately, there were no more miscarriages. But in a sense, I think she felt his loyalty had never truly been tested."

An interesting insight—but not really relevant to today's topic. "How did counseling help with your mom?"

"I had a frank talk with her about respecting boundaries," Franca said. "I also suggested activities for her."

"How'd she take it?"

"It upset her, and that upset me." She sighed. "After a few rough weeks, she reluctantly joined a senior center. A couple of months later, she met a widower, and married him."

"Is she happy?"

"Extremely." Franca folded her hands on the table. "They moved to Reno, where his children live. She's surrounded by grandkids, and except for the holidays, I've become barely more than a Facebook friend. A victim of my own success."

That wasn't the worst thing in the world. "If I were on Facebook, my mother would unfriend me," Marshall muttered.

"Because of you and Nick being brothers? I don't really understand how that happened." Franca broke off as a server offered them each a chocolate chip cookie, courtesy of the café. "Thanks." She set one on her napkin. Marshall accepted his and enjoyed the chocolate melting in his mouth while weighing how much to reveal.

He might as well spill it. The details would soon be all over the hospital anyway. "Nick's parents allowed my parents to adopt me as a toddler. Upton Davis was much more successful financially, while my birth parents were nearly homeless. I gather they hadn't planned on having two kids a year apart."

Quentin Davis had stumbled from job to job, drinking heavily and refusing treatment for his bipolar disorder. Aunt Adina had held a series of low-paying positions, spending money whenever she had it and expecting it to fall out of the sky when she didn't.

"How unusual that they chose to adopt the toddler rather than the baby," Franca said.

"I presume Nick was still breastfeeding. Also, with a toddler, they had a better idea of how well the child was developing."

"Aren't you being a bit severe?" she asked.

"I know my parents." Rather than elaborate, Marshall moved on. "My folks paid Adina and Quentin for an apartment and other living expenses, and insisted on secrecy in return. Until last week, I had no idea I was adopted."

Franca rested her chin on her palm. "How'd you discover it?"

"Uncle Quentin had a crisis of conscience and decided to get it off his chest. He corralled Nick and me and dumped it on us." Marshall pictured the graying, slightly stooped man as he'd sat at a conference table in the medical building just last Monday.

"Your mom must have been upset."

"She implied I'm not her son anymore and refuses to have dinner with me or even talk to me." When Marshall inhaled, his lungs hurt.

"It might be a knee-jerk reaction," Franca said. "I can't believe she means it."

"She didn't leave much room for doubt."

"What about your birth mother? Do you have a relationship with her?"

"Aunt Adina died a couple of years ago. I never especially connected with her," Marshall said. "But at thirty-five, I don't suppose I need a mother."

"Everyone needs a mother." Reaching across the table, Franca cupped her hand over his fist. Instinctively, he relaxed beneath her touch. "Give your mom time. She's hurting, and she lashed out at the person most closely associated with her secret—you."

"If she refuses to see me, what am I supposed to do?" he asked bitterly.

"Write her a letter," Franca advised. "Tell her you love her and that you're here for her. She's a mother, and once her initial shock eases, she'll view things differently. Don't let pride keep you apart."

Pride. Marshall had plenty of that. "I suppose that's good advice."

Her smile froze on her face. Following her gaze, he spotted a little girl with black hair clinging to a woman's hand as they entered.

Anguish transformed Franca's expression, stabbing into Marshall as if the pain were his own. He'd never experienced another person's emotions this keenly

He didn't have to ask what had hurt her. This must be her foster daughter.

EVERYTHING AROUND FRANCA VANISHED. All the light in the world haloed the little girl she loved.

Hard-won self-control barely held her in place. Then Jazz spotted her and the girl pelted across the restaurant screaming, "Mommy Franca!"

In an instant, the child was climbing onto her lap, hugging her. And Franca hugged back, tears flowing.

Bridget stalked toward them. Despite her jeans and cartoon-printed T-shirt, she looked older than her twenty-three years, thanks to her drug use. "What do you think you're doing?"

"I'm sorry." Franca struggled to catch her breath.

"Jazz, get down right now!" Bridget's command whiplashed through the air.

"No!" The child burrowed into Franca.

Marshall sat quietly, observing. Franca felt both his sympathy and his reserve.

Around them, the café fell silent. Everyone was watching.

"Honey, you have to do what your mommy says." Gently, Franca pried the little fingers from around her neck. "Don't worry. I'm keeping your dolls safe and they'll join you as soon as you have room."

"I'm s'posed to stay with you. You promised!" The heartbreak in Jazz's voice tore at Franca.

When she'd joyfully informed the child about the adoption, she'd never imagined that it might fall through. How could a child understand that grown-ups didn't always have the power to keep their word?

"You live with your mother now." Her chest tight, Franca eased Jazz to the floor. "How lucky you are. You have two mommies who love you."

Bridget's steely eyes lit with rage. "No, she doesn't. She has one mother—me!"

Franca forced out the words, "That's right."

"Damn straight it is." Until the man spoke, she hadn't noticed him looming behind Bridget, his muscles bulging beneath a sleeveless T-shirt. Shaved head, coarse features and a scorpion tattoo on his neck. When had Bridget hooked up with this guy?

The notion of him having access to Jazz chilled Franca. But there were no bruises on the girl's face or arms. She wasn't sure whether to be grateful or dismayed that she had no grounds to call the police.

"Come on." Bridget reached for her daughter's hand.

The girl snatched it away. "No."

"You heard your mother!" As if he'd been waiting for a chance to throw his weight around, the man grabbed the child's arm. "Not another word out of you." The man gave Jazz's arm a yank.

"Axel," Bridget warned.

Marshall uncoiled from his seat. He stood several inches taller, but lacked the other man's heft. "You're hurting the child."

The man's lip curled in a sneer. Then, as if becoming aware of the observers around them, he released Jazz. "Yeah, well, do what your mother tells you, kid."

Jazz stood motionless, her tearstained cheeks a match

for Franca's. Clasping her daughter's hand, Bridget led her along the aisle to the other side of the café.

Franca couldn't remain there another instant. "I have to go."

"Understood." Marshall followed protectively as she headed for the door.

Franca supposed she ought to thank him for standing up to Axel, but she could hardly think for the noise in her head. Outside, she said a quick goodbye to him and rushed along the quay, pushing through the midday crowd.

But no sea breeze could dissipate her grief and guilt. She'd failed Jazz, regardless of where the fault lay. It burned like fire.

She lost track of Marshall until he started up the steps to the closest parking area. He paused, his forehead creased with worry. Kind of him, but this wasn't his problem.

On Franca stumbled, toward the more distant lot where she'd left her car. She tried in vain to outrun the realization that swept over her, obliterating the destiny she'd pictured so clearly.

Franca could endure almost anything for a child in her care, but when she'd imagined relinquishment, it had been to a home where the little one could be happy and safe. Not this wrenching sense that she'd betrayed the girl's trust.

She couldn't go through this again, couldn't risk letting down another child and having her heart shredded. But if she didn't foster troubled children, what did that leave? She still wanted to be a mother.

Despite counseling fertility patients, Franca had never considered whether or under what circumstances she might give birth, because she didn't plan to. Nor had she worried about finding the right man to be a father.

Her desire to foster children had struck a chord with her own mom. Franca was a middle child who had often gotten lost in the shuffle at home. It had been exciting and validating to see her mother's excitement. Partly as a result, instead of dreaming about finding Mr. Right as her sister had, Franca had embraced an identity focused on motherhood.

Leaning against her station wagon, she felt confused and lost. At thirty-three, she'd believed she had a firm grasp on the future. Instead, a burning question darkened her horizon:

Now what?

Chapter Five

Franca's heartbroken expression haunted Marshall over the next few days. She didn't contact him about starting the new counseling program, and he let the matter ride.

She must have been too upset about her foster daughter, and he wasn't eager to pursue the matter. Despite her example of how therapy had changed her attitude toward her mother, Marshall doubted enough of his patients would sign up to make the effort worthwhile.

Recalling Franca's advice about writing to his mother, he tried to compose a letter. But after he penned the words *Dear Mom* on crisp gray stationery, nothing else came to mind. Writing, aside from the occasional prescription, had never been Marshall's forte. Perhaps they could gradually resume a normal relationship after the wedding. And if she still didn't return his phone calls, what more could he do? He couldn't force her to care about him.

On Sunday, Marshall accompanied Nick and Caleb to rent matching tuxedos, which Zady had decreed they should wear. While Caleb was being fitted, Marshall asked where the couple planned to go on their honeymoon. "Unless it's a secret." He'd read that some couples hid their destination, presumably to prevent crashers.

"We'd love a week or two in Italy," Nick said. "Gondola rides, Michelangelo and Roman ruins."

"Sounds like fun." As a high school graduation present, Marshall's parents had taken him on a tour of Europe.

"That's a joke," Nick said. "We're planning a three-day weekend in Las Vegas." That was a five-hour drive from Safe Harbor.

"Hard to get away for longer," Marshall sympathized.

"Yeah. Hard when you max out the credit cards, too."

As they left the shop, Marshall presented Caleb with his new bear. "Wow!" Dark eyes shining, the three-year-old inspected the furry animal in its tux.

Nick grinned his approval. "It's a cutie pie, like my son. Thanks, Marsh."

"My pleasure."

Gazing at his brother and nephew, with their dark hair and lopsided smiles, Marshall felt his throat tighten. *If only I had a son.* Before that was possible, though, he had to find the right woman, and not get distracted by one whose approach to life was incompatible with his.

After his breakup with Belle, Marshall had had a few casual relationships during medical school and his residency in Boston. As a fellow in reconstructive surgery at the Cleveland Clinic, he'd tried an online dating site. Of the half dozen women he'd met for coffee, one had lied about her profession, one had asked him to prescribe painkillers for her, and another had talked about how she'd always dreamed of marrying a doctor. The others had been pleasant but uninspiring. No one had generated the kind of connection he'd felt with Franca.

Why did his thoughts keep homing in on her?

As Marshall said goodbye to Nick and Caleb, he recalled the previous day's scene in the café, especially her distress over her foster daughter. It was exactly the kind of trouble that he suspected went hand-in-hand with fostering older children. How frustrating that she insisted on getting involved in such situations.

That fellow Axel could be dangerous, and in Marshall's opinion, to put her daughter at his mercy showed Bridget to be an unfit mother. And there was nothing Franca could do.

The next child she took in might come with an equally risky situation. But no matter how much Marshall wished to protect her, Franca had a right to live as she chose.

How lucky Nick and Zady were, to be well-suited and in love. Over the next few days, Marshall's nurse hummed as she went about her duties.

"What's that you're humming?" he asked on Thursday afternoon as he reviewed the face sheet for his next patient.

Zady's blushed to the roots of her short reddish-brown hair. "Uh…darn. I can't get it out of my mind. It's 'The Teddy Bears' Picnic.'"

"Not a bridal march?" he teased.

"It's Caleb's favorite." She leaned against the counter of the nurses' station. "We were dancing to it with the tuxedo bear you gave him."

"I'm glad he likes the toy." Marshall smiled at the notion of her and his nephew dancing the stuffed animal around.

Kids were resilient, as Caleb demonstrated. The little boy had lost his mother in a boating accident last year, then adjusted to moving from his maternal grandparents' large home to Nick's one-story rental.

Marshall had been surprised when his nurse, who had hardly known his cousin, agreed to move in and babysit during Nick's overnight shifts in exchange for room and board.

She'd explained that it was a great way to save money. Also, she'd been caring for her toddler goddaughter, Linda, for an extended period while the parents traveled on business. Zady had believed the little girl would enjoy having Caleb as a live-in playmate. Marshall, who'd stopped by with an occasional gift, had grown fond of both children.

One example where an untraditional model of parenting had worked out. Although with Zady and Nick getting married and Linda back with her parents, both children were now in more traditional situations. So what did that prove?

Marshall had no chance to dwell on it; his next patient was waiting. On the face sheet, the reason for the visit was listed as follow up. Marshall had performed a vasectomy reversal on the patient eight months ago, and his sperm counts had risen and remained high since then.

"Why does Hank Driver need follow-up?" he asked Zady.

"He requested it," she said. "He declined to state a reason."

"Guess I'll find out." Marshall knocked on the examining room door, waited for a "Come in!" and entered.

A stocky man in slacks and a sport shirt swiveled toward him. "Hey, Doc." The other man thrust his hand out and Marshall shook it firmly. He already knew the patient's age was thirty-seven and his occupation was police detective, but he'd forgotten Hank's disconcerting gaze, as he had one blue eye and one brown.

"Nice to see you," Marshall said. "What seems to be the problem?"

Hank perched on the edge of the examining table. His light brown hair had begun to thin, but he was in good shape, without the potbelly that often signaled the approach of middle age for men.

"Are you sure everything's okay with my sperm, Doc?"

At the computer terminal, Marshall brought up Hank's records. "At your six-month checkup, your sperm count, motility and morphology were normal. Motility, you'll recall, is the sperm's ability to move effectively, and morphology refers to the shape. I can order a retest, but in my opinion, it's too soon. Is there something specific that's troubling you?"

Just because the surgery had succeeded didn't rule out some other medical problem. Any symptom might be meaningful.

"My wife's still not pregnant." Hank blew out a breath. Twice divorced, the other man had obtained a vasectomy in the belief that marriage and fatherhood had passed him by. Then he'd fallen in love with a police dispatcher and remarried. He'd promised his new wife to do his best to reverse the procedure.

"The average period from surgery to conception is about a year," Marshall advised him.

"Maybe so, but she's thirty-five and she's upset that it's taking so long."

Marshall read over the records again. "You told me previously that she had a full workup and no problems surfaced."

Hank began pacing. "Sex with my wife is starting to feel like a race against time. She denies blaming me, but we can hardly talk without fighting."

Marshall remembered the support group. Might as well see how Hank reacted. "Have you considered counseling? The hospital is considering starting a therapy group for male infertility patients."

"Stop right there." Hank scowled. "I'm not seeing some shrink."

"There would be a team running the sessions, including our staff psychologist and me," Marshall said. "I'd address medical questions that might arise."

Hank's expression softened. "Everybody in there would be guys?"

"Yes, except for the psychologist, Dr. Brightman."

"And you recommend this?"

Marshall had to be honest. "I'll admit I resisted when the idea was first raised." He recalled Franca's statements about the benefits of therapy. "However, I understand that infertility is stressful, and stress can have a medical impact."

"Worrying can add to the problem?"

"Yes," Marshall said. "Counseling can help you develop tools for dealing with the pressure. However, if you'd rather, you could both participate in a couple's group."

"Nah." Hank folded his arms. "I like the idea of it being all guys. Less touchy-feely stuff. When did you say this program starts?"

"We haven't set a date," Marshall said.

"Keep me in the loop, will you?" the patient replied.

"I will." Marshall jotted a note in the computer. After further discussion revealed no other concerns, they shook hands and Hank went out.

Marshall hadn't formally committed to co-leading the group. Still, the other man's interest indicated his patients might be more receptive than he had assumed.

Lost in thought, Marshall wandered down the hall. A throat-clearing sound drew his attention to Reid Winfrey, who tilted his head toward a commanding russet-haired figure standing near the nurses' station. "Here to see you," the other urologist murmured.

Fertility program director Owen Tartikoff seemed affable enough as he chatted with Reid's nurse, yet the usually relaxed, wisecracking Jeanine had gone rigid. Surely she didn't find the surgeon *that* intimidating. On the other hand, Owen had once fired a nurse who'd argued with him, Marshall recalled.

"Owen." As he stepped forward, hand outstretched, Jeanine seized the chance to vanish into the break room.

"Marshall." Tartikoff shook his hand firmly. "I heard from Jennifer Martin that you and Brightman might be starting a men's group. Excellent plan."

The director didn't beat around the bush. "I'm surprised Jennifer mentioned it."

"Her office is down the hall from mine. I stop in to keep current on hospital news," Owen said.

His thoroughness was impressive. Also inconvenient, from Marshall's perspective. "I assure you, the talks have been quite informal."

"Let's make them formal." A steely command underlay Owen's words. "It's important for Safe Harbor to stay ahead of the curve."

Talk about tipping points—the project had just flipped from potential to inevitable. "I'll get on it."

"Good man." Clapping him on the shoulder, the surgeon nodded to Reid, who'd remained on the sidelines, and strode out.

"Wow, the big man himself," Reid murmured. "I'll be curious about how this group pans out."

"Me, too." En route to his office, Marshall rejected the impulse to request a meeting with Franca over the weekend. This was business, not a personal matter, and should be conducted during regular hours. After checking his schedule, he wrote her a quick email mentioning Owen's interest and suggesting they confer Monday morning.

Marshall didn't usually schedule surgeries on Mondays so he could be available to patients who'd developed severe problems over the weekend. Although urology involved fewer emergencies than many specialties, they did occur, and he also sometimes received urgent referrals from other urologists due to his advanced training in microsurgery.

He sent the email and received an immediate response. Eleven a.m. Monday, my office, okay?

Marshall sent a confirmation, and squelched an impulse to inquire if she'd heard anything more about her foster daughter. Or to ask her opinion about the toast he'd begun composing for the bride and groom.

He had no reason to involve her in anything not work-related. No reason at all.

SEWING DOLL CLOTHES cleared Franca's mind. The simple tasks of laying out fabric on her cutting board, pinning the tiny pattern pieces, and cutting and then stitching them soothed her.

She jumped whenever her phone rang, though, in case it was news about Jazz. But it was always just the usual telemarketers. She struggled to be polite with them, since she'd read that many worked from home because they were disabled.

This past week, she hadn't been able to start on the doll clothes without breaking into tears. But over the weekend, the turmoil of the previous Saturday's encounter had yielded at last to a resolution.

If your dreams change, change with them. Instead of agonizing, she'd sorted through her options.

At thirty-three, Franca had a good chance of conceiving, but that would decrease with every year that passed while she searched for Mr. Right. Her best choice, she decided, would be to conceive via artificial insemination. She was fortunate to work at a hospital that offered a full range of services associated with AI.

Franca had no illusions about the challenge of raising a child on her own, and she believed fathers had an important role to play in children's lives. Too bad her younger brother, Glenn, lived in Montana and was too far away to serve as a father figure, she reflected as the sewing machine flew along a tiny seam. She planned to research the psychological implications for her baby, but other moms managed.

As her plan formed, her sense of helplessness, of having lost her goal in life, was fading. What a relief.

On Monday morning, however, her cheerful mood faltered when she entered the hospital by the staff door and heard the chatter of parents and children arriving at the day care center. Jazz ought to be skipping ahead of Franca, eager to join her friends.

No other child could replace the one Franca loved. Eyes stinging, she hurried to the elevator, and was grateful not to run into anyone with whom she'd have to converse.

Slowly, Franca regained her calm. Someday in the not-too-distant future, she would deliver a baby no one could take from her.

Her spirits rising, she exited the elevator on the fifth floor and followed the corridor past the administrative offices to her suite. Franca relished working in such a

varied and challenging environment. The regular pay-
check and benefits didn't hurt, either.

Her executive assistant, Maggie Majors, hadn't arrived yet. Since Franca was early and Maggie had to
drop off her seven-year-old daughter at school, she
didn't mind.

In the counseling room, Franca dressed the dolls in
their new blue finery. How precious they looked! If only
Jazz were here to play with them.

Stop torturing yourself. She hurried next door to her
office.

The morning flew by. After administering psychological tests to three potential egg donors, Franca met
with a family about their newborn baby's heart defect.
While surgery should eventually correct the problem,
few people were emotionally prepared for such a frightening diagnosis. Franca offered both emotional support
and information about the journey ahead.

She finished the consultation with fifteen minutes to
prepare for Marshall's eleven o'clock visit. In her computer, she opened a file of ground rules she'd compiled
for therapy groups.

Scanning them, she wondered what minefields lay
ahead in co-leading a therapy group with Marshall. Not
only did he lack experience, but he'd seemed cool to the
idea. His cryptic message requesting today's conference had puzzled her until Jennifer mentioned that Dr.
Tartikoff had leaped on the proposal. Still, if Marshall
opposed participating, he wasn't the sort of person to
let a bigwig push him into it.

Her phone rang. *If he's canceling, I'll call him a cow-
ard to his face...or ear.*

But the familiar male voice didn't belong to Marshall. "Hey, sis."

"Glenn!" He rarely called; he and his wife, Kerry, kept busy running a hardware store in a small Montana town. "What's up?"

"Can't I just call to say I miss you?" She pictured a teasing gleam animating his tanned face.

"Absolutely." She wished she'd had a chance to talk more with Glenn and Kerry at the holiday gathering in Reno. There'd been little opportunity, though, since the group at their mother's home had also included their sister, Gail, and her husband, plus their stepfather, his five children and their families. "But you have another reason, too, right?"

"Okay, so you're psychic. I mean, a psychologist," he said. "I'm calling with news. Kerry's pregnant."

"How wonderful!" she said. "I'm thrilled for you both." And at the confirmation that he was truly putting down roots.

Her brother had had a restless youth, moving from job to job and from state to state. In Montana, he'd fallen in love with Kerry and settled down, eventually winning both her hand and her parents' approval.

"I was afraid this might be painful, because of what happened with Jazz." He'd met her little girl at Christmas.

"Not at all." It occurred to Franca that he might have another reason for caution. "How did Gail react?"

He sighed. "She congratulated us—used all the right words, but her voice was really strained."

"I hope she hasn't had another miscarriage." That would make four.

"She didn't say," Glenn replied. "But she'd hardly bring it up, would she? Now, don't go calling her! She'll assume I put you up to it."

"I won't." Despite all her training, Franca wasn't equipped to comfort her sister's grief.

"I wish the doctors would figure out whether it's genetic," Glenn said. "If it is, maybe she could move on."

Genetic. The word hit Franca like a slap.

Their mother had lost two pregnancies during her first marriage, then gone on to bear three children. One of her aunts, after repeated miscarriages, had remained childless. Because Franca hadn't planned to bear children, she'd never connected the family history to herself. When she'd decided to pursue insemination, she'd assumed that she had a normal chance of carrying a child to term. What if she didn't?

Moreover, miscarriages could be not only heart-wrenching but dangerous for the mother. During Gail's last miscarriage, she'd suffered heavy blood loss and passed out. If her husband hadn't arrived home in time to summon paramedics, she might have died.

Franca struggled to avoid going overboard with her fears. A glance at her watch showed she had only a few minutes before her appointment, and Marshall was frighteningly punctual. "I'm sure Gail's as delighted for you and Kerry as I am. Thanks for calling and not just emailing."

"I love you," Glenn said.

"I love you, too, bro."

As she clicked off, a tall figure filled her door frame. Oh, damn. Despite an urge to run to the privacy of her car, where she could scream and cry and beat on her steering wheel again, she had to pull herself together fast.

"Good morning," she told Marshall, and assumed the most professional smile she could manage.

Chapter Six

Marshall respected Franca's cool manner—that was the right touch in this work setting. Yet he missed her usual warmth. At their meeting, she sat behind her desk, scarcely meeting his gaze. Was she angry at him for some reason?

Briskly, she began outlining protocols for the men's group. The first protocol was to state the group's goal: addressing issues that arose from male infertility and treatment.

"I agree." A mission statement would position the operation on a businesslike basis, which in his experience should appeal to men.

"Good." She'd tucked her hair into what Marshall believed was called a chignon. The style enhanced the heart shape of her face, while escaping twists of reddish-blond hair added an appealing touch. He just wished she'd chosen one of the comfortable chairs beside him rather than keeping a barrier between them.

Clearing her throat, Franca proceeded to item B on their list of protocols, designating the sessions as a safe zone where each participant could speak without interruption, without criticism and without receiving visual negativity such as eye rolling.

The subject of their meeting seemed straightforward,

yet there was an edge to her voice that hinted at tension. Marshall wished she'd explain why. But he'd resolved to avoid personal discussions, hadn't he?

"I'm on board with declaring a safe zone."

As item C, Franca proposed a guarantee of privacy for anything that was disclosed in a group session. "No sharing case histories or anecdotes, even with their spouses."

"Absolutely." While that might be difficult for the patients, they'd appreciate not having *their* personal details bandied about.

He also accepted her suggestions that they restrict participation to six to eight members, allow an hour and a half for each session, and schedule meetings on a weekday evening or on Saturdays. "Wednesday or Thursday nights are fine for me," Marshall said. "I reserve Saturdays for overflow surgeries."

Franca nodded. "I have a standing appointment at my private office on Wednesdays. Thursdays it is."

He entered the information in his calendar. "Anything else?"

"We should encourage a minimum of three sessions." Franca steepled her fingers. That, coupled with the fact that she'd worn glasses today rather than contacts, added to her remote air.

"Okay."

She closed the file in her computer. "May I ask you a question?"

Maybe they'd finally discuss something other than rules and schedules. "Shoot."

"What persuaded you to go ahead with this?" Her amber gaze skimmed his face. "Was it Dr. Tartikoff?"

While he'd hoped to learn what was bugging her, Marshall responded gamely. "A patient requested a surgical follow-up, not for medical reasons but because of personal concerns. When I mentioned this group, he expressed interest." To be candid, he clarified, "Guarded interest."

Franca smiled for the first time that morning. "How precise you are."

"And you, today." Marshall decided to press on. "Is everything all right?"

"What do you mean?"

Her defensive tone signaled him to back off. Instead, he said, "You were understandably upset when we ran into your…" How should he refer to a child who was no longer in her care? "Into Jazz. Is she okay?"

Franca's hands formed fists on the desk. "I'm not privy to that information."

A surge of protectiveness spurred Marshall to continue. "I'm glad you don't have to deal with that lout, the boyfriend. Although I suppose dealing with unsavory characters goes with the territory."

"Which territory?"

"Getting involved with dysfunctional families."

"I suppose it does."

Marshall had never seen her this frosty, nor experienced such a strong desire to push past another person's boundaries. "Surely there are experienced foster parents in a better position to deal with people like that. And group homes, although I don't suppose those are appropriate for such a young child."

"Marshall." Franca's eyes narrowed. "I'm well aware that you never approved of my plans to be a foster mom. There's no need to beat a dead horse."

"That's not my intent." He hated being misunderstood, especially by her. "I'm trying to…" Marshall stopped. He'd been about to say, "protect you."

What right did he have to do that? Judging by her current anger, he gathered her answer would be "none."

"To do what?" Franca prompted.

"Never mind." He rose, towering over her. "I can't expect to get through to you."

She leaped up to her full height, which was eight or nine inches shorter than his. "You're the most infuriating, arrogant man I ever met."

"Seriously?' he retorted. "As bad as all that?"

"Worse."

They glared at each other for about five seconds.

Marshall wasn't sure which of them crumbled first, but suddenly they were laughing. He had no idea what struck him as so funny, except that this was a ridiculous argument between two people who'd always known they were opposites

"Well," Franca said when she regained control of herself. "That cleared the air."

"Are you sure you can work with such an infuriating man?" Marshall quirked an eyebrow.

"Guess I'll have to."

"Suits me. Oh, I'd appreciate if you'd email me a rough draft of our proposal," he said.

"Will do." Franca's mouth twisted ruefully. "I've heard that once Dr. T gets a bee in his bonnet, he expects results pronto."

The notion of Owen Tartikoff wearing a bonnet brought another chuckle. "Let's not provoke the great man any more than necessary." Marshall reached across the desk, and they shook hands. It felt strange, as he wanted to give her a hug. Perhaps it was fortunate she'd kept a barrier between them.

On his way out, Marshall caught a speculative glance

from Franca's assistant in the outer office, who must have heard their loud voices.

An unusual-looking woman with black hair and dramatic bone structure, she was named Maggie Mejia Majors, according to her nameplate. "How alliterative," he said.

"I beg your pardon?"

"Your names all start with the same letter." What was wrong with him? He never joked with strangers. "Have a nice day."

"You, too, Doctor."

If he weren't careful, Marshall reflected, he might soften his edges and become less arrogant. Then what would he and Franca quarrel about?

SHARING A LAUGH with Marshall might have eased their friction, but Franca remained wary of him. In any area other than their professions, they were impossibly far apart.

As if she weren't upset enough already, her attorney stopped by a few days later to report that he'd received a disturbing call from Bridget.

"She claims you influenced Jazz against her." Edmond Everhart's shirt was neatly pressed beneath his tailored suit, and his tie was smoothly knotted, as usual. A family attorney, he consulted at the medical center twice a week, advising patients and staff in areas outside the expertise of the regular hospital attorney. She'd also hired him as her private counsel to deal with the adoption.

"I did no such thing." Franca bristled at the accusation. "After she consented to the adoption, I naturally began treating Jazz as my own child, but I never spoke ill of her mother."

"I believe you." Normally, Franca found Edmond's calm manner reassuring. Today, she wasn't sure anything would have eased her temper. "The issue seems to be her boyfriend. She contends that Jazz is rude to him."

"Rude? He was yanking her around!" At the attorney's startled expression, Franca explained about running into them at the café. "I wouldn't be surprised if he's an ex-con or a gang member. Or both."

"You're probably right." Edmond studied her sympathetically. The father of four-month-old triplets, he also had custody of his eight-year-old niece, Dawn, while his sister served a prison sentence for robbery. His expertise with children of prisoners had been extremely valuable. "If Bridget were on parole, fraternizing with a felon would be a violation. But since her conviction was thrown out, she can associate with anyone she chooses."

"I'm not trying to send Bridget to prison, anyway," Franca said. "What specifically did she say?"

"That Jazz throws tantrums and refuses to call him Daddy," Edmond replied. "I have the impression she's torn between protecting her daughter and pleasing her boyfriend."

"What did you tell her?" Franca asked.

"That it's normal for a child to act up when she's removed from her usual care provider. She cooled down when she heard that. Mostly, she probably just wanted to vent." When his cell jingled, Edmond checked the readout. "I have to take this. But I wanted to inform you that I'd heard from her."

"Thanks for keeping me posted."

During the next few weeks, there was no further word about Jazz. That didn't relieve Franca's anxiety, but she struggled to steer her mind to other subjects so she didn't drive herself crazy.

With Marshall's input, she polished the therapy group proposal. The administrator and the directors of the fertility and men's programs approved it with minor changes. After Jennifer put out the word in the newsletter, referrals began arriving. The start date was set for late April.

Concerned about her older sister, Franca called Gail. Her sister commiserated about Jazz, inquired about Franca's new job and chatted about her husband, an electrician, whom Gail assisted in his business. She didn't bring up any medical issues, and Franca was too tactful to ask. Best to let Gail choose what and when she was willing to share.

Mid-April arrived, and with it the day of Zady and Nick's wedding, scheduled for 4:00 p.m. on a Saturday. It dawned cloudy with a chance of sprinkles, but the weather cleared by the afternoon.

Franca chose a pink dress with a matching print jacket. As she finished applying her makeup, her gaze fell on the last remnant of the blue bridesmaid's gown draped over the sewing machine table. Funny, she'd felt through Belle's entire wedding that Marshall was an unseen presence on the sidelines.

He'd be part of his brother's ceremony today, of course, but his best-man duties ought to keep him busy. There'd be little risk of personal interaction.

Just consider him a casual acquaintance. He wasn't involved in Franca's struggle to figure out whether she dared risk a pregnancy. Although the possibility of remaining childless haunted her, common sense warned her to be realistic. Then there was just plain fear. She'd gone so far as to scan Safe Harbor's computerized material on sperm donors, but whenever Franca started to schedule a consultation, her mind tortured her with scenarios of collapsing in agony, alone in her apartment.

For heaven's sake, she was about to attend a celebration. *Relax and have fun.*

The Seaside Wedding Chapel was perched on the bluffs above the harbor. Inside, a smiling woman handed Franca a printed program. The hum of voices and the tinkling of piano music greeted her as she stepped into the chapel.

Zady had kept the floral arrangements modest, preferring for guests to bask in the glorious view from the arched windows. The sight of colorful sailboats and, beyond the harbor, the blue sweep of the Pacific Ocean refreshed Franca's spirit.

While she was debating where to sit, two women gestured to her. She recognized them as nurses in Marshall's office who worked with Zady. The tall, thin one was Jeanine, Franca recalled, and the short, round woman was Ines.

She slid into a chair beside them, happy to join their banter. They volunteered that they'd leaped at the chance to leave their spouses home with the kids.

"My husband finds weddings boring," Ines said.

"Mine, too," Jeanine added. "Even our wedding, I suspect. Not the honeymoon, though."

"Speaking of honeymoons, any idea where Nick and Zady are going?" Franca asked.

"Las Vegas," Ines piped up.

"For a long weekend," Jeanine said.

A movement near the altar caught Franca's attention. The groom and his brother had emerged, a pair of strikingly handsome men in tuxedos with a mini look-alike trailing solemnly in their wake as the ring bearer.

A murmur ran through the crowd. "Isn't that boy cute?" Ines said.

"He's a doll," her fellow nurse agreed.

"Here we left our kids at home and we're drooling over someone else's child," Ines observed.

"Yes, but my sons don't wear tuxedos and resemble little movie stars," Jeanine said.

"I'll bet you a box of doughnuts he'll spill something on that tux at dinner."

"You're on. Any excuse for doughnuts."

Their banter barely penetrated Franca's awareness. It wasn't Caleb, darling as he was, who transfixed her.

Despite the resemblance between the brothers, Marshall stood out, with his erect stance and chiseled features. Everything about him evoked memories of his tenderness, his annoyance, his humor and his vulnerability.

She'd missed him these past weeks, more than she'd been willing to admit. Since he'd reappeared in her life, he'd become increasingly important to her. And her feelings had only grown stronger because of the recent distance.

Franca realized with a start that she was perilously close to crossing a dangerous line. She had to keep in mind, especially with a man as stiff-necked as Marshall, that however close you might become, ultimately you could only depend on yourself.

Chapter Seven

Marshall envied Nick's easy manner as they stood in front of the assembly. Any public appearance was uncomfortable for him, even accepting an honor. He couldn't escape the notion that he had a stain on his jacket or was about to blurt something idiotic.

You're here to support the groom, not obsess about your appearance.

Staring toward the far wall, he reviewed his ideas for the obligatory toast later this evening. He hadn't decided whether to bring up the fact that they'd recently discovered they were brothers, which would upset his mother. Yet he could hardly refer to Nick as his cousin.

When Marshall's gaze shifted toward his mother, Mildred Davis averted her face. It hurt that she refused to acknowledge him, for her sake as well as his. At seventy-two, she had few friends or relatives. It wasn't healthy to be so isolated.

Abruptly, he became aware of Franca. Wedged between two nurses from his office, she appeared to be listening intently to their conversation. Just knowing she was among the guests helped him to relax.

Marshall wasn't sure why she'd rigorously kept her distance over the past few weeks while they finalized plans for their group, communicating only by email and text. The loss of her daughter was obviously painful, and he supposed his tactless comment about foster parenting still rankled. But she'd always handled their differences with composure in the past.

The pianist finished her rendition of "We've Only Just Begun" and segued to the traditional wedding march. At the entrance appeared a little girl of about three, wearing a rose-colored dress tied with a gold sash and carrying a basket. Marshall smiled at the bride's goddaughter, Linda, whom he'd become fond of during the weeks she'd stayed with Zady.

Linda trotted forward, tossing handfuls of rose petals at the crowd, until she reached the halfway point. There she stopped, panic spreading over her features as if she'd suddenly noticed all the people staring at her.

Where was Zora, the matron of honor? She should have been right behind Linda, prepared to take her hand if needed.

The groom frowned toward the empty doorway as if willing Zady or her sister to appear. Naturally, he didn't want to risk spoiling the bride's big moment by intervening, but someone ought to act.

In the middle of a row, Linda's parents leaned forward uncertainly, also reluctant to intercede. Marshall whispered a request to Caleb, since the child was a natural choice to fetch his fellow Lilliputian, but the boy shook his head.

Might as well make a fool of himself for a good cause, Marshall mused. Up the aisle he strode and bent to take Linda's hand.

"Uncle Marsh!" With a cry, she flung herself into his arms and buried her face in his shoulder. Amid sympathetic chuckles from the crowd, he carried her to the altar.

As he lowered her to the ground, Marshall glimpsed Franca staring longingly at the child. Tears glittered on her cheeks.

She must be thinking of Jazz. It hadn't occurred to him what emotions the sight of a little girl might evoke. Then Franca gave him a shaky, approving smile that warmed him right down to his uncomfortably stiff shoes.

At the end of the aisle, the matron of honor entered belatedly in a swirl of dark pink. Judging by Zora's limp, the cause of the delay must be a hurt foot or ankle.

When she reached the altar, Linda scooted to join her. The music shifted to a familiar bridal melody and an excited rustle ran through the chapel.

The bride floated into view, radiant in a cream-colored gown and a hat trimmed with roses. She held the arm of her brother-in-law, Zora's husband, Lucky Mendez, who was grinning from ear to ear.

The lone sour note was the bride's pinch-faced mother, seated in the front row. At last night's rehearsal, she'd complained loudly about her last-minute invitation, while her husband glowered at everyone. Zady had explained earlier that her manipulative mother had lied to them for years, pitting her and Zora against each other so she could hold center stage. Today, Marshall hoped her grimace at the bridal party went unnoticed by the other guests.

When Lucky relinquished the bride to Nick, Marshall slipped the ring to Caleb. The three-year-old promptly handed it to his father.

"I helped pick it out for my new mom," he announced loudly. Appreciative chuckles rippled through the chapel.

"It was the sparkliest one we could find," Nick said.

"Yeah." His son beamed.

As the ceremony flew by, Marshall's chest squeezed. *My kid brother's getting married.* Too bad he hadn't known they were brothers while they were growing up. Their rivalry might have been less abrasive.

He still wasn't sure how to frame his toast. Well, if all else failed, he'd simply wish the bride and groom a long and happy life together. Boring, but safe.

After the exchange of vows, the minister introduced them as the new Dr. and Mrs. Davis, to the crowd's applause. With the children right behind, Zora and Nick strolled up the aisle, followed by Marshall with a limping Zady on his arm.

"Twist your ankle?" he asked.

"Damn shoes," she muttered. "The men who design high heels must be sadists."

"What about the women who buy them?"

"They're airheads," she responded cheerily. "Like me."

When they passed Franca, Marshall shot her a concerned glance. Her sadness had vanished, however, and she met his gaze with a friendly nod.

After the ceremony, the guests didn't have far to go: there was a ballroom connected to the wedding chapel. Decorated in rose and gold, the room was set up with round tables, a dance floor and long tables at the side for the food. Covered catering dishes indicated that dinner would soon be served.

The photographer had taken family and bridal party shots the previous evening, since Zady didn't wish to keep her guests waiting. She'd also ruled out a receiving line, thus avoiding the thorny problem of whether to include her mother and stepfather in it, as well as the groom's father. Uncle Quentin had attended, but kept a low profile befitting a man who'd abandoned Nick in childhood.

The waitstaff began to circulate with trays of hors d'oeuvres and wine, and Marshall helped himself. He still felt uncomfortable, and keeping his hands full eased his awkwardness. Rather than risk driving after drinking even a small amount, he'd walked to the chapel from his house, less than a mile from here along the bluffside road, and planned to either walk home or call a cab.

Around him, the guests mingled. Many said hello to him, but no one stopped to talk. As for Franca, she stuck close to the nurses.

How fortunate she was, to form attachments easily. Marshall hadn't left any close pals behind when he moved back to California from Ohio, nor had he reconnected with friends from high school or college. His mother was far from the only Davis who lived in isolation, he realized.

Speaking of isolation, Marshall spotted Uncle Quentin lingering uncertainly on the fringes of the gathering. Tall and bony, he'd had his graying brown hair trimmed and held a water glass rather than wine.

It was still hard to think of the man as his father. Upton Davis might have been a workaholic, with rigid expectations for his son, but he'd stuck by his family and provided for them, in contrast to his younger brother. However, Quentin deserved credit for finally seeking treatment for his bipolar disorder and for joining Alcoholics Anonymous.

Marshall sought out his designated spot at the wedding party's table. Zady had agonized over the seating chart, finally putting her mother and stepfather with Caleb's grandparents and Linda's parents. She'd taken care to position Marshall's mother far away from Quentin.

"I just hope my mom doesn't get drunk and act rowdy," she'd said during a break at the office.

"Maybe you should hire an armed guard," Marshall had joked.

"Too expensive," she'd said. "I'll keep a hypodermic handy in case she requires sedating."

"Want a prescription?"

She'd laughed.

Smiling at the memory, Marshall slid into a chair alongside his brother.

Having the ring bearer and flower girl with them added to the wedding party's high spirits. Once dinner was served, Zady and Zora helped the children fill their plates and tuck in their napkins.

Linda ate daintily, while Caleb stayed neat until, for no discernible reason, he poured orange juice down his front. At Franca's table, Marshall saw Ines and Jeanine high-five each other, then enter into a joking dispute featuring the word "doughnuts." Apparently there'd been a bet but neither could recall who won.

Franca settled it with a word and a grin. She seemed to have loosened up since her earlier distress, and she soon joined her companions' giggling. Marshall wished he'd invited her as his plus-one; if she'd accepted, she'd be sitting beside him.

Nick leaned closer. "Do I detect an interest in a certain person?"

"We're old friends," Marshall responded.

"I'm surrounded by old friends. I somehow manage to tear my eyes off them," the groom responded.

Marshall searched in vain for a clever retort. In truth,

he wasn't sure why every man in the room, aside from Nick, wasn't staring at Franca, whose soft pink outfit enhanced her natural glow.

"No smart reply? Wow. You *are* besotted," said his brother.

"Merely appreciative."

"Smooth answer," Nick said. "I wish I had your— what's the word—suaveness?"

"Or savoir faire," Marshall said.

"No normal person uses words like that."

Marshall regarded his brother in surprise. "With your exceptional memory, I'd assume your vocabulary would outstrip mine." His brother had indicated at family gatherings that he almost never had to study. In high school, Nick's easy cruise to academic honors had made Marshall question his own abilities, considering how hard he struggled with some subjects.

Nick ducked his head. "I have a confession."

"I'm all ears."

His brother shrugged. "My memory's pretty good, but I studied like a dog."

"Seriously?" In retrospect, Marshall supposed Nick's bragging had produced the desired effect—stemming his aunt and uncle's criticisms of his sloppy grooming and goof-off reputation. "I don't blame you for exaggerating, the way my parents put you down."

"They were hard on you, too," the groom said. "Damn hard."

"Yes, they were." Marshall had never been successful enough for them. Even though he'd become a National Merit Finalist, that had meant nothing when Nick had been named a scholarship winner. As for Marshall's grades, they'd all been As except for Bs in calculus and Spanish. When his father learned that Nick had earned straight As, he'd tossed Marshall's report card back without comment. His flared nostrils had spoken louder than words.

Did he wish they'd adopted the younger boy? It hurt like hell to think neither Upton nor Mildred had truly loved him because he wasn't perfect.

But why keep fighting a battle he could never win? His tension dissipated.

And, on the plus side, he'd just figured out what to say in his toast.

WHEN FRANCA ACCEPTED the wedding invitation, her focus had been on supporting Zady on her happy day and sharing the event with her colleagues. The sight of the adorable flower girl paralyzed in the middle of the aisle, however, had struck her with a rush of pain.

Where was Jazz right this minute? Was she suffering the same panic and fear, with far more reason than little Linda? Who would help her, when Franca was barred from intervening?

Marshall's actions had stirred her admiration. Not only because he made a handsome knight, riding to the little girl's rescue, but because he'd told Franca long ago of his anxiety at public events.

What a great father he'd be. For his ideal child, of course.

She snapped back to the present as a waiter handed her champagne for a toast. The tinkle of a spoon against a water glass drew everyone's attention to the head table, where Marshall got to his feet. "Someone mentioned that the best man is supposed to say something," he deadpanned.

Smiles greeted his comment. Not from Mildred

Davis at the next table, however. Franca had met Marshall's mother at campus events, and had found her cold. Tonight, the woman was subzero.

"Isn't Dr. Davis handsome in a tux?" Jeanine said.

"If I weren't married, I'd grab him," Ines agreed.

Franca stared straight ahead, wishing the crowd and her companions would settle down so Marshall could get this over with. Yet he didn't appear nervous, she was pleased to note.

"Not everyone here is aware that Nicholas and I were raised as cousins." Marshall spoke steadily. "We were rivals in high school, and frankly, we didn't much care for each other."

Somewhere, a piece of cutlery fell to the floor with a clink. In the silence, it sounded loud as a gunshot.

"Recently, we learned that we are actually brothers," Marshall continued. From the corner of her eye, Franca saw Mildred Davis's mouth open in a gasp.

"It's been said that you can pick your office nurse but you can't pick your relatives," Marshall joked. "Well, I picked Zady as my nurse and I'd do it again in a heartbeat." The bride beamed at him. "As for Nicholas, I'm glad he's my brother, and he's now my friend, too. I wish I'd learned the truth sooner. Here's to Zady and Nicholas and their future as a family."

He raised his glass to cries of "Hear, hear!" Amid the stir as everyone drank, Mildred hurried from the room.

Although most guests probably assumed Mrs. Davis was obeying an urgent call of nature, Marshall's jaw clenched. He stood, glass in hand, for a long moment.

The matron of honor started to rise for her toast, but Marshall signaled Zora with a "wait" gesture. "One more thing," he said.

Everyone quieted.

"It's come to my attention that the couple's ideal honeymoon trip would involve traveling to…what was it?" Marshall pretended to search his memory. "Death Valley? Antarctica? Chernobyl?"

Judging by the confusion on Nick's and Zady's faces, they had no idea what came next. Neither did Franca.

"Oh, yes, Italy." Marshall regarded his brother and sister-in-law. "I realize you have something planned for the next few days, but my gift to you guys is a trip to Italy whenever you have time to enjoy it at your leisure."

"You already gave us a houseful of towels," Zady blurted.

"That was to throw you off the scent," Marshall replied.

"Incredible," Nick said. "That's fantastic, bro."

"Double for me," Zady said. "Thank you!"

Zora sprang to her feet. "Lucky and I can't afford to send you to Italy, but we'll take care of our wonderful new nephew while you're gone. Here's to Nick, Zady and Caleb!"

She raised her glass, and everyone sipped. The bubbly tasted so delicious that Franca accepted a refill.

Her companions did the same. "Our husbands are picking us up," Jeanine announced. "Keep the champagne flowing."

"What's that Dorothy Parker quote?" Ines giggled. "'Three drinks and I'm under the table. Four drinks and I'm under the host.'"

"Someone ought to be under Dr. Davis," Jeanine said. "Not the married Dr. Davis. *Our* Dr. Davis."

"Considering how he keeps peeking at someone at our table, I know who it should be," Ines murmured.

Franca's cheeks felt hot. "I'm not sure why. He had

his chance years ago, but he bypassed me to date my college roommate."

Jeanine seized on the comment. "Who dumped who?"

"He dumped her," Franca said.

"Why?"

"Not brilliant enough to meet his high standards. She struggled with her grades and had to drop a class." Belle had never claimed to be the best student around, especially with the intense academic competition at UC Berkeley, and her goal of graduating early had been for *his* benefit.

"That was it? She couldn't match his level of genius?"

Franca tried to recall exactly what Belle had told her. "He was leaving for medical school at Harvard and she'd planned to graduate early so they wouldn't be separated too long. When she couldn't keep up, he broke it off."

"Maybe he had her best interests at heart."

"That wasn't her impression," Franca said. "And speaking of hearts, it shattered hers. They were practically engaged."

Mercifully, Ines changed the subject. "That was quite a gift he gave Zady and Nick."

"I heard his father left him a bundle," Jeanine said.

"It was still very generous."

"Excuse me. I need to walk around." Her friends were growing tipsy and their remarks becoming more and more personal.

Franca rose too quickly, and had to wait for her champagne-infused body to steady itself. If she stopped drinking now, she hoped to be sober enough to drive in a few hours.

Since there hadn't been a receiving line, this seemed

the right moment to offer her best wishes to the bride and groom before they started dancing.

A lanky man with thinning gray-brown hair reached them first. "Sorry about Mildred," he said. "I'd have pinned her to her seat, but I doubt she'd have appreciated it. Especially from me."

"It's okay, Dad." Nick clapped the man's arm.

So this was Marshall's birth father. Despite a similarity of height and bone structure, he was strikingly different from his older brother, Marshall's adoptive father, whom Franca had met in college. Upton Sinclair had held himself with pride, his shoulders straight, his thick hair a distinguished shade of silver.

"I feel responsible for the disruption." The newcomer addressed his sons. "Can you forgive me for shooting my mouth off?"

The mixed emotions on Marshall's face resolved into a smile. "If not for you, Uncle Quentin, I wouldn't know Zora was my sister-in-law and Caleb was my nephew. I wouldn't be best man at Nicholas's wedding, either."

"You can stop calling me Nicholas," his brother put in. "It sounds too formal."

"Okay, Nicky."

"On second thought, Nicholas is fine."

"Done."

She registered the exact moment when Marshall spotted her. The light in the room brightened, and warmth flowed over her skin.

"Quentin, there's someone I'd like you to meet." Moving to her, Marshall slipped his arm around her waist. "This is Dr. Brightman, our staff psychologist and an old friend of mine. Franca, this my birth father."

"My pleasure." The glint in Quentin's eyes as they

shook hands indicated he guessed there was more to this relationship. But then, the arm encircling her waist told everyone the same.

Franca wondered at Marshall's show of intimacy. Was this a couple of glasses of champagne speaking, or something more? And did she want it to be?

The pounding in her chest might mean almost anything. *Oh, stop kidding yourself.* No matter where this led, for tonight she and Marshall belonged in each other's company.

Beside the dance floor, the DJ took the microphone. "Dr. and Mrs. Nick Davis, how about you lead off the dancing?"

Zady gave a happy little hop. "This is my Cinderella moment! I've been dreaming about this."

Her new husband sketched a bow. "Milady, may I have the honor?"

"Let's go, my prince." Taking his elbow, she tugged him forward.

People gathered to watch the couple swooping around the floor to a romantic waltz. At a gesture from Zady, her sister and Lucky joined them.

Marshall removed his arm from Franca's waist. "May I have this dance?"

Her breath caught. She responded with a low, "I'd be delighted."

Taking her hand, he escorted her into the thickening crowd of dancers. It might be simply a waltz, but there was nothing ordinary about her reaction as Marshall held her close. They'd never had this much physical contact. Their bodies touched, their hands clasped, and an electric current coursed between them as they moved in sync.

Judging by his cheek brushing her hair and his grip tightening around her, Marshall shared her reaction. If this was a mistake, Franca longed to keep right on making it.

And tonight, she suspected she would.

Chapter Eight

Even though Marshall was aware he'd provoked his mother, her fury as she'd stalked from the room troubled him. But it also freed him to be generous with his inherited money in a manner she'd have resented.

What a pleasure to bring joy to Nick and Zady. As for his reservations about Quentin, they'd vanished. Without his birth father's revelation, as Marshall had stated earlier, he'd have missed being best man at this event.

His newfound sense of liberation extended to dancing with Franca, who seemed to have overcome whatever had been keeping her at bay, too. As he held her in his arms, the fresh scent of her hair filled him, and the music wrapped them in a private world. They melted together, and an unfamiliar happiness swelled within Marshall.

Their basic differences hadn't changed. Yet he prized this rare chance to have fun with the only person he could truly be himself with.

The music shifted to a Latin beat. He flowed with its seductive rhythm, and Franca moved with him as if they'd practiced it.

"I had no idea you were such a skillful dancer," she murmured. "Belle said you had two left feet."

Poor Belle! He'd always been tense with her, striving to match her perfection. "I was clumsy because I was trying too hard."

"And with me, you don't have to?"

"With you I'm…" He nearly said "home." Instead, he finished with "…comfortable."

"I'm glad." Quickly, she added, "I'm not sure my feet could take the punishment."

Their swift movements cut off further conversation. Soon, as the rhythm increased, they were both fast-stepping and breathing hard. Others paused to watch them, a development Marshall could have done without.

The music segued into a slower song. He and Franca were adjusting to the pace when people began staring off to the right and sneaking pictures with their phones. Peering over them, Marshall saw Caleb and Linda dancing in a classic waltz position. Both preschoolers wore earnest expressions as Caleb counted aloud: "*One* two three, *one* two three."

Franca stood on tiptoe to watch. "Oh! How cute."

"Priceless." *I wish they were our children.* Or rather, he meant, *my* children. Didn't he?

After a minute, Marshall tugged her into his embrace again. Time faded from awareness as they followed the changing patterns of the music. When other men cut in, Marshall squelched a flare of annoyance. But as the best man, he had other duties. He danced with the bride, the matron of honor and the bride's mother. Red-faced and with a tendency to giggle, Zady's mom, Delilah, brought uncoordinated energy to her dancing. Marshall was glad to relinquish her to her husband.

Another musical transition led to a rock song with the screaming lyrics, "I can't take it anymore!" Startled, Marshall caught Franca's gaze across the floor.

He'd been distraught that night in the parking garage,

wrenched by his mother's rejection. Catching Franca similarly howling had struck him as oddly reassuring. Now they made their way toward each other.

"They're playing our song." Franca draped her arms over his shoulders.

"Feeling better?" He encircled her waist.

"Better than what?"

"That night."

"No comparison." She swayed against him. Although everyone else was gyrating wildly, it was obvious to him that this was a love song.

"I'm six inches off the floor," Franca said. "I drank too much champagne."

"Weddings are magical." Marshall spoke close to her ear. "We could dance all the way home."

"Not me. I have a half-hour drive."

The music stopped. Into his mic, the DJ said, "I'm informed that the bride and groom are about to cut the cake. Don't miss getting your slice!"

People pushed by. Why were they in such a rush? The towering cake took up an entire side table. Did they believe it would run out?

The surging crowd made the room stuffy. Through the large side windows, the night appeared cool and inviting.

"Do you want dessert?" he asked. "Or would you rather take a walk?"

"A walk sounds lovely. Maybe it will clear my head."

After detouring for Franca to collect her purse, Marshall guided her outside. The only person who appeared to notice their departure was Nick, facing them at the cake table with the guests pressing around it. He winked.

Marshall supposed he might be criticized for abandoning his best-man duties, but he'd completed most of them. Besides, if the groom didn't care, why should he?

Marshall wasn't usually one to flout the rules. Now he was ready to crash through a thicket of them.

FROM THE BLUFFS, palm trees screened Franca's view of the sparkling harbor. A fresh breeze filled her lungs, although rather than sobering her, its invigorating effect added to her sense of unreality. She could almost fly, not that she was foolish enough to attempt it.

The scene dissolved her hurt and uncertainty. For tonight, she didn't care that Marshall was too judgmental to rely on as she navigated through an uncertain future. His tender side was exactly what she needed at the moment, so why not enjoy herself?

Marshall's arm anchored her as they strolled along the walkway. When they stopped at an overlook facing the ocean, the music resumed from the wedding chapel, muted but loud enough to serve as a melodic undercurrent. Below, light twinkled from a yacht cruising toward its mooring.

"Some evenings I can hear the music from the wedding chapel on my balcony." Leaning on the rail, Marshall's lean body shielded her from a gust of wind.

"You live that close?"

"Right there." He gestured across the street toward a two-story home atop a rise. With its columns and the lacy trim beneath the eaves, the architecture brought to mind New Orleans.

"On the ocean? That must have cost a fortune!" Franca felt her face growing hot despite the breeze. "I'm sorry. That's the champagne talking."

"It cost a totally unreasonable amount," Marshall said. "But my father left me enough to invest and still buy my dream home. Now all I need is…" The words trailed off.

…*a family to fill it.* She understood. "I've never imagined my dream home."

His low chuckle rumbled through her. "How can you not imagine it, if it's your dream?"

"I'm too befuddled to untangle that sentence."

"Let me simplify," Marshall said. "What kind of house appeals to you?"

"A comfortable one. Warm colors, and a large kitchen." She'd grown up in a modest house with gingerbread-style trim and furniture that, while solid, was so worn that her mother had eventually thrown it out because the thrift shops wouldn't take it. But what had mattered were the gleeful interchanges around the dinner table, and the abundant laughter. "I never fantasized about Prince Charming or the perfect wedding, either."

"How did you and Belle become roommates?" His teeth gleamed in the darkness. "You're totally different."

"The college housing office paired us." They must have seemed similar on paper. Both had been nonsmokers who went to bed early, and they'd been focused on earning their degrees, hers in psychology, Belle's in business administration. "We had a lot in common."

"You could have fooled me." Marshall shook his head. "When she described in detail her plans for her wedding, right down to the cake decorations, I thought I'd strayed into the twilight zone. We hadn't even discussed marriage."

"Is that why you…" Realizing she had no right to pry into his reasons for the breakup, Franca switched to, "Did they include bridesmaid's dresses big enough to eat Chicago?"

He chuckled. "Accurate description." He'd viewed the photo on her phone, she recalled. "It's cold. May I entice you to enjoy the view from my house, madam? Perhaps with a glass of wine?"

"I'm already giddy," she protested, but weakly. It *did* sound like fun.

"You can sleep it off in my guest bedroom," Marshall offered.

Her answer ought to be a resounding no. Instead, Franca replied, "You're just showing off."

"How so?"

"Bachelors don't have guest bedrooms, they have couches," she said.

"There's a couch in my study." Against the moonlight, Marshall formed a muscular silhouette. "But you'd be more comfortable in one of the spare bedrooms."

Franca slapped his arm. "Spare bedrooms, plural? Now I *know* you're bragging."

"In the morning, I'll cook you breakfast in my catering-size kitchen," Marshall continued.

"Why not have your chef do it?"

"The upstairs maid could serve you breakfast in bed." He frowned. "Or would that be the butler's job?"

"Tell me you're kidding!"

"The cleaning crew mucks the house out twice a month," Marshall assured her. "That's the sum total of my staff."

"Don't you rattle around in your mansion?" Franca's curiosity was growing.

"I only bought it a few months ago," Marshall protested. "I've hardly had time to rattle. Or throw parties and create happy memories."

How different he sounded from the guy she remem-

bered from their university years. "You have a senti-
mental side."

"That surprises you?"

"It makes you dangerous." Had she actually said that
aloud?

"You *have* to explain that comment." Taking her arm,
Marshall continued their walk, heading away from the
wedding chapel. When she stumbled on a rough patch
of concrete, he caught her by the waist.

"I can't explain it," Franca said. "I'm not sure what
I meant."

That was a lie. The truth was that a tenderhearted
Marshall threatened her determination to keep him at
bay. Which she hadn't done very well this evening,
had she?

"I'd better head home," she concluded.

"You may not be sober enough to drive," he pointed
out.

"This from the man who just offered me a glass of
wine?"

"And the use of his guest room."

Franca yearned to tour his mansion and to watch this
very masculine man cook breakfast for her. Even though
she was almost certain it was the champagne addling
her brain, she said, "I am a little curious."

"I promise you, the sheets are clean." Marshall halted
at a crosswalk.

"You have guests often?" Franca asked as they
waited.

"Only one so far. Reid—Dr. Winfrey—stayed with
me for a few nights after he arrived from New York,"
Marshall said. "Since he didn't own a car, it was con-
venient for him to ride with me until he got situated."

"That was kind of you."

He shrugged. "Professional courtesy."

The signal changed and they crossed. Nearing the house, Franca saw that what she'd glimpsed so far was actually the back of the house. A concrete staircase led up a rise and around to the front.

There, she discovered, the mansion faced a cul-de-sac. It served a handful of similarly large homes, each with a unique design.

"My first sight of this place gave me pause." Marshall escorted her up the front steps to a broad porch. "I'd been living in hole-in-the-wall apartments, and I'd planned on buying something simpler. But I figured it would be a good investment."

"That's it?" Franca waited as he unlocked the door and deactivated the alarm. "It didn't grab your heart and refuse to let go?"

"That, too." He flicked a switch in the entrance hall. Overhead, a stained-glass chandelier cast amber and green light over the slate-tile floor.

The interior unrolled one delight after another: the spacious living room decorated in shades of aqua and peach, a dining room with a parquet oak table, a study that doubled as a workout room, the family room with big-screen TV—they were better than a showroom because Marshall's spirit infused them.

Nothing prepared her for the kitchen, though. From the oversize cooktop to the double ovens, the built-in refrigerator and walk-in pantry, it would make any caterer catch her breath. Every surface, every window treatment, every lighting fixture contributed to an aura of welcome. Meals would taste better just by being fixed here.

Franca was almost embarrassed by her reaction.

She'd never coveted wealth. But she could scarcely bear to live anywhere else after touring this place.

She searched for a neutral comment. "It's stunning. I'd pictured you in someplace more formal."

"Straight-backed chairs, dark woods and dim sconces?" Leaning against the center island, Marshall quirked an eyebrow. "That describes my parents' house."

A question occurred to her that might ease her sense of being caught up inside his personal realm. "Did you buy it already decorated?"

"The bones were here, but it was far too gloomy," he said. "I worked closely with a designer."

She sighed. "In spite of what I said, it suits you."

"Does it suit *you*?"

Caught off guard, Franca blurted, "I love every inch of it."

Marshall grinned. At ease in his palace, the rangy, rather stiff young man of their younger years had come into his own.

Franca had never experienced such longing around a man, despite the fact that they were spectacularly wrong for each other. Could she truly blame the champagne?

"I should go to bed." She nearly added *alone*, except that might reveal how tempted she was to do otherwise.

"Let's head upstairs."

As they returned to the hall with its curving staircase, Franca sensed that this was her last chance to assert a measure of common sense and beat a safe retreat. Sleeping here, even in a separate room, posed a huge risk. But she'd never felt more protected and sheltered than in Marshall's care.

Her feet barely touched the surface as she made her way up the stairs.

WHEN THE REAL estate agent had lured Marshall inside this house, there'd been a phantom along on the tour. Not that the house was haunted; rather, he'd sensed a woman's reactions.

His future wife, he'd assumed. Didn't everyone carry on conversations with "air people," folks who weren't actually there but who commented or argued in one's head? His usual air people were his parents, constantly criticizing and correcting his actions. But the person in his head when he'd viewed the house, he finally conceded, had been Franca.

Tonight, she more than matched her phantom alter ego, greeting each room with an exclamation. Marshall was proud of the smallest touches: the crown molding, the custom cabinetry, the embellished towels accenting the upstairs hall bathroom, and the low bookshelves and window seat in the room he'd mentally designated as a future playroom. Each cry of admiration was like a caress.

In the doorway to the master suite, Franca stopped ahead of him and inhaled deeply.

"Is anything wrong?" Marshall asked.

"It smells like you," she murmured.

Not the response he'd hoped for. "I assure you, I shower frequently."

"It's a good smell. But it's late, I should head to my own room." She turned abruptly and ran into his chest.

Marshall's arms closed around her. He could feel her heart racing.

She pulled away, and reluctantly, he released her. "Care to see the dressing room? It's equipped with a TV and a great sound system."

"I'd better not. I mean, no thanks." Her amber eyes blinked. "I'm afraid I'm not myself tonight."

She was entirely herself, in Marshall's opinion, the same intriguing person who'd drawn him magnetically fifteen years ago. He'd believed she was wrong for him, but tonight, she sparked magic in his bloodstream.

"Who else would you be?" he teased.

"I'll tell you after I've slept off the champagne." Franca scooted past him into the hall.

Despite his disappointment, Marshall respected her withdrawal. "Let's get you settled in the guest room."

"I'm not sure where it is."

He placed his palm on the small of her back to guide her. "You'll need towels. The linen closet is here, next to the bathroom."

Opening the closet door, he tugged on a china pull to turn on the light and reveal the neatly stacked sheets and towels. He selected a bath sheet along with smaller linens. "Okay?"

Franca smiled dreamily. "Just fine."

He couldn't resist pulling her against him, despite the armful of linens that formed a soft barrier. Their foreheads touched, and as they leaned toward each other, it seemed to Marshall that they completed an electrical circuit.

Or she might be falling asleep.

"The bedroom's just along here." After unloading the towels in the bathroom, he steered her into a peach-colored room with golden-yellow curtains and an oak bedstead. "I hope you'll feel at home. The bathroom's stocked with guest toiletries, but if there's anything lacking, just let me know."

Franca stared at him as if reaching a sudden conclusion. "Marshall."

"Yes?"

She caught him by his tuxedo lapels. "Do you have to be such a frustratingly perfect gentleman?"

"Is that what I am?" If only he had a clue about women. Especially her.

"Damn straight," she said, and tugged him toward the bed.

Chapter Nine

As she toured the house, Franca had become aware of an emotion unworthy of her: envy. Not of Marshall for owning this home, but of the woman who would some-day share it with him.

Why her, whoever she would be? Why had Belle been the lucky one in college, even if that hadn't ended happily? No matter how irrational it was, Franca ached to be selfish, just once. To take what *she* wanted instead of trying to recognize other people's wishes and help them come true.

Tonight, she wanted to act on impulse. To grab Marshall and watch his surprise turn to excitement. To feel his mouth claim hers. So she did.

She stood on tiptoe, her breasts rubbing his chest and her palms stroking his neck while her tongue played along his lips. A deep shudder ran through him, as if a dam had burst. His tux joined her print jacket on the floor and he swept her onto the bed.

Lifting himself on an elbow, Marshall probed her with his dark gaze. "Are you sure?" he asked.

"Aren't you?"

"More than I've ever been sure of anything."

"Then stop talking."

He kissed her again, gentleness shading into ferocity.

Franca treasured the whisper of Marshall's mouth trailing down her throat, the confidence of his hands as he released her dress, the joy of sharing her body with him.

She'd experienced nothing like this with the boyfriends who'd appeared briefly in her past. Why had she imagined Marshall was cold and distant? His passionate response thrilled her. And when he finally thrust deep inside her, Franca yielded to sensation.

Marshall withheld nothing, and neither did she. They became one wild creature, one glorious entity, one soul.

Everything else fell away.

MARSHALL HAD BOTH hoped for and feared the moment when he yielded to his desire for Franca and unleashed his long-suppressed recklessness. He'd always believed at some level that if he completely let go, he'd lose his direction, his purpose, and fail those he cared about. How absurd that struck him now.

The marvel was that Franca sought it as eagerly as he did. Her hands reached for him, her movements encouraged him, and her body invited him into a private dance.

The scent of her perfume intoxicated him; the touch of her skin thrilled him. Soaring together, they crested a giant wave and roared into free fall. Exultation obliterated the last limits of the familiar world.

For too long, Marshall had been caged, mistrusting every vulnerability. Now, a fresh vista unfolded, with Franca at its center.

Marshall held her close as they drifted to a far shore. He barely recovered enough awareness to pull the covers over them before sinking into blissful sleep.

FRANCA AWOKE IN the morning with the sense that she'd forgotten something important. But also that she'd done something wonderful and free.

Beside her under silky sheets lay the man she'd craved for years. Marshall's long body curved toward her, his tousled dark hair tickling her shoulder. In sleep, he had the openness of a young man. Had intimacy changed him, or was it her perceptions that had altered?

An ache at her temples reminded Franca that she'd had more to drink than usual last night. However, she couldn't blame her actions on the champagne. She'd chosen to sleep with Marshall, whatever the consequences.

He stirred. "Good morning." The brightness of his smile rivaled the sunshine glinting between the curtains.

"Hi." Now what? She shouldn't feel awkward, considering how well they knew each other. But in this context, they might as well be strangers.

"I promised to cook breakfast," Marshall murmured.

"That would be lovely." Franca still couldn't shake the notion that she'd been negligent somehow. Was it because she'd left her car at the wedding chapel? That didn't pose a problem; she could walk over to collect it. "Coffee first, please."

"You got it," he said. "I'll be downstairs in a minute." After planting a kiss on her nose, he arose, collected his tuxedo and departed. She missed him as soon as he was gone.

Rising, Franca reflected ruefully on an obvious omission: a change of clothes. She always carried a spare outfit in her car—a habit she'd started after a child client had thrown up on her. No point racing down the block for the clothes, though.

She took a shower and used a toothbrush and toothpaste from the basket of guest toiletries. Then she put on the same dress.

Franca was heading for the stairs when she passed a large, nearly empty room whose mint-green walls brought to mind a nursery. Perhaps that was what Marshall planned for it.

Then it hit her, what she'd forgotten.

Contraception. True, she'd been sleeping alone for the last few years, but how could she have been so careless?

"Oh, hell," Franca said.

She had to go downstairs and drop this on Marshall. That he, too, had been negligent didn't make it any easier. Nor was it his fault that she had a troubled family history when it came to pregnancies.

A remark came to her that she'd almost completely forgotten. After meeting Marshall at college, her mother had commented privately on how handsome he was—and how much he resembled her first husband. "A killer smile and gorgeous eyes," she'd murmured. "But Belle had better watch out. When he turns cold toward her, he'll be pure ice."

Don't get ahead of yourself. She'd better focus on one issue at a time, for her peace of mind as well as his.

MORNINGS-AFTER COULD be tricky, Marshall reflected as he switched on the coffeemaker and began fixing cheese omelets and toast. With other women over the years, there'd been the question of whether they'd see each other again, how often and on what basis. He'd never gone for one-night stands, but a few women preferred them.

Surely not Franca. They belonged to each other now. However fast or slowly their relationship progressed, they were in this together.

With rising anticipation, he heard the brush of footsteps on the stairs. Swiveling from the stovetop, he stared as slim legs and a swirl of pink skirt appeared. Against the soft colors surrounding her, Franca shone like a beacon. Marshall could scarcely breathe.

The sizzle from the stove top broke his reverie. "Breakfast's almost ready," he said.

"I'm not hungry." She scowled.

Uh-oh. "What's wrong?"

Franca crossed to kitchen. "We forgot to use contraception."

Oh, hell. Despite the packet of condoms in Marshall's bedside table, it simply hadn't occurred to him. Thoughts collided, but logic took command. "Is it the right time of the month for you to conceive?"

She glared at him. That must have been the wrong response.

She's a psychologist. Try to think the way she would. "How do you feel about it?" Marshall asked.

"I can't believe neither of us remembered." Striding to the coffeemaker, Franca poured a cup. "We work at a fertility hospital."

All was not necessarily lost. "You could take a morning-after pill."

Coffee sloshed onto the counter. "Easy answer for a guy," she snapped. "Besides, no matter how hard a pregnancy might be, I'd always regret it if I did that."

Her anger puzzled him, since Marshall would love to have a child. Still, he resolved to proceed with caution. "I understand why you're upset," he ventured. "Pregnancy is a huge undertaking for a woman."

"And for a man who'll get stuck with child support for the next twenty years." Before he could reply, Franca raised a hand. "Sorry. That was out of line. My head's throbbing, not that that's any excuse."

Afraid the omelets were getting overcooked, Marshall flipped them onto plates. He served them with a dish of sour cream and chives. "Whatever happens, we'll both be part of the decision making."

Franca splashed milk in and around her cup, adding to the mess on the counter. "I'm sorry, Marshall, but when it comes to my pregnancy, I'm the one who makes the decisions."

The baby that might be forming would be his son or daughter, too. "Legally, that's true, but morally, we're both involved. Please don't treat me like a bystander."

Franca plopped onto a stool at the island. "That doesn't give you the right to run my life."

"Don't exaggerate." This conversation was spiraling out of control. Marshall searched for a way to lower the tension. "It's not that common for a couple to conceive immediately. We might be worrying over nothing."

"Nothing?" Franca poked a fork at her eggs. "For the next few weeks, my entire future is up in the air."

This wasn't how he'd imagined conversing with her this morning. "Why are you picking a fight?" Usually, she was the most reasonable person around. "Let's not ruin a beautiful night together."

Jumping up, Franca carried her plate and cup to the counter. "Thanks for breakfast. I'm just not in the mood for—for whatever." She grabbed her purse.

She was leaving? "Let's not part this way," Marshall protested. "We should talk."

"About what?"

"You're supposed to be the expert."

"On pregnancy?" she asked.

"On relationships."

"Well, here's my opinion," Franca said. "We both know we're not compatible, Marshall. I wish we were and sometimes…no, I refuse to delude myself. Let's just leave it at that."

She barreled out of the kitchen and he heard her footsteps rap across the tile floor toward the door. He didn't deserve her anger, Marshall thought irritably, but he still cared about her. "Wait! I'll drive you to your car."

"I'll feel better if I burn off some energy." The door closed behind her with a loud *click*.

He sat at the counter, bewildered. How could she deny the intimacy they'd shared last night? Yet judging from her words, she didn't just regret the forgotten contraception; she regretted the champagne, the sex and the night with a man she could never love. What had seemed to him a transformative experience had been entirely one-sided.

A knot formed in Marshall's chest. *Well, so what if she rejected you?* He could almost hear his father's voice demanding he shape up and take it like a man.

True, he and Franca had always been opposites. He'd recognized that fifteen years ago. Why expect things to be different now?

This pain in his heart would ease. It had to. Meanwhile, in a few weeks, they'd learn whether they were going to be parents.

And if they were, Marshall had no intention of stepping meekly aside.

As a counselor, Franca often advised clients to take things one day at a time. So that was what she tried to do during the next week.

All the same, her calendar became her foe, announcing that her period was due on the following Friday. It didn't arrive. Not on Saturday or Sunday, either.

She'd been late before. Anxiety could cause that,

Franca cautioned herself, and redoubled her efforts to focus on her job.

It had been unfair to unload on Marshall, yet she couldn't bring herself to apologize. He'd been his usual high-handed self—all right, she conceded, he'd *tried* to understand her, but every word had rubbed salt into her wounds. She'd lost her daughter and then realized she might not be physically able to carry a child to term—and now she faced the prospect of an unplanned pregnancy. For once in her life, she had no compassion to spare.

Mercifully, no one appeared to notice her turmoil. Jeanine and Ines, who'd accepted the explanation that she'd left the reception early because of a headache, filled her in on the mother of the bride's shenanigans. After Franca had left, the woman had tossed a glass of champagne in the face of a waiter who'd accidentally trod on her foot. Lucky and Nick had politely but firmly escorted the miscreant and her complaining husband to a cab.

Attention in the cafeteria soon switched from the wedding to what was termed the Return of the Twins: Zady from her Las Vegas honeymoon and Zora from maternity leave. At lunch, people gathered to admire Zady's ring and coo over pictures of Zora's twins.

Thank goodness they had missed the juiciest piece of gossip stemming from the wedding. Franca shuddered. What a mess it would be if anyone found out what she and the best man had done.

Certainly no one would hear it from Marshall, who'd become cold and formal with her. Through the glass doors that separated the cafeteria from the patio where the doctors preferred to eat, she observed his rigid posture and stern expression.

She missed the warmth he'd shown her, the brilliance of his smile, the ease of his movements. Her anger had driven him into his shell, which she regretted, but she hadn't been wrong. Their differences were too profound to overcome for more than one night of drinking and dancing.

So why did she keep wishing he'd seek her out? Her hormones must be running riot. That was probably what had delayed her period, too. No, wait. If her hormones were surging, that might indicate pregnancy.

A week and a half later, she was still in turmoil. She sat at her desk and buried her face in her hands. Quickly recalling where she was, she straightened her shoulders. No weeping and wailing for a professional, especially since tonight marked the start of the men's counseling group. She had to project confidence and control.

In the therapy room, she cleared away the toys and drawing materials and arranged chairs in a circle for the half dozen men scheduled to participate. After communicating solely via email and text, she and Marshall would again be in the same room, side by side. Normally, Franca enjoyed meeting clients and beginning a journey with them. Now she simply hoped she could weather the session without a meltdown.

Someone tapped on the door. "Am I intruding?" Edmond adjusted the squarish glasses on his nose.

"Not at all." Franca gestured for the attorney to enter. "What did you find out?" She'd asked him to check on Jazz.

He came into the room but remained standing. "Bridget's moved into a two-bedroom apartment."

"Good." That meant Jazz had a room of her own. There'd be a kitchen, too, and a chance for healthier meals. "Does she want me to bring over Jazz's stuff?" Most of her clothes and toys remained at Franca's.

Edmond gave a regretful head shake. "They're sharing the apartment with her boyfriend. Axel doesn't want a bunch of toys littering the place, according to Bridget."

They were living with that awful man? "I'm sorry to hear that."

"There's more."

"More?" Her throat went dry.

"The district attorney has declined to refile the charges."

Franca's heartbeat thundered in her ears. Despite Edmond's cautions, she'd drawn comfort from the idea that she could bring her daughter home if Bridget was sent to prison. This development shattered that hope.

"There's nothing you can do?" As she stared at the attorney in his impeccable suit, an unreasoning anger tempted her to lash out at his smugness. But he was on her side.

"I'm afraid not. I'm sorry, Franca. You and Jazz deserve better."

She forced herself to politely acknowledge Edmond's sympathy. It was a relief when he left.

Despite a prickling behind her eyelids, no tears flowed. This cut too deep.

After a while, her breathing slowed. It was nearly five o'clock, which left an hour to grab a bite before the six o'clock session. Oddly, Franca discovered she had a ravenous appetite.

Typical of a mother-to-be.

In view of this fresh blow, she'd forgotten her other concern. Although it was early for results, she decided to pick up a test kit at the hospital pharmacy. She'd wait until after the counseling session to use it, in case the result was positive. Her emotions were tumultuous enough already.

Sucking in a deep breath, Franca headed for the elevator.

Chapter Ten

The past ten days since he and Franca made love, Marshall had instinctively watched for her everywhere. He'd listened for her voice, while mentally replaying their last scene, trying to figure out how it could have ended differently.

But he never managed to find the right responses for her. In many ways, she seemed contradictory, fearing a pregnancy yet refusing to consider a morning-after pill. Did that spring from her deep love of children? He wished he understood her.

Distracted at lunch that day, he'd struggled to join the laughter as Nick related funny incidents from his Las Vegas honeymoon, and been reduced to nodding vaguely because he scarcely heard what his brother said. It was as if Marshall had landed in a foreign country where he more or less understood the language but couldn't grasp its nuances.

Had Franca's period started? Surely she'd inform him. Until then, in view of how touchy she'd become, he decided to wait.

Meanwhile, he'd had no luck reconnecting with his mother. A few days after the wedding, Marshall had called to invite her to dinner again, but she'd declined curtly, citing prior plans. Much as he hated to abandon his efforts, he didn't see what else he could do.

His work had been his refuge. In the examining room, Marshall knew how to evaluate symptoms to reach a diagnosis, while for each operation, he had a carefully mapped-out strategy. At tonight's therapy group, however, the circle of men left him at a loss. Judging by the uneasy shifting in chairs and folding of arms, the clients were equally uncomfortable.

Keenly aware of Franca beside him, he scanned her out of his peripheral vision. She'd tucked her reddish-blond hair into a bun and put on dark-rimmed glasses. In spite of the buttoned-down impression, no one could miss the ripe curves beneath her suit or the softness of her lips.

Especially not me.

"Let's get started," she said. Around the room, the men slouched lower in their seats. Hank Driver, the detective whose vasectomy Marshall had reversed, was checking his phone. "Please mute your electronics."

"Sorry." He tapped the screen. Marshall was glad he'd remembered to put his own phone on vibrate.

"Let's set a few ground rules." Franca outlined the protocols. Everyone agreed about keeping the discussions private and listening without interrupting. "Do you have anything to add, Dr. Davis?"

He did. "Like most men, I was brought up to hold my emotions inside. I admire everyone for participating."

"Good point." Her gaze returned to the clients. "Let's introduce ourselves—first names only—and then you're welcome to raise any issues related to infertility or treatment."

What if no one spoke? However, after the introductions, a man named Cory broke the ice. "How do we

tell our in-laws to butt out? That's our biggest problem.
I mean, besides not having a baby." There were nods
of recognition.

"Would you mind sharing your story?" Franca asked.

His mother-in-law called daily, advising her daughter
to relax and let nature take its course. "After my wife
hangs up, she bursts into tears," Cory said. "She's been
through in vitro twice. Implying that she just ought to
relax is cruel."

"Has she explained to her mother how hurtful these
comments are?"

"She's tried," Cory said. "But her mother insists she's
trying to make sure her daughter is happy. Well, that's
my job, not hers."

Since Marshall's parents had been the opposite of
over-involved, he had no idea what to recommend.
Franca asked if anyone else had similar problems.

"We had to cut off contact with my sister-in-law,"
said a fellow named Burt. "She had the nerve to suggest my wife hang out with her to absorb her hormones,
because she's pregnant with her third child."

Beside him, Marshall registered a wince from
Franca. At the sister-in-law's insensitivity, or at the
prospect of being pregnant?

"Can a woman really absorb someone else's hormones, Doc?" Hank asked.

Marshall wished Nick were here, with his experience in obstetrics. However, he was fairly certain of
the answer. "There aren't any pregnancy pheromones
that increase other women's fertility. If there were, I'm
sure we'd be providing them to our patients."

Several men chuckled. Franca didn't crack a smile.

"Well, family interference appears to be a sore point

for many of you," she said. "Let's consider how infertility affects your family members."

"It's none of their business," Cory declared.

"That may be," she said. "But imagine how it would affect you if a person you love, especially your child, was suffering and hurting."

"I never considered it that way." He frowned. "I suppose I'd want to fix things for them."

"I wish our relatives didn't act as if this is our fault," another man said.

"Even if my sister-in-law has good intentions, that's no excuse for flaunting her pregnancy," Burt put in.

"Families are far from perfect," Franca said. "Any crisis, and infertility *is* a crisis, can highlight problem areas."

"My cousin went through infertility treatments and described it in detail on her Facebook page," one man said. "When she started urging us to do the same, my wife nearly strangled her."

"Each couple has a right to choose their own level of privacy," Franca said. "Let's discuss ways to set boundaries."

She recommended that, after making sure the partners were in agreement, they talk to each offending relative, stating explicitly what had to change. "Be polite but firm, and stay calm," she said. "Don't let people manipulate you by claiming you've hurt their feelings. And don't forget to reinforce their positive behavior."

"How do we do that?" Cory asked. "Give them treats, like my dog?"

Laughter rippled through the room.

"One reward might be spending more time together," Franca said. "Also, show an interest in what's happening with *them*."

Marshall admired her perceptiveness. He wished he had more to contribute, but aside from emphasizing a point here and there, he simply observed.

Toward the end, Hank Driver shot him a curve ball. "Do you have children, Dr. Davis?"

"No," he admitted. "I wish I did."

Franca's forehead furrowed.

"Just curious," Hank said.

After surveying the room in case anyone else wanted to speak, Franca said, "We've gone past our scheduled hour and a half. If you guys want to talk informally afterward, the cafeteria is open 24 hours."

"Thanks, but I had a long day," Hank replied. The rest of the men echoed his sentiment.

Finally the session ended. Chairs scraped as the men rose. Several shook hands with Marshall and Franca.

"I'm glad you're here, Doc," the detective told him. "No offense to Dr. Brightman, but having a medical expert gives it a stamp of authenticity. And it helps to hear a man's perspective."

"That's why we're both here," Franca said.

Once they were alone, Marshall gestured to the chairs. "I can put these away for you."

"The cleaning crew will straighten up tomorrow." She fidgeted with the strap of her purse. "Don't you have to be up early for surgery?"

"I'm in no rush."

"I'm tired, and the powers that be have requested I write up my observations on tonight's session for the morning." She peered at her notes. "Whatever you'd like to include, please email me ASAP."

"I'll do that." He recognized she was giving him his cue to depart. But she sounded shaky, and he couldn't leave her.

After she locked the office, Marshall accompanied her along the hallway. Near the elevators, she said, "Don't bother to wait," and vanished into the ladies' room.

Although it was only 8:00 p.m. and security patrolled the hospital, a woman alone could be vulnerable. Taking out his phone, he leaned against the wall and checked his email.

PINK. FRANCA STARED at the stick. According to the directions, that meant a 99 percent chance she was pregnant.

Most of her clients would be delirious with joy at such a result, but pregnancy posed a major risk to her health. All the same, it was miraculous, Franca thought as she rested a hand on her abdomen. A life had started that depended utterly on her—on a woman who hadn't planned for it and whose womb might not be able to nurture it to term.

Take it one day at a time. Oh, dear. That advice had been hard enough to follow during the past ten days. Now it frustrated her, because, ready or not, Franca had to prepare for the future.

She wished her stomach weren't churning, from hormones or anxiety or both. The awareness that she'd brought this about by practically dragging Marshall into bed did nothing to ease her discomfort.

Marshall. Oddly, she longed for his presence—until she recalled that he'd suggested a morning-after pill. Despite her fears, she had to give any child its chance. Didn't he? The man certainly sent mixed signals about wanting to be a father.

Franca had to pull herself together. It would be unprofessional to lurch downstairs, visibly upset. There might not be many patients wandering about at this hour, but staff members would see her.

She splashed water on her face, too upset to be careful where it splattered. As she stretched for the towel dispenser, she felt her foot slip on the wet floor.

She grabbed the edge of the counter, but its smooth surface defied her. She couldn't be falling. Not now. Not in this condition. Not like an idiot, flailing and struggling for balance.

With a shriek, Franca lost the battle.

THE SCREAM SENT adrenaline shooting through Marshall. Thrusting his phone into his pocket, he yanked open the door.

"Are you okay?" He rushed to kneel beside Franca on the floor, registering the water around her that must have been what sent her tumbling. "Did you hit your head?"

"No, my hip." She levered herself into a sitting position. "Clumsy as usual."

"Careful or you'll slip again." Assessing how best to aid her, Marshall noticed the box she'd knocked to the floor as well as the small stick nearby. The stick that had turned pink.

That was why she'd been in here so long. This was the news they'd both been waiting for. He'd been aware this might happen. Why didn't he feel prepared?

Because such a miracle didn't seem possible.

Franca followed his gaze to the pink stick but didn't comment. No explanation was necessary.

Marshall dragged his attention to the present situation. "While I always enjoy having a nice sit on the floor of the ladies' room, we should get up."

"By all means." When he helped her to her feet,

Franca winced and rubbed her thigh. "Don't worry, it isn't fatal."

"You didn't hurt the…?" His mouth refused to form the word *baby*.

"At this stage, no. I'm one big bundle of insulation."

After wiping the floor with a paper towel to prevent injury to anyone else, Marshall escorted Franca into the hall. "We should talk," he said. "Do some strategic planning."

"I just got the news." She ducked her head. "I'm not ready for this conversation."

"I'm not sure I am, either." Glancing down at her scalp, he noticed a thin line of hair that was a brighter shade than the rest of her strawberry-blond locks. "You should stop dyeing your hair now that you're pregnant."

"Excuse me?" Franca pulled away.

He shouldn't have blurted that. "Sorry."

"Marshall, I didn't mean to snap at you that morning at your place," she said. "I was upset about a lot of things. And I know you're trying to be supportive. But the fact is, your instincts are all wrong."

"I've been told that before." Damn, he was tired of walking on eggshells. "The bottom line is, we're about to become parents."

"Yes, I got that." Franca folded her arms.

Why avoid the obvious? Marshall thought. The right path was clear.

"Marry me," he said.

To HER ASTONISHMENT, Franca almost agreed. Despite the evidence of Marshall's controlling nature—he'd ordered her to stop coloring her hair, for Pete's sake!— she longed to lean on his strength.

What a batty idea. If she miscarried, that would remove the entire reason for his offer. Even if she carried the baby to term, their differences would sooner or later make them both wretched. Franca had witnessed the destruction divorce caused on children and on adults, above all her mother. The best prevention was to avoid marrying the wrong man.

Still, judging by the intensity in Marshall's dark eyes, she believed his proposal was sincere. Marshall had a strong sense of duty. Thank goodness he didn't whip a ring out of his pocket. She wasn't sure what she'd have done—probably fallen over laughing and *really* injured her hip.

"I have to say no." With sadness, she watched his eagerness fade. "While I appreciate your desire to help, I don't need a man to lean on."

"I'm the father," Marshall said quietly. "I should provide for you and the baby."

Franca chose to be realistic. "I'll accept support for the child's sake. As for sharing custody, we can work out the details later."

"Once you recover from the shock, you should reconsider," he said.

"My brain cells are fully functioning." She didn't mean to be hurtful. "Marshall, you're a great guy, but as I said before, we're incompatible. We've always been honest about that."

"People can adjust their expectations," he replied tightly.

"And a few years later, they end up in my office, fighting like cats and dogs," Franca answered. "Now I'm heading home."

"If you have any pain, call me," Marshall said. "Correction: call 911, then me."

"Okay." His concern felt unexpectedly reassuring.

And given her shaky state, Franca was glad when he insisted on walking her out to the nearly empty parking structure.

A little over a month ago, they'd been distant acquaintances howling to music in this same garage, united only by frustration with their individual problems. Now they were bound by a quirk of fate. That, and their own negligence.

As she drove away, Franca checked her rearview mirror. Marshall stood motionless, watching.

If I'd accepted his proposal, we'd be planning our wedding.

Instead, she faced a half-hour drive to a lonely apartment and a cold bed. An apartment filled with memories of a little girl who would never return.

It didn't feel like home at all.

Chapter Eleven

To Marshall, asking advice meant showing weakness. He ought to be able to solve his own problems. But no matter how much research he did on the internet, it failed to produce a workable strategy for persuading Franca to marry him.

By Saturday, he was almost ready to drive to her apartment and demand she reconsider. However, besides the near-certainty of rejection, he had no good counter to her argument that people who married for the wrong reasons ended up hating each other.

Except that they *wouldn't* be marrying for the wrong reasons. A child, and a friendship of many years' standing, formed a basis they could build on. And shuttling between custodial parents was far from an ideal situation for a kid.

And, as if he weren't struggling enough already, the world was suddenly filled with pregnant women and infants in strollers. At the hospital, they jammed the elevators and the hallways. On the street, he passed parents gathering outside shops and urging their toddlers to hurry.

Easy to grasp why patients couldn't compartmentalize their fertility issues. Reminders intruded everywhere.

As a last resort, he might as well seek advice, and how many men had a brother who'd been in basically the same situation? Nick's girlfriend Bethany had become pregnant four years ago and, while Marshall had never met her, he'd heard she, too, had refused to marry the father of her baby.

Nick's experience might offer clues about what *not* to do. Also, his success with Zady indicated he'd learned from his failure.

At the office, Marshall had heard Zady inform the other nurses that she and her sister planned to attend a movie this evening, leaving Nick and Caleb alone at the house. Playing with his nephew would be fun, and after the boy went to bed, the men could talk.

He called Nick. "Sure, stop by," his brother said.

"I'll bring pizza," Marshall offered.

"You hate pizza."

"Correction: I *used* to hate pizza," he said. "You converted me."

"Okay. We usually order from Krazy Kids Pizza," Nick replied. "Pepperoni's a big favorite around here. Wait—you're paying. Make that two large pizzas, one pepperoni and beef, the other mushroom and olive with extra cheese."

"My source tells me that Papa Giovanni's pizza is superior, but otherwise, I agree to your terms," Marshall said.

"Your source?"

"Cole Rattigan." The head of the men's program claimed to have a refined palate.

"I bow to his expertise," Nick said. "Also, Papa Giovanni's is more expensive, so knock yourself out."

A few hours later, Marshall arrived laden with pizza

boxes. Roses edged the front walk of Nick's cozy ranch-style house.

When the door opened, Caleb rushed forward. "Uncle Marsh! Yay!"

"Pizza. Yay," Nick said. "We worked up an appetite playing ball." That accounted for his mussed hair and grass-stained T-shirt.

"Sorry I missed it." Marshall caught his brother's skeptical expression. "Not really."

At the kitchen table, they polished off a good portion of the pizza. A child's card game followed, with Caleb triumphing.

With a little prompting, the three-year-old brushed his teeth and changed into pajamas. To Marshall's pleasure, the boy climbed into his lap and handed him a picture book.

The child dozed off halfway through. Marshall carried him to his pint-size bed, its headboard painted with fairy-tale characters. Nick pulled a patchwork quilt over his son, and they crept out.

"He's fond of you," Nick said. "There's no accounting for taste. Beer?"

"Sure. Thanks."

In the living room, Nick sprawled on the couch and Marshall chose an armchair. "I have to admit, I had a second motive for coming tonight, besides seeing my nephew."

"Seeing your brother?" Nick asked.

"A third motive."

"Shoot."

"I was wondering how you handled it when Caleb's mother refused to marry you," Marshall said. "This isn't idle curiosity."

"Got a girl pregnant, did you?" Nick must have

picked up Marshall's involuntary start, because he hurried to add, "Sorry, man, that was harsh. Am I right?"

Marshall shrugged. "Mind answering the question?"

"I'll start at the beginning."

"Go for it."

Nick and Bethany had met at a party. She'd been pretty, lively and wild. Unattached and blowing off steam after completing his residency, Nick had jumped into an affair.

"We were both careless," he said. "When we found out she was pregnant, she nixed my proposal and insisted on adoption."

"Adoption?" That obviously hadn't happened.

"Her parents talked her out of it because they longed for a grandchild," Nick explained. "Beth still refused to marry me. She preferred living with them."

"Why?"

"Big house. Free babysitting, laundry and housekeeping," Nick said. "Besides, Beth and I weren't in love."

"You stayed involved?" Marshall probed.

"I visited and contributed to Caleb's expenses, as much as I could." Nick hadn't inherited wealth as Marshall had. "After Bethany died in a boating accident last year, I brought him to live with me."

"Yes, I remember." But none of that gave Marshall ideas for how to proceed with Franca. "In retrospect, do you think if you'd tried harder you could have won Beth over?"

"Doubtful, though the romantic approach never hurts." Nick plopped his feet on the coffee table. "How did you propose to your girlfriend—I'm assuming you did, right?"

"It went something like, 'We should get married.'"

"No wonder she said no, Uncle Marsh." At the high-pitched pronouncement from across the room, Marshall's hand jerked, spilling a few drops of beer on his slacks.

"Hey, sport. You're supposed to be in bed," Nick gently scolded his son.

Caleb folded his arms over his teddy-bear print pj's. "Dad, tell him how we did it with Zady."

"We?" Marshall asked.

"It was a joint proposal." Nick grinned. "And you can do it better than me, kid."

"You go down on your knee." Caleb demonstrated. He looked adorably earnest. "You need a ring, too."

"As sparkly as possible," Nick said.

"Yeah." Caleb nodded vigorously. "Like in the movies."

"We'd watched a romantic comedy, which taught us the proper method." Nick grinned. "Okay, killer, back to bed. Uncle Marsh and I are having a grown-up conversation."

Caleb arose with a show of dusting off his pajamas. "Don't forget."

"Thanks for the tip." Marshall listened until he heard his nephew's door close. "I had no idea he could hear us."

"Zady says men's voices carry in this house," Nick admitted. "Let's adjourn to the kitchen."

At the table, they finished their beer with slices of cold pizza. Marshall was glad his brother understood how hunger could strike again so quickly. "So the key is a romantic presentation?"

"Depends on the woman and how she feels about you." Nick's fingers tapped the table. "It's Franca, isn't it?"

"That's private."

"Please remove the stuffing from your shirt and answer again."

"Yes," he said.

"And she turned you down?"

"Let's just say I won't be lining up a best man anytime soon," Marshall replied. "I don't understand women."

"If you did, you'd be the first guy ever," Nick said. "You have to take your cues from her."

"But it makes more sense for her to live at my place. With a baby coming, it's crazy for her to be driving so far every day and living alone," Marshall protested.

"May I speak as a doctor?"

"What else would you speak as?" Grumpily, Marshall added, "Not to mention that I'm one, too."

"You work with men. I work with women," Nick said. "Pregnancy does weird things to their bodies. Their hormones fluctuate, their ankles and breasts swell—drag your mind away from that image, right now—their hearts and lungs work harder, and let's not forget the throwing-up part. All day, not just mornings."

While Marshall had learned all that in medical school, he hadn't considered the impact on Franca's moods. "That sounds seriously unpleasant."

"As I tell my patients' husbands, your job is to be there for her," Nick said. "In your case, you should be more flexible."

"I suck at being flexible."

"Do it anyway."

Marshall reminded himself that he'd come here for counsel. "Your input is appreciated."

"Glad to hear it."

On the way home, Marshall wished for some of the synchronicity that, in his college days, had often landed him face-to-face with Franca. But if he did run into her by accident, how did a man demonstrate flexibility when his gut insisted he was right?

WHILE EVERY OBSTETRICIAN at Safe Harbor was well qualified, Franca wanted to choose one who'd be on her wavelength. She decided on Dr. Nora Franco, whose four-year-old son, Neo, had attended day care with Jazz. She and Nora had broken the ice when, noting the similarity in their names, they'd joked that if Franca married into Nora's husband's family, she'd be Franca Franco.

During one of their chats, Nora had confided that she'd gotten pregnant by accident. Although her policeman boyfriend was now her husband, Franca believed the obstetrician would understand the challenges she faced as a single mom.

Despite a busy schedule, Nora was able to work Franca in late on Monday. After greeting Franca warmly, the tall blonde physician asked a few questions, reviewed her medical history and performed a physical exam.

She confirmed a pregnancy of five weeks' duration, based on the start of Franca's last period. Now she was staring at the computer terminal.

Shifting uneasily on the examining table, Franca tugged her skimpy robe tighter around herself. "Is anything wrong?"

Nora shook her head. "The only thing concerning me is your blood pressure. It's 130 over 80. That stops short of the danger zone, but it's a little higher than your usual pressure, and normally BP drops during early pregnancy. That's because progesterone relaxes the walls of the blood vessels."

"Could this cause problems?" Franca pressed.

"Not unless it worsens significantly. Even then, we

can treat it." Nora wheeled her stool closer. "Are you under stress? Of course an unplanned pregnancy is stressful, but each person reacts differently."

Despite her worries about Jazz and her medical issues, what popped into Franca's head was the bill she'd received for the next three months at her private office. The landlords had raised the rent, and she wasn't sure she could justify the cost.

"I'm weighing whether to continue treating private clients." In fact, she had to rush there in a few minutes to keep an appointment. "But I can't bear to let down people who're depending on me."

"It's wise to reduce any unnecessary strain." Nora regarded her questioningly. "Do you have support from the father?"

That's too personal. "Some. The bottom line is, it's my baby and I'm dealing with it."

"Any close family?"

"Not around here. But I'm fine." She wasn't ready to notify them. Franca didn't wish to upset Gail after what her sister had endured, and as for Mom, her fussing might drive Franca crazy.

More than ever in the ten years since her father's death from heart disease, she wished he were here. A psychologist, Evan Brightman had checked his kids' homework, listened to their problems while smoking his pipe, and cracked jokes at the dinner table. Just a whiff of aromatic smoke could slam Franca's heart with nostalgic longing.

The doctor didn't appear convinced that Franca was fine. However, she moved on. "I estimate your due date as December 15. You should have a baby for Christmas."

Last year's holidays had been joyous, with Jazz's

adoption seemingly a done deal. Franca couldn't bear to imagine what the holidays would be like without her. Was it possible she'd have her precious Baby Bright— short for Baby Brightman—or would she fail to save this child, too?

Nora frowned. "How about sharing what you've been holding back?"

Might as well go for it. "My mother had two miscarriages before carrying to term. My sister, Gail, has lost three pregnancies, and the doctors can't find a reason. I'm afraid I've inherited the same tendency."

"While I don't see any warning signs, let's review common causes of pregnancy loss." Franca was relieved Nora didn't dismiss her concern.

She cited chromosomal abnormalities in the fetus or bacterial infections, but those were usually onetime events, not repetitive. There was no untreated diabetes or substance abuse, either.

"What does that leave?" Franca asked.

"Polycystic ovary syndrome is associated with abnormally high levels of the hormone testosterone. We can test for that," the doctor said. "Another risk is if the mother's immune system attacks the embryo, viewing it as a foreign object. I'll order extra blood work." She tapped notes into the computer.

Franca remembered that she had to rush to meet her client. "Do I have to do the labs today?"

"Tomorrow or Wednesday would be fine." Nora glanced up. "If you suffer cramps or severe abdominal pain and bleeding beyond a little spotting, call me at once."

"By then it will be too late, though, won't it?" Nora sighed, and Franca added, "My sister had heavy bleeding. Fortunately her husband was there."

"Do you live alone?"

"Yes."

"Keep your cell phone within reach," Nora said.

Franca thanked the doctor, scheduled her next checkup and accepted a plastic bag of vitamins and product samples. The drive to her Garden Grove office took forty-five minutes in rush-hour traffic, and she narrowly arrived by six o'clock.

Franca jogged into the one-story white building, where the receptionist was preparing to leave. The woman regarded her apologetically. "Your client just canceled."

"What?" Franca had to pause to catch her breath. "She didn't call my cell."

"She phoned here." The receptionist pulled on a sweater. "People tend to be evasive when they break commitments at the last minute."

"Did she ask for another date?"

"She said you've done such a great job, she and her husband don't need any more counseling."

If the decision was financially motivated, Franca would have offered a discount, but she might not be able to keep the practice open anyway. "Thanks for filling me in," she said. "While I'm here, I should check my mail."

"It's in your drawer. Do you mind locking up? Everyone else is gone."

"No problem."

After the woman left, Franca keyed open her private office. Not so private these days since she only used it some weekends and evenings, and she shared it with another counselor.

In the drawer, she found only flyers and other junk. The rest of the room had an impersonal air. She'd moved most of the toys, books and drawing materials to the medical center.

Nora had been right that she should be reducing her stress levels. Why had she clung to the notion that she was indispensable?

Franca was locking the inner office when a sharp pain in her side sent her doubling over. Groping for support, she banged her leg against a chair.

As she sank onto a couch, she registered that she might be suffering a miscarriage alone in an isolated building. In a panic, Franca took out her phone and instinctively tapped the first number that showed—Marshall's. What was she doing? She should dial 911.

Struggling to end the call, she fumbled the device. As she reached for the symbol to cut off the connection, she heard his voice say, "Franca?"

"I think I'm losing the baby," she blurted.

Chapter Twelve

A dark tide of worry surged through Marshall as he exited the freeway. True, Franca had reported after a moment that she'd experienced a single cramp and suffered no bleeding. But she still might be in danger.

She'd claimed she was well enough to drive the short distance to her apartment. "I overreacted, that's all. I'm sorry for disturbing you."

"For your sake and the baby's, wait for me there." Ultimately, she'd provided the address.

In the clinic parking lot, Marshall broke into a run, his mind conjuring up a horrific scene of Franca collapsed on the floor. Yanking open the door, he was overjoyed to find her on a sofa, calmly leafing through a magazine. "No further problems?"

"Just boredom." A smile softened her mouth. "It was kind of you to rush over, but unnecessary."

"How do you feel?" He ached to touch her.

"Embarrassed," Franca said.

He dropped into a chair. "Are you sure you're both okay?"

"Yes." A pucker formed between her eyebrows. "But if it was over, I imagine you…that you might be… relieved."

"What?" Marshall shot to his feet. How had she developed such a disgusting idea about him? "Do you really have such a low opinion of me?"

Franca's small, warm hand caught his wrist. "Of course not. I misunderstood your reaction to the pregnancy."

"That's one hell of a misunderstanding!"

"You mentioned the morning-after pill." She stroked his arm. "Sit down, Marshall. I'm getting a crick in my neck looking up at you."

He obeyed stiffly. "I brought that up for your sake. I had no idea how *you* felt about having a baby. I still don't."

She wrapped her arms around herself. "While I wouldn't have chosen these circumstances, I love this baby."

Then marry me! However, issuing commands might provoke a fight. How frustrating. When he'd tried to be empathetic and suggested the morning-after pill, she'd assumed he didn't want the baby. If he pressed her to marry him, she'd assume some other wrongheaded thing.

"Now that you can see that I'm fine, I'm heading home," Franca said.

"I'll follow, okay? If you have any problems, flash your lights."

Her lips pressed together. Then, with a sigh, Franca conceded, "That's kind of you."

"I'm on your side," Marshall said. "Whether you believe that or not."

Her gaze searched his face. "You do have your moments."

What did that mean? Marshall refused to prolong their fruitless discussion. "Lead the way, madam."

Franca arose with no sign of pain. Marshall allowed himself to breathe again. She really was okay.

As SHE LED Marshall into her apartment, Franca tried viewing the place from his perspective. Compared to his house, the living room was small, with plain, thrift-store furnishings. "Pretty far from a mansion at the beach," she conceded.

He smiled. "Yes, but it's yours. Did you make the comforter?"

"My mom crocheted it," She fingered the bright colors thrown over the back of the sofa.

"I can't imagine my mother crocheting anything."

She remembered Mildred Davis stalking out of the wedding dinner. "Have you reconciled with her?"

"Afraid not." He studied the scenic photos. "Do these have special meaning for you?"

"My brother shot them near his home in Montana." She stretched, then froze when she felt a twinge in her abdomen.

Fear flooded her, wildly out of proportion. *You are not having a miscarriage.* But the terror she'd experienced at the clinic hadn't entirely dissipated. How desperately she loved Baby Bright, and how helpless she'd been to protect her child.

"What is it?" Marshall caught her shoulder.

"A minor aftershock from the spasm I had earlier. Nothing to worry about."

When he released her, Franca missed his support. Her knees had gone liquid, and she wanted to sit. But sinking into a seat would be like inviting him to stay.

"You're certain?"

She searched for a neutral remark. "I'm just sore

from lying on the examining table at Dr. Franco's office."

"You had an appointment? I presume she's running the appropriate tests." Noting her dubious expression, Marshall elaborated. "When I broke the news to my brother, he reminded me how hard pregnancy is on a woman's body."

He'd told Nick? Franca could have kicked him. "I was hoping to keep this quiet a while longer."

"Sorry. He isn't a blabbermouth, though." Marshall reflected on that. "But I suppose he'll mention it to Zady."

"Who'll spill to her twin."

"Who'll inform her husband and housemates," he conceded.

"Next stop: the internet." Franca's irritation yielded to amusement at how readily she and Marshall fell into their usual banter.

"Are you mad that I spilled the beans?"

"I bow to the inevitable." They ought to figure out how to respond to the inevitable gossip, but she had no energy for strategizing. "Let the chips fall where they may. Our colleagues will move on to fresh gossip soon enough."

Judging by his frown, Marshall hadn't considered how others might react. Then he nodded. "You're right. They'd find out, anyway."

"Exactly." Casual tittle-tattle didn't bother Franca. But if she miscarried, every sideways glance or attempt at consolation would turn a knife in the wound. Just as she was sure it did with her sister.

Restlessly, Franca paced past Jazz's room. Little doll faces and teddy bears peered back as if asking when their mistress was coming home.

Marshall followed her gaze. "The fairy-tale theme reminds me of Caleb's room."

"I'll bet his isn't pink and sparkly."

He smiled. "You must be saving everything until she comes home."

Ouch. "She isn't going to. The DA dropped the case against her mother."

Marshall spoke in a deep rumble. "I know how much you loved her."

Loved her, past tense. Franca almost railed at him for dismissing her grief, almost protested that her love for Jazz would last until the day she died. But he was trying to comfort her, not minimize her loss.

And she was grateful for his presence. Why did she have the urge to strike out at the man who'd run to her side when she called him? *Because it would be too easy to lean on him when ultimately, the only person I can count on is myself.* Doubly so if she miscarried.

"You shouldn't have to carry this burden alone," Marshall told her. "I realize I speak at the risk of getting my head bitten off."

Franca would have laughed if she hadn't hurt so much. "I don't mean to be touchy. But I can handle it. I'm a big girl."

"Not a superhero, though."

"What does that mean?"

"That you can't do everything," he said. "Commuting, working two jobs, living by yourself. All while growing a baby."

"You can't help being bossy, can you?" she protested.

"I'm trying to be flexible, but it goes against my nature." Taking her hands, Marshall chafed them lightly. "Since I'm lousy at it, let me jump in with both feet.

Move in with me. I have plenty of space and I live close to the medical center."

"We'll argue. Like we always do."

"I'm sure you won't hesitate to point out when I'm being a pain in the ass," he said. "Like *you* always do."

Franca had to admit that was true, and that he'd been remarkably patient with her outbursts. "You promise not to resent it when I tell you off?"

"I may growl and sulk, but I'll let it go," he said.

"Growl and sulk," she repeated. "How can a woman refuse such a great offer?"

Was it really a bad idea to move in with him, as long as she knew it wouldn't last? Franca's mother had been crushed by her first husband's abandonment because she'd relied on his support after she'd lost two babies. And Belle had reorganized her class schedule and her future plans trying to please Marshall, only to be tossed aside when she fell short of his expectations.

But forewarned was forearmed, as the old saying went. The man owned a dream house, he cooked breakfast, and he was studying her with enough heat to melt chocolate. Despite all that, Franca might have still resisted if this apartment wasn't so achingly empty and if she hadn't resolved to resign her position at the clinic. With the sense of stepping onto a shifting ice floe, she said, "I'll have my own room?"

She detected a flicker of disappointment in his eyes, but it vanished in a blink. "Of course. You can furnish it with your stuff. I'll put the bed and dresser in the garage."

Replace his gorgeous furniture? "No, we can store *my* old junk." What else should she address? "I'd be happy to pay rent."

"Rent?" His eyebrows shot up. "Not unless you want me to donate it to charity."

She already supported her favorite causes. Besides, having a child wasn't cheap. "I'll buy my own food, drive to work separately, and it's only for the first trimester."

He'd been nodding along until the last part. "Why?"

"By then, I'll find a place of my own nearby." Franca refused to risk letting her emotions tempt her to stay. Better to establish a limit up front.

Marshall released a frustrated breath. "When does the trimester end?"

"The middle of July."

"That's less than two months!"

"Take it or leave it."

A couple of heartbeats passed before he said, "Done."

He'd folded fast, perhaps believing he still had time to change her mind. Well, he'd fail. Meanwhile, moving in with him would solve a lot of problems.

And by July, there might not even be a baby. *Don't worry about that.*

They shook hands and agreed that she'd move in the following weekend. Only after Marshall left did another notion strike Franca.

Despite the dismaying news from her lawyer, she'd kept the apartment intact for her daughter in case things changed unexpectedly. Choosing her future baby's well-being instead felt like she was truly giving up on Jazz.

Any reasonable person would approve of Franca's decision. But that didn't dispel the sense of disloyalty that dogged her.

THE NEXT WEEKEND's transition went smoothly, to Marshall's satisfaction. That happened partly because he had hired professional movers, and partly because he worked out a floor plan in advance.

With Franca's approval, Jazz's bed and curtains went into the playroom. They could change the pink color scheme later if the baby happened to be a boy. Her brother's photos brightened the upstairs hallway, while her mother's crocheted afghan enlivened the family room.

They had a minor disagreement about her habit of leaving appliances out on the kitchen counter, which he preferred uncluttered. This was resolved when Marshall cleared space for the appliances in the lower cabinets. He conceded that she couldn't reach things higher up, and he certainly didn't want her climbing on a footstool.

Franca's acceptance of his invitation and her willingness to compromise should have been gratifying. Instead, her responses made him uneasy. She was treating him as a roommate, and a temporary one at that. No wonder she didn't bother fighting over minutiae.

How disturbing that she remained cool to him, when awareness of her disturbed his attempts to sleep at night. His skin prickled with longing whenever he heard her stirring down the hall, awakening memories of soaring to the heights with her in the very room where she was sleeping.

During their lovemaking, Marshall had plunged off the emotional deep end, and the resulting cascade threatened his hard-won inner calm. He had to admit, it was wise to withdraw, but not to this extent.

Franca didn't seem to be experiencing any emotional turbulence. On Monday, Marshall had to wake her as she snoozed in complete indifference to her alarm clock's jangling.

"Must be pregnancy hormones," she said over her breakfast cereal.

"You sure you don't want a ride to work?" To hell with what everyone would say when they arrived together. "We can save gas."

"It's only a few miles." Morning light through the French doors cast a rosy glow over her face. "Besides, don't you normally have to be in earlier than me, for surgery?"

She had a point. "Every day but Monday."

"And my Tuesday afternoon counseling group often runs late," Franca said. "Also, it would be a pain to have to coordinate about every last-minute patient or stop at the supermarket. There's also the matter of preserving our privacy."

She was right. But if either of them imagined they could keep their situation secret, Marshall soon learned better.

At work that day, he caught curious glances from Zady. Finally, his nurse poked her head into his private office. "I hope you don't mind, but Nick mentioned… I mean, congratulations!"

"For…?" he asked.

"Fatherhood," she prompted.

He'd forgotten his disclosure to his brother. "Oh. Thanks."

She must have told the other nurses, because he heard them chattering, then fall silent as he approached their station. Marshall was glad to depart for a late-morning meeting to review suite assignments in the new building.

Interior work on the floors would begin soon, with the opening scheduled for late summer. To avoid any further conflict, the administrator had decided that

Marshall should represent the urologists and Dr. Jack Ryder speak for the other specialists as they firmed up specifics.

The two men met in a conference room in the administrator's office. That way, they could call on him should they hit an impasse.

Jack shook hands warily and scanned the tentative floor plan Marshall had prepared on his laptop. The dark-haired obstetrician suggested only one switch, allotting a larger suite to the pediatricians.

"That does reduce the space for urology fellows," Marshall noted as he visualized Jack's suggestion.

"They'll be newcomers," Jack said. "And the pediatricians are crammed into tight quarters right now."

Marshall and Cole Rattigan had labored hard to win fellowship money and attract the best candidates to their program. However, he doubted anyone would reject a fellowship simply because it meant accepting a small office. "That's reasonable."

"By the way, congratulations," Jack said when they'd finished. "I hear you're about to be a dad."

"Thanks." Marshall regarded him questioningly. "Where'd you hear that?"

The other man grinned. "Speaking of being jammed together, I'm in the same suite with your brother."

"Who has a big mouth." Marshall closed his laptop. "I'm surprised you aren't trumpeting the news to all and sundry."

"Why would I do that?"

"Because parenthood is the greatest experience ever," Jack enthused. "My daughter, Rachel, just hit the seven-month mark and watching her develop is a high."

"I'm sure she's a doll." The desire for fatherhood that had grown in Marshall these past few years had taken on almost tangible form since he saw that positive pregnancy test. There'd been distractions—mostly his worry over Franca's health when she feared she was miscarrying—yet day by day, he'd begun to picture his child as a real person, a little boy or girl cradled in his arms. Someone to laugh with, to regale with stories of his childhood and to build a future for.

"It's hard to believe Anya initially wasn't keen on keeping the baby," Jack said. "I had to win her over for Rachel's sake *and* mine."

How amazing that the other man spoke openly about such private matters. Could Jack's experience help him to overcome Franca's resistance? "How did you change her mind?"

"She assumed I'd dump the burden of child rearing on her." The other doctor leaned back with a dreamy expression. "I ran errands to show that I'd be a real partner. What put me over the top was my cooking."

"I fixed an omelet for Franca. She wasn't impressed," Marshall said.

"Think big," Jack advised. "I prepared dinner for Anya and her housemates on a regular basis. They're picky eaters, but I won them over."

"I have no idea how to fix a complicated meal." Nor could he spare the time to take a class.

"There's a ton of recipes on the internet, with step-by-step instructions," Jack said. "Cooking is similar to surgery. If you assemble your tools and ingredients, and follow the directions, you can't go wrong."

"Or if you do, nobody dies."

"Precisely."

Marshall departed with his head buzzing. For maximum impact, he decided to pick a fancy recipe. One of his favorite dishes was chicken mole, a spicy Mexican dish that combined hot peppers with a dash of chocolate.

At lunch, he found a recipe on the internet, along with the pronunciation—*MO-lay.* The long list of ingredients daunted him, but he was willing to go the extra mile to dazzle Franca.

She'd mentioned that she'd be home late tomorrow night. What a perfect opportunity for him to experiment in the kitchen.

As Jack had said, if you followed the recipe, you could hardly go wrong.

Chapter Thirteen

The days had no business passing so rapidly, Franca reflected on Tuesday. True, she'd received positive news: the results of her blood test had come back normal, and a recheck of her blood pressure showed it had dropped slightly. She'd also arranged to leave her old clinic as of June first.

But in her sixth week of pregnancy, this tiny dot within her was growing rapidly, and she felt unprepared for what lay ahead. She hadn't informed her family, because that would require dealing with their reactions. She'd simply sent them her new address, noting that this place was closer to work.

At the hospital, however, secrets didn't stay hidden long. In the cafeteria, Ines and Jeanine flagged her down.

"We heard your news," Ines said over her sandwich. "Congratulations!"

"Is this our fault?" Jeanine asked.

Puzzled, Franca toyed with her chef's salad. "How could my pregnancy be your fault?"

"We figure that's where you went after the wedding," Ines noted.

"We kept talking about how handsome Dr. Davis

was and how somebody ought to—what were the words from Dorothy Parker?" said the taller nurse.

"Somebody ought to be under him," Ines filled in.

"Oh, that." Franca chuckled. "Yes, I took your comments to heart. I went right out and jumped into his bed."

Receiving wide-eyed stares from both women, she realized her attempt at humor had missed the mark. Perhaps because she *had* done just that.

"How was he?" Ines inquired.

Jeanine poked her. "I can't believe you said that!"

Franca popped open her carton of milk. "Use your imagination."

"It's already running wild," Ines said.

"This is none of our business." Jeanine held on to her high moral ground for a few heartbeats before asking, "Are you in love?"

"What kind of question is that?" Heat crept up Franca's neck. Too bad toning down her red hair hadn't reduced her body's tendency to blush.

As for her feelings toward Marshall, she couldn't have described them if she'd wanted to. She'd moved in with the conviction that it was for her health and safety, and that she'd been armored against her susceptibility to him. Yet watching him arrange toys and picture books in the playroom, Franca had been surprised by the tenderness in Marshall's expression.

"I never had toys like this when I was a kid," he'd said when she entered.

"None?" How was that possible in such a wealthy family?

He'd traced a finger down the spine of *Goodnight Moon.* "Just nonfiction books, a microscope, building sets. I intend to do things differently."

"For a lot of us, having a baby is a chance to repeat our childhood and make things turn out right." Immediately, Franca wished she could erase her words. Sometimes a counselor knew too much—and in this case, blurted it out at the wrong moment.

The pain that had flashed across Marshall's face stunned her. Despite her familiarity with his rigid nature, glimpses of vulnerability threatened to suck her in.

He'll be devastated if I miscarry. His gentler side would slam shut, and she'd lose him emotionally, even if he forced himself to stick around from a sense of duty. That would almost be worse than an outright rejection, because postponing the process of healing only encouraged the wound to fester.

But she wasn't going to reveal any of that in this lighthearted conversation with her friends. "How could I be in love with a man who irritates me so much?" Franca countered.

"Dr. Davis may get cranky under pressure," Jeanine acknowledged. "But no guy is a sweetheart all the time."

"My husband can be a real pain," Ines agreed. "He gets over it and so do I."

Franca was weighing how to end this conversation when the nurses solved the problem by noticing they were due back on the job.

"More details later?" Ines prompted as she arose.

"No."

"Spoilsport."

Franca was finishing her salad when Jennifer Martin slipped into the seat opposite her. "Don't worry. I'm not here to pry," the public relations director said. "I witnessed something and I wanted you to know about it."

That sounded ominous. "What is it?"

"We ran into Jazz at the beach on Sunday."

Black hair, blue eyes and a small, worried face filled Franca's mind. "Is she all right?"

"Quieter than usual, but after she and Rosalie started playing, she pepped up," Jennifer said. "They built a sand castle with a little help from Ian. He adores kids." Jennifer's husband, who hosted a video blog called *On the Prowl in OC*, had written several books about fertility treatments and parenthood.

"Did you have a chance to talk to her mother? How'd she strike you?" She feared Bridget might be using drugs again.

"She was with a rough sort of man."

A knot formed in Franca's stomach. "That must be her boyfriend, Axel." Recalling their encounter at the café, she asked, "Did he jerk Jazz around?"

"Not in front of us." Jennifer swallowed. "But when he ordered her to leave the beach, she jumped up in a hurry, like she was afraid of him."

Franca wrapped her arms around herself. "Oh, no."

Jennifer leaned close, shielding their conversation from the busy room. "Bridget was wearing a turtleneck, despite the warm weather. Ian believes he saw a bruise on her neck."

Abused women often wore long sleeves and high collars to hide their injuries. And if Axel was beating Bridget, he might be hurting her daughter, too. "Was Jazz bundled up?"

"No," Jennifer said. "I studied her as closely as I dared without being too obvious. I wish you could get custody."

"Me, too." Franca shook her head regretfully. "I can't do anything without proof." She had to walk a fine line and avoid antagonizing Bridget. If the authorities took the child away from her mother, no matter what the reason, Franca had no legal claim on her.

"I hope I didn't upset you," Jennifer said. "You have to take care of yourself and your baby."

"I will." Still, if she'd measured her blood pressure at that moment, she feared it would have shot through the roof.

That afternoon, Franca was too busy to dwell on what Jennifer had reported. There were job-applicant screenings, educational sessions for patients and endless paperwork to document treatments. The counseling group that met at four o'clock ran late, and afterward, a participant distressed by the topic needed an extra hour of counseling.

Marshall had texted that he planned to cook dinner. Since Franca had made spaghetti last night, that seemed fair enough. What a joy it would be to come home to such a beautiful house and find dinner waiting for her.

Or so she anticipated, until the smell of burned chocolate hit her as she entered from the garage. Had something caught fire? Despite her exhaustion, Franca flew past the laundry room into the kitchen. "Marshall? Are you okay?"

Dismay radiated from the tall man who swiveled toward her. His apron, his face and his shirt sleeves were smeared with goo, while encrusted pans and bowls littered the counter and stove top. Dark glop filled the blender, while the scents of scorched peppers, cloves and anise augmented the pungent chocolate odor.

"What on earth?" Franca had an urge to grab a washcloth and scrub Marshall like a toddler. She doubted he'd appreciate it.

"I had no idea things would burn so quickly," he said.

"If I'd had nurses to hand me stuff like in the operating room, I'm sure I could have pulled it off."

"In other words, you could use a sous-chef." Reassured that nothing was currently on fire, Franca surveyed the mess. It seemed impossible to dirty up this many pots with a single recipe. "What were you making?"

"Chicken mole." He handed her a printout.

Franca scanned it. "There are sixteen, no, seventeen ingredients. That would put me off right there."

"If it were easy, it wouldn't be much of an accomplishment." Marshall stared bleakly around, apparently too overwhelmed to start cleaning.

Franca did her best to hide a smile. Training her attention on the recipe, she noted multiple steps involving browning and blending to create the peppery sauce. "You must have been at this for hours."

"Completely wasted," Marshall said.

"It's a noble failure," she assured him. "You aimed high."

As if taking her words literally, he glanced upward and groaned. A dark brown substance was dripping from the hood above the burners.

"When did you say your cleaning crew comes?" she asked.

He sighed. "I'll ask if they can schedule an extra visit for tomorrow. Franca, I'm sorry. You must be starved, and I was planning something special."

"You were?" She'd assumed he was merely experimenting.

"Jack Ryder suggested…" He broke off.

"What does Jack have to do with this?" The obstetrician had a gung-ho personality, she recalled. That didn't explain this culinary disaster.

"This was how he wooed his wife." Marshall ducked his head.

"By burning down the kitchen?"

"By cooking for her."

"You tackled this recipe for my benefit?" The notion gave Franca a fluttery sensation. "What a sweet thing to do."

"But we have nothing to eat."

She spotted a platter covered by a clean dish towel. "If I read the recipe correctly, the chicken might have escaped damage. Where is it?"

"Right here." Marshall lifted the towel to reveal a pile of poached chicken pieces. Pale and bland without sauce, they should nevertheless be edible. "I forgot about them."

"Is there a salad?" she ventured.

He retrieved a bowl from the refrigerator. "Right here."

"Perfect!"

"That's gracious of you." Marshall stared down at his smudged clothing. "I suppose I should change."

"Let's wash our hands, soak the pans in the sink and call it even."

"You're sure it's legal to leave such a mess?" he asked with an uptick of spirit. "My mother would require smelling salts if anyone left her kitchen in this state."

"It's your house and your rules."

"Our house," he said. She didn't bother to argue.

They set places at the kitchen island, where the chicken proved reasonably tasty. The only disadvantage was that after dinner they had to face the stove.

"From here, it reminds me of a volcano eruption," Marshall observed.

"I'll bet you blew up a few science experiments with

those kits you got as a kid." Franca poured herself a second glass of white grape juice.

He flexed his shoulders, no doubt stiff from hours of chopping and stirring. "I nearly demolished the garage once."

"How old were you?"

"Ten or eleven." He grimaced at the memory. "I wasn't sure my folks would ever forgive me."

"It was their own fault. They should have given you a teddy bear," she said.

"I'd probably have dissected it."

"Like any proper future surgeon." She raised her glass. "Here's to surviving our childhoods."

He clinked with her. "But I'm sure yours was happier than mine, not that this is any sort of contest."

"It *was* happy," Franca said. "Except that… No, I shouldn't complain."

"Complain away." Marshall's steady gaze encouraged her to continue.

"I was the infamous middle child." She tried to avoid clichés, but this one held some truth. "My big sister seemed more accomplished and prettier. My brother became the baby of the family. I tried to win our parents' approval by being a better student and more compliant."

"Did it work?"

"In an offhand way," Franca said. "They praised me, but there was something missing. Until I started working with troubled kids when I was in high school."

"Why did that make a difference?" Marshall asked. "It certainly wouldn't have with my folks."

"My mom identified with my dream of becoming a foster parent. She loved the idea of being surrounded by kids," Franca recalled. "Also, working with youngsters made me want to understand their family dynamics.

That's when I decided to follow in my father's footsteps as a psychologist."

"I imagine he appreciated that."

"Yes, he did."

Rising, Franca stored the leftovers while Marshall called and arranged for the cleaners to arrive the next day. With a sense of skipping school, they left the wrecked kitchen and carried their glasses to the patio.

In the few days since she'd moved in, Franca hadn't had a chance to enjoy the outdoor areas of the house, which included a patch of emerald lawn and a curving flower bed bursting with blooms. Beyond the bluffs, she glimpsed the harbor and the midnight-blue ocean beneath a darkening sky.

In the cool evening air, Franca had an urge to scoot her lounge chair closer to Marshall's. Her hand drifted to her abdomen. How incredible that she carried a part of him merged with a part of her.

"Does it hurt?" He propped up on his elbow to face her.

"No." She peered down at her still-flat stomach. "I was just thinking about how Baby Bright combines both our heritages."

"Cute name."

"Short for Brightman," she explained.

Marshall's expression sobered. "You don't want to give it up for adoption, do you?"

"Certainly not!" she said. "Why?"

"That's what Jack Ryder's wife planned, initially." The glow of outdoor lighting emphasized Marshall's high cheekbones.

"You discussed my pregnancy with him?" In fairness, Franca conceded that plenty of staffers were gabbing about the situation. "Never mind."

"I apologize if I was indiscreet," Marshall said. "I'm a bit overeager."

She couldn't bristle at a guy who'd covered himself in chocolate sauce on her behalf. "I appreciate the good intentions."

Marshall tugged her arm. "Come here. You deserve a massage."

"You're the one who must be sore from all that cooking." She didn't resist, though, when he pulled her onto his lap and his large, skilled hands played over her muscles, releasing the tension.

Awareness of his hard thighs beneath her reawakened sensations she'd tried to drive from her dreams, and desire rushed over her in a heated surge. When Marshall's hands slid around to the front and cupped her exquisitely sensitive breasts, Franca hovered on the edge of surrender.

A gust of sea air snapped her back to reality, though. Embarrassed, she drew his hands away. "I'm tired. I've had a long day."

Marshall cleared his throat. "I didn't mean to go too far."

"It's as much my fault as yours." Shifting position, she cupped his stubbled cheek with her palm. "We've always been attracted to each other."

"You have keen powers of observation." His mouth quirked as he tried to lighten the mood. It looked like it hurt.

Franca could barely keep from kissing this earnest man. It was surprising how appealing she found his smeared face and clothes, sacrificed in an attempt to please her. But she knew how swiftly he could switch gears. "There's a reason we never followed through on it until now." She rose clumsily on stiff knees.

"Fear?" he guessed, catching her hips to aid her balance.

"Or wisdom." Franca eased away. "We have to stay on an even keel for our baby's sake as well as our own."

She could see the struggle as he searched for words. Finally he said, "You're worn out. Go rest."

Franca took her glass inside. What a strange reversal, she thought, that Marshall's emotions had become transparent, while she was the one holding herself in check.

Her maternal hormones must be screwing with them both.

MARSHALL REMAINED SITTING on the edge of the lounge chair, missing Franca's warmth where she'd cuddled against him. How unexpected, that his catastrophe in the kitchen had brought them closer rather than offending her.

He'd moved too fast, though. Lesson learned: relationships progressed best when allowed to unfold gradually. In retrospect, it was clear that after he and Franca had thrown caution aside the night they made love, the experience had driven her to retreat. But although their mutual amusement tonight had furthered their détente, he'd overplayed his hand.

How to proceed? Clearly, his upbringing and instincts weren't up to the task of persuading her to stay. But, by luck, Marshall had stumbled upon helpful advice, first from his brother and then from Jack. While things hadn't played out as anticipated, their suggestions *had* helped.

According to the stories circulating at the hospital, a number of colleagues had won their wives despite initial reluctance. Surely he could glean more useful tips from them. How to do that without baldly declaring himself a hopeless case, he wasn't sure, but he'd stay alert for opportunities.

Marshall had to convince Franca that while they might not be destined to fall madly in love, they could find happiness sharing a partnership as parents and friends.

The sooner, the better.

Chapter Fourteen

Soliciting advice turned out to be a challenge. Neither of the urologists who shared Marshall's suite was married, and he couldn't ask the nurses, who often ate lunch with Franca and would no doubt blab about his clumsy inquiries.

At Thursday night's counseling group, he half expected the men to stand up and accuse him of fraud. After all, he needed advice as much as they did.

However, when he tuned in to the discussion, he was pleased by how much the men had gained from the previous meeting. Several had successfully confronted troublesome relatives, and had an increased sense of teamwork with their wives. Cory reported that not only had his mother-in-law stopped showering them with offensive suggestions, she'd been relieved to learn she didn't have to offer solutions, just sympathy.

Once they wrapped up that topic, Hank Driver brought up another issue: his belief that his wife blamed him for their infertility. It had been his choice to undergo a vasectomy, and the reversal hadn't yet paid off.

Marshall jumped in. "You're convinced she blames you, but she claims she doesn't. Is it possible you blame yourself?"

The detective's forehead furrowed. "You're right. I

do feel like I'm letting her down. Also, I cheated on my previous two wives, which Sarah is aware of because she's a dispatcher in our department. I'd never cheat on *her*, but I'm not sure she trusts me."

"Have you brought that up with her?" Franca asked.

"It never occurred to me," Hank said. "I guess I should."

Being able to contribute to the session cheered Marshall, and he was glad to gain more insight into family dynamics. Still, he hadn't learned anything that would advance his personal quest.

Help came from an unexpected source. On Friday morning, his surgeries ran long. In the cafeteria, he'd barely started to eat when Owen Tartikoff dropped into the vacant seat opposite him.

Marshall's hand jerked, nearly dropping his sandwich. For heaven's sake, the fertility program chief didn't intimidate him. Much.

"How's it going?" The russet-haired doctor had a disconcerting manner of seeming casual while conveying steely resolve.

"We're settling in fine."

The surgeon's cinnamon eyes blinked. "That's an odd way to describe therapy."

Oh, he meant the men's counseling group. "I'd call it productive," Marshall said. "The clients seem to be benefiting."

"How, exactly?"

"I wish I could describe the process to you, because it's very interesting. However, anything revealed in our sessions is confidential."

Owen's fingers drummed on the table. For a guy accustomed to being in charge, having a door slammed in his face must be hard to take. Marshall hoped the surgeon wasn't about to pull rank. As a medical supervisor, he might insist on reading Franca's or Marshall's notes, but that didn't seem right.

He searched for a diversion. "When I spoke of settling in, I was referring to Dr. Brightman and me. You've probably heard the scuttlebutt."

"Yes." Tartikoff leaned back in his chair. "Reminds me of when Bailey and I were housemates while she was pregnant. We fought like cats and dogs for a while."

The distraction appeared to be working. "Your twins are how old?"

That brought out the photos. "Here they are at their third birthday party, in January." The image showed a boy and girl with curly light brown hair, both grinning impishly. "Their names are Julie and Richard. That's for the heroine of the musical *Carousel* and its composer, Richard Rodgers."

Marshall examined the image. "They're quite a pair. You and your wife must be big fans of musicals."

"We sing together. It bridged the gap between us." After a fond gaze at the screen, Owen slipped the phone into his pocket. "That's how I won her over."

Owen had dropped a suggestion right into Marshall's lap. The only problem was that while he could, with an effort, carry a tune, he doubted he'd win Franca's heart by breaking into song.

However, the chocolate-pepper-sauce disaster had amused rather than offended her, hadn't it? "Do you recommend any song in particular?"

"'You'll Never Walk Alone,'" he announced. "That's from *Carousel*, too."

"What about accompaniment?" If success required mastering the guitar, Marshall was lost.

"In my case, there happened to be a pianist handy,"

the other man said. "You could download karaoke music."

"Great idea."

"I figured you for a smart man, and I was right."

How ironic, Marshall mused as they parted. Many of the doctors at Safe Harbor turned themselves inside out trying to score points with the big man. Little did they suspect all it took was agreeing to belt out a tune.

And make a complete fool of yourself.

He decided to start by finding a karaoke-style arrangement in the right key, whatever that was, and hoping for the best.

ON SATURDAY, FRANCA held her final sessions with private clients: a family of four and a married couple. Although they were sad to learn she was closing her practice, they had progressed enough to continue with another counselor or, if they preferred, on their own.

What an emotional experience, the end of an era. Joining this office five years ago after working at a larger clinic had been a financial risk that had paid off. How exciting and validating to her as a professional, only in her late twenties, to establish her own practice.

Over the years, however, the increasing burden of paperwork along with cuts in insurance payments had taken a toll. When she learned of the opening at Safe Harbor, Franca had leaped at the fresh opportunity.

And now she was cutting the cord on her private practice. It meant saying goodbye to her youthful dreams, even as she embraced new goals.

She'd have liked to confide her mixed reaction to Marshall, but after returning home from surgery, he closeted himself in his study. Despite his occasional openness, he remained opaque in many ways. While she respected his privacy, it reminded her how easily he could withdraw.

By dinner, which they prepared together, they were too tired to do more than chat about the suggestions circulating for the as-yet-unscheduled opening ceremony of the new medical building. On the cafeteria bulletin board, notes had proposed a light-and-sound show and a band playing music from around the world. A few ideas had been hilarious but in poor taste, inspired by the Porvamm's function of providing men's fertility care.

"Giant balloons shaped like the male anatomy?" Franca chuckled as she dished up stir-fry and rice.

"Don't laugh," Marshall grumbled. "When I chose urology as a specialty, I figured there'd be teasing, but I had no idea how many people would consider me a weirdo."

"I can imagine." *Easily.*

"I don't mind the comments at my expense." He doused his rice with soy sauce. "It's poking fun at my patients that bothers me. Those guys go through a lot."

"As I've seen from our group," Franca said. "And you know what? I'm impressed with how protective they are toward their wives."

"Of course." He regarded her steadily. "A man ought to protect the people he cares about."

She had no answer. In truth, his comments spurred her to consider how much he'd changed from the uptight, moralistic young man she'd met in college. Had her fears about him ultimately shutting her out been misplaced? Or had he simply not yet been tested?

They watched a movie that night on the family room's large screen. Although his preference ran to documentaries and science fiction, and hers to roman-

tic comedies and costume dramas, they both enjoyed a
fast-paced thriller with a love story.

Living here was more fun than she'd expected,
Franca conceded as she got ready for bed. She'd been
determined not to drift into a long-term relationship
based on physical attraction and an accidental pregnancy. Was there more than that between her and Marshall, or was proximity clouding her judgment?

Mid-July was only six weeks away. She wished she
had someone to help her gain perspective on the situation. Mentally she considered, and ruled out, everyone
she'd met at the hospital.

On Sunday afternoon, the urge to talk had grown
so strong that after lunch, Franca sat in the kitchen reviewing the names in her phone. In the old days, she'd
have called Belle.

Guilt surged inside her. By sleeping with Marshall,
she'd violated the unwritten girlfriend code. Okay, it
used to be unwritten, until someone posted it on the
internet.

The rules included never canceling important plans
with your friends for a guy, protecting confidences,
showing sympathy rather than saying I told you so and
sticking with a friend at a social event where you'd arrived together. But the most serious commandment was
not dating your close friend's ex.

Since the wedding, Belle had posted charming photos
of her new home in Denver and sung the praises of her
husband. That didn't mean she'd erased Marshall's rejection entirely.

Eventually, Franca would have to fess up, but not
yet. Nor could she use her mother as a sounding board.
Mom would only urge Franca to get married.

That left her sister. In view of Gail's devastating

losses, news of the pregnancy might be painful for her. Yet Franca hadn't talked to her in three months.

If the conversation worked around to pregnancy, fine. If not, they could catch up in other areas. Often, clients who'd suffered trauma commented how hurt they were by friends who avoided them, presumably too uncomfortable to stay in touch. She'd hate for Gail to believe that was the case with her.

Since Marshall was in his study and potentially within earshot, Franca carried her phone outside. The far-off murmur of the surf provided a soothing backdrop.

Tapping her sister's number in Arizona, she perched on a chair. Gail answered on the third ring, "Yes?"

"It's your long-lost sister," Franca said.

"The one with freckles?"

"No, the other one."

They both giggled. Franca's Raggedy Ann coloring was no longer the sore point it used to be. Two years younger than Gail, she'd longed for her big sister's confidence as well as her creamy complexion and chestnut-brown hair. Gail had poked fun at her freckles until one day Franca started to cry. Apologetically, Gail had admitted she envied her little sister's vivid appearance.

"Sorry I haven't called," Gail said. "I've been busy, but that's no excuse."

"Yes, it's entirely your fault," Franca replied. "Except for the part that's my fault."

"Now that we've got the apologies out of the way, tell me how it's going at the hospital. You aren't still on probation, are you?"

"I've passed that stage, thank goodness." Franca relayed her further adventures at Safe Harbor, including the establishment of the men's group. "I'm closing my private practice," she said.

"Wow! I remember how excited you were about having your own office," Gail said. "I got your new home address. Do you have roommates?"

Here goes nothing. "I'm living with a guy."

"Do I hear wedding bells?" Gail asked. "Scratch that. I do *not* want to pry."

"It's too early to answer, anyway."

"Who's the guy?"

She should have prepared herself for that. "Do you remember Marshall Davis?"

"Belle's boyfriend?" Gail let out a whoop. "Have you told her?"

Franca sighed. "No, and I'm a little uncomfortable about it."

"Well, she *is* married."

"Still, it might be a sore point."

"I always thought he and Belle made a handsome couple, but they were shallow, like a set of dolls," Gail said.

"That's interesting." Franca had considered them well-suited. As far as she could tell, they'd never argued, unlike her and Marshall. "How about you? How're things in Phoenix?"

"Hot," Gail said. "Which is great for business, because everybody's air-conditioning needs fixing." Her husband, Tim, repaired heating and cooling systems, while she handled the bookkeeping and scheduled appointments. "How's Jazz? Any chance of getting her back?"

"I'm afraid not." Franca explained about the DA's decision. "Losing her broke my heart. I always dreamed of adopting a foster child but I don't think I can try again. It's too painful."

"Don't give up on your dream," Gail urged.

"At this point, my dream is to have a family." Franca could no longer hold her anxiety in check. "I'm afraid of pregnancy, too. With our family's medical history..." She stopped, distressed at having blundered into sensitive territory.

"I'm well aware of our family's medical history, as you put it," snapped her sister. "To me, it's more personal than that."

"I didn't mean to be tactless."

Franca sensed Gail struggling for control. "Let's not discuss it," she said at last.

"I agree." Franca felt selfish for getting so caught up in her desire to confide that she'd offended her sister. "I'd appreciate your not mentioning Marshall to Mom yet."

"I can protect a confidence." Gail's tone was frosty.

"Give my love to Tim." After they said goodbye, Franca ended the call with a sigh. Instead of reconnecting with her sister, she'd opened a gap between them. And informing Gail about the pregnancy, when she eventually did, would be that much harder.

Her throat tightened. It hurt to keep secrets from the people whose support she valued most.

The scrape of the French door jerked her attention to Marshall, who stood in the opening. "Would you mind coming to my study? I have something to show you."

She could use a change of pace, Franca thought, rising. "What is it?"

"A surprise." With a smile playing around his mouth, he held the door for her.

DURING SURGERY, MARSHALL had the proverbial nerves of steel. Performing a song was entirely different.

He'd arrayed a couple of bouquets around the room to set a romantic scene. It hadn't been easy sneaking them in, but he was satisfied to see they aroused Franca's curiosity. "Pretend it's a bower," he said. "Okay, a bower with exercise equipment."

"I'm afraid to ask what this is about. Why is it so dark in here?"

"Just go with it, okay?" Marshall had tilted the blinds to reduce the light spilling across his monitor. "Hold on a sec."

On the computer, he clicked to the downloaded music. The speaker on this system wasn't great, but it beat the tinny one in his phone.

Marshall pressed start. After a few bars of introduction, he launched into the song. "When you walk through a storm..."

Franca's mouth fell open.

Despite an urge to hide under the desk, Marshall poured his soul into the lyrics about holding up your head and hanging on to hope. A chill ran through him; he wasn't sure whether it sprang from the moving message or from anxiety.

The song reached its crescendo. While practicing, Marshall had murmured the melody and lyrics to keep from being overheard. Singing full-out proved more difficult. Still, he was doing okay until he hit, and shattered, a couple of high notes.

Finally, it was over. Franca stood motionless, staring at him. Stunned, or on the cusp of dissolving into laughter? Should he follow up by presenting her with a bouquet?

That would look ridiculous. *Even more ridiculous than this entire serenade?*

Finally, she spoke. "That was adorable."

"Adorable?" he repeated, unsure how to interpret that remark. "As in cute and childish?"

"It was totally…" She swallowed. "I would never have…"

Marshall ventured closer. "Should I hire an interpreter?"

"It was fine," Franca said. Then she did the one thing he hadn't anticipated.

She broke into tears.

Chapter Fifteen

When Marshall wrapped his arms around Franca, she felt wonderful, and foolish. Why had she searched through her phone for someone to confide in when he'd been here all along?

Planning this wildly out-of-character ballad for her sake. Buying flowers to create a romantic mood. Pushing past his inherent restraint to reach out to her.

Embarrassingly, her tears yielded to sobs. When Marshall guided her to the sofa and onto his lap, she collapsed against him.

"Was I that bad?" he asked.

Laughter battled with her ragged emotions. Franca gulped for air before saying, "Of course not."

Marshall reached for a box of tissues. As Franca accepted one, she thought of how often she'd performed the same kindness for her patients. And how wonderful it was to know that someone cared. Especially when that someone was Marshall.

They both spoke at once. "Why did you…?" And stopped.

Franca leaped into the gap. "Why the serenade?"

Marshall's arms tightened around her. "The advice about cooking brought us closer, so I asked for more suggestions."

"Someone advised you to sing to me?" Franca couldn't imagine who would do such a crazy thing.

He nodded. "Owen Tartikoff."

"*The* Owen Tartikoff?" As if there were more than one. "You're telling me he sang to his wife?"

"He claims he did."

Franca tried to picture the imposing surgeon crooning to his lady love. A hilarious scene, but touching. "What about the choice of music?"

Marshall's cheeks colored. "He suggested it."

"That very song?"

"It worked for him."

Marshall had hit on exactly what she needed through dumb luck rather than insight. But they'd always had a tendency to stumble into the same place, whether physically or emotionally. "It worked for me, too."

"Your turn," Marshall said.

"I have to sing?" Aside from lullabies to an uncritical toddler, Franca hadn't sung since college karaoke parties.

"I meant, to explain. Why are you crying?"

As excuses sprang to mind, Franca realized she'd become accustomed to deflecting difficult questions. Marshall deserved the truth.

Scooting off his lap, she sat beside him on the couch. "I've been talking to my sister."

"Is she okay?"

"Yes, but…" *Just go for it.* "The women in my family have a history of miscarriages."

"You mentioned your mother's troubles," he said.

"Well, she's not the only one who's had difficulties. My sister, Gail, and my aunt had repeated losses, too. Although no cause has been diagnosed, it might be genetic. That would mean I'm at an increased risk of losing the baby."

Marshall stiffened. She could feel him pulling away. "Has your doctor found anything wrong?"

"No. But neither did Gail's."

"That's a serious concern."

"You've been generous, inviting me to move in while I'm pregnant," Franca said. "If I lose the baby…" Well, the rest was obvious.

When she lost the child, she'd lose Marshall, too.

HE UNDERSTOOD NOW why a few abdominal twinges last week had sent Franca into a panic. Also, a miscarriage on top of losing her foster daughter would devastate even the strongest person.

"This is a lot to hold inside," Marshall said.

"As a counselor, I know the importance of sharing one's burdens. But I'm supposed to be a source of support for others," Franca countered.

With his thumb, Marshall wiped moisture from her cheek. "As the father of your baby, I'm on your team."

"If I miscarry, you won't be the father anymore." She drew in a shaky breath.

"You assume that would be the end?" He wished she had more faith in him. "After all these years, I'm not going to stop caring about you."

"If this pregnancy falls apart, I may not be up to attempting another one," Franca said. "Having children is very important to you. And I'm aware that you'd never choose to be a foster parent."

Marshall couldn't deny that children were central to his planned future, and to his happiness. As for fostering, her experience with Jazz had if anything reinforced his aversion to taking in a child who might never bond with him or might ultimately be taken away. That didn't mean he'd abandon Franca.

"We don't have to decide anything yet." Marshall saw no point in battling about something that might not happen. "I'm glad you shared this with me."

She smiled. "That was very sweet, singing to me. You showed me a new side of yourself."

"Let's build on that."

Franca clapped her hands. "I don't believe it! You sound like me during a group session."

"Consider me a convert to therapy." In the interest of truth, Marshall qualified: "To a modest extent."

"All the same, I'm thrilled." Her tears appeared to be forgotten.

"Moving forward," Marshall said, "what shall we burn for dinner?"

"It's only three o'clock."

"We have to plan the menu and hit the supermarket."

"Let's go figure it out."

At the store, Marshall goofed around, loading up the cart with cake mixes and tubs of icing "for all the parties we'll throw." French vanilla, triple chocolate, red velvet—how could he resist?

He didn't specify that those parties might be for children. After all, grown-ups could enjoy them, too.

At home, while Franca napped before it was time to begin cooking, Marshall wandered into the playroom-turned-nursery. Usually when he regarded the princess-pink bedspread, the dolls and the stuffed animals, happiness coursed through him. Today, Franca's disclosure made him keenly aware of the fragility of his dreams.

From atop a toy chest, he picked up a stuffed rabbit with floppy ears. Its button eyes peered at him wistfully.

The little girl it belonged to was gone, and with her a big chunk of Franca's heart. How dreadful if she—and he—had to face another loss.

From the window, Marshall gazed down at the cul-de-sac, serene in the lingering sunlight of early June. A small boy rode his tricycle along the sidewalk under his father's supervision. At another house, two school-age girls sat on the porch with cell phones in hand. Judging by their laughter, they were texting each other.

From the day he'd discovered this house, Marshall had imagined his children growing up in it. When he'd learned Franca was pregnant, he'd thought his dream might finally be coming true.

In this quiet moment, he had to assess the implications of what she'd revealed. While miscarriages weren't uncommon, most couples grieved and then renewed their attempts to have a family. What if Franca couldn't do that?

Below, the boy's mother called him and her husband inside for dinner. Marshall's chest ached with longing to be like that man.

He visualized a Norman Rockwell painting of an idealized family gathered around the table, with just enough mischief to avoid mushiness.

Franca had been right that he sought parenthood to compensate for his own childhood. He yearned for the joy and acceptance he'd missed from his judgmental parents. Yet there'd been love, too.

Too bad you couldn't buy a prepackaged future at the supermarket in the flavor of your choice. Instead, he and Franca would have to make the best of whatever fell into their cart.

If necessary, he'd be willing to adopt a healthy infant, not that he expected the process to be easy. Most importantly, Franca would have to accept him for who he was: a traditional guy whose idea of home didn't include losing control to a system that could destroy your family without warning.

Franca awoke bathed in fading light touched with gold as it sifted through the curtains of her bedroom. Marshall's song ran through her head: "You'll Never Walk Alone."

It was reassuring that she truly didn't have to walk alone. Until recently, Franca had steamed ahead, expecting help from no one. But pregnancy, coupled with distance from her family, had left her vulnerable. Things that had never bothered her before, such as the prospect of living alone in an apartment, scared her. In Marshall's house, she felt safe.

The scents of broiling salmon and asparagus floated through the partly open door. Her stomach rumbled.

How luxurious, to sleep while Marshall fixed dinner. Franca washed up and smoothed the wrinkles out of her knit top. While her jeans had grown tight, she was reluctant to invest in maternity clothes just yet.

When she descended the stairs, a thrill of anticipation ran through her as she caught sight of Marshall's lanky form moving about the kitchen. At the doorway, she halted to watch him.

Since college, she'd headed off any potentially serious relationship with a man to concentrate on her career and foster parenthood. She'd volunteered at a home for abused women, and taken in several foster children on an emergency basis before Jazz. She'd believed her lack of enthusiasm for the guys she met indicated she was fine without them.

She'd been deceiving herself. Without realizing it,

she'd compared them to a man who attracted and stimulated her even when he infuriated her. A man they couldn't match and whom she had never expected to grow this close to. *This* man.

His lazy smile enveloped her. "Welcome, beautiful dreamer."

"Is that your next song?"

"There's a song called 'Beautiful Dreamer'?"

"You bet. Let's search for the lyrics," she said. "*After* we eat."

"Everything's ready." With a few strides, Marshall reached the kitchen table—more comfortable than the island where they usually ate—and pulled out a chair for her.

He'd already set their places, Franca noticed. "You'll spoil me."

"That's the idea."

He eased her chair forward, his arms reaching around her and his cheek close to hers. Franca rested her head against his chest and wished she could stay there forever.

Hunger prompted her to straighten. "Okay, Chef Davis. Let's sample your creation." Earlier, she'd planned meals for later in the week while he'd kept tonight's menu to himself. At the market, she'd been too amused by the variety of cake mixes in their cart to pay attention to what else he'd put in.

"Hope you like it," Marshall said.

The salmon and asparagus, served with a salad, were delicious. "I'm glad you didn't give up on Jack Ryder's advice," she said.

"Sorry?"

"About preparing dinner for me."

Marshall paused with his water glass in hand. "I forgot about that. I wasn't trying to impress you."

"Even better."

To her, the meal tasted better than anything she'd eaten in a restaurant. Once they'd finished, he brought out his laptop to search for "Beautiful Dreamer." They listened to the Stephen Foster melody a couple of times, then found karaoke accompaniment and joined in together to sing.

Their voices rang through the house, the blend masking most of the muffed notes, in Franca's opinion. Moving to the family room couch, they relaxed side by side with the laptop on Marshall's knees, and ran through a series of other favorites.

"Be sure to thank Owen Tartikoff for me, if you dare," Franca teased.

"My other source of advice scored a home run, too," he said.

"You mean Jack?"

"No, my brother. He told me to be flexible."

"Amazingly, it worked." Curling against Marshall, Franca tipped up her face to his. He set the laptop aside and drew her into a kiss.

How natural it was to taste his mouth and ruffle his hair. Then to rise and climb the stairs hand in hand.

They made love in his king-size bed, more slowly and gently than before. Her pregnant body had developed a heightened sensitivity, so that simply inhaling the scent of his skin sent her floating to the heights. The climax seemed to last for an hour.

Franca drifted off to sleep, snug and free of cares.

MARSHALL LAY AWAKE musing on this astonishing change in their relationship. Bonding with Franca had combined the best of the old days with their increased maturity.

If he'd had a clue how valuable advice could be, he'd have written to Dear Abby long ago. Maybe he still ought to, regarding how to handle his mother. But the answer was obvious: eventually, he'd have to confront her.

Perhaps she'd soften when she learned she was going to be a grandmother. He wasn't eager to mention that to her, though. If Mildred dismissed this miraculous occurrence with a nasty comment, he might never forgive her.

He was dozing off when, dimly, he heard a phone ringing. Blinking awake in the darkness, Marshall took a few beats to register that it must be Franca's phone. She didn't move. Her hormones must have sent her into an unusually deep sleep.

On the carpet, he scrambled for her jeans and drew the cell from the pocket. The readout said *Unknown Caller.*

Should he answer? When she stirred, he clicked to answer and handed her the device. "It's for you."

Franca held the phone to her ear. "Dr. Brightman." After a moment, she said, "Yes, I know Bridget. Please don't call child services. Where is she?"

Who was calling and what had happened to Bridget? From the bedside table, Marshall took a pad and pen, and jotted the address as Franca spoke it aloud.

She listened with only a few comments such as "Really?" and "I understand," before concluding, "Thank you, Hank. I'll be there as fast as I can. Ten, fifteen minutes at most."

It must be police detective Hank Driver, Marshall registered as Franca climbed out of bed. "What's happened?"

"Bridget's been arrested." Franca grabbed her clothes from the floor. "She asked for me to take Jazz."

Though it would be embarrassing for Hank to see them together, Marshall couldn't let her go alone. "I'll drive, if that's all right."

"Thanks," Franca said, and hurried to the bathroom.

No time to consider how they'd deal with this development. Right now, Marshall's job was to protect Franca, and to stay—he was starting to hate the word—flexible.

Chapter Sixteen

The address Hank had provided lay in the town's northeast quadrant, adjacent to the freeway. En route, Franca couldn't resist pressing her foot against the floor of Marshall's silver sedan, as if to speed it up from the passenger side. It was fortunate that he'd offered to drive, because otherwise she'd have been a danger to herself and others.

He'd leaped into action without comment, calmly but swiftly closing up the house and taking the wheel. She was grateful he didn't speak, because she needed the silence to sort out her turmoil.

According to Hank, Axel had been arrested with stolen items in his car. After obtaining a search warrant for his apartment, police had found enough evidence to put Bridget under suspicion as well. He'd provided no further details, saying the case remained under investigation.

The Safe Harbor police were trained in sensitivity to arrestees' children, Franca was aware. Unless they observed signs of abuse or neglect, they entrusted a child to an alternative caregiver designated by the parent rather than handing them to protective services. Mercifully, Bridget had requested her.

Did Bridget intend for Franca to keep the four-year-old long-term, or was her request a stopgap measure? That might depend on whatever the charges were against Bridget and whether she was released on bail.

How were these events affecting Jazz? Having police officers search her home and confront her mother must be frightening, no matter how sensitively they handled it.

At the apartment complex, Marshall slotted his car into a space marked for visitors. "I'll come in with you."

"Okay." His willingness to stand by her without complaint or criticism was a good start. A good start to what, she had no idea.

In her haste, Franca knocked on the wrong door. Marshall caught up with her. "It's 214, not 114," he said. Since no one answered, she was spared an awkward apology.

With a hand on her spine, he guided her up the outdoor staircase. His strength steadied her.

Hank must have been watching, because the stocky detective opened the door at their approach. "You got here fast." He nodded at Marshall, although the detective must have been surprised to see him. And curious.

"It felt like forever." Stepping past him, Franca took in the cluttered living room, the coffee table covered with beer cans and take-out containers. On the walls, someone had tacked posters of tattooed motorcyclists and video game–style warriors. Bits of paper littered the worn carpet.

Where was Jazz? Franca was about to ask when she spotted Bridget huddled in a chair, her light brown hair askew. "Are you all right?"

"I screwed up." Bridget frowned past her at Marshall. "What's *he* doing here?"

They'd run into each other at the café, Franca recalled. "I hope you don't mind. Dr. Davis was with me when I got the call." She kept her tone professional but gentle. Offending Bridget, especially in her fragile state, might affect her decision about Jazz.

"He's a doctor?" Bridget shrugged. "I guess that's okay."

Marshall seemed about to reply, but apparently thought the better of it. His natural reticence was the perfect attitude in this situation, a counterpoint to Franca's tendency to over-empathize.

"Do you want me to call a lawyer?" she asked.

"I already did." Tears glistened against Bridget's lashes. "That stupid Axel. And stupid me." She said nothing further, probably aware that Hank was listening.

Franca couldn't contain her anxiety any longer. "Where's Jazz?"

"In her room talking to Officer Jorgas," Hank said. "If you'll hang on, I'll check on the child."

Before he could move, however, an inner door flew open and a black-haired sprite darted out. "Mommy Franca!"

Behind her appeared a uniformed police officer, her brown hair pulled into a bun. "She heard their voices. I couldn't stop her."

"It's okay, Jorgas," Hank said.

Everything else vanished from Franca's awareness as she dropped to her knees on the carpet. She barely had time to brace before Jazz flew into her arms.

ON ENTERING, MARSHALL had been struck by the odors of beer and food scraps. While people might suffer financial hardship, they didn't have to live in squalor.

You aren't here to judge. He shifted his attention to

Bridget. Her wilted demeanor formed a contrast to the aggressive manner she'd shown several weeks ago at the café, yet in the jut of her chin he read a touchy pride. He wondered what she and her lout of a boyfriend had been involved in.

In charged a little bundle of fear and joy. Although he couldn't see Franca's expression, he sensed her happiness as she hugged the girl.

A glimpse of Jazz's tearstained face above Franca's shoulder wrenched Marshall's heart. If only he could lower a shining globe of protection around them both.

In her chair, Bridget shivered. When she glanced his way, he ducked his head to hide any hint of criticism. He didn't want to arouse any further resentment from her.

Franca addressed the girl in her arms. "Your mommy's asked me to look after you for a while."

"I have to go with the police," Bridget told her daughter. "I should be able to come get you soon."

That spelled another emotional rollercoaster for Franca, exactly what a pregnant woman didn't need. And more disruption for Jazz.

Marshall's job was to soften the blows. Meanwhile, he forced himself to keep his peace.

"Did I do something wrong?" Jazz asked her mother. Releasing her, Franca straightened.

"Of course not." Bridget reached out for her daughter's hand. "Sweetheart, when grown-ups mess up, it isn't a child's fault."

To Marshall, that seemed like something Franca might say. Perhaps Bridget had learned it from her.

Hank, who'd been talking with the other officer, swung around. At the sudden movement, Jazz shrank against her mother. "Make him go away!"

"He won't hurt you," Bridget said.

The detective squatted down to the child's level. "Hi, Jazz. I'm Hank. You're going home with Dr. Brightman—Mommy Franca," he said. "While we take care of the paperwork, Officer Jorgas will help you pack, okay?"

With a nod, Jazz went into the bedroom, followed by the uniformed woman. Hank addressed Bridget. "Please fill in Dr. Brightman about your daughter's schedule, medical issues and habits."

"She's more familiar with those than me," the woman said. "Just show me where to sign."

Watching as Hank handled the paperwork, Marshall admired his patience. This was a far cry from the way TV shows portrayed law enforcement. The detective even checked that Franca had brought a car seat. Fortunately, she'd put one in Marshall's car before they left.

It was late by the time they hit the road. Franca sat in the rear next to Jazz, who drooped against her. The little girl hadn't responded when Franca had introduced her to Marshall. He must seem like one more faceless adult drifting through her turbulent world. She had a lot to process, and was obviously exhausted.

When they reached his driveway, Jazz stared at the house in confusion. "Is this a hotel?"

"No, honey, it's our new home," Franca said.

"Oh."

After parking in the garage, Marshall rounded the car to Jazz's side. "Shall I carry her?"

"Who're you?" Jazz demanded.

"This is my friend Marshall, remember?" Franca unbuckled the child. "He's a doctor."

Jazz scowled. "I want him to leave."

"He lives here, too," Franca said.

Marshall held the car door for them. "I'm glad you're staying with us."

Scrambling out of the seat, Jazz refused to meet his gaze. "Let's get you to bed." Holding the child's hand, Franca took her inside. Marshall followed with the suitcase, a doll and a stuffed animal.

He wondered how the house appeared to Jazz. Big and strange, no doubt. And from her past experience, she knew not to consider it permanent.

His emotions were being tugged in opposite directions. While he could hardly wait for life to return to normal—the new normal in which he and Franca were lovers—he understood how upsetting it would be for Franca when and if her daughter left. Also, now that he'd visited the unkempt apartment on top of having met the brutish Axel, it troubled him to picture Jazz living under those circumstances.

"Are you hungry?" Franca asked.

The girl's dark hair shook no.

Upstairs in the playroom, Marshall set down the suitcase. Surely Jazz would relax when she found her familiar items arrayed around the space.

Instead, her body went rigid. "Why is my stuff here?" Her voice trembled. "I want to go home!"

Which home did she mean? Apparently Franca understood, because she answered, "When I moved here, I brought your stuff with me."

"I want my room!"

Franca knelt beside her. "Honey, I live here now. This is a much nicer place. And tomorrow you can go to the hospital day care and play with your old friends. They miss you."

That did the trick. "Okay."

"Anything else I can do?" Marshall asked.

"No, thanks. You've been great." Franca's weary

smile reminded him of the tender moments that had been interrupted.

"See you in a few minutes?" In front of Jazz, he stopped short of inviting her to his bedroom, but surely she'd be happier sleeping in his arms. And they could talk about the evening's events.

"It may take a while for Jazz to get settled."

"Of course." He said good-night and went out.

In his suite, Marshall left the door ajar and sat down to read a medical journal. But he couldn't focus on the words as he listened to noises from down the hall. Franca's soothing tones accompanied their movements as she showed the newcomer to the bathroom and took out sheets and towels.

Would Bridget drag her daughter back and forth as she went through the legal process? It wasn't fair to treat Franca as a free babysitter or subject a child to such uncertainty.

The memory of that sour-smelling apartment twisted inside him. Taking in a foster child hadn't been part of his plan, but he could never send Jazz back to that place. Marshall forced his attention on to an article about new techniques in freezing and thawing ovarian tissue. It offered the potential to preserve fertility for women facing chemotherapy.

A shriek yanked him from his reading. Leaping up, Marshall broke into a run.

FRANCA WAS WELL aware that she ought to remain calm and reassuring, no matter what the provocation. That didn't offset her physical exhaustion or today's emotional strain.

After reading a picture book aloud, she could barely stay awake. She was tucking Jazz into bed when, for the thousandth time, the little girl demanded to go "home" to their old apartment.

"This is home now," Franca snapped.

"I won't sleep here!" The tantrum reminded her of Jazz's toddler days. "Take me to my mommy."

"Not tonight." Franca barely refrained from pointing out that Bridget was no doubt at the police station this very minute.

"I hate you!" the little girl lashed out, and swung her doll by the leg.

When pain flared, Franca screamed. Instantly, she saw Jazz's horror at inflicting injury on Franca. Then she heard heavy footsteps racing toward the playroom.

Marshall. He'd been a pillar of strength for her, but to Jazz, he was a large, menacing stranger.

Whatever he said or did now would make all the difference.

THE SIGHT OF Franca's bleeding forehead sent rage jolting through Marshall. "What the hell?"

On the bed, Jazz stuck out her lower lip. "My dolly hit her."

He took in the plastic figure the girl was clutching by its leg. "That's a lie. *You* hit her."

"Marshall, she's been through a lot." Franca's warning tone did nothing to assuage his anger.

"Don't make excuses for her." Oddly, he heard his father's voice infusing his, as if he were repeating words heard long ago, although he didn't recall Upton Davis ever yelling at him. To Jazz, he roared, "Shame on you!"

Her glare matched his. "Leave me alone. You're a meanie!"

Franca's hand on his elbow tempered Marshall's fury as her earlier words sank in. What did he expect from a kid who'd had such a rough upbringing? More quietly, he said, "Apologize."

"No!"

Franca's grip became insistent. "I'd like to speak to you outside."

His jaw clenched, Marshall accompanied her to the hall. She shut the door and led him far enough away that their voices shouldn't carry.

"I snapped at her, and she reached her breaking point," Franca said.

"That's no excuse for hitting you."

"It isn't serious."

"It could have been." While Marshall didn't wish to exaggerate, neither would he tolerate an out-of-control child who, at age four, was beyond the toddler stage. "What if she had kicked you in the stomach?"

"She didn't."

In view of the blood welling along the cut in Franca's forehead, that failed to reassure him. "You're in denial about how vulnerable you are. While I understand that she has to stay here for now, she's big enough to harm you and the baby. Think about the future."

She stiffened, and when she tried to speak, no words emerged. Maybe she was gripped by mixed emotions, too. Being struck must have shocked her almost as much as him.

"Let's treat that cut." In the bathroom, Marshall took antiseptic and an adhesive bandage from the medicine cabinet. After washing his hands, he cleaned the area around the injury and applied the bandage.

"Will I live?" Franca asked wryly.

"Hopefully for many years." She still hadn't responded to his comments. "What are you thinking?" he asked.

"That what you and I share is precious, but I love Jazz." She swallowed. "Don't force me to choose."

"I hope it won't come to that." How could he risk alienating Franca? Also, she'd be in even more danger isolated with this unruly girl.

Marshall understood the necessity of making allowances for a child in crisis. Nevertheless, he refused to abandon his basic values regarding his family, and those didn't include tolerating physical violence. If Jazz behaved this way now, how much worse might she become around a baby, a rival for Franca's affection?

"It may not be our decision if her mother gets out on bail," he said.

"I realize that." Franca folded her arms. "Marshall, there's a lot about you that's terrific."

"Hold on to that thought." He didn't ask about the "but" implied in her statement. No sense revisiting the fact that she considered him insensitive and unbending when he was only doing his best for her.

She nodded, acquiescing. "I'd better go reassure Jazz that I'm not angry."

Although dubious about the risk of another tantrum, Marshall had to trust her judgment. "Call me if you need me. I promise to hang on to my temper."

"Will do."

They kissed lightly and held each other. Then she returned to the playroom.

Filled with apprehension, he went to bed alone.

"ARE YOU OKAY, Mommy Franca?" Huddling beneath the covers, Jazz studied her anxiously.

"Dr. Marshall fixed me up." Franca sat on the edge of the bed.

"My dolly was bad." Blue eyes watched for her response.

Marshall hadn't been entirely wrong, Franca conceded. Jazz had picked up bad habits, such as blaming others for her actions.

"Sweetheart, your dolly didn't hit me. You did," she said. "Even when you're frustrated, it's wrong to hurt others."

Jazz hugged her knees and stared fiercely at the wall.

"When you get mad at your friends, you can't hit them." At day care, Jazz could be expelled if she lashed out physically.

"I won't."

"Now will you apologize?" Franca asked.

Jazz bit her lip before saying, "What's *apologize* mean?"

She must have refused as a reflex. "It means saying you're sorry."

"I'm sorry, Mommy." The girl threw her arms around Franca and snuggled close. In a way, it reminded her of hugging Marshall a few minutes ago.

She treasured his kindness, yet she couldn't expect him to change his basic attitude toward parenting. Nor was it possible to transform a troubled child with a snap of her fingers. How could she care so deeply for two people who were utterly incompatible?

If push came to shove, Franca had to choose the one who needed her most. And that was the child whose arms were wrapped around her right now.

Her heart ached.

Chapter Seventeen

In the morning, Jazz demanded doughnuts for breakfast, which was what Bridget had been feeding her. When Franca refused, the little girl knocked over her glass of milk.

Franca's throat tightened at the sight of Marshall's scowl. *Not another showdown, please.*

Jazz righted the glass and mopped at the spilled milk with her napkin. "I'm sorry."

"Apology accepted," he replied.

That wasn't easy for Marshall to say, Franca guessed. She was glad Jazz now understood what an apology was and when to offer one.

While he cleaned up, the little girl ate her oatmeal and fruit without further protest. She got dressed for day care promptly, too.

Franca wasn't naive enough to believe the storms had ended. She was grateful for the break, though. *Take one day at a time*, she repeated silently.

At the hospital, eager greetings from friends brought out Jazz's sunny side. Later, Franca got good news when she had her blood pressure checked. Despite recent events, it was within acceptable levels.

Her nausea remained mild and she'd gained a healthy, modest amount of weight. Her assistant, Maggie, who'd been thrilled to learn of the pregnancy, recommended a visit to the Baby Bump for maternity clothes.

"It's early," Franca responded as she headed into her office. "I still fit into my looser stuff."

"You'll be sticking out to here before you know it. I did with my daughter." Maggie had both a seven-year-old daughter and a teenage stepson.

"You did a fine job of dropping the weight," Franca replied. At nearly thirty, Maggie had a great figure.

"I could still lose a few pounds." The assistant shrugged. "Don't worry. I'm not jumping into some diet fad."

Franca was pleased at having ducked the subject. No sense buying a bunch of clothes she'd have to donate to the thrift store if she miscarried.

She had to stop thinking that way. A negative mind-set might affect her health. Also, she faced more urgent matters.

Shortly after lunch came the nervously anticipated call from Bridget. "You're out on bail?" Franca asked, after assuring her that Jazz was fine.

"The judge released me on my own recognizance."

"I'm glad to hear it." In her office chair, Franca tried to prepare for a demand to hand over the girl. She hoped Bridget grasped how hard it was on the child to be dragged back and forth. "I don't want to pry, but are the charges against you serious?"

Bridget didn't flare up. Instead, she spoke candidly. "Axel got caught stealing packages off people's porches. When the cops searched his car, they found fake IDs and other stuff." She sucked in a deep breath. "We were stealing people's identities online. I was dumb to let him talk me into this, but we were broke. Anyway, my lawyer says I might be able to cut a deal by testifying against him."

What did this mean for Jazz? Franca wondered. "A deal would let you avoid prison?"

"That's up to the DA."

"What about Axel?"

"That's the scary part," Bridget said. "If he finds out I'm a witness, there's no predicting what he'll do."

Franca shuddered at the idea of that abusive man on the loose. "Isn't he still in jail?"

"His gang buddies might raise bail for him," Bridget said. "I'm staying at a women's shelter in case he gets out. Will you hold on to my daughter a while longer?"

"Of course." Although Marshall might not like this, he'd indicated he would let Jazz stay, at least temporarily. "Have you considered the long term, though? I'm not trying to push you."

The silence on the other end worried her. At last Bridget spoke. "I figured it would be easy to raise her now that she's older, but she can be stubborn. Let me think it over, okay?"

"Sure."

"Oh, I have a new phone number." To prevent Axel from harrassing her, Franca presumed. "Ready?"

"Yes." As Bridget recited the number, Franca entered it in her cell.

"I'll be in touch soon. Tell Jazz I love her."

"You bet."

Swiveling her chair, Franca stared out the window. From five stories up on a clear June day, she had a view over the bluffs to the Pacific Ocean. Her thoughts were far from peaceful, however.

If Axel were freed, Bridget might take her daughter and disappear, before or after the trial. Or she might agree to relinquish her permanently, in which case Franca would gain a daughter and lose the man she loved.

She dreaded both possibilities.

AFTER FRANCA TEXTED that Jazz would be staying a few more days, Marshall resolved to make the best of the situation. If he tried hard enough, perhaps he'd break through the little girl's shell and find the kind of loving spirit he treasured in Caleb and Linda. Her apology at breakfast had been a good sign.

That evening, he offered to babysit while Franca shopped for maternity clothes. Jazz raised such a ruckus, however, that Franca took her along.

"I'm the only stable person in her life," she explained when he questioned her decision.

"Aren't you teaching her that it pays to throw a tantrum?" he asked.

"Give the kid a break. She's having a rough time."

So was Franca, he observed. However, arguing was pointless.

At the office the next day, Zady asked Marshall to bring Franca and Jazz to a start-of-summer party she and Nick were throwing for Caleb that Saturday. "We've invited his grandparents and a bunch of his friends."

"Terrific." Surely Jazz would enjoy a party, and seeing Marshall with Caleb might reassure Jazz that he wasn't an ogre. "I have surgery that morning, so I'll be late."

"Oh, it doesn't start till noon. Nick works the overnight shift on Fridays and he sleeps in."

"That'll be fine."

That evening, before Marshall could convey the invitation, Jazz refused to sit down to dinner. "I want a new dress!" She stamped her foot.

"A girl at day care wore a pink dress similar to one she used to have," Franca told him. "I gather it got stained and Bridget tossed it out." To Jazz, she said, "When I have a chance, I'll sew one for you. We can pick out the fabric together."

"I want it now!"

"No, honey. Let's eat."

It took ten minutes of stomping and pouting before the girl accepted defeat. During dinner, Marshall remained on edge in case Jazz knocked over her glass or otherwise created an uproar.

However, she behaved, and went to bed calmly. "She's behaved well this evening," Franca said. "Maybe I should slip out and buy her the dress."

"You've got to be kidding." Noting the concern on her heart-shaped face, Marshall understood the impulse to indulge someone you loved. But he didn't believe that was the way to raise a child.

"I suppose you're right." Franca curled beside him on the family-room sofa, her cheek on his shoulder.

Remembering Zady's invitation, Marshall repeated it to her. "It should be fun."

"I'd love to go." Franca sighed. "I suspect a party is more than Jazz can handle at this stage, though. Any frustration will throw her off the rails."

Reluctantly, he agreed, and texted their regrets.

Franca arranged for Jennifer Martin to babysit Jazz at her house during Thursday evening's group session. The little girl jumped at the idea, excited about playing with Jennifer's daughter, Rosalie. Her friend, being a year older, attended kindergarten rather than day care.

At the session, the group received the happy news

that Hank Driver's wife was pregnant. "Also, we're communicating better now," the detective said. "She *does* trust me not to cheat, but she appreciated my reassurances." He added that he'd decided to leave the men's group. He and his wife planned to join one as a couple.

After the session, he shook hands with Marshall and Franca. "How's the little girl doing?"

"Pretty well," Marshall said.

"I appreciate your calling me," Franca put in.

"This kind of situation is tough on kids." Hank broke off as another client came up to talk to them. They had no chance to ask the detective anything more about the case.

At home, a weary Jazz let Marshall carry her into the house. In his arms, she felt small and helpless, her face soft as she dozed.

"Jennifer said she and Rosalie had a ball," Franca told him on the way upstairs. He'd waited in the car while she went into Jennifer's house to pick up Jazz.

Marshall gazed down at the child cradled against him. Perhaps he could grow to love her.

On Friday afternoon, Cole Rattigan took Marshall on a private tour of the remodeled Portia and Vincent Adams Memorial Medical Building across the drive from the hospital. The new features included a curving front portico and a graceful, high-ceilinged lobby.

The upper stories housed labs and operating suites for the men's program. Despite the lack of carpet and furnishings, the two floors of office space were invitingly spacious.

"It's on track to be finished ahead of schedule," the eminent surgeon said as they descended in the whisper-quiet elevator. "We decided to move up the official opening." He provided a date near the end of June.

"Isn't that rather soon? There's a lot of interior work unfinished."

"We won't be able to move in by the opening." The doctor finger-combed his overgrown brown hair. "But many staff members schedule vacations during July and August, and we'd like a full complement at the ceremony."

"That makes sense." Marshall recalled the suggestions he'd read on the bulletin board. "Will there be a band? A light-and-sound show?" *Or weird-shaped balloons?*

"Still to be determined." Cole smiled. "Speeches! You can count on plenty of those."

As they left the building, it occurred to Marshall that while seeking advice, he'd never asked how Cole had won his wife, Stacy, who'd been his surgical nurse. According to the grapevine, she'd been pregnant with triplets but had initially rejected Cole's proposal. "May I ask a personal question?"

"Shoot," Cole responded cheerfully.

"You've heard that Franca and I are having a baby?"

"Congratulations!"

"She refuses to marry me," Marshall admitted. "I could use ideas."

"You're asking me?" Despite being nearly forty, Cole radiated a gleeful innocence. "I'm honored."

"Any tips from your experience?"

The surgeon paused on the sidewalk. "Stace considered me clueless on how to be a husband, and she had a point."

"How'd you fix that?"

"It was a steep learning curve," the other doctor said. "I just kept plugging away at figuring out what she expected from me. I also had to accept that being a god figure in the OR didn't mean I was one at home."

"So I've discovered."

"By the way," Cole said. "If Owen Tartikoff suggests singing to her, ignore him."

"Why?"

"He has a fantastic voice," Cole explained. "Most of us are less gifted."

"Too late."

But the surgeon's remarks echoed in Marshall's mind. He *was* growing more aware of Franca's emotions and views, and she seemed to be opening up to him. Perhaps eventually she'd accept him as being husband material, too.

It would be easier if Jazz's mom reclaimed her, yet the prospect troubled him. The child he'd carried to her room last night deserved a mother *and* a father, and showed signs of beginning to accept him. Once she adapted to their routine, she might not be so highstrung.

At the end of the day, he was walking to his car when Zady phoned. "I'm picking up Caleb at day care. You should get over here."

In the background, he heard a little girl screaming, "Take me home! Our real home, not that new house!"

He heard Franca's voice responding. While he couldn't discern the words, her tone was ragged.

"I'll be right there." He thanked his sister-in-law and reversed direction toward the hospital.

The day care center lay on the ground floor adjacent to the cafeteria. Near the entrance, Franca knelt beside the howling preschooler. The center's director, Maureen Arthur, watched with folded arms, her glasses halfway down her nose.

"We'll go out to dinner," Franca coaxed. "How about Waffle Heaven?"

"No!" the red-faced girl cried. "I won't go!"

"You're bribing her with junk food?" Marshall asked.

Franca shot him a mind-your-own-business glare. "Waffle Heaven has salads."

"You're rewarding misbehavior," he said. As a psychologist, surely she knew that, but he supposed stress and emotions had the power to short-circuit rational thought.

The day care director nodded.

"Go away!" Jazz yelled at Marshall. "I hate you!"

So much for warming toward him. It hurt to discover that while he'd believed they were making progress, the little girl still viewed him as the enemy.

"We could eat at Krazy Kids Pizza," Franca offered.

"It's best not to negotiate," Maureen told her gently. "When a child throws a tantrum, try to distract her."

Or give her a swat on the bottom. That was what his parents would have done. Still, spanking a child who might have witnessed her mother being abused seemed like a bad idea.

"Maybe I have a toy in here." Franca dug through her purse.

"I don't want a toy!"

Marshall addressed the child in a level tone. "This is a hospital. There are sick people here and your screaming hurts their ears."

Jazz appeared to be weighing his comment. Mercifully, she stopped shouting.

Franca's cell jingled. Plucking it from her purse, she scanned the readout. "Oh, dear. This is important."

"Dr. Davis and I will handle this," the director assured her.

"Thanks." Franca retreated to a secluded corner.

"Can I see them?" Jazz asked.

Marshall focused on the child. "See who?"

"The sick people."

"When you're sick, do you want strangers coming in your room?" he asked.

"I guess not."

"It appears you have this under control," Maureen murmured. "You have a father's instincts, Dr. Davis."

The compliment pleased him enormously. If only Franca had heard it, but she was absorbed in her conversation.

"WHEN I WAS growing up, I kept running away from foster homes," Bridget said to Franca over the phone. "I had this fantasy about living with my mother. When I finally found her, though, she was a mess. Like I am now."

"That must have been awful." Franca nearly held her breath, afraid Bridget would retract what she'd said moments earlier: that she'd decided to let Franca adopt Jazz after all.

"I can't handle being tied down with a kid. Maybe some moms can do that at twenty-three, but not me." Bridget coughed. "And I'm scared."

"Is Axel out of jail?"

"No, but I saw one of his gang buddies near the shelter." Her voice trembled. "The address is supposed to be secret but... Maybe he was just in the neighborhood by accident."

"Did he recognize you?"

"I can't take that chance. I moved to another shelter, but what if he finds me again? This is no way to raise a kid." Bridget went on to say that as soon as her legal troubles were resolved, if she didn't land in prison, she planned to leave the area and start over. "I don't want to haul Jazz halfway across the country. She deserves a real home."

Unexpectedly, doubts gripped Franca. How was she to raise two children alone, especially with Jazz lashing out? Well, she'd manage. She would never break her commitment to the little girl.

"I can set up an appointment with Edmond." He'd been invaluable during their previous adoption proceedings.

"I like him," Bridget agreed. "The sooner you can set it up, the better. And bring Jazz, will you? I want to assure her I love her, that this is for her sake."

"Of course. Let me call you back."

To Franca's relief, she reached the attorney, who set a meeting for midday Saturday at his private office. After notifying Bridget, Franca clicked off with the most turbulent feelings she'd ever experienced.

She stiffened her resolve. There was no turning back from the path she'd set herself on, regardless of the fallout.

Now she had to break the news to Marshall.

Chapter Eighteen

When Franca told him what had happened, Marshall was glad for her sake and for Jazz's. Unless the girl's unstable mother reneged again, Franca would finally get what she'd yearned for since that night when they had both howled their distress into the cavernous parking structure.

Yet an icy rock formed in his chest during Franca's summary of Bridget's remarks. Marshall could summon only rote responses—"I see" and "Uh-huh." Even if his coldness disappointed her, how could he explain his reaction when he didn't understand it himself?

A grumbling Jazz stopped playing with a tablet the day care director had lent her. "I'm hungry."

"We all are," he said. And tired, and standing in a corridor within earshot of passersby. "Krazy Kids Pizza has play equipment." Marshall often drove past the place on Safe Harbor Boulevard. "Let's stop there for dinner."

"I thought you objected to bribing a child with junk food," Franca remarked.

"Since she's no longer throwing a tantrum, this isn't a bribe," Marshall said. "It's an executive decision."

"Might as well," she conceded. "I'm in no mood to cook."

Since they'd arrived in separate cars, he didn't get to listen while Franca broke the good news to Jazz.

At the box-shaped restaurant, its interior teeth-achingly bright with primary colors, the little girl clung to Franca's hand. If she was bursting with excitement or consumed by fear, Marshall couldn't tell. Perhaps, like him, she was struggling to adjust to this development.

The pizza lived up to its bad reputation: overly sweet tomato sauce and thin toppings on a cardboard crust. Jazz loved it. After downing two slices along with a few sips of juice, she dashed off to the welter of tunnels and platforms.

His legs cramped beneath the red table, Marshall squinted in the lingering sunshine. They'd chosen an outdoor spot to be near the play equipment. It was also near exhaust fumes and traffic noise, although those shortcomings didn't appear to bother their fellow diners. Young couples, middle-aged duos and grandparents chatted, played with their phones and watched the kids clambering about.

Other people had a quality that Marshall seemed to lack: the ability to accept life with all its flaws. After surviving the ups and downs of the past weeks, he'd hit a brick wall. It would be dishonest to pretend he could tolerate a household without boundaries, or that he was the right father for a troubled child.

Across the table sat the woman he'd struggled not to love for fifteen years—and fallen for anyway. Despite everything that had occurred between them, though, he couldn't be the man she needed, and she didn't love him the way he was, with all *his* flaws.

They ought to be discussing the future. But the fact that they wouldn't share it weighed on Marshall so heavily he could hardly breathe.

FRANCA SEARCHED IN vain for a hint of the warmth she believed lay beneath Marshall's hard surface. Where was the man who'd carried a sleeping Jazz into the house with tenderness transforming his face?

Whatever love he was capable of had evidently reached its limits. She'd never understood how he could have thrown away his relationship with Belle after behaving as if he meant to marry her. And for such a petty reason as having to drop a class.

She'd hoped, foolishly, that he'd changed. Now, confronted by the reality of raising a difficult child, he'd closed up like a fortress.

Still, they couldn't simply walk away from the situation. "We have to make some decisions," she said.

Marshall roused from his reverie. "Let's start with the fact that you shouldn't be alone while you're pregnant."

"That's all you care about, my pregnancy? Not Jazz?" It was hard to accept his indifference to the little girl, who was giggling as she played hide-and-seek with another youngster. But it reminded Franca of the fragility of the thread that linked her to Marshall, a thread that would snap if she miscarried. "I'll buy a medical alert system."

"That isn't enough, although I'll be happy to pay for one." He spoke stiffly, as if addressing a not-very-cooperative patient. "We can work out an arrangement for you both to live at my house."

"What kind of arrangement?"

"We'll establish rules that Jazz has to abide by, with consequences if she doesn't," Marshall said. "That may seem strict, but if she can't accept discipline, she'll pose a danger to you and our baby."

This was wrong on many levels. Franca started with

the most offensive one. "You act as if she's a juvenile delinquent who should be sentenced to jail. A four-year-old accepting discipline—what does that even mean? Marching in lockstep and never having a meltdown? And what do you suppose it will do to her self-esteem to live with a man who views her as his baby's enemy, who dotes on his child but cracks down on her?"

"That's not what I meant." His jaw tightened until she wondered how he could force out the words. "A child has to respect authority. If she doesn't obey her parents, she'll never succeed in school or in society."

If she doesn't obey like a well-trained puppy, she'll never succeed? Incredible. He was ready to write off a preschooler as a hopeless case on the basis of a few temper tantrums. "Jazz is my responsibility," Franca said. "I'll make the rules for her."

"She should be *our* responsibility."

"Not as long as your idea of parenting borders on medieval." This discussion was about to degenerate into a nasty argument. Time to call it quits. "Jazz and I will leave as soon as I can rent a place."

His chest heaved. "If you insist, I can't stop you. But what about after the baby's born? We'll be sharing custody, I presume."

"I can't plan that far ahead." Especially since, like her mother and sister, she might not make it past the first trimester. "We'll deal with how to co-parent the baby later."

They didn't realize Jazz had returned to the table until she asked, "What baby?" As the girl reached for her unfinished juice, Franca chided herself for not paying closer attention.

Marshall ducked his head. "Little kids, big ears. Reminds me of Caleb."

Franca did her best to answer simply and openly. "I'm pregnant," she told the girl. "If everything goes well, the baby should be born by Christmas."

Jazz paused with the cup in hand. "Where will I sleep?"

"You'll have your own room as soon as I find an apartment. We can't move back to our old place. It's too far from where I work," she said. "And the baby will have a room, too."

Jazz looked confused, understandably. Franca would have preferred to delay the news about her pregnancy.

"We won't live in Marshall's house?"

"It'll be better this way," Franca said. "Then you and he won't fight about things. It'll be fine."

"No!" Judging by her rebellious expression, that juice was about to get tossed.

"Stop!" Marshall barked.

The girl flinched and set the cup on the table. Although the command had achieved the desired result, Jazz's fearful reaction shook Franca.

"Let's go." She didn't add "home," because Marshall's house no longer fit that description.

AWAKENING IN THE middle of the night, Marshall did something he hadn't done since childhood. He went to sit on the top of the stairs and listen.

No house was completely quiet, and in this one he always heard the murmur of the surf from below the bluffs. Also, despite the sturdy construction, the twitter of night birds penetrated the house's walls, along with the distant rumble of trucks along the coast highway.

After a while, those noises faded, and he discerned the creak of a bed as Franca or Jazz shifted around. The soft sigh of breathing drifted to him.

He used to sit this way because he was lonely. His awareness of his parents safely tucked in bed had reminded him that no matter how angry they got, they'd still be there.

Now his loneliness had grown as large and solid as a tumor. He hadn't meant to force Franca to choose between him and Jazz. She was the only woman he'd ever loved and maybe the only one he ever would. He knew she cared for him, too. Sadly, not enough to meet him halfway.

How could he resolve their differences when she was supposed to be the expert on relationships? While the day care director had complimented him on his parenting instincts, Franca disagreed.

Tonight, the house vibrated with her presence. But already, Marshall felt it throbbing with the emptiness to come.

SATURDAY MORNING, FRANCA awoke on the edge of a dream. It faded instantly, but she recalled that it had featured Bridget.

How would the other woman react to seeing her daughter at the law office? Would her unpredictable emotions once again tip in the other direction, like a boat on a stormy ocean?

As she and Jazz ate breakfast with Marshall, Franca had an irrational impulse to lean on his strength. She almost wished he could accompany them to Edmond's for moral support, which was a ridiculous notion. If anything, having him around would probably antagonize Bridget and upset Jazz. Besides, he had several surgeries scheduled today.

The little girl didn't throw a tantrum, for once. Surprisingly, she helped Marshall set the table, and when he poured her milk, she thanked him.

"You're welcome." He regarded the child with an unreadable expression.

Franca couldn't assess what their interaction might mean. She was too worried about what lay ahead.

After Marshall departed, she let Jazz watch cartoons while she reviewed the material she'd saved from the last adoption effort. They had agreed that she would provide Bridget with twice-yearly reports on Jazz's development, including photos. Once Jazz reached high-school age, she could choose whether to have regular visits, assuming that Bridget was available.

Those stipulations seemed fair. They reminded Franca that Bridget could be quite reasonable—under the right circumstances.

The rest of the morning passed slowly. They read picture books and played with dolls and stuffed animals, which Jazz arrayed on the staircase. She objected when Franca instructed her to put them away for lunch.

"They're waiting for Marshall," she said. "He'll carry them to my room."

What an odd thing to say. "We have to clear them away ourselves. He might…" She shouldn't assume he'd be angry. "…trip over them."

"Okay." Jazz addressed her toys as she gathered them in her arms. "You guys be nice. No tantrums."

Was she that frightened of a scolding? The sooner they moved out, the better, Franca thought, and hurried to fix lunch before their appointment.

Except for the two half days a week when he consulted at the hospital, Edmond practiced family law at Geoff Humphreys and Associates. It was located on the ground floor in a strip mall between a dentist's office and a convenience store.

As soon as they parked, Bridget appeared from around a corner. Her flip-flops slapping the sidewalk, she sped over and grabbed Jazz's hand.

"Let's go," she said. "Now!"

The little girl peered up at Franca pleadingly. Despite Franca's attempts to prepare for the worst, she hadn't anticipated this.

The session was over before it had begun.

THE CONCERNS THAT Marshall had suppressed during the morning rushed back as he left the hospital. His instincts urged him to drive to the attorney's office, to lend whatever help he could to Franca.

But if he'd learned anything from her, it was to mistrust his instincts. This morning, Jazz had tried to please him. Was it possible she was changing, or, as Franca seemed to believe, was she simply afraid of him?

For most of his life, Marshall had kept his anxieties to himself, viewing emotion as a weakness. Yet recently, he'd found that when he sought advice, no one scorned him. And in fact, their advice had been useful.

The person who knew him best, in a clear-sighted if not necessarily flattering sense, was his brother. When he reached that conclusion, his car was already headed for Nick's house.

A cluster of balloons tied to the mailbox puzzled him, until he remembered that his brother and Zady were hosting a party. *Great timing, Marshall.*

After wedging his sedan into a spot down the block, Marshall drummed his fingers on the steering wheel. He couldn't leave. He had to talk to his brother.

He pressed Nick's number on his cell. "Can you meet me outside? I need your opinion, and it's urgent."

"My medical opinion?" his brother asked.

"No. Personal."

"I'm your go-to guy on personal matters?" Nick crowed. "Wouldn't miss it for the world."

Leave it to his brother to preen at his expense. If Marshall had anyone else to consult... But he didn't.

As he approached along the sidewalk, Marshall heard the clamor of children's voices from the rear yard. In the living room, the curtains fluttered, marking the presence of additional guests inside.

Nick emerged from a narrow side yard and stopped in the driveway, out of sight of the living room. "Hey, bro. What's up?"

"It's Franca." Hands jammed in his pockets, Marshall sketched the situation about the forthcoming adoption and her plans to move out. "I'm trying to accept Jazz, but how can I when she throws tantrums, and I mean big ones? She whacked Franca in the forehead and drew blood."

"How much?" Nick asked.

Although the sight had jolted Marshall, the cut had healed quickly. "A trace."

His brother leaned against the garage wall, heedless of dirtying his already-soiled T-shirt and jeans. "Caleb was rude to Zady when I took him away from his grandparents. He never hit her, though."

"She might outgrow it." Marshall paused as a motor home rumbled past. "But with a baby coming, how can we risk its safety?"

"You really believe she's that dangerous?" Nick probed.

Marshall hated to think the worst of a small child.

However, he couldn't afford to be naive when he was responsible for protecting his family. "What if Jazz has violent traits that keep re-emerging as she gets bigger? We won't have a chance of curbing them as long as Franca refuses to accept that we have to establish rules. Children have to learn respect and self-control."

"You sound like your parents," his brother said.

"My parents were strict, maybe too strict," Marshall conceded, "but they didn't have to cope with a violent kid."

"That's not true!" said a familiar, dry voice. From the front walkway, Mildred Davis marched into view. Marshall hadn't heard the door open; the motor home must have covered the sound. Her thin face radiating fury, his mother rounded on Nick. "You told me he wouldn't be here."

Her words stung. Why did she dislike him so much?

"He wasn't supposed to be," Nick replied mildly. "Sorry, Aunt Mildred."

"I didn't know you were going to be here, either," Marshall said. "And I don't understand what you mean about violent children."

His mother stared toward a black car at the curb, as if debating whether to ignore him and drive off. Instead, her eyes narrowing, she responded. "You were a selfish little brat when we took you in. You broke my favorite china platter and bit Upton's arm when he gave you a spanking."

He'd bitten his father? "I was, what, two years old?"

"Old enough to respect other people and their property," his mother snarled. "I nearly sent you back to your crazy father and his ditzy wife, but Upton reminded me that you were our nephew. He insisted discipline would bring you around, and it did."

"That's why you were so strict?" He'd assumed it was simply how they'd approached parenting.

"Someone had to keep you on the straight and narrow." Her nostrils flared. "You never appreciated how much we sacrificed."

"Sacrificed?"

"You were a handful when you were small," Mildred said. "You should have been grateful for what we gave you."

"How could I, when you didn't tell me I was adopted?"

"You have no business throwing that in my face!" Pain throbbed beneath her fury. "I knew that as soon as you found out, you'd never see me the same way again. You'd consider me a failure, just as Upton did. I didn't have a career, and I couldn't do the one thing a man wants most from his wife. Well, now you've learned I'm not really your mother, so that's the end of that."

What decades of outdated notions she'd endured about marriage, childbearing and her own self-worth. "Mom, that's not true. There's a lot I'd like to share with you, if you'll let me."

"Share with me?" She spoke the words as if they were an insult.

For heaven's sake, she was about to become a grandmother. "Franca and I are..." His phone shrilled. *Just ignore it.* Except that as a doctor, Marshall had to be available for emergencies. Also, he'd rather not toss out the news of the pregnancy in a rush. "Sorry. Hang on."

His mother tapped her foot in annoyance. Nick gave him a sympathetic look.

The caller was Hank Driver. "I can't reach Franca Brightman," the detective said. "Is she with you?"

"No." She must have muted her phone at the attorney's office. "What's wrong?"

"I just learned that Axel Ryerson is out on bail," he said. "I have reason to believe he's hunting for his girlfriend, and since Franca has the little girl, she could be in danger, too. Any idea where they are?"

"Yes." After providing the attorney's address, Marshall called out, "Sorry, emergency," to his mother and brother, and he ran toward his car.

Chapter Nineteen

The session with the lawyer had accomplished everything Franca had hoped for. Far from intending to cancel the meeting, Bridget had wanted to hurry it along. She'd learned of Axel's release and it had intensified her desire to sign over permanent custody.

"He'll do anything to hurt me, and maybe Jazz, too," she'd said as she'd rushed them inside. "I hid my car around the corner in case he and his friends are cruising the area. I can't risk being spotted out front."

They'd confirmed their previously agreed-upon terms, and Edmond had promised to schedule a court date as soon as possible. The adoption was back on track.

After shaking hands with Edmond, they emerged into the outer office, which was empty on a Saturday afternoon. Bridget peered out through the blinds. "Hold on. There's a silver car driving by that I don't recognize. It's gone behind a pickup and I can't see the driver."

"He might be stopping at the convenience store," Franca pointed out.

"Or not."

Between them, Jazz fidgeted. Earlier, the receptionist had helped entertain her, and after the woman left, the little girl had played on her tablet. However, her patience had clearly frayed.

"Hang on another minute," Franca told her.

"No." Jazz ran toward the exit. "You promised me ice cream."

"Yes, but not yet."

"Someone's getting out of the pickup," Bridget warned. "Damn! It's Axel. How did he know I was here?"

Fear seized Franca as Jazz thrust open the glass door. "Jazz, stop!"

"You can't make me!"

Surely she could outrun a four-year-old. But not in time to catch her before a bulky figure—shaved head, scorpion tattoo—hurtled forward to grab her. "Got you, you little worm."

Jazz screamed. After yelling to Edmond to call the police, the two women raced outside.

"Let her go!" To Franca's dismay, the words squeaked out of her constricted throat.

"Bridget, get in the truck or that's the end of your brat." A knife gleamed in Axel's hand.

"She's not mine anymore. So beat it!" Bridget shouted, and ducked inside the office.

Surely the police would be here any minute. But until then, Franca was alone with Axel and a terrified Jazz. And a wickedly sharp knife.

If only she knew more than rudimentary self-defense. If only she were bigger and stronger or had a gun.

Instead, disbelief held her motionless.

FROM THE FAR side of the pickup, Marshall couldn't see what was happening, but he heard the panic in Franca's voice, followed by Axel's deadly threat. Seizing his flash-

light from his car, the only item at hand that might serve
as a weapon, he circled the truck.

Before him, Franca stood in Axel's path, her face
ashen. Another step and Marshall spotted the shaking
child with a knife to her throat. Didn't that bastard understand how easily his hand could slip?

Fury roared in Marshall's ears. Only an awareness of
how vulnerable they all were held him in check.

"You're frightening the child," he said.

Axel bared his teeth, his neck swiveling as he took
in this new arrival. "What the hell are you gonna do
about it?"

"The police are on their way." As if to underscore
Franca's words, a siren wailed in the distance.

"You're going back to jail." Since that didn't appear
to penetrate the jerk's thick head, Marshall added, "Any
idea how prisoners treat an inmate who hurts children?"

When Axel's hand tightened on the knife hilt, Marshall's chest ached. Then the man lowered the knife. "I
ain't hurting her."

"Give her to me," Franca commanded.

Stay out of it! But it would be counterproductive to
engage in a side argument. Instead, Marshall moved
slowly to stand between her and Axel. "This isn't our
fight. Just release Jazz."

The man shoved the girl forward. "I don't care about
the damn kid anyway." Marshall scooped her up. She
huddled against him, shivering.

Holding Jazz and using his body to block any attempt at Franca, Marshall registered Axel glaring toward the law-office window. He half expected the man
to try to crash through it, not that that would work outside of the movies. Why didn't he flee? Though, if the

man had more sense, he wouldn't be in such a mess in the first place.

A police cruiser swept into the lot, lights flashing. Not far behind followed a second cruiser, then a beige sedan with Hank at the wheel.

"I didn't do nothing!" At a command from the officers, Axel set the knife on the ground and raised his hands.

As the officers secured the scene, Marshall carried Jazz to Franca. When he tried to set the little girl on her feet, however, she clung to him.

"You saved me, Marshall." She hiccuped.

"It's a daddy's job to protect his family," he told her. When he glanced up, he could have sworn tears glittered in Franca's eyes.

After that, they were kept busy providing statements. The female officer who'd been at Bridget's apartment a few days ago spoke to her briefly, disappeared around the building and returned with a small metal box. "Magnetic GPS case."

"That's how he tracked my car!" Bridget said. "That must be what his buddy was doing near the women's shelter."

"Are you okay?" Franca asked.

Bridget stroked Jazz's dark hair. "Yeah, but I'm not proud of myself. You're the one who stayed out here and risked your life. You really are her mom." She regarded Marshall admiringly. "And I'm glad she'll have you for a dad."

"Daddies protect their families," Jazz repeated.

"They sure do," Marshall said.

He still wasn't sure where he stood with Franca. He only knew that, after today, he felt as if Jazz was his daughter, too.

IT WAS LATE afternoon before they arrived home, picking up take-out roast chicken with vegetables and salad on their way. After dinner, Marshall volunteered to bake cupcakes with Jazz.

"Might as well use some of this cake mix." He indicated the row of boxes in the pantry.

"Chocolate!" Jazz peered at the display eagerly, then tempered her demand with, "Or some other kind."

Her old defiance had vanished, although Franca expected it to crop up occasionally. Children didn't transform into angels in a single day.

"Chocolate it is." Marshall removed their paper plates from the table. "Franca, you can be our taste tester."

"That means I get to eat whatever you bake," she told Jazz.

"Cool," the little girl said.

Franca took a seat at the island. She kept reliving the earlier scene, trembling at the memory of how close she and Jazz had come to serious injury or death. Yet the sight of Marshall moving easily about the kitchen reassured her.

His courage and strength had saved them, despite Axel's loud claims to police that he'd never intended to harm anyone. Moreover, much as she might question Marshall's stern approach to discipline, she had to admit that she'd overindulged the little girl. Otherwise, Jazz might not have ignored her command to stay inside.

Sipping a cup of tea, Franca watched Marshall with fresh eyes as he tied aprons around himself and Jazz. She listened as he patiently cautioned about the hot oven and the importance of washing their hands. *Just like a father.*

If only doubt didn't still nag inside her. Could she really trust him completely?

He brought a stool so the four-year-old could reach the counter. After they'd cracked the eggs and stirred in the dry mix and water, he helped her position the hand mixer. Although Franca considered the child too young to handle the device, she resisted the urge to intervene.

Jazz held the mixer fairly steady for a few minutes. When her hand wobbled, Marshall praised her and gently took charge of the mixer to finish the job. The girl beamed with pride.

As they lined cupcake pans with fluted papers, she peppered him with questions. "Will you teach the baby to bake, too?"

"Not for a few years," Marshall said. "By then, you might be big enough to teach her. Or him."

"I'll be the big sister, right?"

"You bet."

Amused as Franca was by this exchange, she wasn't sure they should let Jazz assume the baby was a sure thing. The week's events had pushed the pregnancy to the back of her mind. Now, she touched her palm to her midsection, and her abdomen felt larger and firmer than she recalled. She was, she realized, entering the ninth week. According to the material Dr. Franco had provided, Baby Bright was an inch long, its hands meeting over the heart.

Would there truly be a new baby to hold and love? No use worrying about it now. They'd had enough scares for today.

With Marshall's help, Jazz began spooning batter into the papers. "Are you the baby's daddy?" she asked.

"Yes."

The child stared up at him. "Are you my daddy, too?"

"I want to be," Marshall said. "And watch that spoon. You're dripping."

"Oops."

He reached for a paper towel. "Allow me to demonstrate the fine art of mopping up."

"What's *demonstrate*?"

"It means *to show*. As in, let me demonstrate how to hug." Putting down the towel, he gathered her against him. Jazz giggled.

Franca's heart squeezed. Was it possible they could bond into a family?

"Can I live in your house?" Jazz asked. "If I promise no more tantrums?"

Marshall finished cleaning the spilled batter. "None?"

"Mostly none."

He planted a kiss atop her head. "I don't expect you to be perfect. I wasn't so perfect myself when I was a kid. But I figured you weren't happy here."

"Yes, I am," Jazz said.

"Why were you so determined to go home?"

"I thought you'd kick me out," she said.

"Why would I do that?"

"'Cause I'm bad a lot."

"Not bad. Just naughty. You can learn to do better, like I did."

Jazz clutched her hands together. "And you might take my toys."

"Wow, I'd have to be a mean guy to do that." Opening the oven, Marshall slid in the trays of cupcakes. "You were making a preemptive strike? That means you pushed me away before I could do it to you."

The little girl nodded.

"I wouldn't throw you out over a few tantrums," Marshall said as he set the timer. "Or for any reason, because, remember, daddies protect their families. Good daddies do."

"Unfortunately, not all men are good," Franca said. Bridget had described how Jazz's father had sent them packing when the child was a toddler, only allowing them to throw a few items into a suitcase. Afterward, Bridget and Jazz dropped in and out of shelters and friends' homes, often with little notice. Jazz must have had to leave toys behind more than once.

"So can I stay?" she asked.

Marshall's eyes met Franca's. How could she respond? She wanted for them to stay, too, yet a long-term commitment meant relying on Marshall to have truly changed from the rigid man she'd known years ago. Despite all the promising signs, how could she be sure?

"The grown-ups will talk about this later," he told Jazz. "Please don't worry, okay?"

"Okay."

While the cupcakes were baking, Jazz climbed into Marshall's lap and he read one of her favorite picture books. Then the three of them enjoyed the chocolate treats, barely cooled long enough to hold icing.

Marshall stored the remainder in a plastic container. "We can have them for breakfast," Jazz announced.

"We'll eat cereal and fruit for breakfast," Marshall corrected. "And save our cupcakes for dessert tomorrow night."

She folded her arms. "I want another one now."

"You've had three. Any more and you'll be sick."

Jazz grabbed her half-full glass of milk. "Give me another cupcake!"

For a frozen moment, both adults regarded her indecisively. Aware that the child must be exhausted, Franca had an impulse to spring to her defense before Marshall could react. But he was right.

She closed her hand over Jazz's on the glass. "You've had a rough day, but if this is how you repay Marshall for baking with you, why should he ever agree to make cupcakes again?"

"You're mean!" Jazz replied.

Marshall sat down across from them. "No, she's a mommy who loves you and wants what's best for you. She also deserves your respect. We would never call you names and you shouldn't call us mean or bad either."

Jazz heaved an exaggerated sigh. "Boy, you're *both* saying the same stuff. I give up."

Franca's gaze connected with Marshall's. "That's because we're a team," she said.

Astonishingly, she realized it was true.

HE *HAD* TO win over Franca, Marshall reflected as they descended the stairs after tucking Jazz into bed. He yearned to be both her husband and Jazz's father. But if he said or did the wrong thing, he might drive her away.

I nearly sent you back to your crazy father and his ditzy wife. His mother's words, almost forgotten in the rush of the day's events, popped into his mind. Jolted, he missed his footing and had to grab the banister.

"Are you okay?" Behind him, Franca touched his shoulder in concern. "Confronting an armed man is a traumatic experience. It must be catching up with you."

"Among other things." Reaching the bottom of the stairs, he gestured toward the living room. "Mind joining me in here? There's something I want to share."

"Of course."

Early-evening light drifted through the front windows, augmented by the glow of etched-glass lamps. Marshall had furnished the room elegantly but comfortably with armchairs and a sofa grouped around a patterned rug.

He chose the couch. Franca perched on a chair.

From habit, he sought to phrase his thoughts cautiously. Oh, to hell with caution. He'd lay everything out and if she rejected him, at least he'd done his best.

"I ran into my mother today," he began.

"Where?"

"At Nick's." *Don't stop to explain the details.* "She vented about what a little monster I used to be and how they had to crack down on me."

"How cruel," Franca said. "I can't imagine you were ever difficult."

"Apparently I was a destructive toddler," Marshall said. "That's why they were so strict."

"From everything I've heard, they overdid it."

Her sympathy encouraged him. "I've always believed that there was something fundamentally wrong with me," Marshall said. "That when I'm most myself, I don't deserve to be loved."

"That's awful!"

"The only way I could deserve love was to be perfect," he went on. "Now I understand where that stems from."

"What a burden to carry." Franca leaned forward.

Even if what he was about to say offended her, Marshall couldn't stop. "You said once that my instincts were all wrong. Well, I may have a gift for putting my foot in my mouth, but my instincts *aren't* all wrong. To raise children together, we have to find a balance between my strictness and your nurturing." He halted, his throat tightening, awaiting her reaction.

"You're right." At close range, the pupils of Franca's eyes seemed unusually large. "At Edmond's office, Jazz defied me and ran outside. If you'd been there and ordered her to stop, she'd have obeyed."

She understood. Finally, they'd reached common ground.

Then she averted her gaze. "What's bothering you?" Marshall refused to let her withhold anything. They'd come too far. "Whatever it is, please trust me with it."

Franca took a deep breath. "It isn't really my business, but..."

"Go for it."

"Why did you dump Belle?"

Marshall blinked. "What?"

"I never understood how you could love a woman for years and then dump her because she fell short of your expectations," she said. "So what if she couldn't keep up with her increased class load?"

"You believe I dropped her because she wasn't brilliant enough?"

"That's basically what she told me." Franca clenched her hands in her lap.

Marshall had used her grades as an excuse to avoid hurting Belle's feelings. Instead, by disguising the truth, he'd misled her, and consequently Franca.

"It was her idea to graduate early and move to Boston," he said. "I realized I didn't want her to. I wasn't in love with her and never had been, but it would have been cruel to say that. So when she began struggling academically, it seemed the perfect reason to split. I claimed we both needed to concentrate on our studies."

Franca swallowed. "You weren't in love with her, ever?"

"The woman I really belonged with was you," Marshall admitted. "Only, at that age, I wasn't ready for such an intense relationship."

Franca appeared to be reflecting, perhaps replaying events in light of what he'd just disclosed. "The first time I saw you, at that party, I thought you were coming over to talk to me," she said.

"I was," he admitted. "Then you got klutzy and I could hear my parents announcing you weren't my type."

"They had a lot of nerve." Smiling, she noted, "I mean their alter egos."

"Air people," Marshall said. "That's my name for those voices in our heads."

"Air people," Franca repeated. "I like that."

"I'm sorry for hurting Belle," he said. "I'm not sure she ever really loved me, either, though. How could she, when I never showed her who I was inside?"

Franca considered this for a moment. "My sister described you and Belle as a handsome couple, but shallow."

"Your sister's a perceptive woman. Especially the handsome part." He sobered. Without realizing it, he'd withheld something, too. "Franca, you're the right woman for me, but I can't be a perfect guy. I am who I am. I'm stricter than you, with a different viewpoint on some issues. I'm willing to work things out, but we can't sustain a relationship where I have to walk on eggshells."

Franca sat silent as his words sank in. Maybe he'd gone too far. He'd had no choice, though.

At last she spoke. "You told Jazz you don't expect her to be perfect. I don't expect that of you, either."

Then she did something utterly unexpected. She got down on her knees and asked, "Marshall Davis, will you marry me?"

Chapter Twenty

When Marshall proposed to her weeks ago, Franca had been wary. She'd been convinced Jazz and the baby depended on her alone to shoulder the responsibility for them, and had viewed Marshall's rigidity as a threat.

But since then he'd opened up emotionally, overcoming the restraint that had served as his survival mechanism all his life. And although he might have been unfair to Belle in some ways, he'd been young and inexperienced—and had done his best to spare her.

She loved this man. He'd let her view his scarred soul, and had accepted her despite *her* flaws. He'd matured into a partner Franca could count on. The confrontation with Axel had proved that.

She no longer believed he'd run out on her if she miscarried. After all, she'd been honest about her family's history, and it hadn't fazed him. And now he'd accepted Jazz as his child, too.

Yet his answer to her proposal was taking an awfully long time. "Marshall?"

The corners of his mouth twitched. "It's my understanding that a proposal should be accompanied by a ring and preferably flowers."

Was he mocking her? "I beg your pardon?"

"I love you," he said.

"And I love you." She'd made that clear, hadn't she?

"Now as to this proposal business, let's improvise." Pushing the coffee table aside, he knelt facing her. "Since neither of us was clever enough to buy a ring, we'll have to create our own."

Franca's uncertainty vanished as he reached out. Although it required a bit of scooting, soon they'd encircled each other in their arms.

His masculine scent, a hint of aftershave lotion with an undertone of surgical soap, buoyed her. How exhilarating to be sheltered and loved. "This is the best kind of ring," she whispered.

When his lips touched hers, Franca forgot everything but her precious connection with this tender, wonderful man.

"The best kind of circle, indeed," Marshall said when the kiss ended. "As long as we don't topple over."

Franca smiled. "It feels heavenly, no matter how awkward we look."

"No one's watching," he assured her. "Except for that security camera over there."

"What!" She stared upward. "I don't see it."

"Oh. Guess I forgot to have it installed."

Torn between laughing and poking him in the ribs, Franca lost her balance and would have collapsed except for his support. It seemed a symbolic start to their future together.

"We can shop for rings tomorrow," he said. "Whatever style you choose."

"I'll enjoy that." They moved to sit side by side on the couch. She stroked his cheek, and he drew her against his shoulder.

As she relaxed, Franca recalled their earlier topic. "You didn't finish telling me about your mom. Did she explain why she cut you off when you found out you were adopted?"

"In a way." Marshall's deep voice vibrated through her. "She's convinced my father considered her a failure because she couldn't have kids. And she assumed that once I learned she wasn't my birth mother, I'd cast her off."

"A preemptive strike, like Jazz?" Franca murmured.

He rested his cheek on her head. "That's right."

What a dark place Mildred Davis must inhabit, where her self-worth depended on two men whose love she didn't trust. "I hate to think how sad her own childhood must have been that she had such a low opinion of herself even into adulthood."

"I'm not sure how to break through that," Marshall said. "But I want her to enjoy being a grandmother. She's earned that chance."

"You didn't tell her I'm pregnant?"

"Not yet," he said. "But I will."

"Speaking of children," Franca said, "shall we see if Jazz is still awake? Regardless of what she said to you, I'm sure she's worried."

"Absolutely."

The moment they entered the playroom, the girl sat bolt upright, dark hair wild around her face. "Oh, it's you!" She held out her arms. "I was afraid it was that bad man."

Franca should have anticipated that the trauma would linger in Jazz's mind. She hurried over. "We're here because something great has happened."

Marshall pulled up a chair, since the bed was too small for them both to sit on the edge. "Franca and I are getting married. You'll be our daughter and we'll live here forever."

"With the baby, too?"

"You bet," he said.

"Yay!" After hugging them both, Jazz asked, "Can I sleep with you guys tonight?"

Franca wasn't sure how to answer. Like her, Marshall must have been looking forward to making love again.

"Will that help you feel safe?" he asked.

Jazz nodded vigorously.

"Just for tonight," Marshall warned. "So you won't be scared." He glanced at Franca and mouthed, "Okay?"

"There's nothing more important than our little girl," she confirmed. "But it's only for tonight."

"Okay, Mommy and Daddy." Jazz scrambled out of bed.

They walked down the hall hand in hand.

THE NEXT DAY, the three of them went to Nick and Zady's house to bring them and Caleb up to date. Later, while Marshall and Jazz played a game with their hosts, Franca slipped out to the patio and placed the first of several important calls.

Her mom responded with excitement when Franca gave her the news about the baby. Then she asked, "Have you mentioned this to Gail yet?"

"No. I'm nervous about that," Franca admitted, stretching her legs.

"She'll be delighted for you," her mother insisted. "Don't put it off."

"I won't." As soon as they finished, she inhaled the fresh air, perfumed with jasmine from bushes surrounding the small yard. Then she pressed her sister's name in the phone.

After exchanging greetings, Gail said, "Have you talked to Mom?"

"I just did," Franca answered, puzzled.

"So she broke the news."

"Uh...what news?"

"She didn't share that I'm four months pregnant?" Usually, their mother would have spread the word near and far.

Four months meant her sister was well into the second trimester. "That's terrific! I guess she figured you'd rather break it to me yourself." Might as well go for it. "Marshall and I are engaged."

"Congratulations!"

"And I get to adopt Jazz after all. We saw the lawyer yesterday."

"Fantastic!"

"And I'm nine weeks pregnant."

There was a stunned silence. Then: "Our kids will be almost the same age. And Glenn's, too."

"That *is* a bonus." Although the three cousins would live in different states, they'd spend many holidays together as a family.

"What aren't you saying?" Gail pressed.

No use avoiding the subject. "I'm worried about the pregnancy. Not that there's anything wrong, according to my doctor."

"Because of our family medical history, which I was so rude about when you brought it up?" Gail said. "I've never reached the fourth month before. My doctor says the miscarriages might have been a fluke, or a problem that self-corrected."

"I feel as if a curse has been lifted," Franca ventured.

"Me, too. We can both hope for the best."

A few minutes later, she completed the family notifications. Her brother congratulated her and added that his wife's pregnancy was progressing well, also. He, too, was thrilled that the three cousins would be close in age.

After she clicked off, Franca wished she could stop there. However, she had to place one more call. *Just get it over with.*

Belle answered on the second ring. "Franca! I was about to call you. I have fantastic news."

Franca broke into laughter. "You can't be!"

"I can't be what?"

But she'd known the instant she heard the joy in Belle's voice. "You're pregnant."

"How did you guess?" Without waiting, her friend said, "I'm two months along. I'd have called you sooner but you were so sad about losing Jazz."

"I haven't lost her," Franca said. "Her birth mother changed her mind."

"That's great!"

"And I'm pregnant."

"Oh." Belle seemed to be searching for polite phrasing. "Is there a father? I mean, in the picture?"

"Yes, and we're getting married." *Now for the hard part.* "It's Marshall."

A pause. Then a disbelieving, "Marshall *Davis*?"

"We ran into each other at the hospital where we're both on staff," Franca explained. "He's changed over the years." She had no idea what to add, except, "I hope this isn't uncomfortable for you. I want us to stay friends." While she didn't believe Belle would hold a grudge, she might not be able to help feeling betrayed.

"Good," Belle said. "It's way overdue."

"What?"

Her friend must have shifted the phone, because there was a moment's static before she continued, "I sensed he was drawn to you, only I was too selfish to call him on it because I was afraid I'd lose him. Well, I lost him anyway. Seeing you alone year after year, I kept wondering about what might have been."

"If Marshall and I had had a relationship in college, we'd have ended up hating each other," Franca told her.

"Really?"

"We had a lot to work out even now," she assured her friend. "You're truly okay with this?"

"It stings," Belle admitted. "For me, Marshall was a romantic dream. But the truth is, I have the best possible husband. When he looks at me, there's no other woman lurking behind his eyes."

"You deserve that, and more." It was brave of Belle to be honest, and generous of her to understand.

"You do, too."

Now they could move on. "I just talked to my brother and sister. They're both expecting babies within a few months of mine, and yours."

"This will be quite a Christmas!"

"It sure will."

At last the calls were over, the old hurts healed. Yet there remained one family member to bring into the happy circle.

When they got home, Marshall tried calling his mother, but reached only her voice mail. He composed an email apologizing for running off abruptly at Nick's house, and then explained about the confrontation at the lawyer's office. He informed her of the engagement, the pregnancy and Jazz's forthcoming adoption. Seeking neutral ground, he invited her to join them for the opening ceremony of the new medical building, and to go out to dinner with them afterward.

After proofreading the email for him, Franca hoped the prospect of becoming a grandmother would overcome Mildred's reticence. Also, Marshall had emphasized in the email that he considered himself just as much a father to his adoptive daughter as to the baby Franca was carrying. He hoped his mother would grasp the message that it didn't matter how a child came into the family.

Her response arrived later that evening. He forwarded the email to Franca.

I'm pleased that both my nephews have found brides and that you'll be able to experience fatherhood, Mildred wrote. Since you will have a baby of your own, perhaps raising an adopted child won't be as difficult as it was for me. That part of my life is behind us. I'm sure you'll understand why I don't belong at this ceremony or at your family dinner.

"She's sticking to her guns." The sorrow on Marshall's face resonated inside Franca. "We'll invite her to other events, of course, but she seems resolved to regard me as nothing more than a nephew. I'm honestly not sure she ever loved me."

Was that true? To Franca, the words "I don't belong at this ceremony" indicated pain rather than rejection. Still, Marshall might be right.

Yet the separation troubled her. Later, while checking her own mail, Franca decided that, as the woman's future daughter-in-law, she ought to write to her and add her insights. As to whether her words would make a difference, Franca figured it was a long shot. After asking Marshall to be sure he didn't object, she composed a message and hit Send.

Then she went upstairs with her future husband to put their daughter to bed. And, finally, to make love again.

Chapter Twenty-One

Banners and a band ushered invitees into the elegant lobby of the Portia and Vincent Adams Memorial Medical Building. Its acquisition and renovation had been a long, difficult, even tragic process, involving the bankruptcy of the former dental building's owners, a competitive sale when it seemed unaffordable and then a financial commitment by the wealthy Adams couple just before their deaths in a car crash.

Marshall had only joined the staff last fall. Yet stepping inside with Franca and Jazz, he felt his heart expand with warmth and pride. Not only did his professional future lie within these walls, but the crowd filling the folding chairs included warm, familiar faces. Nick, Zady and Caleb had saved seats for them. Jennifer Martin, who as public relations director was helping run the event, left her five-year-old daughter with them—much to Jazz's joy—while her husband assisted with the sound equipment.

People stopped by to say hello, people with whom he had formed connections. They included Zady's twin sister, Zora, and her husband, Lucky, as well as other urologists and nurses.

Throughout his education and training, Marshall had isolated himself from those around him. Many had considered him cold and snobbish, while the truth was that he'd longed to be a part of their easy camaraderie. How had this happened, that in the span of a few months he'd bridged the gaps of a lifetime?

When his hand covered Franca's, she tipped him an understanding smile. On his other side, Jazz was giggling as she chatted with her little friend Rosalie. Then she rested her cheek against Marshall's arm.

He belonged here. The awareness lifted his spirits as high as the bright clusters of Mylar balloons.

Yet a heaviness dragged him down to earth, because a key person was missing. How could a man accept that his own mother didn't love him? Mildred Davis *was* his mother—except that, apparently, she no longer wished to be.

At the front, Owen Tartikoff and Cole Rattigan took places of honor alongside the Adamses' daughters, both of whom were in their early teens, and their grandmother. After the band finished a rousing number, the hospital administrator rose to speak.

A powerfully built fellow who inspired confidence, Dr. Mark Rayburn uttered a few words of welcome before unveiling a statue commissioned for the building. The bronze figure of a man in slacks and a sport coat, lovingly holding a baby in the crook of his arm, occupied one end of a park-style bench. The bronze sculpture was so realistic that Marshall imagined visitors sitting next to the man before realizing he wasn't an actual person.

Applause surged, and the artist took a bow. Mark proceeded to thank the Adams girls and their grandmother for the bequest from the Vince and Portia Adams estate, stirring an ovation.

Next up was Owen Tartikoff. The surgeon energized the people in the lobby with his description of the growth of the Safe Harbor fertility program and its cutting-edge successes.

He introduced Cole Rattigan as head of the men's program. What a contrast, Marshall thought: where Owen was forceful and commanding, Cole was reticent and self-deprecating.

"I'm surprised they let me speak in public," he told the crowd. "The last time I lectured, I mentioned declining sperm levels worldwide and the media claimed I'd predicted the end of life on earth. Reporters were camped out on my doorstep for weeks."

Laughter rippled through the room. Marshall recalled reading about that episode a few years ago and pitying the doctor whose remarks had been sensationalized.

Cole summarized the issues facing infertile men, tossed out a few statistics and concluded, "The key to any program is its personnel. We're bringing on board distinguished younger surgeons and there's one in particular I'd like to introduce who's been intimately involved in the planning of this building. Dr. Marshall Davis, please come up and say a few words."

The old fear of making a fool of himself held Marshall motionless. Then Jazz said, "That's you, Daddy."

"It sure is." Loud clapping, led by Franca, propelled him to the podium. En route, he quickly considered what he might say. He might list the fellowships they'd secured, or review the discussions the staff had had about allocating office space. But why risk boring the audience to death?

At the microphone, Marshall plunged right in. "I've never terrified the public like my distinguished colleague Dr. Rattigan, but the public used to terrify me.

I had a fear of public speaking because I feared if I said the wrong thing, the audience would rise up and mock me en masse."

Sympathetic murmurs greeted this admission. On his brother's lips, he read the words, "You're kidding!" Apparently Nick hadn't suspected what lay behind his mask.

"This hospital is about creating families," Marshall said. "For the community, for our patients and for our staff. To my astonishment, it brought me together with my brother and with an old friend who's soon to be my wife, Dr. Franca Brightman."

More clapping followed, with a notable clatter from his office's nurses. Ines poked two fingers in her mouth as if to produce a wolf whistle, until Jeanine knocked her hand away.

"As many of you know, my fiancée and I are setting an example of how to form a family, both by having a baby and by adopting our adorable foster daughter, Jazz." He grinned down at Franca, who resembled a fertility goddess in her forest-green maternity dress. Jazz wiggled happily in her chair.

He was about to wrap up his remarks when a movement near the entrance caught his attention. The rail-thin figure of Mildred Davis, clad in a gray suit that matched her upswept hair, edged inside.

Should he acknowledge her? At his brother's wedding, she hadn't hesitated to stalk from the banquet hall in front of everyone. A rebuff here would be embarrassing and hurtful. But she'd come, hadn't she?

Trust your instincts.

"Very importantly, let me thank the woman who raised me to be a man of accomplishment, whose rock-solid adherence to her principles taught me to stand by what I believe in and fight for it." Marshall regarded her directly. "My mother, Mildred Davis."

In her stunned expression, he read the same fear that he used to experience, of being ridiculed. Then Franca and Nick rose to their feet, turned toward her and cheered. The rest of the audience joined in enthusiastically.

Tears ran down his mother's cheeks. He didn't recall ever seeing her cry before.

To hell with decorous behavior. Down the aisle Marshall went, greeting his mother with a hug. Barely reaching his chest, she responded with a powerful grip of her own.

"Well, I can't top that," Mark Rayburn said from the stage. "I now declare the Portia and Vincent Adams Memorial Medical Building open!"

The band broke into "Happy Days Are Here Again." Around the room, chairs scraped and clothing rustled as people prepared to leave.

"I'm proud of you," his mother said. "By the way, you're marrying the right woman."

"I know, Mom." Marshall released her. "What changed your mind about today?"

Mildred glanced past him, as if to be sure they weren't overheard. "Franca emailed to say how much you love me, that every memory you have of growing up involves Upton and me as your parents."

"She wrote all that?" He'd assumed Franca was sending a simple courtesy note.

"She explained how hard it was for you to accept her foster child, but that you'd eventually forged a bond as strong as any parent's. And she urged me to be a part of your family, in any role I choose."

"That sounds like quite an email."

"It inspired me to take out our old scrapbooks, the ones we made after vacations and holidays." His mother had spent many hours assembling beautiful, quilted volumes of photos and memorabilia. "I'd forgotten how happy we were. I realized that I'd become locked into my anger, even when it was counterproductive. I'm afraid I'm not a very flexible person."

"Me, either," Marshall said. "I'm working on it, though." Franca and the others were approaching, with Jazz trotting ahead. "Here comes your granddaughter."

"I always envied my friends who were grandmothers," Mildred admitted. She hugged the little girl without reserve, and Franca, as well.

"You'll join us for dinner, won't you?" Franca asked.

"If I'm still invited."

"Absolutely," Marshall said.

"Don't worry about the cost," Nick added. "My brother's paying."

"I certainly am." Marshall offered his mother and his fiancée each an arm. Caleb crooked his elbow for Jazz, who gave him a dazzling smile.

As they emerged into the summer evening, he heard the others making various restaurant suggestions. Since it didn't matter to him where they ate, he let the names flow by: Papa Giovanni's, Fu Manchu's, Salads and More, Krazy Kids Pizza, Waffle Heaven.

How ironic that, for all these years, he and Franca had avoided involvement because of their contrasting personalities, Marshall mused. Thanks to her, he'd found the acceptance and the love he'd always craved.

Opposites could not only attract, they could bring out

the best in each other. He and Franca and their family members were the living proof.

Now if they could only agree on where to eat dinner…

* * * * *

MILLS & BOON®

Cherish™

EXPERIENCE THE ULTIMATE RUSH OF FALLING IN LOVE

A sneak peek at next month's titles...

In stores from 11th February 2016:

- **The Greek's Ready-Made Wife** – Jennifer Faye *and*
  Fortune's Secret Husband – Karen Rose Smith
- **Crown Prince's Chosen Bride** – Kandy Shepherd
  and **"I Do"...Take Two!** – Merline Lovelace

In stores from 25th February 2016:

- **Billionaire, Boss...Bridegroom?** – Kate Hardy *and*
  A Baby and a Betrothal – Michelle Major
- **Tempted by Her Tycoon Boss** – Jennie Adams *and*
  From Dare to Due Date – Christy Jeffries

Available at WHSmith, Tesco, Asda, Eason, Amazon and Apple

Just can't wait?
Buy our books online a month before they hit the shops!
visit www.millsandboon.co.uk

These books are also available in eBook format!

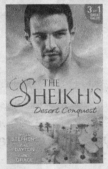

MILLS & BOON®
The Billionaires Collection!

This fabulous 6 book collection features stories from some of our talented writers. Feel the temperature rise with our ultra-sexy and powerful billionaires. Don't miss this great offer – buy the collection today to get two books free!

Order yours at
www.millsandboon.co.uk
/billionaires

MILLS & BOON®

Let us take you back in time with our Medieval Brides...

The Novice Bride – Carol Townend

The Dumont Bride – Terri Brisbin

The Lord's Forced Bride – Anne Herries

The Warrior's Princess Bride – Meriel Fuller

The Overlord's Bride – Margaret Moore

Templar Knight, Forbidden Bride – Lynna Banning

Order yours at
www.millsandboon.co.uk/medievalbrides

MILLS & BOON®

Why shop at millsandboon.co.uk?

Each year, thousands of romance readers find their perfect read at millsandboon.co.uk. That's because we're passionate about bringing you the very best romantic fiction. Here are some of the advantages of shopping at www.millsandboon.co.uk:

* **Get new books first**—you'll be able to buy your favourite books one month before they hit the shops

* **Get exclusive discounts**—you'll also be able to buy our specially created monthly collections, with up to 50% off the RRP

* **Find your favourite authors**—latest news, interviews and new releases for all your favourite authors and series on our website, plus ideas for what to try next

* **Join in**—once you've bought your favourite books, don't forget to register with us to rate, review and join in the discussions

Visit **www.millsandboon.co.uk**
for all this and more today!